Rafael's Wings

Rafael's Wings

Sian Mackay

Published by
Kennedy and Boyd
an imprint of
Zeticula
57 St Vincent Crescent
Glasgow
G3 8NQ

http://www.kennedyandboyd.co.uk
admin@kennedyandboyd.co.uk

First published April 2006
Reprinted July 2006
Copyright © Sian Mackay 2006

Sian Mackay asserts the moral right to be identified as the author of this book.

This novel is entirely a work of fiction. Any resemblance to actual persons, living or dead, is entirely coincidental. The names, characters, organisations, places and incidents portrayed in it are the work of the author's imagination.

Cover photograph of *Easter Angel*, by Beral Anderson
© Sverre Koxvold 2006.

ISBN 1-904999-27-1 Paperback
ISBN 1-904999-28-x Hardback

For Angus Sinclair

And also, hereabouts, worshipers disguised as gods and as gods in the disguise of birds, jumped from platforms fixed on long poles, and glided as they spun by the ropes - feathered serpents and eagles too, the voladores, *or fliers. There still are such plummeteers, in market places, as there seem to be remnants or conversions or equivalents of all the old things.*

Well, given time, we all catch up with legends, more or less.

Saul Bellow

1

On a sunlit roof terrace, her Mediterranean drying green, she pegs up her laundry and keeps a lookout for the hawks. The first time Rafael Vargas led her here through the low wooden door, the eye-level spires, gargoyles and finials of the neighbouring church had made her gasp. The church dominated the roof and all the other roofs surrounding it, where abandoned adobes, distressingly in need of a lick of paint, opened onto similar terraces with identical washing lines. Once upon a time these dwellings had housed, she supposed, maids who had serviced the flats in the grand turn-of-the-century buildings below. However, these days - decades after their rich Barcelona owners deserted the city centre for the new suburbs - the flats were grand only in dimension, their huge rooms having been demoted to rather austere bedsits and studios inhabited by impoverished tenants like herself.

Up here, released from her dreary quarters below, she breathes easily, imagining the roofscape as her private oasis. And the hawks are her guardian angels, whose otherworldly presence has reassured her during weeks of waiting for news: *where* is my field base to be - the Atlas Mountains, the Picos, the Pyrenees? - and *when* am I to go? Intimately, she knows these hawks: *Falco naumanni; small, elegantly proportioned, nests colonially on cliffs or old buildings like this church.* Yesterday, she had come up here at sunrise, in time to see a dozen Lesser kestrels flying from their cave-like roosts above the gargoyles, and her spirit had soared with their flight, as it has done with every wildlife discovery since, at the age of nine, she stumbled upon a nest of newly-hatched larks, miraculously embedded in a frost-girt hawthorn hedge near her childhood home.

If I'm lucky, they'll come again, she thinks, a red plastic peg clenched between her teeth: *Falco naumanni* . . . . Then, all of a sudden, with a woosh of wings and a crystalline cry, an immature hawk swerves over the washing line.

Her pulse quickens when it rings up, rufous, against the honey-coloured façade of the church and the blue sky that seems to vibrate with its passage. Birds are her business, a passion she acknowledges with a surge of elation at the same moment as a breeze lifts the hem of her rust-coloured skirt. She wants to dance in it, this gust . . . several hawks are out flying now, their wheeling grace prompting thoughts of Rafael Vargas – bird-man, beggarman, performer, magician – what *was* he? Her landlord, certainly, although they'd hardly exchanged a word since the day she arrived to rent a room of her own here in Barcelona. Her mouth curves, remembering how in a rare conversation Vargas had told her of years spent in South America before he returned to Europe to devise the winged costume he wore these days for his performances in Barcelona's main square. 'I'm a kind of Robin Hood,' he said, 'extracting euros from rich tourists and transferring them across the Atlantic Ocean to help small agricultural projects in Third World pueblos.'

She had been intrigued, and often took the longer route back to the flat from the university to watch Rafael Vargas performing in Plaça Major. He was the best by far of the many 'living statues' there that sprang to life like Doctor Faustus's dolls when someone dropped coins into the receptacles at their feet. He didn't see her concealed among the spellbound tourists, but at least her landlord was some sort of reference point in this lonely city filled with surprises: these living statues, the professor's Catalan (when she had expected *Castellano*), Gaudí's weird Sagrada Familía, and even the massive church looming over this diminutive roof where her morning laundry flaps in a Spanish breeze.

The breeze gathers strength, ruffles her cropped brown hair when she turns to leave the terrace. Don't forget to secure the door, she reminds herself; otherwise thieves, *ladrones*, might break in across the roofs. As a stranger, *una forastera*, you must get it right. Get everything right! This door: padlock it; the professor's lectures: understand them; the scientific papers: get

12

high marks. You didn't leave the north . . . all that dourness tinged with splendour . . . to get it wrong. Yet often she feels exasperated, since although she is fluent in Spanish, she is learning that language doesn't make you one of them. No effort, no getting it right, seemed to lift her into the embrace of Spain, where everyday a different saint is celebrated, and where people are forever hugging and kissing each other. Only not her, not yet.

Downstairs again, she enters the Art Nouveau hall tiled in shades of butterscotch, pink and green. The beige phone hangs mutely on the wall and she pauses beside it, willing the professor to ring. *If only there had been a lecture or a tutorial today he might have called me aside to reveal my destination.* She frowns, turning into the long passageway where her own room is the last. As usual, the silent flat is deserted. She seldom encounters the other tenants who keep to their rooms and go away every weekend. Last week she had come in through the front door to find them, six people including Rafael Vargas, lined-up in the hall, all wearing anoraks and walking boots, with rucksacks, tents and sleeping bags at their feet. They had stepped aside to let her pass and she had slunk away down the gaunt hall to her room feeling like the one kid in the school excluded from a playground game.

When she reaches the long window banded with coloured fanlights that admits the only daylight to the hall, a frond of the date palm rooted in the courtyard below feathers her cheek and the warm air feels like an embrace. Transported momentarily into an exotic future, the shining date strands become jewels in a desert bazaar and, dreamily, she leans out her hand and places among them a dun-coloured warbler.

The bird had been nothing to write home about, but it had captivated her when its image had filled the screen during Professor Bauza's slide lecture last term. *A diminutive warbler that had winged its way hundreds of miles over inhospitable deserts to land outside my cell,* the professor had said. That had been a long time ago, when – a doctoral student like herself – his first field base had been an Egyptian monastery, and the next slide proved it.

'1962. Here you see the monastery in the Alexandrian desert, where the Melodious warbler, *Hippolais polyglotta*, feasts on the seeds of the oasis palms before its northern migration. Soon, you will all be setting off to carry out field work, and I give you this counsel: see everything, hear everything, and above all, *document everything*, even things that might seem unimportant in the larger scale of things, like the Melodious warbler.'

She had impressed the professor's mantra on her mind. His words had inspired her. In this hiatus, she needed direction. So now, in her room, she takes *Warblers of the Eastern Mediterranean* off her desk. A substantial volume bound in faded burgundy leather, an important contribution to ornithological knowledge. Fine gold lettering on its spine, the mottled frontispiece signed: *R. R. Bauza, Egypt 1962,* and she remembers. Faded, not quite sepia, the next grainy slide had appeared on the screen, and the mud walls of the monastery had puckered under the well-aimed prod of the professor's pointer.

'The Coptic fathers, robed and bearded, came out through the ancient baked courtyard to greet me in my battered old Plymouth, thickly covered with *khamsin* sand,' he said, almost reverential. 'When I told them I had come to study one of the habitats of *Neophron percnopterus,* the Egyptian vulture, they took me in.'

The evidence was there for his students to see. Six monks in chimney pot hats, crucifixes gleaming against their black gowns, gather round the stranger in their midst. Smiling, sunhatted, shirtsleeves rolled, a large box camera in one hand, a leather satchel in the other, R. R. Bauza stands among them as if he has fallen from another planet. One of the monks must have taken that shot, a fellow student had whispered in Luisa's ear. And she supposed it must have been so. A moment that would have been lost forever *except in the professor's own memory* if nobody had snapped him half-a-century ago. And, as the lecture drew to a close, her heart had leaped with longing to get off the lecture theatre's hard seat and go immediately to that desert. 'Here in the desert where there is only dark and light, the first disciples of Christendom rehearsed their feeling for opposites; for night and day, sin and forgiveness, and life, of course, and death,' the professor said.

Yes, she, too, craved opposites, startling contrasts, rather than this endless waiting in Barcelona. Unused to cities, she longed for open countryside, for sea and mountains. In time snatched from studying, sometimes she trailed to the British Council to hear a talk by a visiting author, drink the wine provided and borrow books from the library. One poet, new to her, had seemed to speak to her and her alone when he recited lines she has learned by heart:

this is where one's false and tawdry self
starts to drown

How grey, she thought, her mouth a grim line glimpsed in the silver framed mirror hanging above her desk, how stale life has become. I am drowning here. I need to move on from this city, from this wretched flat where I find myself nearly always alone. The professor's bound to be around today. I'll make some excuse to see him before his office closes. And she hurried to the university only to be told by the professor's secretary, you've missed him, I'm afraid, but I'll tell him you called. Nothing to do then but wait, wait, wait. But I *will* make something happen, she resolved, returning to the flat determined to stay cheery. I'll make a sandwich, take it to my room and document the leaving of Scotland. In the refrigerator, a sticky label marks her shelf 'Luisa Ross' as if she had been an inmate of some institution. Rafael Vargas and the other tenants have them too: Lola, Jaume, Ricardo, Lidia, and the rest. Unlikely companions in a *tableau vivant*, frozen in space and time. She grimaced at the thought. Frozen as my footprints in the snow that morning I walked out of Scotland.

Lying on her bed a little later, notebook and pen to hand, she looks over the start she has made. '*Leaving the North*. At the edge of the territory Dan tended (with my assistance) there was always wind and sea-spray; rock pools, wrack and mussel beds.' It was a small start, but a start, nevertheless, and she mustn't weaken. Wasn't the yellow file on her desk marked *Luisa Ross b. 1965. BSc Glasgow University 1991. MSc 1998*, proof she'd come far, and would go further as soon as her field base had been determined?

The importance of documentation. But words are one thing, atmospheres another, she worries, pummelling the pillows against the carved Catalan bedhead. How to recapture atmosphere, release memories, bring back Scottish dunelands after all those weeks? An island cut off by the tide. A kitchen in a bothy where nervously, noisily, I'm piling plates, pans, mugs into the sink. But listen, defying distance and time, isn't that Dan's voice I hear . . . Dan's angry voice? 'So that's it then, after all these years, I'm not enough for you to stay for!'

Suddenly, she's writing down his words and, at the same time, a vivid image engulfs her. There she is, a solitary figure perched on the rocks of the North Shore, near cormorants hanging out their wings to dry in patchy sunlight. The roof of her bothy home peers over the dunes half-a-mile away, a conning tower . . . watching . . . waiting for her return. A plume of smoke rises from its squat chimney even in summer. Tormented by indecision, she sits with the letter from Barcelona on her lap.

'The sun, emerging from a screen of grey cumulus, almost blinded me.' She writes swiftly, desperate not to lose the thought. 'And, at that moment, a mirror of silver stole, as-if-by-magic, across the briny rock pools. It was a slight alteration of nature, barely discernible, yet this was the moment, the turning point when everything changed forever. I knew the time had come for me to leave Dan for good. The letter on my lap offered me a place on the professor's doctoral programme; the opportunity to become an ornithologist in my own right, not merely Dan's assistant. Yet I sat there thinking, I'm about to ruin Dan's life in order to save my own. And that frightened me. I had never put myself first before.

'I'm not enough for her to stay for' . . . Dan's cry came borne in the wind with the strident piping of the oystercatchers far across the bay. Then, *don't listen! don't listen!* the birds seemed to cry. *Harden your heart!*

Lapsing into the bower of pillows, she pictures herself half-way across the bay. Sand-bearing winds sting her face.

She cradles in her hands an immature auk, newly dead from exhaustion. Usually she wouldn't have given a dead bird a second glance – there were so many – but that day had been different, and she gropes for a way to explain it in words.

'If I had left its still-warm body on the shingle, a fox would have had its heart. So I dug a hole in the sand, laid the bird in, found flat stones to make a roof, and, looking back over my shoulder as I walked on, the little cyst looked somehow sacred, partly concealed by apricot sand and sea lavender. Then, almost immediately, a fox came skulking on the tide line. A young vixen, terribly thin. Down wind, I watched her through my binoculars, realising, that's what *you* feel like inside: achingly hungry to be released from serving Dan with soup, stews and sex (trying for the child we couldn't seem to conceive), typing up *his* research notes, despite your own M.Sc. and five year's teaching experience in the biology department of a Glasgow comprehensive before you even met Dan.'

Wistfully, she hears music. Somewhere in the Barcelona streets below, a distant accordion.

'Dan was playing the piano when I slipped into the bothy, expressing the sensitive side he usually concealed under the macho demands of official conservation work: digging trenches, pulling up sparta grass, felling trees and planting new ones. A never-ending, small-corner-of-the-planet-maintaining programme. But, poor man, was he playing the wrong tune that day! The impromptu, *Rosamunde*, so redolent of love and loss. Stuff the rose of all the world, I muttered, clapping the black kettle on the Rayburn stove. Harden your heart! If Dan knew what you were about to tell him, he'd force his hands down on as many notes of the keyboard as possible, black and white in a terrible discord, and slam the piano lid shut.

'I waited by the kitchen window. Sometimes we used it as a makeshift ornithological hide for observing the scrubby sycamore outside. There we could view at close quarters the occasional migrant bird. When I looked out that day, six baby swallows were twirping urgently to be fed on a limb of the tree, and, despite my agitation - *Dan's going to stop playing any minute*

17

now! - the intimate delicacy of the scene made me realise I would miss the island and its wildlife far more than I would miss Dan. Vigorously, I rubbed a roundel in the dusty window with the cuff of my jersey. As if I might fly off and away through that shining circle before I had to confront him. Then the music stopped and Dan came into the kitchen.'

Vividly she remembers the day she left Scotland and headed for Barcelona.

Dan was so angry. And I was so afraid. Looking back over my shoulder, my footprints meandering across the snow-covered dunes read like manuscript notes for a lament. And when the snow melted, I would have ceased to exist in the north.

§

The undulating mountain barrier they call La Serra de Tramuntana runs parallel to the north coast of Mallorca and accounts for almost a third of the surface of the island. If you study a relief map you might imagine some giant hand had moulded the limestone peaks, or *puigs*, of the sierra. She noted the highest peaks, a trio called Major, Massanella and Tomir, and lesser piles with curious names like El Teix and El Roig, and verdant hills between the mountains and the open plain known as El Raigeur.

Professor Bauza has suggested she take a look at a large volume bound in black and gold and illustrated with coloured plates: *La Serra de Mallorca.* They would examine the territory on a large scale map the following day. Any one of mainland Spain's high wildernesses could have been the professor's choice for her fieldwork: the Picos, the Sierra Nevada, the Sierra Moreno. But Mallorca? Sex, sun and sangria - wasn't that how the cliché went? The despoiled holiday destination of Northern Europeans? However, the centrefold map in the book intrigued her. For a start, the island was logistically interesting. Mainland Spain – Barcelona to be specific – was around eighty miles north of Mallorca; and North Africa – Algiers was the nearest city – a similar distance south.

A chapter titled *The Environment* informed her that the sierra – *la serra* in Catalan – was an ornithologist's paradise, home to large raptors and a strategic landing site for rare migrant birds.

'The mountains display limestone caves, gorges and underground springs. The sierra contains the main water reserve of the island,' she read with mounting fascination. 'Holm oak thrives in humid valleys with dense soil where ghostly reminders of the charcoal industry remain. Circles of stones (*sitjas*) and dormant lime kilns half-hidden by rosemary, briar, mock-privet and rockrose. At heights over 1000 metres the *pseudomaquis* sustains kermes oak, rockrose, prickly juniper and alpine plants on its silvery rock.'

Now she stands in front of the 1:25,000 military survey map of the island affixed to the wall of Professor Bauza's tutorial room. His pointer fixes one red dot on the map after another. 'These are the towns the conquerors built on the plain in the fourteenth century,' he tells her. 'Mallorcans call the plain, *Es Pla*.' His mouth opens wide pronouncing *'Pla'*, then he recites an evocative litany of the names of the towns on the plain: *María de la Salud, Ariany, Llubi, Sineu* . . . She smiles like a child at a magic show, and, certain of her interest, he shifts his rod to the north. 'That's the town of Inca, by the way, larger by far than the others, the centre of the island's leather industry. Inca was the Moorish capital of the island but, after the fourteenth century conquest, Palma became the seat of power and the countryside became known as the *Pars Forans*.'

She nods, then, with a graceful gesture towards the top edge of the map, he draws her attention to a chain of settlements strategically placed along the foothills of La Serra de Tramuntana and replaces the pointer on his desk. When she feels his touch on the small of her back, urging her closer to the map, a shiver runs through her. The moment has come. This is where I'm to go. She keeps her eyes glued to the gnarled twig of his index finger hovering above one of the mountain towns.

'You see that town? You could live there at weekends during your field study.' He squints sideways, catches her nod, and his finger shoots up beyond the cultivable reaches of the mountain foothills to a tiny red square on the edge of the white and green grid. 'That's the nature reserve, the project base,' he confides, peering at her over his spectacles. 'Can you make out its name?'

'Ca'n Clot,' she obliges with a nervy, excited cough.

They move closer to the map, bonded for a few moments in silent collusion while she absorbs the cartographic evidence for the terrain surrounding the field base.

'What does 'clot' mean?' eventually she asks.

'*Clot*' is Catalan for *hoya*. You know what *hoya* means, I suppose.'

Sí, of course, she wants to protest. Has the old man forgotten, I was brought up bilingual in Scotland? That my mother was Spanish? But this was neither the time nor the place to confess that Catalan, the language of Barcelona with Provençal derivations and Arabic admixes, had come as a surprise. A severe challenge in fact, after she discovered the professor's doctoral programme would be conducted in Catalan. These past weeks she had struggled to follow his lectures, though, greatly to her relief, the textbooks he prescribed were in Castilian. Reading far into the night had helped her to keep up with her fellow students.

'*Hoya*.' Thoughtfully she repeats the word. 'Doesn't it mean a geographical depression. The literal translation of Ca'n Clot must be 'the house or finca in the depression'?'

'Quite right.' The pressure of his hand comes again, this time below her shoulder blades. 'I may say, *clot* also means a *grave* in Catalan.'

She moves a little beyond his touch, hiding her irritation at his odd insinuendo. '*Clot*' meant 'grave'. So what?

Gradually, she was getting the hang of her mentor who, indeed, seemed to hail from a different planet. Or, more mundanely, she thought, he can never resist revealing the other side of a coin. Surely he doesn't think I'll be put off by his peculiar, insistent play on words? Maybe that's something characteristic of Catalans? In any case, I'll soon be out of his

20

orbit. To this refuge, this Ca'n Clot, set high on the very edge of the tree line, on the brown and white shot silk contours of the mountain called Massanella.

She prided herself on her map-reading ability. She could define the territory as a hovering hawk might. This wasn't easy terrain, that much was clear. The territory of rare warblers, of raven, falcon, kite and eagle and Mallorca's fabled Black vulture, *Aegypius monachus*, that nests in high wildernesses, far from human interference. If she stood in front of the map for a few more seconds, she would be able to give a detailed account of the area to anyone who asked. Only, it would not be a poetic description. That must wait until she ventured onto the wild mountain itself. The Puig Major de Massanella was 1367 metres high at its summit. Even its neighbouring peak, the Puig Major de Son Torrella, at 1445 metres, was higher than Ben Nevis, higher than Snowdon.

'Well, there you have it, that's the project base. The question is, do you want to go? I may say, it's a tough assignment.'

She wonders if the professor will add 'for a woman', for the phrase is surely on his lips. His dark olive eyes search her face but to her relief he says nothing more. Momentarily she wavers, her own eyes seeking the reassurance of her yellow file lying nearby on the professor's desk labelled *Luisa Ross* . . . it would not be easy . . . . Her thoughts raced. Can I really carry this off?

'Yes, I *do* want to go to Mallorca,' she said, with the same sort of startled longing she had felt as a child, daring herself to jump from one riverbank to another.

'For long periods you'll be quite alone up in the mountains, though always in contact by mobile phone with the reserve wardens who routinely visit Ca'n Clot. They'll help you in every possible way.'

After that, the old man handed her his copy of *La Serra de Mallorca*. 'This book is my gift to you, and what more is there to say? If it pleases you, the assignment is yours. And, I may say, that's the end of the matter. You'll fly to Mallorca next week and stay until *Navidad*, return to Barcelona over the holidays to write up your first report, and go back to Mallorca in January to undertake a three-month field study.'

Before she left for Mallorca, Professor Bauza booked a room for his student at Bar Solitario in the mountain town. Jaume the barman, and his wife, Paquita, would help her to find a house to rent over the winter. The professor insisted Luisa would need a comfortable retreat at weekends and whenever bad weather hit the mountains. And he told her something personal for the first time, as if reciting a well-loved story.

'I myself come from this area of Mallorca. From the mountain town closest to the finca of Ca'n Clot, the field base. My father was a carbonero there, Ramón Rafal Bauza. I was named after him. The town was poor when I was a child. There was no such thing as electricity and we had few things that were not basics of life, I may say. We made soap and candle wax and much else besides from the products of the olive industry. Although the manufacture of charcoal, from the holm oak woods, and olive oil production were the main sources of the town's income, there wasn't enough work to go round. A lot of people had to emigrate to Central and South America to find work. Nowadays tourism and building, building, building everywhere, with European Community grants, has altered the face of the island. The Partido Popular even wants to destroy part of *Es Pla* with yet another motorway. Everything's changing now. There's so much greed around. Though I think you will find that my town has changed far less than other places and retains its character.'

§

In Bar Solitario, loosely named after the Blue Rock thrush, *Monticola solitarius*, (whose loud, melodious song, heard in rocky vantage points, changes to a sharp *tak-tak* when alarmed) two men order *carajillos*. Jaume, the barman, pours out the coffee then turns to take a glistening brandy bottle off the shelf behind him. It is not yet noon in the mountain town.

'We need a stiff one this morning,' the older man jokes.

The barman knows why but says nothing as he pours a

measure of brandy into each cup. If he waits long enough Julio Valente will confirm his supposition, and, sure enough, he does.

'We're on the way to the station to pick up Bauza's student,' Valente says and the barman nods. Unable to disguise his boredom, Valente's companion, Felipe Tamarit, taps out a rhythm with a one Euro coin on the brown melamine surface of the bar.

The barman knew all about it. Señorita Ross was due to arrive today on a reconnaissance trip and would be staying in one of three rooms they let out above the bar. They were to help her to find a house to rent when she returned in January. Ramón had phoned a few days ago to book the room himself. A señorita hand-picked by Ramón Rafal Bauza, their local hero. Everyone was eager to meet her.

All the same, another woman is on Julio's mind. A woman who arrived in town a few months ago but who, like the Blue Rock thrush, prefers not to show herself much. *La Solitaria.* He calls her this because he doesn't yet know her name, but he likes her mature, womanly looks. She's proud, that's for sure, yet he suspects she has a big case of the blues. Surely *he* could make her happy? Driving past her orchard on the edge of town he has caught fleeting glimpses of her, raking and weeding between the trees. A singer of songs of lonely desolation. He downs the brandy-laced coffee then touches the sleeve of his sullen companion.

'C'mon, let's go. *¡Hombre!* put on your cap. We're part of the welcoming committee for Luisa Ross's train.'

The Arabs who first dug this land called it *azahar*, Anita Berens muses, stopping her work to savour the heavenly scent of citrus blossom wafting through her orchard. Then she stiffened. Was somebody calling my name?

Anita? Lourdes?

Her head spun round towards the minor road that skirted her land, but no one was there. No car, no farm vehicle, no green jeep driven by that mountain conservancy guy she liked the look of. Wouldn't mind at all if he got out for a chat. As it was, her only human contact since she had bought the orchard had been with the ancient proprietor of the neighbouring smallholding who taught her how to harvest the almonds from her trees, hitting the branches with a stick - *click! clack!* - until they scattered down on the fine green net he insisted she borrow.

'New vines must only be planted during a new moon,' he had told her. 'And if you decide to develop your *caseta* into a house to live in make sure the windows face south-east to catch the rising sun. No need for an alarm clock then, señora!'

Her spade hits a small rock in the red earth where she's digging, jarring her instep so that she curses out loud and her terrier rushes to her side. Chrissakes! she cries again, this is all I need. Now I'll bloody well have to dig the thing out with my hands. Down on all fours and dig. She thrusts her hands into the friable red soil. With small yelps of pleasure the dog gets the hang of it, digs maniacally with its forepaws, sends showers of earth all over her. Soon earth is in her eyes, in her mouth, in her hair, yet she has to laugh at the animal's touching display of enthusiasm. After that, the rock set aside, she carries on working with the spade. And when all the earth has been turned in the channel between the vines, she straightens up to look at the mountain, her boot resting on the spade, her left hand massaging the small of her back.

Her smallholding is one of many set in a lovely fertile valley below the mountain of Massanella, each the size of a small field, each with a small sandstone building. According to her old neighbour, the pattern of land division here went back to the conquest of Mallorca, when the six ancient gnarled olive trees on her land must have been planted, making them over eight hundred years old.

These earthly paradises seldom changed hands. Someone had to die first, but soon after she arrived in the town, she had been lucky enough to hear about this one that had belonged to the grandmother of Magdalena in the grocery shop. A hand-written notice in the shop window had alerted her to its sale, and she had acted fast to secure it with funds wired from her Swiss bank account. Around here, the old people were dying off fast. When a neighbour near her town house, Alejandro Ferrer, died, as soon he must, the neglected land to the east of her orchard would be sold off too, or inherited by one of his relatives. Let it be someone, she prays, who will not disturb the peace with a loud transistor radio or a barking dog.

She can tell by the sun, it's almost noon. Thrushes and warblers sing among the tumbled thorn bushes above the torrente where she works. Anita! Anita! Or Lourdes! Lourdes! for that matter, but no one calls my name. She rakes seeding grasses into a bundle, hoists it up with both arms, carries it to the compost heap at the back of the house. One day she might improve the two-storey building, *la caseta*, to create a dwelling-house and move out of town. If only they would let her. Then the remains of her life might be carefully glued back together, as if by a restorer repairing an Oriental bowl.

Oh, dream on, what's the harm, she thinks, vigorously scrubbing embedded earth from her nails under the cold water tap at the stone sink outside the cottage. The dog lies curled up on a shaggy pile of almond branches she pruned only yesterday and she goes muttering over to it. Never mind, little dog, our nice friend Colin will be with us after Christmas. The only person in the world these days who calls me Lourdes. No one else on this God forsaken island has the remotest interest in knowing my name far less calling it. She puts down a tin plate of scraps for the dog, takes her lunchtime sandwich from her basket, kicks off her boots and sits on the old bench outside the *caseta*. Feet up on the table, relax, enjoy! How magnificent Massanella looks today. Wow, what a view!

Some days the mountain landscape here reminds her of Colombia and makes her heart sing. Other days, cloudy days, the sight of it makes her homesick as Ruth weeping alone among the alien corn. But whatever her mood she prefers to be out here in the countryside, where she can be at peace. At the house in town she feels tense, always waiting for the knock on her door she dreads. The knock of the passing stranger who has found her hiding place. One of Andreas' honchos.

It's only a matter of time . . . in the meantime, *this* is what keeps me going, this contact with the earth, inhaling *azahar*, seeing the difference my work makes. An old vine rescued from near-decay at the far end of the plot; the herb garden newly created at the door of the old *caseta* where pots of marjoram, hyssop, verbena and thyme nestle; the embryo formal garden, on a modest scale, a riot of roses, lavender, bay and carnations. My hand in all this creation. Hand, heart and head.

She laughs dryly, and the dog leaps onto her lap. Sometimes I wish they'd damn well come, she whispers to the quivering animal, to break this impasse, this absurd waiting in no-man's-land. The dog cocked a velvety ear and gazed at her soulfully. Then, stricken by remorse that she had never given the dog a name, she told it, here and now I name you Azahar. A beautiful name. Yes, let's make the best of it! Cut some creamy roses to take back to town. That's right, into the back of the car with you and let's be off to town.

She knew the route so well, the return journey was usually seamless. Only today, when the track leading from her finca joined the road to Inca, she had to pull up sharply to avoid colliding with the conservancy jeep speeding up to town. It swerved, and the driver gave a sharp warning blast on the horn. The guy she liked the look of, who made her want to wave. Today the jeep is filled with people and she wonders who they can be as it flashes past.

Luisa Ross had arrived on the Palma-Inca train fifteen minutes earlier. Julio Valente and Felipe Tamarit immediately stepped forward to pick up her rucksacks. Then the alcalde of the town came thrusting out his hand to introduce himself.

'Call me Raúl if you like,' he blustered before he embraced her, flushed as an excited schoolboy. 'Welcome to our town,' he enthused, a small, stocky man whose ancestors had tended the olive terraces with the Bauzas, Luisa supposed.

The welcoming committee had taken her by surprise. Julio Valente and Felipe Tamarit, the two nature reserve wardens she must work alongside, Señor Caubet, and Mónica his efficient looking assistant, all waiting with a press photographer. Hiding her confusion, Luisa made a joke of looking round for the band while flashing bulbs captured for posterity the eventful day of her arrival.

'The photo's only for the town newsletter,' Mónica said, almost apologetic.

Yes, after all, Luisa Ross' credentials were impeccable. Hadn't she been hand-picked by Ramón Rafal Bauza, the town's local hero? Ah, yes, the importance of documentation. *See everything. Hear everything. Document everything.* Bauza's mantras.

'I'll ride in the jeep with our guest,' Señor Caubet told his assistant with a dismissive yet kindly flourish of his hand, and Mónica strode away in her beige trousers suit towards a new Opel parked near the wardens' jeep in the otherwise deserted station.

Then the conservancy jeep started up: Julio Valente with Felipe Tamarit in the front and Luisa riding in the back with the alcalde who reeked of garlic and the cigarillo he lit up as soon as they pulled out. He knew his job. 'PR' was the key to getting and keeping votes. It was the same in any language. Today he would wear one of the many hats his senior position in the town required of him: environmental tour guide. Only Luisa couldn't help wishing he'd pipe down and let her concentrate on the countryside whizzing past the window. Low stone dykes, deeply green grass, thousands of geometrically planted trees, everything shimmering in sunlight. And sure enough, in the midst of this astonishing beauty yes, there they were, geopoetic now, the red dots between Inca and the mountain town she had seen on Professor Bauza's map; idyllic ochre cottages snug among orchards of almond and fruit trees, roses, daisies and bean rows. Her excitement mounted, seeing ahead the rockbound town clinging with its seventeenth century church to the mountain foothills. Higher still, a convent, institutional and austere, dominated the town from a geological cone that must have split off from the mountain. And then, at last, she saw with startled recognition, rearing above it all was the mountain called Massanella.

The enthusiastic alcalde, craning out of the speeding jeep, pointed everything out, and Luisa's euphoria felt boundless as the jeep swept up the road towards the town. Such a warm welcome, such a contrast to Rafael Vargas' unfriendly flat. Rafael Vargas had intrigued her, though his lack of interest in her had been perplexing. Still, what did he matter now she was off on tracks of her own? She had left behind the professor's tutorial rooms, too, with its maps of Egypt, Saudi, South America and Spain. Her new life was to be defined here, on a red dot on a map of this island.

The alcalde drew her attention to an impressive high crag near the town's entrance, its terracotta flanks austerely etched and pitted with shallow black caves.

'Lesser kestrels nest there,' he said, eager, proud.

Falco naumanni. I'll make a note of that, she thought wryly, suddenly nostalgic for her Barcelona angels. And where the Lesser kestrel nests, the swift is sure to follow in late spring, bound perhaps for Scotland, on its northerly migration.

Raúl Caubet drew closer with a confiding air: 'The crag is more than it seems. Far more.' Then, all of a sudden, Julio Valente was braking hard and pressing on the horn to avoid collision with a car emerging from a side road. 'Phew! that was a near one,' he exclaimed. But the drama failed to deflect Señor Caubet. 'Indeed, señora, that very crag is a sacred site associated with the worship of bulls.' His hand flapped so energetically his fingertips brushed her knee. Putting down this moment of over-familiarity to an excess of enthusiasm, Luisa shifted away a little, amused. After all, wasn't she among warm-hearted romantic people now? People who didn't fear human contact and didn't hesitate to touch a stranger. Yes, now she was among the Mallorcans.

'It is true, señora. The place is named the Bull Mountain because in the 1950s the buried statuette of a bull was unearthed by some boys playing there. It was donated to the Palma museum.'

'Then I'll make a point of going to see it when I'm in the city,' she says.

The crag was the last prominent feature of the plain before the road twisted steeply up toward the first houses of the town.

Solid mountain homes. Uncompromised by decoration or *bijoux* floral pots at the door, they clung to their steep terrain.

'It's a *small* town . . . or is it a large village?' she wonders aloud. Only, when she sees Felipe Tamarit's shoulders heaving with suppressed laughter, and turns to meet the alcalde's sudden frown she thinks, oh, great, I've just made my first blunder.

'It is certainly not a village, señora. It is a town with three shops, two bars, an olive manufactory and an important church . . . .'

Thinking fast, eager to make amends, she observes that the town *belongs* to the mountain in a most remarkable way.

That seemed to do the trick. Señor Caubet beamed. 'Yes, our town and the mountain are one. It is a beautiful relationship.'

It was all a matter of climate and weather, she supposed. This mountain begins right here on the edge of town; town and mountain are part and parcel of one another. Whereas Scottish mountain towns characteristically lurked on low foothills. From here on, everything rises steeply in the lee of Massanella. She had known from the professor's map, Massanella would not be a jagged mountain, nevertheless its sheer amplitude, reminiscent of a curvaceous recumbent female nude, surprised her. And now she was within its orbit, she realised its surface would be anything but yielding. No, it would be a boulder strewn wilderness, a brute to climb. After all, wasn't the entire sierra a raised beach squeezed up like toothpaste from the depths of the sea, with all its rocks and fossils, even before the Mediterranean Sea was formed, after the Earth's tectonic plates shifted aeons ago?

Representatives of the mountain town are waiting to meet her in an old olive processing barn, converted now for lectures and exhibitions as Raúl Caubet informs her. A formal reception must be endured. From the bottom of the steps when the jeep pulls up, she sees her hosts foreshortened under the arched entrance, their clothes old-fashioned to her eyes, comfortable rather than smart, and, among them, one or two more trendily dressed in T-shirts and jeans. Everyone stands very still, as if posing for a group photograph.

Up the steps she goes beside the alcalde who stretches both arms wide to usher everyone inside. Like a shepherd, Luisa thinks, driving his flock from one field to another. For her benefit, he gives his short welcoming speech in Castilian rather than the Mallorcan dialect of the town. Then, he guides Luisa towards people she must meet: representatives of the area's conservation groups, members of the local administration and the various political parties. And, after Mónica reappears to inspect with painted nails the impeccable table covered with a white cut-lacework cloth, he declares the buffet open.

A long table is laid out with glasses for cava and plates of green and black olives, sliced bread, various cheeses and *sobrasado* which, someone explains, is a local delicacy prepared from pig's blood, paprika and herbs. Pressed to try it, although she is practically a vegetarian, Luisa cannot refuse. She spreads a morsel on a slice of bread and swallows it in one gulp. *¡Delicioso!*, she tells the watching congregation, then accepts a glass of cava from Raúl Caubet. Everyone claps enthusiastically and, surrounded by laughter and animation, suddenly she feels happy.

Unused to being the centre of attention, the sparkling cava fortifies her. But when the alcalde says, 'it takes ten years for a foreigner to learn Mallorcan, even if that person practises every day,' she feels a small stab of pain. Although she is half-Spanish, try as she might, she could never be truly one of them.

Later, when she leans out to close the shutters of her upstairs room at Bar Solitario, the mountain air smells pure and sweet. The evening sky is a masterwork painted in smooth washes of duck-egg blue and rosy-gold before, as if in a deep-held breath, its colours retreat in the face of inky night and the stars come shining out. All through the tranquillity of the night nothing stirs except an occasional eagle owl marking the limits of its territory in the woods behind the town.

The town lies sleeping, but Anita Berens' house in Calle Luna has become the haunt of raucous ghosts. Around three am she jerks awake in a turmoil. Fearful apparitions always wakened her in the middle of the night in her Colombian prison. The fear has diminished but, still, she hardly ever sleeps through the night. Fear and frequent nightmares haunt her life and the most persistent nightmare always ends with her running down dark corridors, waking with the scream in her head: *Elena is dead!*

Fumbling for the matches beside the candlestick, she drags her body off the bed. *¡Elena está muerta!* The dog comes to her but she bends over to shove it gently aside and gropes under the bed for her slippers. As if a dog could help me now! She steals onto the terrace through the half-open French doors. Another sort of prison. How long can this be endured? Warm wet face lifted to the mocking half-moon. A night sky so clear you could smash it like a plate-glass window. *Verklartenacht.* Cypress and date-palm silhouettes against an indigo sky. Starry, starry *nacht.* Anita Berens. Are there no angels up there to hear when I call in despair? Waking, shouting: *¡Elena!*

Shivering now, she pulls on the thick orange robe hanging on the back of the door, and, cosseted in its hopeful colour, picks her way downstairs. One guiding hand traces the wall as the steep flight of stone steps descends. She curses the ghosts she struggles to keep at bay all day long, only for them to get the upper hand in the small hours of the night. Elena is *not* dead, she makes herself say. Elena is almost twenty years old, in good health as far as I know, married to someone I have never met called Bartolomé, and living in New York City.

Pallid moonlight invades the night house through its small windows. Her daughter's number lies on the face of the telephone. No need even to look as she taps in the digits like a blind person expert in braille. *Three-thirty am Mallorca time. Nine-thirty pm New York time.* The dialling tone rings on interminably. Then Elena's sweet voice on the answering machine: *Hello, this is Elena. Please leave a message after the beep and I'll get back to you . . .* Some sort of comfort, crumbs of words, all she expects. I am your mother, she whispers under her breath into the handset, hearing the repetition of the message in Spanish: *¡Hola! soy Elena. En este momento no puedo atenderte . . .* At least Elena hasn't forgotten to deal with the world in Spanish. Don't forget me, the one person in the world whom you can't phone back, the one person who daren't leave a message, *cariño*, because, sure as hell, they've got your phone tapped.

En este momento . . . she slips the receiver back on its cradle, then encounters a face staring out from the gilt-framed mirror hanging above the telephone table. She shouts out with fright. Then, *idiot!* she cries with a dry hysterical laugh. Of course no one's there but you. And just as well there's no one living next door or they'd think there was a madwoman in here! Pushing damp strands of hair off her forehead, she moves closer to the mirror in another of her frequent searches for herself. For Lourdes Herreros, who lives on behind the image of the stranger she has been forced to invent and must strive continually to believe in. Anita Berens, the stranger she feels no love for yet whom she has to live with day in, day out.

Mi nombre es Lourdes, pero me llaman Anita.

Anita Berens, part-Dutch, part-South American like Lourdes Herreros, but as far as the people up here in this little town are concerned I am German. What's the difference to them? They've already sold out a big slice of their inheritance to thousands of Germans and other foreigners living on this island. What's one more? Anita Berens speaks Spanish, German, Dutch and English fluently, the languages of the ancestors of Andreas and Lourdes Herreros. If they had half a chance to get to know me, Lourdes, they'd be proud to make my acquaintance.

Hah! little do they know that Anita Berens' neat haircut masks Lourdes' dark-brown hair, worn once upon a time in a chignon, or left hanging loose below her shoulders. Whereas now it's dyed blond and cut rather severely at shoulder length with a chiselled fringe. My own hair, Lourdes' hair, had hung loose the night of the party, above a Scarlett O'Hara-style evening dress. And the next day I had arranged it in a sophisticated French-roll and put on my Colombian gold-hooped earrings.

So long ago and far away; that last time I was truly myself. In Colombia. In each and every moment before that split second before I was brutally removed from my own life, just as Andreas' parents had been. In Berlin. After *Kristallnacht.* The shadow of repeated history. Only his parents never returned to tell their tale as I do mine.

This is where my story begins: It happened with the speed of lightning . . . say it in Spanish, why not? *ocurrió a la velocidad de un rayo* . . . yet I've relived the precise moment the hooded men burst into my car, relived it times without number. Trailing back to my moonlit room in this two bit Mallorcan town, I can see Pedro waiting beside the limousine as if it were yesterday . . . cap under his arm, outside Broadcasting House in Bogotá . . . raining lightly, I remember . . . then the unimaginable struck . . . *un rayo de entre la nada.*

Back in her bed, she swallows a couple of sleeping pills and blows out the candle. The terrier retreats to his cushion in a corner of the room.

At that same forlorn hour of the night, the cabin hostess slips through the silent plane to fetch Colin Cramer a second brandy. He looks out over the Pyrenees at what lies far below the wings of the Boeing 727 bound for Mallorca. He can't sleep but, then, flying always makes him feel wide awake. And tonight his excitement is heightened by the relish he feels for the role he's taken upon himself as a sort of Santa Claus, even if his surprise visit to Lourdes will be a little early for Christmas. The Apple Mac stowed in the hold of the plane will transform her existence as Anita Berens, at least a little. This will be a short visit, very short. A one-nighter snatched from the hubbub of his London life. Over the years he has flown out to Mallorca many times. Long before he met Lourdes Herreros, occasionally he would join laddish parties of golfing friends for long weekends near Andratx. Once he had spent the entire month of August chilling out with media folk in a romantic hilltop town to the north of the island whose name he couldn't recall. He had sowed a few wild oats in these good old days and, in more prosperous times, had brought the wife and kids over to Mallorca on villa and sailing holidays.

Tonight, a night of astonishing clarity, the aeroplane is coasting low above the Pyrenees and he can see tiny pinpricks of lights from hamlets, villages and towns dispersed like microchips on inky black valley heads, deep plains and river mouths. It was only relatively recently that humans first discovered the essential bedrock of their world, he muses. First, the early pilots, followed by all sorts of scientists, geologists, biologists, anthropologists, etcetera, and then the first rich owners of private planes had

33

looked down in astonishment, from heights in the sky where they had never been before, at the strata of stone and sand and salt that underpinned their little lives. Where life itself, Colin recites to himself, like a patch of moss deep in hollow ruins, flowers here and there where it dares.

He doesn't have to look up the words of Antoine de Saint-Exupéry. He has known passages from the book by heart ever since his final year at the London School of Economics when he discovered *Wind, Sand and Stars* in a bookshop on The Strand. And, after that, he became obsessed with the idea of becoming a pilot rather than a journalist, only the examining board of the RAF had rejected him because he was short-sighted. When, despite claims for their efficacy by the US Air Force, his eyesight hadn't improved after a year of chewing concentrated blueberry tablets, he'd had to accept it. He was grounded for life, reduced to a mere mortal indulging his flights of fancy from business class. A frequent flyer with a passion for the history of aviation.

He adjusted his rather comfortable seat into reclining position and settled back, relieved for these few precious hours to be beyond the reach of work colleagues and family. In the dimly lit fore cabin of executive class there were only two other passengers, both sleeping as far as he could see. No one will chat to him, he is free to let his thoughts wander.

The poet Marlowe's words come to him, not for the first time: *Is this the face that launched a thousand ships, and burned the topless towers of Ilium?* Aegean terrorism centuries ago. Had nothing changed? After the devastation of Manhattan's Ilium, the illustrious Twin Towers of the most powerful nation on earth, for a whole day Lourdes had been unable to confirm that her daughter Elena was safe. In great distress she had phoned him at his London office and he had sent his New York correspondent, Rob Greenaway, to Elena's apartment on 42nd Street to make sure she was okay. That was when he had realised the way round the communication glitch that caused Lourdes so much anguish was to get her up and running on the InterNet. She and Elena could safely, well, relatively safely, send each other e-mails. But Lourdes had resisted the idea. She refused to learn a new skill in her present predicament. If something went wrong with a computer in Colin's absence, who could she trust to help her out? However, lately she had come round to the idea, after he persuaded her they'd make faster progress on the book he was writing about her kidnapping. Who could tell? Circumstances might change. *Flight into Exile* might even be in the shops in time for next Christmas.

Better late than never, he sighed, and the brandy went down, hot in his throat. He peers out at the sea under the wing of the plane where the occasional mast light gave away the presence of fishing boats plying the Mediterranean. He remembers again, Saint-Exupéry: 'thus do we now assess man on a cosmic scale, observing him through our cabin windows as if through scientific instruments.' Marlowe and Saint-Exupéry, my imaginary flight companions. But not in their wildest dreams could the innocent early pilots have imagined using their planes as *weapons*. Oh, no! Aeroplanes were magic carpets transporting them to 'faerylands forlorn', avoiding bad weather, mountain tops and the metaphorical towers of Ilium. How he has always envied the pilots, like Saint-Exupéry, who, early on in the history of flight, dared to fly their flimsy transport over deserts, volcanoes and seas, steering a careful course between Cassiopeia and the Great Bear. These days we're being forced to read our history anew, he thought wryly. One of the important subtexts of *Ecco!*, the magazine he edited, was that human beings consistently failed to learn from history.

The 'fasten seatbelt' sign flashed on the deck above his head. Prepare for landing. Return to the present. He stole a last look at the fishing boats below, their lights pinpricking the inky sea surrounding Mallorca. Had any of them a more sinister purpose than bringing in fish? His thought prompted him to set aside his brandy glass and take out of his briefcase a press release concerning a Spanish seizure of cocaine from a boat out of Colombia. It had arrived on his desk in London minutes before he headed for the airport. Scanning the text, he wondered, isn't it just possible Andreas Herreros has had a hand in this?

2

The south-east facing windows of the silent town turn to gold in the rising sun. The driver of Colin Cramer's airport taxi brakes sharply at Anita Berens' door, and, not much later, Luisa Ross rises in her simple room above Bar Solitario to prepare for her first trip to Ca'n Clot.

Struck by an odd reversal of history - my mother arriving in Britain from Spain almost half a century ago, a probationary exile like myself - thoughtfully she hangs up in the wardrobe the skirt, blouse and tan leather jacket she had worn for her arrival yesterday. Then, overcome with nostalgia, she has to sit down on the edge of the bed, remembering.

Mother . . .

a slim young woman wearing a floral dress under a brown grosgrain coat with padded shoulders, nipped in at the waist, and a cap with a feather in it. According to the silver-framed photo that lived on top of our piano at home she arrived at Tilbury Docks with one old suitcase.

Mother . . .

a teacher of piano, decided to abandon Franco's Spain because the culture was stultifying and young women had limited choices: marriage under a patriarchal system, frustrated spinsterhood, or entering a nunnery. And she told you she could never get out of her mind what she had seen with her own eyes in childhood. Her father, Manuel Frutos, being led out of the town hall in handcuffs beside the most interesting men of the town who had been his friends since childhood, teachers, a painter, a transvestite poet, a homosexual actor. All of them poets of life in their own way, taken to the outskirts of town, blindfolded, shot and piled in an unmarked common grave. And in our attic her battered brown suitcase lay empty and forgotten until I found it, covered with dust, during the forlorn days after her death in Scotland, in 1984.

And, is this why I find myself in Spain? To deal with my Spanish side, see where I fit in? Excited by a sudden thought, she jumps off the bed. Fastening the buttons of her green woollen shirt, she wonders, why not take my grandfather's name? Call myself Luisa de Frutos after this fieldwork placement's over. Why not? After all, I'm in Spain now, and today marks the start of my new life. A new name for a new phase of life. She puts on a padded beige jacket with a sturdy zip and lots of pockets, such as fishermen wear, and goes down to the bar where Jaume's matronly wife, Paquita, serves up eggs, bread and cocoa and, after that, Julio and Felipe arrive to collect her. The jeep slips eastwards out of the waking town, past a straggle of new villas, each fenced off within landscaped grounds, and her head spins round amazed when, at one house after the other, ferocious guard dogs fling themselves at the fences.

'I curse the owners of these dogs,' Julio Valente asserts, turning in his seat to see her. 'I just hope these owners have been wakened under their duvets by the horrible din of their own dogs!'

Startled by Julio's outburst, Luisa wonders what the owners of the villas need to protect.

'It's no joke being a guard dog in Mallorca, señorita,' he goes on. By way of the driver's mirror she catches his frown, the puckered moustachioed lips, the dark brows indrawn above sharp yet tender brown eyes. Felipe, reading a magazine, says nothing.

'It's high time Spain was brought into line with the rest of Europe over cruelty to animals,' Julio adds. 'The owners of these dogs drive away to work every day, leaving the animals isolated, untrained and unloved, chained and underfed, just to protect their TVs, videos, family jewels, etcetera.' He gave a disdainful laugh. 'A lot of dogs are left alone for days, even in the blazing heat of summer. If they happen to remember, someone comes to throw down food for them. No wonder the dogs are savage.'

Was this man, Valente, testing her? Hoping to tease an opinion out of her? Well, it was far too soon for that. She didn't reply but recalled something she had read in a guide book to the island: 'Mallorcan dogs sound ferocious but love their owners'. The odd phrase had stuck in her mind. Now it made sense. Food meant survival to all creatures. These dogs had no choice but to love the hand that fed them but, left chained up all day, it was small wonder they were ready to attack anyone except their owners. The dogs were terrorists and terrified, both at once.

They reached the countryside and turned sharp left onto a minor road where a sign nailed to a tree read: *Coto privado de caza*. Private game reserve. Luisa asked Julio, 'what goes on here?'

'The territory we're driving into, señorita, is reserved for the hunt, *la caça*. It takes place every year between October and March.'

'Hunting? Are there wild animals here, apart from mountain goats?'

Both men turn their heads to look at her, Felipe smirking.

'No! no! no! Not bears, or wild cat, or anything like that,' Julio says. 'Wild animals were hunted out of existence centuries ago. *Thrushes*. They shoot and net thrushes for the local speciality, *Tords en Col*, thrush wrapped in cabbage leaves.'

Bird hunting? Surely not in Professor Bauza's territory, she thinks. The chained dogs were bad enough, but the prospect of innocent songbirds being slaughtered near her field base filled her with dismay. How would she be able to stay silent about an important topic on the agenda of every European ornithologist she had ever met? Thousands of migrant birds killed in the fray along with the thrushes, just as dolphins and tropical fish are slaughtered every minute of every day by commercial fisheries round the world. She stifles the remark: do Mallorcans eat larks' tongues too? and wondered what the men, Julio and Felipe, guardians of nature, felt about bird hunting? Far too soon to ask. As a newcomer she must wait and see, and curb her indignation lest it spoil her journey to Ca'n Clot, the finca in the depression.

Finding a space for her feet on the green metal floor among boxes of supplies, rolls of wire netting and wooden stakes, she fishes for her binoculars in a side pocket of her rucksack. How will I get on with the men, she wonders? Muscular Julio, a salt-of-the-earth type; wiry Felipe, golden-skinned, perhaps with Arab ancestors? I'd bet they'll be pretty much like country blokes I'd meet at Lanark, or Berwick, or Inverness, whose wildlife politics are often a bit 'iffy'. A bit in your face, too, but the important thing is their hearts seem to be in the right place. Julio, the senior warden, a little older than me, calls me señorita. Salt-and-pepper, curling hair escapes the confines of his cap. The younger man, Felipe's head's in a magazine; he calls me señora and, from where I sit, I can almost touch the light brown coil of his ponytail.

She looks away to see Massanella rearing up under a wash of pure blue sky, noticing how the sharp morning sun has erased its dimensions, its gullies and swellings and shadows. It resembles a surreal stage-flat waiting for action, for *me*, she thinks, her excitement reviving as they drive on a straight asphalted road, through private lands which slope up to an ancient Arab settlement Julio tells her is called Casas Viejas . . . she translates the name as 'the old houses', and, indeed, as Julio adds, the conglomeration of manorial house, with Italianate overhanging eaves and adjacent outbuildings, was built in the seventeenth century on foundations dating back to Moorish times.

She notices a man on top of a ladder working on the pantiled roof, and, at that moment, with a loud yawn, Felipe tucks the magazine under his seat and says, 'the family that own the place descend directly from one of the fourteenth century conquerors of Mallorca.'

Julio gets out in the dusty farmyard, scattering an assortment of fowls and ducks: 'Hey! Pep! How's it going?' he calls, and the man starts climbing down the ladder.

Felipe stretches languorously, making triangles of his arms above his head. 'The owners moved to town last year. Like many Mallorcans, they prefer the comforts of a new-build home. It's one of these villas we passed, as a matter of fact, guarded by a Doberman.'

Shifting uncomfortably in her seat, she looks away out at the old farmstead, where Julio and the man stand chatting.

'That's Pep Oleza,' Felipe says, turning to look at her. 'A sort of gamekeeper-cum-manager. They call them *'amos'* here.'

Amos, she thinks. Lovers of a place that belongs to someone else.

'If you ask me the Arabs made a better job of ruling Mallorca than their Christian successors,' Felipe continued. 'The Arabs knew what they were doing, built in high places where there was water, *sabes*? Water for agriculture, horticulture, and domesticity. Clear, cool, mountain spring water, not the terrible chlorinated water they pipe into town houses nowadays.'

Surely not, with lovely spring water up here in the mountains? Luisa wants to say it, but she won't be drawn on the water issue either. Nothing must be allowed to threaten the world she was about to enter . . . a world she has invented in her dreams ever since the day Professor Bauza gave her this assignment.

Julio gets back in: 'Pep tells me the estate's being viewed by rich foreigners.'

Felipe let out a groan. 'See what I mean, señora? We're losing our heritage. Everything from old barns and garages to ancient estates like Casas Viejas snapped up and developed into luxury retreats with big blue swimming pools in the old orchards.'

Felipe the disgruntled, Julio the sanguine, Luisa thinks, her mouth curving as they drive on. Then almost immediately she hears muffled shots coming from the forest high above the track.

'There it is, señorita, *la caça*,' Julio says.

More shots follow, then the sharp cry: '*¡ven aquí! ¡ven aquí!*'

Leaning out of the window, she looks up to see a distant shooter on the terraced hill calling his pointer, then another hunter emerging from the woods with more dogs. The scene resembles an eighteenth century print, and the practice should have been confined to ancient history long ago, she thinks glumly.

'They shoot, in these parts, in the early morning and at dusk during the season,' Julio says, briskly shifting gears to accommodate a hilly stretch of the track.

They're doing their best to induct me, when really they would rather not have to, Luisa thinks, sitting back, determined not to dwell on the slaughter of the birds. Not now, anyway. Yes, they were doing their best, and she was doing her best to like the men, but she dreaded to think how she would feel about them if she discovered they favoured this so-called hunt.

They travelled in silence through the sheer lee of a thick pine forest, her eyes tracing stony lineaments drawn on the mountainside that reminded her of Scottish drystone dykes. Each Scottish dyke is like a signature. Local people used to be able to tell, by looking at a drystone dyke, the man who built it.

'Are these boundary walls?' eventually she wonders, leaning towards Julio for enlightenment.

'No, they are covered *canalettas*, channelling water from underground springs near Massanella's summit to irrigate the plains.'

Picturing the rushing rivers and waterfalls of home, she realises how lucky Scots were to take their water for granted. She knows from studying maps of the island, Mallorca has no rivers, only underground springs, these *canalettas* and the *torrentes* that direct flood water and melting snow down to the plain.

Soon the road becomes a trail of compacted earth, strewn with rockfall, that wends in and out of deep dank valleys, darkly wooded with holm oaks and reeking of fungal mould. For fifteen minutes they have seen no-one but Pep Oleza. As they climb higher, air smelling of pine and mountain camomile ruffles her hair through the open windows and, the hunt left far behind, her elation mounts to be in the midst of such unfamiliar beauty.

Yet, I could describe this route with my eyes closed, how perfectly it emulates its contour map . . . it's as if Professor Bauza's standing in front of his map at this very minute, his thick finger tracing this very journey I'm taking across its silky brown and white contours, like some all-seeing God.

'They say you are from Scotland?' suddenly Julio says.

'*Sí, eso es.*' She catches his glance in the mirror.

'They say Scotland is very beautiful. Is it as beautiful as Mallorca?'

How to reply? Scotland is the most beautiful place in the world, given the right weather in the right place?

'Both are beautiful, though in different ways,' she says tactfully. 'I hope you'll visit Scotland one day and judge for yourself.'

But when they emerge out of a gloomy valley into the vast silence of the luminescent wilderness she has to draw in her breath. How spectacular it was up here. Rather like the first time I opened the door to Rafael's drying roof, and saw in front of me - *loom!* - those spires and bells and hawks. Here was a seemingly limitless silver plateau, strewn with boulders, serene under an expansive sky, and Massanella reigning overall. A vision of eternity. She can't take her eyes off it and finds herself longing to cross the meseta on foot, alone.

After that, no one speaks until they arrive at a high metal gate secured with a massive padlock. Felipe fumbles for the key in the tool compartment, jumps out and holds the gate back until the jeep passes through.

Waiting for Felipe to get in, Julio pushes his green cap off his forehead and turns to Luisa: 'You can't drive up further than the gate unless you have a key to the padlock. The nature reserve begins here.'

'But can you walk up to the finca on foot, along the mountain tracks?'

'Yes, of course, you go from this gate. I'll show you the route myself one day. The paths are not shown on any maps. They're donkey tracks, laid down by old carboneros working in the holm oak woods long ago. You have to *feel* for the paths, grope around a bit in places. It takes much longer to go that way, of course, than driving or even walking to Ca'n Clot on this road we're on. Around two-and-a-half hours from the town, I'd say, if you keep up a steady pace.'

Felipe tosses the key back into its nook and they head north to the heart of the reserve. At the edge of the last oak wood, Julio halts the jeep and points to a gaunt, spreading tree. 'In the old days local people said that tree stood at the very edge of the world. They still call it the Tree on the Edge.'

He turns off the engine and they sit for a few minutes looking out at a vast, living candelabra, a gnarled ancient marvel of sculpted bark. Julio knew I would appreciate this wonderful tree, she thinks, moved by his gesture. Even Felipe looks out. So mysterious here on the edge of the wood. Pulsating energy, tangible silence. Reach out and you can touch it, but draw your fingers quickly back. You never know . . . yes, something might lurk hidden in the wood surrounding this Tree on the Edge. A little shiver runs through her. Fear? Excitement? She herself could hardly tell what she felt, staring up into the canopy of the tree, wondering how she would fare up here on the edge of the world.

Julio starts up the engine. 'That tree should never have grown so large. Maybe a previous owner of Ca'n Clot imported the seeds of a different sort of oak to Mallorca. That's my guess, but I'm no botanist, I'm afraid.'

Her throat feels dry, knowing any second she'll see it, and when Julio says, there it is, there's Ca'n Clot, an ochre structure with attached outbuildings rises in the landscape ahead, its back turned to a crag around two hundred metres high. Her pulse quickens. It's certainly wild and lonely up here; can I really carry this off? . . . So far from anywhere, my field base for the foreseeable future.

'They call the crag El Escarpado de las Cuevas Negras,' Julio says, steering with one hand, pointing with the other.

'Yes,' she says, thoughtfully. 'We could see the crag from another angle, earlier, when we crossed the meseta.'

He smiles. 'You are very observant, señorita.' Then drives fast over the small stones that pepper the approach to the finca. They bounce up, hit the jeep as if it were a xylophone. The music of the morning with the distant added refrain of a barking dog. Julio shouts over the racket. 'That's Perro you hear. Our old guard dog. We train birds up here. Some are precious, so we have to make sure no one steals them or the eggs of the nesting birds, come to that.'

Eager to hear about an unexpected sideline to Ca'n Clot's activities she wonders what breeds of birds are trained here.

'Quite a variety. You'll see for yourself. Mostly birds of

prey for display at country fairs. Though Felipe here trains his favourites to hunt.'

At that, Felipe's arm crooks up on the back of his seat, and he turns to catch her eye.

So, he's a falconer, she thinks, avoiding his gaze.

He lays his chin on his arm and fixes her with a sideways look out of near-Oriental eyes. 'At the moment I'm training my eyas. You can help me fly her?'

§

At that moment in the house of Anita Berens, Colin Cramer sat reading *El Pais,* where he had found another version of the press release he had brought with him from London. The mingled aromas of bacon and coffee permeated the salon where he lounged on the white leather sofa, recovering from his journey.

'Listen to this,' he called, and Lourdes came through from the kitchen where she had been clearing the breakfast dishes into the dishwasher. With a practised eye, he scanned the text. He could read Spanish to his own satisfaction and, when Lourdes came to sit beside him, haltingly, he translated: 'A thirty-two meter-long trawler, the *Vega II,* carrying cocaine from Colombia, was brought into a small fishing port near La Coruña last week under the escort of a high speed Spanish Customs vessel.'

But his efforts failed to impress Lourdes: 'here', she said, playfully nudging him: 'give it to me,' and she rattled off the rest of the article in English. 'At first officials were unable to find the haul. Then, twenty-four hours later they discovered a false hull stashed with five tonnes of pure cocaine . . . .'

I'll use that story, Colin privately vowed. I'll get young James on to it as soon as I'm back in the office tomorrow. The world has become so *magnetised* by events in the Arab world it has forgotten - if, indeed, it ever cared about - the terror that occurs every minute of every day in Central America so Europe can have its drugs.

With a sigh, Lourdes folded up the newspaper, and said, 'Colin, if you're sitting comfortably, shall we make a start on your book?'

Colin had wanted to begin at the beginning. He had showed her how to open and close files on the computer, and after she had demonstrated her competence they labelled a file: *Colombia 2000*. He intended to get Lourdes to dictate exactly what had happened at the time of her kidnapping. She had protested, 'but you've heard it all before, Colin!' Yes, maybe, he had replied, but what happened has never been written down, that's a different kettle of fish altogether. No detail she might remember was to be left out. But, although she was eager to co-operate, sitting beside him in the upstairs guest room that now housed the Apple Mac - so grateful was she for his unexpected arrival with the gift of the computer (they had already sent an e-mail to Elena and had received a reply) - this method failed to work. It was as if he had asked her to drag up a heavy body in a sack from the bottom of a deep sluggish river.

'It happened with lightning speed,' she started to say, sitting obediently, like a child on the stiff chair beside his . . . *como un rayo*, she muttered in Spanish. . . 'yes, it happened with lightning speed.' Then, flinging her arms wide, she protested: 'oh, it simply won't work this way, Colin. I sound so *stilted*.'

'Try again, my dear,' he urged. 'If we succeed in recording how ghastly it was, won't you feel a great weight has been lifted?'

It had been Lourdes' idea, after that, to work with a tape recorder. 'We could sit and chat as we usually do, having a drink or two beside the fire? Then, if I start to flow, you can switch on the recorder. After that, in the next few days, I'll type what I've said into the computer, and edit it if necessary.'

Now, with the recorder well placed on a side table at his elbow, they sat close together on the sofa, not quite touching, and he judged she was as ready as she would ever be. 'Okay, my dear,' he said gently, 'tell me how it began?'

Lourdes was sitting bent forward a little, her arms wrapped round herself. She stared at her feet and said slowly, 'As usual,

Pedro was waiting beside my limousine, cap under his arm, outside Broadcasting House. It was raining lightly.'

She paused, looking sideways at Colin. He nodded encouragingly and she went on. 'I'm going straight home tonight, I told Pedro when he was opening the rear door for me. I was dog tired after a late party the night before, followed by a hard day's work, so I dropped into the creamy upholstered seat with a sigh of relief and shook off my high-heeled shoes. I remember thinking I must be getting old!' She gave a dry laugh, and Colin said softly, 'you're doing fine. Go on.'

'Pedro put on his cap, got in and drove away. Playing safe had become second-nature because of recent Bogotá kidnappings . . . I stretched over to lock each door of the car in turn. When I looked over my shoulder through the rear window I happened to notice three other cars pulling out; one was a Mercedes directly behind us, two others left the kerbside opposite, a Renault and a white van. Could be coincidence, I thought. Still you could never be too careful.'

Every time she recalled that terrible night, even after all these months, her brain sent out a warning signal - *un rayo*. Adrenalin coursing through her. She paused to light a *Ducados*, begging Colin's forbearance with a small frown. He said nothing, but gave her hand a squeeze. They both knew she would soon be describing the worst moment of her life.

'Stiff with exhaustion and worry about the cars, I leaned forward and slid back the communicating window in case I needed to speak to Pedro. The traffic was lighter than usual on the Avenida heading west towards the suburb where I lived with Andreas and Elena . . . we were making good headway . . . I turned to look out of the rear window again, only the road we had travelled had become an impressionistic blur of red, green and halogenic lights behind the rain-spotted window.'

She fell silent again until Colin prompted, 'what happened then?'

'It's possible we're being followed, eventually I told Pedro. At the same time I wondered, is tiredness making me edgy? Is this just paranoia? For safety's sake or simply to avoid traffic jams, Pedro often varied the route home. So it wasn't unusual that we swerved suddenly right, into a minor *carretera*, and drove some way along the deserted street before he turned left, and left again, and eventually stopped at a red traffic light that would lead us, he assured me, back onto the Avenida at a different junction.'

Como un rayo . . . it happened with lightning speed. Yet she relives the precise moment times without number, every time she wakes with the fear in the night. Maybe, after I've told it to Colin, it will go away? She wonders, but without conviction. In her head, she sketches out a sentence in Spanish. The language of her entire adult life in Colombia. The second language of her life that became her first. *Un encapuchado aparece de entre la nada en la ventana del conductor.* Thoughtfully, she repeats the sentence out loud, noting her side-step into the present tense with an impatient growl. But Colin reassured her, 'it doesn't matter, sweetheart, you're doing really well', and - for his sake - she translates the sentence: 'Out of nowhere, a hooded man appears at the driver's window . . . .'

'But, how can you replicate in words the experience of losing a valued comrade?' Suddenly angry and tearful, both at once, she laid her head on Colin's shoulder. 'I'm a little panicky to have arrived at the moment when I must describe Pedro's assassination,' she confessed in a low voice, as a child might to a sympathetic parent. 'After all, Pedro was the right-hand man of the Herreros family for over twenty years.'

'Of course it's upsetting,' Colin said kindly: 'I understand.'

'Pedro slumped over dead from a silent bullet discharged through the window,' she went on flatly. 'And, that was that. From one moment to the next . . . *de entre la nada,*' she mutters . . . 'he was dead and I was their prisoner.'

Tears well up, remembering, and when Colin hugs her, they overwhelm her.

'Hold it right there,' he says, briskly switching off the recorder. He goes to the kitchen and brings back paper towels. 'You're doing *so* well, Lourdes. Let's have a pause, blow your nose, dry your tears and I'll get us another drink before we go on.'

She is brave, she is beautiful, he thinks, watching her, waiting for her to recover. Not for the first time, he felt a rush of love for her and wanted to wrap her in his arms. Often he fancied her inordinately. It wasn't easy spending time in such close quarters with this passionate woman. But he knew the score. He could, from time to time, take her hand. Kisses and hugs on arrival and departure were permitted. Now, in this role as a sort of father confessor, he felt closer to her than ever.

'I'm ready. Turn the machine on again?' she says, interrupting his thoughts, taking the wine he hands her.

'When one of the thugs gets in front, fear makes me wet my knickers. Through the communicating window he shouts at me to open the rear doors. I do what he asks without question. I'm trembling . . . the fate of my colleagues who *didn't* survive their kidnappings uppermost in my mind: Carmen, Diana and the others, all of them colleagues and friends. Two men, also hooded - *encapuchados* - get in on either side of me. A fourth opens the left-hand door in front, hauls Pedro's body out into the gutter, then they drive off. The man on my right pushes my head down onto his leg and keeps his hand there.'

She glanced at Colin, pulling a face, and he smiled sympathetically. 'Ugh!' she exclaimed, 'the mingled odours of stale food, urine and tobacco, the fact of my cheek pressed against his thigh bone . . . I can feel it to this day, that bone, hard under muscle and flesh, and every time I remember that night I wonder how I managed not to retch or faint, or both. My feet, naked under the thin veil of my stockings, started to fumble around the floor of the car for my cast-off shoes.' She gave a little laugh. 'If only I can get my shoes back on I'll feel safer,' I thought. 'But the man shouts:"keep still, do nothing, say nothing, above all, don't scream!"'

Lourdes leaned back into the sofa, confronting the past with a vicious frown while Colin waited calmly, knowing the worst was over.

'He sounded menacing. I couldn't see him,' she said softly, 'but I could smell the stale tobacco and too much wine on his breath. Then he commanded:"*¡No hagas nada, no digas nada, sobre todo no chilles!*"

'I remember as if it had all taken place in slow motion only yesterday. People say they remember precise details after a serious accident, and, after all, this was a near death experience

for all I knew. On good days I feel lucky to be alive. *"'Sobre todo"*
. . . near-paralysed with fear I was ready to comply with any
instruction. . . . *"¡no chilles!"* He needn't have worried! The
last thing I would've done was scream! All I could think of was
Elena, my baby, almost grown up and about to go off to college
in New York State. Sweet seventeen. As the car sped away, I
heard muted street sounds, the patter of rain on the roof, and
my shocked brain asked one question over and over again. Will
I ever see Elena again?'

§

Every morning the wardens collected Luisa at Bar Solitario
and drove her up to the territory she would have to get to
know like the back of Professor Bauza's hand. They had taken
her on foot one day to see a devastated pine wood, high in the
mountain foothills west of Ca'n Clot. In November, when she
had still been in Barcelona, winds of up to 120 miles per hour
had buffeted the island for days on end. The forested mountain
slopes had suffered tremendous tree loss. When they arrived in
the wood she could scarcely believe the nightmarish mayhem
of trees lying side by side or on top of each other just as they
had fallen. And it was eerily silent up there, where no birds
sang. Greedy sunlight penetrated to the floor of the wood,
highlighting the arboreal carnage. Very few birds are interested
in dead woods, Julio said.

His nature conservancy bosses were out of their minds with
worry. How to deal with the crisis. They couldn't risk leaving all
that tinder lying about until summer when it might catch fire
and create the most god-awful inferno. The only answer was to
clear the forests of the deadwood. Following Julio and Felipe,
Luisa clambered over gigantic tree trunks, some shoulder high,
almost shuddering at her own insignificance in comparison with
the few trees, still standing, that loomed above their heads. It is
as if they mock our slow human passage through a devastated
battleground, she thought.

Teams of men were being organised for the daunting task
of clearing the fallen trees and hauling them by rope and tackle

down the mountainside, then transporting them to a field the size of a football pitch, not far from the mountain town. Nobody had decided what to do with all the wood, Julio said, but perhaps it would be exported and turned into furniture.

During those days when she returned to town with Julio and Felipe at dusk, she ate her evening meal at Bar Solitario where the town's older population gathered to watch television, gamble at the fruit machine or sit in groups playing cards or dominoes. And every evening she was the centre of the attention of well-wishers ready to entertain her with anecdotes, legends and even the occasional line of Mallorcan poetry before she retired upstairs, heavy with the need to sleep.

The bar was the town's social club. Its uncompromising interior contained around a hundred chairs set at oblong wooden tables. Here and there, dusty arrangements of plastic flowers romped in gilt vases, a wooden booth in the far corner displayed lottery tickets, a side table carried sets of chess, draughts and dominoes and, above the mantelpiece in pride of place, hung faded framed photographs of men at work making carbon from holm oak wood and gathering olives. She searched weather-beaten group portraits captured for posterity by early box cameras until she discovered a man with a striking resemblance to Professor Bauza, only this old cabonero wore the traditional black banded sunhat, collarless shirt and baggy black pantaloons of countrymen. She wondered if he could be the professor's father.

By chance, Jaume, on the lookout for a house Luisa might rent, received a fax from an absent German resident. In high excitement, Paquita brought the news to Luisa's table, where she was eating vegetable casserole in preference to *Tords en Col*, the bar's speciality.

'Señora Lehmann wants to rent out her small house. This might be the very place for you, Luisa.'

A Mallorcan family by name of Ferrer would be her neighbours to one side, Paquita explained, and, on the other side, a German woman 'who keeps herself to herself so that none of us even know her name'. Next morning, Jaume and

Paquita took her to see the house at number twelve Calle Luna and the deal was quickly sealed with a return fax to Munich. Luisa would rent the house from early January when she came back from Barcelona. The name of the street nearly broke her up with pleasure. Calle Luna. The street of the moon. Could anyone even imagine a street in Scotland being named after the *moon*?

That evening in the bar Paquita introduced her to the Ferrer family who lived in number thirteen and, since it was obvious no one else was going to, she decided to introduce herself to the neighbour in number eleven. After supper one evening she slipped out of the bar and went up the hill to Calle Luna where, for the past hour, Lourdes had been working upstairs at the computer, blessing her fluency, this ability she had to set her story down rapidly on the computer page. Her broadcasting background helped. As Colin had persuaded her, the computer was 'user friendly', and after his tuition she had the hang of it. Colin was waiting in London at this very moment for the text he had dragged out of her during his brief visit. He had nearly convinced her that something must happen soon to break the impasse she was held in. Andreas Herreros had only to make one false move to bring down his house of cards, Colin said. Then she would be free to travel wherever she chose - New York! - and he could publish the book. She hadn't been so sure, tended to think these days that she was imprisoned for life, but when things were going well, like now, she told herself, one never knows.

Hearing a knock on her front door, then a pause before it repeated, she hesitated. No one has knocked on my door since I arrived, so this must be the neighbour I am to have in January, who's in town for a few weeks. She had heard all about the plans of the Scottish woman, Luisa Ross, via a fax from Gerda Lehmann. They communicated in German. Gerda had no links with Colombia as far as she knew. Sending and receiving faxes was safe enough. Besides, the woman was old, with bad hearing and poor eyesight, so it had been easy to get on quite friendly terms before Gerda had left Mallorca for Munich last month.

51

Not such good news that next door's to be rented, she thought. And I won't open my door to this person . . . *yet*. I don't need *more* worries, so, *por favor*, Señorita Ross, allow me to play for time. Unlike you, I have a lot to lose.

The knocking ceased and Lourdes went back to work. It helped to know that Colin, already back in London, would receive the text straight away, via a system called Apple Share. Reaching out for her packet of cigarettes lying on the table, she relished the prospect of working on the book, getting back in touch with a long lost aspect of her professional self. The radio journalist she had been in Bogotá, with her own programme, inspired by the BBC's *Women's Hour,* a hotch potch of features, music, stories and poems aimed at housebound *colombianas*. The content of the programmes had to be chosen with great care, of course, for there was always someone out there listening, waiting to pounce on anything that could possibly be construed as subversive, even if she was the wife of Andreas Herreros. Always, at the back of her mind, were the 1990s kidnappings of several journalists, including her friends Carmen Filgueira and Diana Montoya who had never come back. Thinking about Carmen and Diana brought on her nervousness. Depression threatened, she recognised the signs, so enough was enough. She saved the work, turned off the computer and decided it was time for a stiff drink downstairs.

Obviously I won't be able to completely ignore Luisa Ross when she becomes my next-door-neighbour, she thought, negotiating the steep stairs that led directly into the kitchen. No, I'm sufficiently well practised in the niceties of life to share a cup of tea with her from time to time. Reaching in the cupboard above the sink, she found the bottle of Prozac pills, then went into the salon to pour herself a brandy, turned on the CD player, and sank into the sofa. When she kicked off her shoes and stretched out against the embroidered cushions, the terrier gave a little yelp and jumped up beside her.

On good days I can even find myself wondering if I missed my true vocation. Acting! Mallorcans pose little threat, I can conceal Lourdes Herreros from them any day of the week. Besides, they've no interest in looking beyond the surfaces of incomers. Why should they? Yet a *northern* European, this Luisa Ross, living in such close proximity will be a different ball game from Gerda. I'll have to plan, invent, evade with the greatest care - oh! take endless measures to protect my identity. Already I'm wondering if she'll hear me wailing in the night through the walls, after she moves in.

On the fourth day Luisa told Julio she was ready to stay alone overnight at Ca'n Clot, and that, before she returned to Barcelona, she intended to live up at the base the following week. From that moment on she would be her own boss, and, far from feeling worried and anxious, she felt she had arrived at a place where she might rediscover and reinhabit the part of her soul bequeathed to her by her warm-hearted Spanish mother. Now, she was beginning to realise how deeply she had drowned in adolescent grief, first over her mother's death, and, two years later, over the death of her sister, Eva. She was beginning to understand, too, that her father's recent death had freed her. They were all gone. She was an orphan, free to embrace Spain at last.

In a state of unfettered contentment and curiosity, notebook and binoculars to hand, she explored the territories of Ca'n Clot. All that week there was time to start putting names to the birds, insects, trees, shrubs, flowers and grasses that shared the wilderness. At night she slept in a simple gallery room, one of several reserved for visiting ornithologists like herself. And when she stayed indoors she preferred to sit reading and writing in the small studio, at the rear of the finca, Julio told her had been named 'the den' by a previous inhabitant.

To begin with, the irascible Felipe, constructing a new weathering for the captive birds out of the wire and stakes they'd brought up in the jeep, had no time for her. It didn't matter; the aviary intrigued her but she was prepared to wait to be invited in. Her enthusiasm for her new home buoyed her through an entire night when a raging storm gave the surrounding plateau a fantastic beating and brought down several small pines near the base of the crag. Another evening, Perro's barking alerted her to the presence of a stranger in the vicinity of the finca. At first she had been alarmed, catching sight of a distant horned figure through the shutters. Then she had laughed aloud when she saw through her field glasses that he was only a tourist in a silly hat who had lost his way. She gave him a bed for the night in one of the rooms off the gallery and phoned to ask Julio to come and drive him to the train station next morning.

One day, she had felt very uncertain, approaching the wire and wood structure behind Felipe, whose curt invitation to visit the aviary had come as a surprise. Once inside, she heard the grate of gravel under their heavy boots and turned to watch as Felipe, sinewy in his dark green uniform, a pail filled with hunks of red meat in one hand, a leather gauntlet in the other, locked the gate behind them.

'Can't be too careful,' he muttered, drawing on the glove, frowning in the glare of the midday sun.

Luisa hurriedly put on her brimmed canvas hat. Not much hope of escape from here, she thought, anxious for the well-being of the captive birds she was about to see. She followed Felipe deeper into the oblong aviary that abutted Ca'n Clot's gable end. Here was her chance to get the measure of the man. The long row of pens, covered with a sloping pantiled roof, faced a parallel chicken wire fence, and the far end of the enclosure was also made of wire. Through it she could see the substantial black heap of Perro's body lying fast asleep, not inside, but on top of his cave-like kennel. The old labrador was a touching sight that somehow reassured her.

Pausing at the first pen, the half-closed eyes of a medium-sized raptor flickered back at her. Partly concealed in its bundled feathers, its yellow legs clung to a perch as high as her hip.

'Black kite,' Felipe announced over his shoulder: '*Milvus migrans*, not a native bird of Mallorca, although the Red kite is present most of the time.'

When he sauntered off to set down his pail in the middle of the patio, she thought she might draw him one day, on a white page of her notebook. A proud oval for his face, a long avian nose, dark brows meeting in the middle over eyes like

54

almonds, the neat Don Carlos beard. In profile, his face was all promontories. The cone of his Adam's apple, the jutting chin below full thrusting lips. She kept her hands in the pockets of her jacket and waited until he came back towards her, all energy, clicking the fingers of his outstretched hand with the irritating nonchalance of a ringmaster.

'Is *Aegypius monachus* here?' she asked.

'Yes, of course, but have patience. Our next exhibit is the Griffon vulture.' He held a small piece of bloodied meat in his gauntlet.

The griffon was a huge raptor with brown body plumage and darker flight feathers, miserably hunched up on its perch, and she felt sorry for the bird until she remembered an illustration of griffons from one of her *National Geographic* magazines. Hadn't they been hunched like this one, waiting their turn to clean up the carcasses of *wildebeest* from their perches of tree limbs in the African bush? Griffons are *meant* to be hunched. Reassured a little, nevertheless she wondered what to make of this bird prison.

With a click of his fingers, Felipe continued his rounds, and she straightened up and went coolly after him.

'Egyptian vulture,' he announced and, seeing it, she brightened. Bauza's speciality, *Neophron percnopterus*. Far smaller than she had imagined, its bald yellow face stared out impassively as it squatted on pinkish-yellow legs, not on its perch but in a corner of its cage. Yet, after a few seconds, it seemed to her that, as she watched, it blinked a secret greeting and she smiled.

Catching the exchange between Luisa and the bird Felipe said: 'You know, I suppose, that the Egyptian vulture is one of very few tool-using birds?'

'I didn't know,' she asserted. Professor Bauza had never mentioned that fact. Was Felipe pulling her leg?

'Yes, it's true. Gyp vultures pick up stones in their bills and break open eggs with them.'

'Why don't you show me?' she challenged.

'Sure, no problem. They love ostrich eggs. I'll buy one from the ostrich farm near Inca and give you a demonstration one day soon.'

They moved together to the next cage where a bright-eyed, sleek creature, with a massive bill and shaggy, ruffed throat was jerking on its perch.

This inmate was easy to name. 'Raven!' she got out before Felipe had a chance.

'Yes *Corvus corax*. We call her Cora,' he said, bending a little towards the cage. 'There are loads of ravens around here, of course. Not all as clever as her. C'mon, girl, let's hear what you have to say for yourself today!'

As if on cue, *Kway! kway!* came the high-pitched call, and when Luisa laughed Felipe confided, 'Cora's the star performer in the Fest of Saint Anthony. You'll see her amazing tricks in January, that is, if you come back to town in time.'

She admitted to herself, a little anxiously, that for all his cocksureness she was warming towards this man who undoubtedly had the welfare of the birds at heart. After all, presumably it had not been *his* decision to run a concentration camp for large avians up here.

Now they stood outside the pen of the Mallorcan vulture, *Aegypius monachus*. She had observed many of its kind this past week sailing high above Ca'n Clot and its territories, and, stopping in front of this one, a young bird, fallen to earth and imprisoned by man to become a caricature of itself, she felt very sorry for it. Immensely hunched on the perch, its small head daft in proportion to its body, its plumage dark brown rather than the black she had expected, it made no movement and she turned from it sadly. Although the birds looked in good condition, they seemed to her unnaturally passive. Again, she delved for a reassuring thought. *Vultures are among few birds of prey that breed happily in captivity.* Surely she had read that somewhere? Perhaps this one didn't feel so bad after all?

Felipe had disappeared into a cage at the end of the weathering and she found him crouching down beside the perch of a buzzard-like bird, dark with pale feathers on its upper wings. It must be a little eagle, she thought, staying at the gate, unwilling to break the seance between the man and the bird whose piercing eyes were assessing him. He spoke to the little raptor with utmost gentleness, then stroked her back with a feather until she perked up her feathers with a zizz of energy and shifted from one claw to the other on the perch.

Luisa kept very still. What a beauty this was. A bib of golden feathers streaked with brown, a fluffy golden bridge above the cere of the hooked beak, and slanted eyes. When she entered the cage, its head spun round and these eyes seemed to run through her like daggers.

'¡Qué bonita!, ¡qué bonita!' Felipe sang to the bird, at the same time as he held Luisa with a sideways glance. 'Meet my eyas,' he said in a low voice, and offered the red meat to the bird. 'I trained her myself from a wild bird.'

The earnest raptor pounced on the titbit and deposited it on the perch under her fluffy Turkish knickers where her merciless talons held it fast and her rapier beak tore into it. Luisa watched the little eagle ravening through the blood-running meat, a little awed. There's something almost *religious* in this primitive act of survival, she thought.

'Meat is how you tame them,' Felipe said, getting to his feet.

'What kind of eagle is she?' Luisa whispered, anxious not to disturb the feasting bird.

'Booted eagle. *Hieraetus penatus*. Summer visitor to Mallorca. But I detained her here and she's happy.'

She supposed it must be so. The bird was the very picture of avian health and vigour. 'Did you capture the bird yourself?'

'Yhep, as a nestling . . . after you've tamed them, you can hunt with them. Birds that hunt have to be struck, that is, they have to be hooded. You put the hood on when you take them into the field and then you loosen it and take it off before you release them to rise in the air and wait up there until they spot game.'

She was prepared to be told. She knew nothing of the art of falconry.

'Before this one would take the hood she had to be thoroughly mastered. She resisted the hood for a long time. One day she wounded me.'

Felipe rolled up the sleeve of his right arm to the elbow. Sure enough, the well-rounded muscle below his elbow bore a livid purplish scar. He crouched down again and she resisted a small temptation to sympathise, troubled enough by her attraction to this other world. Indeed, sensing a sort of surrender to veils of illusion she thought she had developed the power to resist, she took a step backwards.

But Felipe noticed, held her with a sharp glance, and said: 'I call her Aquila. Soon she started to come onto my fist for meat and eventually she submitted. The first time she let me slip on the hood I flew high as a kite myself.' He looked so radiant as he spoke, Luisa found herself envying his passion. 'She's much more docile when her eyes are covered with the hood. I'd no problems with her after that.'

On the way out he threw a hunk of meat from the pail into each pen and Luisa, trailing behind him, saw the Egyptian vulture flutter in its corner, then each bird in turn jump lazily down off its perch, stretch its jesses and totter towards the false carrion.

Another day, she watched him setting two galvanised metal baths in the centre of the patio, one filled with sand, the other with water - 'some prefer sand, others water,' he said, and opened all the pens, one by one, to free the birds. 'Bath time', he called out, and two birds immediately flitted to one of the outside perches positioned near the baths.

'I generally leave them to it,' Felipe said surveying his charges from the other side of the chicken wire fence, where he stood beside Luisa. They saw no bathing at first and after a few minutes he explained, 'some take the whole day to make up their minds to have a bath at all. Others bathe quickly, dry their feathers in the sun and return to their cages.'

Then all at once Luisa gasped, seeing a peregrine falcon flitting through its open cage and dropping eagerly into the water, ruffed and ceremonious, with a great stirring of wings. And the bird's posturing took her back to Plaça Major, to Barcelona, where she had so admired the representative fidelity of the young Central American men enacting their tribal bird dance alongside Rafael Vargas in his winged costume.

'This area of Mallorca fell under the district, the *juz d'Inken*, in Moorish times,' Felipe told her as they stood watching. And when he said, 'you look a bit Arab yourself, señora,' she was pleased, but not surprised. Her mother had told her often about Spain's Moorish legacy and loved to describe the wonderful palaces of La Alhambra and Al-Andalus. Combing out her daughter's wavy brown hair before school, she would say, 'we both have Spanish-Arab blood, darling, I'm sure of that; whereas Evie looks more like her father.'

'The Moors knew everything about falconry,' Felipe was saying. 'Hunted in these mountains with eagle and peregrine falcons they called *shaheens*. There was far more game for the birds to hunt in those days. Now that small mammals are rare on the mountains, trained birds like Aquila have to rely on catching other birds.'

Pleased to have an audience, a pupil, here where he was a master of the legacy of the *juz d'Inken*, Felipe showed her the small workbench where he manufactured the bird hoods, jesses and leashes. To begin with, he fiddled about with the gear that hung from hooks above the workbench, uncertain how to engage her, then he handed her a small oblong of leather pierced by two eyelets.

'Falconers have to make their own aylmeri anklets to fit their own hawks.' He stood close, to demonstrate how a thong is threaded through the eyelets: 'The thong's called a jesse. I make them . . . and these bewits, too.' He pulled off a hook a finer, pointed thong: 'Bewits attach the bells to the hawk's leg, *sabes?*'

Then he dropped a silver bell into the palm of her hand, and she admired its acorn shape that was fixed, she now knew, to scrawny bird legs by means of jesses and bewits.

'I ordered Aquila's bell from America. The bell you choose depends on your own ear. In my opinion, you can't beat Asborno bells from the USA.'

He picked up a bell and gave it a lusty blow so that she backed off, covering her ears against the piercing blast, half-groaning, half-laughing.

'See what I mean? Asbornos have an excellent pitch few other bells can match. They're the best, the most discordant, and the more discordant the ring of a bell, the further the sound carries. That's important when you're flying the bird over distance in open landscape.'

Cúanto más discordante es el tañir de la campana
      the more discordant the ring of a bell
más lejos llega el sonido
      the further the sound carries . . .

How well the phrase sounded in Spanish, and she knew, repeating it to herself, that it would linger in her mind. And she felt her thought become almost a physical thing that lodged in the cochleae of her eardrums when she turned away, discomfited, to admire through narrowed eyes five tiny leather caps hanging above the workbench.

Felipe swelled a little and grinned. 'Oh, I didn't make these. I *collect* hoods other falconers don't want.' With evident excitement, he showed her. 'This is a Bahraini hood, specially made for Aquila, but not by me. I've not the skill.'

Arabian? she wondered, admiring its tasselled leather topknot, and he nodded, picking up another. '*Sí, correcto,* señora! And this one's an Anglo-Indian hood. See, it has what's called a Turkish topknot.' He trilled the short, upright tassel through his fingers. 'But my favourite is the Dutch hood,' he said and lifted it off its hook. It was a diminutive hood of dark olive-green leather with snakeskin side panels and a topknot of mixed plumes, and he laid it on her palm.

Can he tell, she wondered, avoiding his eyes, that he's winning me over with all this evocative bird gear?

'It's a bit of an antique, to tell the truth,' he insisted, almost urging her to agree with him.

'I think it's exquisite,' she protested. 'I mean, the object, the hood. I'm not so sure I like the idea of hooding birds, though . . . in fact I *detest* it!'

'Oh, don't let it upset you. They love wearing hoods, really, they do.'

Momentarily, they fell silent and when, impetuously, he added: 'I want you to have the Dutch hood,' she hesitated. And only when she affirmed that she couldn't possibly take it did he fall to persuasion.

'Don't worry, you'd be doing me a favour. I need to get another,' he said, lifting her hand and laying the hood on her palm. 'The Dutch hood's far too heavy for a small eagle like my Aquila. And I'll never use it on any of my other birds, so what's the point of it gathering dust. Tell you what, take it in exchange for helping me to exercise Aquila?'

Later, in the aviary, when she put on the gauntlet he gave her, a strange sense came over her that she was about to participate in something forbidden, almost arcane. Yet she forgot her nervousness, and her enthralled heart sang when, with an otherworldly, near inaudible whirr of its spread wings and pinions, Aquila ceremoniously left her perch to mount Felipe's arm. The little eagle hopped onto his gauntlet, unconcerned, blinking as if nothing much was happening. Then Felipe drew close with a loud whisper, *Hold your arm steady*! And the bird stepped obediently from his gloved hand to hers, its fluffy legs trailing the jesses which Felipe hooked to Luisa's gauntlet, and she, watching, held her breath like someone bewitched until the eagle's talons tweaked the skin of her hand under the glove. Before she could protest, quick as a wink Felipe dropped the hood over Aquila's head. Then, holding Luisa with his gaze, he drew tight the thonged fastening with one end fixed between his teeth and the other held delicately between his fingers.

I've seen that look before, she thought. Yes, in the jeep that first day we drove up here. 'I'm training my eyas. You can help me fly her?' The moment had arrived. She had become an indispensable player in the action.

The bird's determined grip strained her hand, but Felipe reassured her, Aquila's talons wouldn't rip open her glove. After that the clinch of the little raptor was a steadying influence that encouraged her not to weaken. I can do what Felipe asks of me, she resolved, and they climbed with the bird to the crag of Cuevas Negras. Before he left her to wait there alone in the cool air, he struck Aquila's hood.

And now, one hand thrust into the pocket of her jacket, her other arm bent at the elbow, aching, she holds the little eagle aloft on the tasselled gauntlet. The weight of the bird amazes her. All those feathers and bones: *metatarsals, talons, carpals, metacarpals* . . . raptor anatomy in my hands. She couldn't get over the wonder of it. Its head turned away from her, she studies the gorgeous mantle, the intricate detail of upperwings decorated with pale v-shaped feathers.

She waits with the bird as Felipe has instructed, on El Escarpado de las Cuevas Negras. North, east and west the boundless grainy mountains unroll, and she hugs to herself the sense that the drama she waits to play a part in matters not a jot in the enormous scheme of things, but to her seems acutely prescient. For what seems like an eternity, she watches Felipe's matchstick figure stealing about the plateau. Indrawing her breath through her teeth with the challenge of Aquila's weight, she waits for the signal to free the bird.

At last it comes, Felipe's discordant whistle, his arms waving wildly below.

 Slip the leash!

 the echo of his voice ringing round the hoya . . .

 Slip the leash!

He whirls the lure above his head, a rustic bundle of rabbit meat and feathers. Her fingers fumble urgently to loosen the jesses. Almost sick with apprehension lest she lose the moment, at last she sets the eagle free. With a sudden clap of huge wings it puts forward its breast. With a whirr of wings it stirs a rush of wind into her face, then it sails higher and higher into the pure air of the mountains. Up it goes, cutting through the quivering blue air. Then, dropping her numbed arm with relief, she brings up the binoculars to follow the brave little eagle as it speeds on desperate, flapping wings until it turns . . . hovers . . . and for a moment seems to sit in the air. Then, like a streak of lightning, it falls towards Felipe's bait. Luisa stands mesmerised: . . . *a la velocidad de un rayo* . . . with elegant braking and up-drawn wings, the taloned feet precisely bond to land on Felipe's lure.

She watched the magnified ravening bird until Felipe looked up at her, waving his free hand above his head, skipping a little triumphantly before he returned Aquila to the cadge. It *is* splendid, she thought, dropping the binoculars, sensing her reservations dissolve with the relief of her thought — it's as if my own imprisoned spirit has flown out of some dark tunnel, off and away. Her boots slithering on treacherous stones, her gauntleted hand grasping the support of lentisca and myrtle branches, she sped down the crag. When her feet hit level ground Felipe raced towards her and she to him, elated by what they had helped the little eagle to achieve. Unthinkingly, she accepted Felipe's embrace, but then, when his mouth seized hers and her body raged with ferocious desire, in her struggle to free herself she stumbled and fell to the ground. A chilling sense of dismay ran through her. Grim-faced she got up with a show of rubbing her still-aching arm and suddenly struck him hard on the side of his face. For a few seconds they glared at each other, their breaths coming in short astonished bursts, and she saw his cheek was livid with the imprint of her hand.

A smirk played on the corners of his mouth, perspiration shone on his forehead. 'Something new, you liked it, didn't you?' he said, mocking her with half-closed eyes.

As if in a dream, in the middle of nowhere, she sought words to express what she felt. Disgust with myself, she thought, for wanting to succumb to his voracious anemone mouth? Not entirely his fault then that he seized the advantage? Displacing her confusion, she dusted the earth off her trousers. *That* wasn't part of the bargain,' she said coolly, 'and if you so much as lay a finger on me again you'll have hell to pay.'

Felipe gave a scornful laugh and turned away towards the cadge, while she – vowing the impossible, *I will put this incident out of my mind forever* – went down the path in the opposite direction, back to Ca'n Clot.

However much she wished to stay in Mallorca, she must return to Barcelona to write the report the professor required. Rafael Vargas would have to be given notice, too, that she would be quitting her room. The day before she left town, she revisited the house on Calle Luna to discover what she might need to bring back with her in January. It was so well-equipped she couldn't think of anything at all. After that, she was warmly welcomed into the Ferrer family's kitchen where she shared coffee and *magdalena* cakes with María and her old mother, Francisca. Passing number eleven, once more Luisa attempted to introduce herself, but her knocking was in vain.

3

Tendrils, seed-pods and buds, sedge-green, beige and pink on a dark ochre ground. As if for the first time, she delights in the Art Nouveau decoration of Rafael Vargas' tiled entrance hall and plucks a rosebud from its abundant ceramic garden. Inwardly she's dancing. She has mapped out the territory surrounding her field base, survived a storm in the mountains and resisted the lure of the falconer.

Through the open window at the far end of the hall, the date palm rustles to the cadenza of advent bells . . . *cuánto más discordante es el tañir* . . . Felipe Tamarit's words come back to her as she walks towards the window, as they had done when she waited in patient astonishment on the high wooded crag. Aquila on her arm, the blast of the Adorno whistle echoing round the hoya. She will always remember this, yet the Barcelona bells ring out as if nothing at all has happened. Her first trip to Mallorca, something fantastical, like a brief contract between the *juz d'Inken* and their conquerors. She had spent so long in a sexual desert, Felipe's allurements had come as a severe test, jesses, aylmeris, bewits and that lithe body of his. Casually, Julio had dropped into their conversation before she left that Felipe would be marrying a girl from Inca during the Christmas holidays. Did Julio know about Felipe's advances, then? Had he observed them through his binoculars from some high plateau? Now, she could laugh at Felipe's sultry epilogue — *something new, you liked it, didn't you*? Yes, he had struck a discordant note, accompanying the wild dance she had mercifully resisted - *un sonido discordante* - that might have cost her the assignment at Ca'n Clot.

All the way down the silent corridor she anticipates her return to Mallorca, no longer minding the challenge of a couple more weeks of solitary life here in Barcelona. Even the thought of a lonely Christmas fails to dismay her. After all, isn't she is one of Bauza's chosen now, embraced by the people of the mountain town? These holidays, *Navidad*, will pass swiftly; there is a report to write, research papers to read on migrant birds that traverse Spain en route to Scotland and other parts of Northern Europe, and this Barcelona life to pack away.

One day she stopped by the university to see the professor and returned to the flat by way of Plaça Major where she noticed Rafael Vargas had changed his act. He was only one among many 'living statues' disguised as clowns, fakirs, gods and goddesses, devils, pirates and magicians who performed in the square and its surrounding streets. There were Central American musicians wearing head-dresses of eagles wings, too, and young men dressed up as buzzards, hooting and swooping in a grotesque dance that fascinated and unnerved her, both at once. An ancient dance, which one of them had told her, is reserved for *Quinquagesima* Sunday, a religious festival, in their own pueblos. European tourists thronged to see it.

Rafael Vargas was dressed a little differently, though still fantastically, with a jousting stick tucked under his arm and another laid on the ground at his feet. Evidently he had come up with a new idea for his performance, and she soon got the hang of it. Instead of simply dropping a coin into his collecting tray (when he would spring at you with crustacean claws such as you could buy in the *Mercado*) anyone in the audience could start the action by picking up the combat stick. For some time Luisa stood watching until a boy went forward to challenge Vargas, and after it was over, when the crowd was applauding the youngster's bravura, something made her push through to the edge. A little startled, she found herself picking up the stick the boy had relinquished. Rafael Vargas' eyes lit-up behind his leather mask. The stick felt heavy in her hands and she wondered at her temerity.

Clack! clack! came the sound of wood against wood.

'*Go for her, mister!*' the boy who had gone before her was calling out and his goading made her all the more determined to pit herself against Vargas with everything she'd got.

Eventually they locked sticks and the silent crowd held its

breath. She felt the power of the charge between them . . . *now he knows I exist!* . . . if not in his flat with its Art Nouveau tiles, then publicly in this square. As if by silent mutual agreement they disengaged and began again. She had never done anything like this before. Scenes of combat from children's comics filled her mind — *take that, and that, and that*! as *clack! clack*! went their sticks, and the Amerindian musicians on the other side of the square accompanied their performance with strident pipes and drums and she laughed aloud. Then, just when Rafael Vargas was about to force her backwards, he slipped. A gasp ran through the crowd. She couldn't believe it. There he was on all fours at her feet. Mister Big, looking up at her. You see me now, she thought, a little triumphant, and when she stretched out her hand to help him up, the crowd broke into loud applause. Rafael dusted himself down, became a statue once more as if nothing at all had happened. But she knew better. Something important had happened. After tossing a coin into the plumed helmet at his feet, she addressed the silent statue. 'I am leaving for Mallorca after the holidays. My rent is fully paid up and I shall leave a forwarding address on the kitchen table.'

That afternoon, when a soft click of the entrance door announced someone's return to the flat, Luisa stiffened, closed her notebook and decided to make a dash out of the kitchen to the sanctuary of her room. But Rafael Vargas was already filling the door frame, blocking her exit. 'You were angry in the square,' he said. 'It was astonishing . . . your energy.'

Who wouldn't be angry, she wanted to say, avoiding his eyes. Didn't I have to jump off a psychological cliff to get myself to Barcelona in the first place? Didn't I abandon Dan, home, the wild things, only to be totally ignored by you lot here. So now, although our debacle was quite unplanned, I've had my mild revenge. I exist for you at last. Instead, her mouth puckered to prevent a grin. 'It was bad luck you slipped and fell at a crucial moment,' she said.

'All in a day's work, señorita. Part of the performance. And now won't you join me in a glass of wine?'

Bemused by his not unwelcome presence, she folded her arms thinking isn't this too little, too late?

He was opening the refrigerator, turning to smile at her: 'The crowd loved our performance, and I dare say you earned me a few more euros today. So what do you say to a glass of wine?'

She trailed back to the table.

'So, you're leaving Barcelona for Mallorca . . . ah, yes, Mallorca, home of the Black vulture,' he said, uncorking a bottle with a flourish.

She kept her voice steady. 'Not just vultures; the mountains are a haven for many species of birds.'

'Maybe so, however vultures are special to me. They were my constant companions during my travels in South America.' Now he was fumbling in a cupboard for glasses, saying 'they were omnipresent in the skies high above the wilderness, magnificent wheeling creatures.'

'The American birds are unrelated to Old World vultures,' Luisa asserted, returning to the chair she had recently vacated. Only occasionally had she seen Rafael Vargas without his bird mask and winged costume. One of those times had been when he interviewed her for the room. Now his near presence disarmed her; the curly brown hair, greying and receding a little, yet framing so well his broad forehead, the muscular face with eyes that narrowed when he spoke . . . blue eyes, of that peculiarly arresting blue found only in Mediterranean people.

He came to the table. 'I didn't know the vultures were unrelated . . . in what way?'

'Well, globally, groups of vultures have evolved quite indepenently. Condors and smaller American vultures, for example, are descended from the same ancestors as storks and other water-birds. Whereas, most Old Word vultures, in Europe, Africa and Asia, share the same ancestry as birds of prey.'

'That's certainly a surprise to me,' he began, his eyes narrowing, and as if they realised they risked sparring - verbally this time - they smiled awkwardly at each other and her tension began to dissipate. Maybe it's not too late for us to become friends, she thought, mentally rearranging the ceramic rosebuds of the entrance hall. After all, he's a man you don't meet every day — bird-man, performer, magician even, but also an anthropologist who's devoted years of his life to field work in Central America.

'As I mentioned before, I think of myself as a bit of a Robin Hood, robbing rich tourists to benefit the Third World poor.' He slides her glass across the table. 'My performances in Plaça Major help to finance small agricultural schemes in Amerindian pueblos.'

'Tell me about your costume, the claws, the wings, the helmet,' she encourages, surprised by their unexpected camaraderie. Some stirring emotion impossible to name, an attraction this kindred spirit's previous lack of interest in her had forced her to deny, seems to enlarge her now.

'Well, let's see, I invented the gear from different sources. One inspiration was, in fact, the pueblo Indians who dress in winged costumes to impersonate the condor's spirit.'

'Like the ones in the square?'

'Yes, well, unfortunately their dance has gone a bit Disneyland. When you witness the real thing, in a mountain pueblo, for instance, it's much more primitive. It's otherworldly, quite eerie.' He looked thoughtful for a moment. 'There's evidence from pre-Colombian times that condors were given ceremonial burials, you know, to the accompaniment of ritual dances. In time, I learned that Toltec practices survive to this day in which people bury themselves underground in an act symbolising their desire to transform their lives. I learned how these people harness *las poderías*, the nature powers – of wind, water, fire, sun and earth – to ceremonies that are always enacted round a fire. And I came to see that so-called 'civilized' westerners – I was one – had become so divorced from nature, they felt trapped in meaningless, dead-end lives. So I came back to Barcelona determined to write a book and develop a training programme for Europeans called *El Arte de Vivir con Alabanza*. . . .'

The art of living with praise, she translated, remembering with a start how she had buried the auk on her Scottish island. But now he was saying: 'You've changed a lot after your trip to Mallorca.'

She stiffened a little, suddenly defensive. 'Changed? How could you possibly know that?'

'You can tell a lot about someone just by looking at them,' he smiled, raising his glass to his lips, and she, attempting to read his face, looked into eyes disconcertingly magnified through the wine glass.

That was true, you could tell a lot by looking. After all wasn't it her own habit to observe people in the same way as she observed wildlife. So what of Rafael Vargas? *A man powerful in mind and body who probably practises Chi-gong or some other Oriental art, who is uncompromising, committed, idealistic, and therefore probably quite pigheaded* . . . .

'Have I changed for the better?' she dared to ask, after a small silence.

Leaning a little forward, he made a playful show of inspecting her. 'Well, your mossy eyes are not so embedded in grief, and your shoulders are no longer humped.'

She gave out a small laugh and he nodded with a crooked smile. For a split second they held each others eyes, his careful, narrowed, hers with a glint of defiance. Then, aware that the silent room was darkening, unsure of what to say, she glanced away to the rain soaked window before she looked at him again.

'This training you were telling me about, is that what you're doing when you and the other tenants go off with camping gear. Like the day you were all in the hall?'

'Yes, we go to the woods and hills most weekends, but everyone works hard, here in the flat, too.'

'Behind their closed doors?'

'Yes, they practise tasks and exercises designed to throw off the wounds of their pasts . . . you know, what we call 'conditioning' these days . . . so that afterwards they can experience life more fully. Anyway, after several weeks the training process culminates in a burial ceremony. Next weekend they will be burying themselves overnight in dug outs covered with branches round an open fire in the Garaff hills north of Barcelona. Like the Pueblo Indians I mentioned earlier, they hope to emerge from this final ritual after their arduous training programme with a sense of renewal.'

'To someone uninitiated, that all sounds terribly dramatic.'

Rafael leans across the table to light the advent candle set between them at the centre of the kitchen table and says, 'Oh, you're not uninitiated. You've been throwing off the past, too.' Taken by surprise, sharply she meets his eyes. 'Like the rest of us behind our closed doors,' he continues. 'It's painful, isn't it, remembering the people and events that have shaped us in the past, people who have caused us both joy and suffering? On more than one occasion I heard you crying in your room.'

So suddenly, so unexpectedly, the mood of their conversation has shifted. *What!* she wants to blurt out . . . tears rise, hot in her eyes, but he mustn't see. She is Luisa the strong now, not as she was last month, that lonely, anxious creature.

'But the doors are so thick, I didn't think . . . .' Filled with an obscure sense of something she cannot name – embarrassment? shame? loss of face? that someone, anyone else, let alone Mister Big, should realise her fragility – she clings to the edge of the table, sees white knuckles that seem to belong to someone else.

When she hears him saying, yes, the doors are thick, but the walls are thin, she knows his room must be next to her own and she wants to rush away out of the kitchen. Terribly discomfited by his revelation that he *had known all along* this intimate stuff about her touches a raw nerve, makes her drain her glass, get up, replace her chair under the table. It was horribly upsetting to be reminded of an awful time when you thought you had put it behind you.

Jolted into flight: 'I've got to go, got things to do in my room,' she says coolly.

He gets up so energetically his chair clatters backwards onto the floor. Arriving at her side he holds her arm. 'Look, I didn't mean to upset you, quite the opposite. Please stay a little longer?'

71

His solicitous expression only intensifies her vexation. She smells the waxy scent of his woollen sweater before she pulls away, rubbing her arm where he had held it.

'On more than one occasion when I heard you crying, I almost came to you,' he says.

Couldn't he just stop it? She didn't want to be hearing this. Now wouldn't it come pouring out of her, all her pent-up resentment. All those solitary sleepless nights waking up shouting, drowning in dreams of the cold North Sea. Even behind my impenetrable door, had he heard this?

'Christ, you're presumptuous! What are you like?' She can't control the words that come or the anger in her voice. 'I was a stranger in your house, yet you made no effort whatsoever to make me feel welcome and, added to that, you *listened* . . . like some cheap nasty voyeur, through the walls at night!'

'It wasn't like that,' he insists, almost stern. Then, as if trusting she would stay, would listen, he moves a little away, towards the window. It had stopped raining. Silvery droplets reflected the streetlights below onto the windowpane.

'What you didn't know, couldn't know,' she hears him saying, 'is that *everyone* in this flat was suffering alone behind their closed doors.' He chooses his words carefully as if leading up to something he's determined to make her understand. 'You see, it's an important part of the training programme, of *el arte*, that participants keep a vow of silence. Although you weren't a member of our group, you were unwittingly acting out the game plan the rest of us were up to our necks in. When I interviewed you for the room I thought, here's a tough woman who'll be totally caught up in getting her doctorate, self-sufficient, undemanding, not in the least bit interested in what we're up to. I had no idea you were so lonely . . . until I heard you crying. That was just before you left for Mallorca. You, Luisa, were reviewing *your* past, were you not?'

Yes, she thought; I was up to my neck in scenes from childhood, and, later, in the quicksands of those grey years after mother and Evie died. After we were bereaved, two now, not four. Just Dad and I, resenting each other because he knew

I knew he had lost his favourite, Evie, his darling. And more recently there had been Dad's death . . . and . . . *so I'm not enough for you to stay for!* . . . the break-up with Dan.

'All human beings review their past during important transitions in their lives,' Rafael Vargas was saying. 'That's a fundamental, healing use of memory . . . I'm very sorry indeed you felt the flatmates were hostile when, in fact, they were going through pretty much the same as you.'

Then she feels it, something like affection in his voice calms her a little. 'Why don't you join us on our trip next weekend? You might learn something about the mountains, Luisa . . . Have you thought what it'll be like living in the mountains of Mallorca alone? . . . have you ever experienced the brute power of nature? Winds, cyclones, thunder lighting, snowstorms? In winter it snows in Mallorca. People have been known to fall into snow-holes in the mountains there, never to be seen again.'

'Snow holes in Mallorca? I didn't think . . . look,' she said, her animosity reviving, 'I'm a scientist studying bird habitats, not some New Age hippie. I don't need *training*.'

He went to refill his glass and she noticed how glass and bottle were touched for a brief moment by reflected glints from the candle flame. How expert I've become at dousing my emotions under blankets of fact, she told herself. Her thought was edged with despair, but she carried on: 'No doubt what you're up to is valuable, but I'm too old to be drawn into New Age happenings and I'm long past being committed to any one ideology. After all, I did all that sort of stuff when I was a student.'

She lied. She hadn't been committed to anything other than getting a good degree and had been well known by her fellow students as a loner. I've spent my life avoiding people, she thought, her eyes fixed to the flame of the candle. All my life shrinking from life.

Rafael went back to the window. Into the silent kitchen came the girn of accordion from the street far below. 'Come over here and see how lovely the night is beyond the window,' he said, beckoning her with his hand and she knew it would be churlish to resist. They stayed silently looking down through the crowns of the plane trees, down to the flower booths and the rain-slicked pavement, listening to the lonely musician in an old raincoat and black fedora playing his lament filled tangos.

'What a host of memories must stir the old accordionist's mind every time he plays,' Rafael eventually said, turning to her. 'Forget how difficult it was when you lived here last time, Luisa. Forgive us, please. Don't be alone anymore. Come to the Garaff as my guest at the weekend. I promise you, there's no need to take part in any of the group's activities unless you want to. After all, you have already buried your old life in Scotland.'

Only he knew how true that was, she thought. And what he had said earlier had helped her to understand that her act of burying the little auk on the North Shore had been a symbolic leave-taking of her old life.

'Friends?' he said, holding out his hand to her. 'Can we be friends, Luisa?'

She gave him her hand, and, when he captured it for a few moments, a comforting warmth ran through her. It's going to be alright, she thought. In the next stage of my life, a man with wings will watch me with careful eyes.

'Next weekend, isn't that Christmas weekend?' she said, returning her glass to the table.

Even with the settled prospect of Mallorca in January, and with her kestrel angels flying over the roof for company, hadn't she been fooling herself that she could handle a lonely Christmas in the deserted city?

'Yes, Christmas, if you like. Although Christmas has become synonymous with consumerism, so much so that people who live what you might call alternative lives prefer to call the festive season the winter solstice.'

'Okay, the solstice. It falls more or less at the same time as Christmas though, doesn't it?'

Thank you very much for your invitation, but I'm far too preoccupied with papers to write up to accept it, eventually she told Rafael Vargas. However, after he returned with the others from the hills on Christmas day, what a party there was in the kitchen. They were radiant, the reborn flatmates, whooping with exultation. It moved her to see how they danced and sang with such gusto. Candles were lit, someone played a guitar, Rafael fastened his winged cloak about her shoulders and someone took photographs. They invited the ancient accordionist (a veteran of the Spanish Civil War) to eat and drink at their banquet, and Rafael taught Luisa some tango steps.

The next day he took her to see the Master of Pedret's *Vision of Ezekiel* in Barcelona's Museo de Arte de Cataluña. Painted on wood at the end of the eleventh century; Indian red, olive green, ochre, the colours echoed the Catalan landscape. The pigments the painters used would come directly from the landscape of the Mediterranean, he said. Earth, flowers, moss, bark – and the sea, of course, always the sea. Every time he told her something about the Romanesque Catalan paintings that surrounded them, jewel-like against the whitewashed walls, she wanted to know more.

'Pedret's vision was another inspiration for the costume I wear in Plaça Major,' he said.

She stood in front of one of the strangest images she had ever seen, and the curious thing was that it might have been a portrait of Rafael. A keen, considerate power emanated from the face. 'Ezekiel's wearing not one, but three pairs of wings,' she remarked. The wings looked jagged, the opposite of soft and angelic. The pair folded over his body and the pair rising behind his head had peacock feather eyes.

'The wings spreading from his shoulders resemble the wings of a bird of prey,' he said, 'and look, there's a wheel of fire to the right of the painting.'

Seraphim's wings scattered with eyes. A wheel of fire.

What did it all mean? He told her what he knew. That the paintings were designed to be seen by candlelight in the early churches of Catalonia. That the early painters borrowed narrative subjects from the Gospels and the Old Testament, from allegories, visions of hell, monsters and folklore. That

Ezekiel was one of their favourite inspirations, whose vision sometimes showed God surrounded by the symbols of the Evangelists, a winged man, a bull, an eagle and a lion.

He said she would find thirteenth century panel paintings in an identical style in the museum of Palma de Mallorca. And she remembered her promise to the alcalde to visit that very museum to see the bull figurine from the mountain town.

The evening before she returned to Mallorca they went to a tapas bar off Las Ramblas. They sat in the half-circle of a varnished booth lined with mirrors, buoyed up by their camaraderie and the wine and food temptingly displayed before them, tortilla, *ensalada, caracoles*, olives in terracotta dishes. From every angle as he spoke she could watch him, reflected and unreflected against glinting burnished brasses and polished glass. She sat thinking, how odd; I seem to have known this man all my life whereas a few days ago I knew him not at all, and thought I didn't much like him.

'In the Americas early human societies invented complex rituals involving condors as sources of shamanistic power,' Rafael was saying, getting back to a subject that enthralled them both. 'I suppose their ability to detect death and appear mysteriously as if from nowhere whenever a death occurred gave them magical associations. Shamans were, and still are, healers and predictors of future events with the power to intervene between humans and supernatural forces.'

Then and there she called down some shaman to intervene, to turn round her lingering cynicism, to help her to build on this fantastical start to the New Year. The auk in its sea lavender cyst lingered like a talisman at the back of her mind. Burial of her old life, an action, a memory only Rafael Vargas could fully appreciate, and she realised she had found, if not a lover, an extraordinary friend.

'Your clear voice reminds me of plainsong . . . plainsong sung in Spanish with a Scottish accent,' he smiled.

In a dark corner of the bar, a guitarist sang flamenco songs of life and love, and she returned his smile, taking her bearings from ordinary Spanish faces. Laughter, grimaces, a cigar being lit, a newspaper being read, a couple kissing blithely.

§

After the New Year's break, Colin Cramer briefed James Denton about the seizure of the *Vega II* and other related matters. As a trainee journalist on *Ecco!* magazine, already James had been put to work on genetically modified crops, organic farming, animal rights including fox hunting, and wind and wave power. All-British stories. Now he could cut his teeth on something more tasty. It was time James wrote his first foreign news article for the magazine, and it was high time *Ecco!* started featuring hard hitting stories. As a treat they went from the office to his cafe, where they got down to business in the seclusion of Colin's favourite corner. His young companion, casually but smartly dressed in dark jeans and a grey sweatshirt that declared 'Cambridge' in large white letters across his chest, made him wonder with almost parental affection - after all James' father had been his close friend from childhood - was this a signal? Did James nurse a lingering regret that he'd opted to work at the bottom of the ladder in journalism - 'alternative' not mainstream journalism, at that - rather than go up to University?

He peppered the beige froth in his glass with a burst of brown sugar. 'What d'you know about the drugs racket, James?'

'I know a bit, obviously, from films and media reports.'

'Ah, that's good,' Colin said affably. How he loved the naive passion of the young. He'd had it once himself. 'Now let me tell you about one particular case out of literally hundreds that occur every month. The *Vega II*, a bit of an old rusty tub, I believe, was originally registered in Falmouth, Cornwall, before she was sold to her present mafia owners.'

Colin hesitated before he sat forward to impress upon James the importance of what he had to say. 'The *Vega* must have had another name, an *English* name, before that. Perhaps you can find out what it was from the shipping registers?' Then, amused and gratified, he watched James making a note on his writing pad.

77

'Last month the ship was seized in the Atlantic, 350 miles off the Canary Islands to be exact. It was coming from Colombia with a haul of five tonnes of pure cocaine worth upwards of 150 million pounds at street level. '

James gave a low whistle and scribbled again.

'The incident was a splendid example of international co-operation. A feather in the cap of the Spanish customs and police working in co-operation with the United States Drugs Enforcement Agency.'

When James nodded Colin asked: 'What d'you know about the DEA?'

'Not a lot,' he replied with engaging modesty, bending towards his coffee. He sat back wearing a frothy moustache and when Colin pointed it out, James blushed and wiped his lips vigorously with the back of his hand. There, is that better? his winning grin seemed to say. James Denton, nineteen years old, a year or two younger than Colin's eldest son, Titus, who had no interest whatsoever in journalism but had gone north, to Scotland, to become a shepherd.

'Okay, so I'll tell you a little more. The *Vega II* was heading for Galicia on the north coast of Spain. For centuries that coastline's been a smugglers' paradise. Early in the twentieth century they specialised in spirits and tobacco, perfumes and silks, brought in by fishermen and by the owners of schooners. However, it's a sad fact that nowadays the Spanish coastline attracts drugs smugglers using fast rubber boats, fishing smacks, trawlers, battered old freighters, fancy yachts, sometimes working alone, sometimes in tow with mafia gangs.'

'Did that ghastly oil spill on the coast - I've forgotten it's name - deter the smugglers?

'The *Prestige* disaster? No, nothing deters the mafia gangs. They find ways round any disaster, their credibility and power depend on it. They control and export vast quantities of cocaine and hashish as well as smaller hauls of heroin that make them huge fortunes. But only for as long as they keep a step ahead of Spain's increasingly vigilant Civil Guard and Customs Service and the DEA. Every day suspicious vessels are shadowed by long range spotter planes whose satellites check their progress.'

Briskly, James turned to a fresh page.

'So, okay, James. I want you to find out more. Start building up a dossier of information on the DEA, initially for your own reference. The Drugs Enforcement Agency of the United States of America monitors, among other things, the activities of cocaine cartels world-wide . . . including Colombia, for example. Get working on background information about the history of drugs dealing in Colombia.'

'Colombia . . . cocaine,' James interrupted, visibly excited. 'Hey, Colin, have you by any chance seen that film partly set in Colombia where Harrison Ford played the president of the USA? The film was called *The President*.'

Colin sighed inwardly. How very, very young James was. Still referring to virtual reality. But, come to think of it was not all of life virtual reality for many young people nowadays, and, wasn't film often as real as real life for them? He found that disturbing. TV was *real* to them, films were real and these youngsters seemed incapable of observing that much of today's media actually *distorted* reality.

'No, my boy, can't say I've seen the film,' he grunted, unwilling to develop that theme. 'Let's stick to reality. And it's not pretty.'

'The film wasn't pretty either, Colin. Quite tough, as a matter of fact.'

'Be that as it may, James. Where was I . . . you're making me lose my thread,' he frowned. Was age making him lose his memory, too? 'Oh, yes, as I was saying, many boats slip through the net . . . more, perhaps, than are ever caught . . . with millions of lines of the white powder that'll eventually be sniffed up nostrils in homes, bars and toilets all over Europe from Manchester to Mallorca. As you know many kids who strike or shoot up end up dying.'

His recalled the fishing boats he'd seen from the plane in the Mediterranean that night he'd taken the Apple Mac out to Lourdes. Only, he wouldn't let James loose on that other dimension of the story. No, not yet. Later, perhaps, when James had built up the background he had just suggested he might direct him to the human suffering on the fringes of the drugs barons' vile trade. The collateral damage of urban warfare. Thousands of innocent Colombians had fled for their lives to Europe and elsewhere. *Evil . . . vile . . .* these two words teased his brain and he only half-heard the questions James was flinging his way.

He raised the palm of his hand with mock defensiveness. 'Hold on! Let's talk about all that another time!' He had thrown James a lead or two, and now he needed to get back to the office to clear his desk for a ten day break in Mallorca where he intended to complete, as near as damn it, the first draft of *Flight into Exile*. 'You're asking me the very questions I want *you* to discover the answers to. Make a list of your questions, James.'

'Yes, Colin, sure thing.'

And for a few moments Colin sat waiting patiently for the list to be recorded. One day James won't have to make so many notes, he thought. As an experienced journalist he'll *remember* the important verbal details of an interview. And one day, not yet, but when the time was right - and the right time would come only when it was safe for Lourdes to live a normal life - he would ensure that *Ecco!* took the lead in reminding the public of the many dimensions of Colombia's tragedy. Andreas Herreros was an odd case, though. A sort-of *aristocratic* drugs baron, definitely not a thug. Not that that excused anything; far from it. Only the man didn't seem to him to be inherently criminal like the late Paco Escobar or his rivals, the Rodriguez brothers, thugs whose recent early release from prison by a Colombian judge had appalled American officials. No, Andreas Herreros made a tiny fraction of the fortunes these guys raked in from the Medellín and Calí drugs cartels. For him it was no more than a lucrative hobby. At the height of its success in the early 1990s the Calí cartel was estimated to be earning *twenty-two million dollars a day* whereas he doubted if Herreros had made more than a million dollars a *year* from his dabbling on the side. Still, added to his shipping interests, that tidy sum had enabled him and Lourdes to live like aristocrats. There had been something odd about the revenge Herreros had taken against Lourdes, though, something too extreme that puzzled him, and every time he went to work on the book with her he hoped she'd drop a clue as to why her husband had behaved so outrageously as to have her kidnapped. On the other hand, perhaps she herself had no idea. Still, it bugged him; there was something about the way the kidnapping had been handled that didn't square up . . . something . . . .

'Let's go, James,' he suggested firmly, 'Put your notebook away.'

One day the puzzle's bound to solve itself, he thought, straightening up, remembering to pull back his shoulders as they walked to the office. How speedily James walked, how tall the young were nowadays. Why, James's a head taller than me! But then, perhaps I'm shrinking! He felt quite virile, damn it, in the company of his peers; but the presence of the young always made him feel like an ancient mariner, hoary and enfeebled, and the very thought of old age made him shudder. He shifted his thoughts with forced amusement back to 'evil' and 'vile' until, in a triumphant flash, he realised why his brain had been toying with the words.

'We were talking earlier about the evil trade . . . *evil* . . . *vile* . . . . Both words share the same letters; they're anagrams, James. Don't you think that's curious?'

'And l-i-v-e, too' James replied without a pause. 'In fact 'evil' is a palindrome of 'live'.'

'Fancy that! Well I never, you certainly . . . .' Colin hoped his chortle didn't sound too forced. However, James probably hadn't heard. His lean and slightly swaggering frame was already on the other side of the swing doors of the building where *Ecco!* magazine shared offices with half-a-dozen other small publishing houses. And Colin was left thinking, boy, do I need a break. Just as well I'm headed for Mallorca next Sunday.

4

The train slips through Palma's brash new suburbs. Impatient to see again the dramatic sierra and the textures and rich colours of the plain, Luisa wishes it would go faster. On the overhead rack is her largest rucksack, closely packed with all her belongings, removed now from Barcelona. On the seat beside her an elegant blue case, on her lap an envelope from Dan, delivered by the postman this morning just before she left. She opens the envelope, but there is no letter. Only a few press cuttings. Her mouth curves. *He has forgiven me.*

She unfolds the largest item. REVEALED AFTER 130M YEARS: THE FACE OF A DINOSAUR runs the headline under a gruesome illustration of the creature's head reproduced on grainy newsprint. Was it a vulture's head? Huge eye cavity, a great beak for ravening, but no, according to the caption it's a *dromaeosaur's* head. *A spectacular dinosaur fossil,* she reads with amused fascination. *Its entire body covering, still intact, has been discovered in China, by scientists who believe it represents conclusive evidence that these extinct animals 'invented' feathers long before they were used by birds for flight.* Prominent eyes, hooked beak set in a preposterously small head the better to get under the skin and into the organs, muscles and sinews of its meat. The earliest ancestor of European vultures? It *invented* feathers. *The fossil shows unequivocally that the dinosaur grew feathers over its entire skin.*

The train stops, picks up a few suburban passengers at the next station. She takes the blue leather case onto her lap. Lapis lazuli, an exotic gift Rafael surprised her with when they had been saying good-bye. 'Not to be opened until your birthday in February,' he had smiled, handing it over at Sants Station. 'I'll post the key to you nearer your birthday.' Her fingers explore the exquisitely tooled brass lock. She can't get his parting words out of her head. 'Never forget, Luisa, *praising* is what matters; we can at least rejoice in the world we live in and try to prevent it being mutilated any more than it is.' That was a good sign - *try!* - he doesn't feel he has all the answers, doesn't think in black and white.

Last night in the tapas bar he had confided, I'm trying to end a relationship that no longer works. We're holding each other back. Gently, he said. I want to end it gently. Sometimes gently isn't possible, she had held back from saying. Dan and I . . . breaking-up is always a miserable business.

When she looks up the train is cutting through the almond and citrus orchards of the plain, parallel to the hills of El Raigeur and the slate-blue sierra. Soon she would re-enter the professor's ancestral territory. Not far from the university's zoology block, she had been hailing a taxi when, quite unexpectedly, the professor had arrived at her side, his oval head a pensive, polished acorn under its neat black beret.

'So you're off then?' he said, leaning a little towards her on his walking stick, examining her face as if to determine how she was handling the transition from Barcelona to Mallorca. 'In remote places the spirit soars highest, Luisa. There you have glimpses of worlds unknown to most mortals. But never forget, too much isolation makes the heart plummet. A bit like a hawk falling on its prey.'

'Hawk' and 'prey'. Her mind spiralled to Cuevas Negras. Did the professor *know* about Aquila's flight - those yellow talons seizing Felipe's lure? Had someone told him? Did it matter? Releasing herself from the old man's gaze, she had handed her laden rucksack to the taxi driver. 'I'll be *fine*, Professor,' she reassured him brightly. 'Your people will look after me.'

Now the train charts a course through rich agricultural lands, veers slightly north, turns west again, and the rounded summit of Massanella hoves into view. A *lion couchant* against the vibrant sky. A mass of undulating limestone whose unyielding nature is totally disguised from this perspective. The very place where I'm to be tested. But what could make my heart plunge? I already know about thunderstorms . . . that spell of tormented weather during my reconnaissance trip . . . to begin with I felt defiant, elated even, when the Tramuntana winds whipped up as if from nowhere, spiralling ferociously round the finca. I can handle this, I thought. Only, when the storm hit, searing and thrashing the darkened plain it was as if I stood at the mouth of Hell itself. I'm no coward, but if it happens again I'll be off like a shot, straight back to town.

She cranes round as if someone might have arrived in the carriage who could read her thoughts. Then, reassured by its emptiness, takes an uneasy breath and calculates her chances of returning to Barcelona with an exemplary field study in three months time. It was difficult even to imagine thunder storms on a day like today. Yet this time there might be snow to contend with as well as storms. Hadn't Rafael mentioned snow-holes? . . thunderstorms . . . snow . . . isolation. Yes, isolation on the mountain. But I'll guard against that with frequent trips to town. Perhaps I'll make friends with the German neighbour? If not, it won't really matter. The townsfolk who welcomed me last December, Bauza's tribe, will be there for me.

§

At that very moment Anita Berens, on the way to the bread shop, *Gloriosa*, comes face-to-face with the man she had seen Luisa Ross go off with in his jeep last December. An attractively solid man, not originally from the mountain town but probably *Andaluz*. She has spotted him a few times, driving the jeep along country roads and past her finca. Quite spontaneously she turns to him. '*Buenos días*, señor. I understand Luisa Ross will be back soon. Have you any information?'

'*Sí*, señora,' the man replies cheerily, doffing his cap and stepping off the narrow sidewalk to stand beside her. 'My assistant, Felipe Tamarit, is on his way to pick her up at the station as we speak.'

In retrospect, her unguarded action, one Lourdes Herreros might make, not the aloof Anita Berens, took her aback. The people up here thought of her as a northern European

- a German woman, or so she hoped - whose Spanish was reasonable, yet full of the hesitations and mistakes she made a point of inserting. Not only she, but her language, too, must be disguised to conceal the geographical roots of her adulthood. All that was such a strain, usually she drove to the supermarket in Inca rather than shop in the village. Bread was the exception. She liked her daily bread to be fresh and locally baked and that's why she had been down at *Gloriosa*.

So many people from these Mallorcan mountain towns had emigrated last century to Central and South America, to get rich in the sugar cane industry, and had returned on vacations with children and grandchildren, showing off their new found wealth, speaking a subtly different language, much the same as her own Colombian. The townsfolk knew that language and that's why she couldn't be too careful. She always made a point of avoiding South American words. Words that weren't common parlance in Spain. Words that might betray her. Watching Julio Valente get into his jeep and drive away, she worried a little, then she thought, *ach!* what's the harm in a few spontaneous words to a fellow who seems a good guy? So, Luisa Ross gets back today, and just as well I know.

The terrier, so touching in its displays of energy, jumps into the back of the car and they drive out of town to the orchard where she is creating the paradise that will belong one day to her soon-to-be-born grandchild. Yes, *grandchild!* The news had come via an e-mail from Elena. The Internet, what a fantastic system! Now she's able to outwit her predators for the first time since she fled Colombia. This morning her joy spills over into every thought, into every glimpse of the countryside, into every intention however small. The flower-filled meadows of the lyrical countryside. Live each day as fully as you can, she urged herself continually. This was the line that helped her survive this tedious exile. She could never be careful enough. Eighteen months of relative freedom; the first year moving from pillar to post - Switzerland, England, Spain - and then to Mallorca. As she and Colin often reflected, it was unlikely Andreas himself would come looking for her, because the moment he set foot outside Colombia he risked extradition to the USA and a lengthy sentence for his history of drugs dealing. No, he was more likely to send someone else to do his dirty work, just as he did when he had her kidnapped.

Man doesn't have many predators, she reflects, speeding along the road out of town: Polar bear, White shark . . . other human beings, and what else? Often the thought enraged her, *one of those days Andreas' honchos might catch up with me, take me by surprise in my orchard.* Now that same thought turns her elation to dread. Bastard! she hisses under her breath and her foot went down on the brake pedal. She had narrowly avoided hitting a stray lamb lost on the road. Its tremulous bleats seemed somehow to echo her own predicament. She watched it wandering helplessly for a few moments, until it took a leggy leap over a low stone dyke into a daisy strewn meadow, where its mother came bustling forward to claim it. She drove on thinking, if Andreas Herreros *were* to walk behind Anita Berens, he'd notice immediately the subtle curve of *my* hips. And he'd recognise the way I hold my head, *my* particular style of walking, the very footprints of Lourdes Herreros. She swore under her breath. He's ruining my life! Yet, once upon a time, when we were desperately in love and young and foolish, when the world seemed to be perpetually in springtime, my body was his. *Lourdes's* backside, not that dumb blond Anita's.

The sky was overcast, it was surprisingly cold and, after a quick look round the car park, Luisa felt disappointed. The conservancy jeep was parked there alright, only there was no sign of a driver and she wanted to get up to the town before the shops closed for the weekend. Perhaps they've forgotten I'm arriving today? No reception committee this time, no flashbulbs, no band. Only a young woman coming towards me, a portrait by Ingrés. *Petite, curvaceous, cheeks like russet apples, thick dark curling hair pulled severely to the nape of her neck, lustrous darting eyes in a brick-like face. A little hunched and apprehensive, pulling on the handle of a rather battered brown suitcase . . . .*

They exchanged greetings then stood side-by-side in silence, quite alone on the station platform, edged with date palms and whispering red pepper trees.

Suddenly the woman said: 'D'you know where the toilets are? There weren't any on the train.'

Luisa looked around, then shrugged: 'There's nothing that looks like a toilet to me.' And when her companion said, '*Es urgente*,' she pointed to a nearby bougainvillaea bush: 'You could always go there.'

But she didn't move, and after a small silence Luisa introduced herself. The woman replied: 'And I am Rosa Sanchez.'

Luisa looked at her watch. Damn it! Would Julio or Felipe never come. 'Who're you waiting for, Rosa?' she asked.

'A señora from Inca. I'm to work as her housekeeper, cleaning toilets and terraces, cooking and everything else. I only arrived in Mallorca last week. I'm an immigrant from Colombia. A nurse really, but until I get my Spanish papers I'll have to work at the bottom of the heap.'

Colombia? I couldn't even put it on a map, Luisa thought, uneasily recalling footprints in the snow, her own leavetaking of Scotland.

When Rosa sat precariously on the edge of her suitcase, Luisa noticed a gorgeous red rose tucked into her hair and felt a sudden longing to wear such a rose herself. 'Why did you leave your country?' she said,

'Because of the violence, señora. My town is small, in the mountains, where the old people still think the world is flat. But the town became a cell for the drugs cartels . . . at any moment, any one of our doors could be battered open by guerrillas carrying Kalashnikovs.'

Luisa thought weakly, drugs cartels, Kalashnikovs? This was like the hearing an interview on a radio news programme. No wonder the woman speaks in that high, excited, chattery tone . . . the voice of a frightened child.

Rosa shrugged then said after a small silence: 'I inherited my grandparents' finca in the countryside, and I went there every weekend, to show my poor neighbours how to grow better crops. My grandfather had helped me to understand the nature of the land.'

Luisa nodded, thinking of Rafael, and the villages he supported from his earnings at Plaça Major. Evidently, the Atlantic Ocean heaved with interchange between South America and its motherland, Spain. How different her own perspective on the globe had been, how narrow her outlook all her life, with Scotland as the centre of her small universe. She had never met anyone like Rosa before, or Rafael, the professor, Felipe, and Julio, for that matter . . . the *dramatis personae* of this new life.

'Everyone knew, at any moment we could be herded out like animals and taken away if we knew too much or said the wrong thing.' Rosa's dialect was so rapid and elided that Luisa had to concentrate hard to understand it. 'So many people had gone missing. *Sí, señora.* Someone found a cave in a forest beyond the town filled with the bones and rotting flesh of *campesinos* who had disappeared.'

Surging with an obscure sense of guilt at her own privileged life, and shame that her own knowledge of world politics was virtually zero, she urged Rosa Sanchez to tell her more.

'Well, it happened one day. My own door burst open. Thugs in balaclavas, holding rifles ordered me out of the cottage. It's our place now, they hollered . . . they roared with laughter . . . don't think you can come back here, *hija de puta*. They called me a slut, a whore. They were riffraff.' Rosa's eyes narrowed: 'They were nothing but *cholo*s.'

This certainly puts my own anxieties into perspective, Luisa grimaced inwardly. Thunderstorms, snow, isolation, indeed!

'Then the door of my own house banged shut in my face. *¡Sí, señora!* They forced me to leave all the family possessions behind, these thugs, and I had to walk ten kilometres through the night back to town, through the countryside that smelled of cut grass. How good it felt, though, smelling that grass as I walked. You see, it could have been worse, they could have *raped* me, they could have *killed* me! At least I was still alive!'

When Rosa fell silent, staring out at the countryside with

a sad, stony expression, Luisa found herself saying, 'you'll be safe here in Mallorca'.

Rosa turned to her with glistening, grateful eyes. 'You think so, señora? I hope so.'

At that moment a car pulled up beside the white buildings opposite where the women waited. To Luisa's surprise, Felipe Tamarit got out and the matronly driver rolled down her window. *'¡Ven aqui! Rosa,'* she called out and Felipe rushed to open the boot.

The thought of the thrush hunters imperiously calling their dogs: *¡Ven aqui! ¡ven aqui!* roused Luisa's indignation on Rosa's behalf.

'The woman I'll be working for,' Rosa confided with a resigned air. And when she bent down to pick up her suitcase she couldn't help noticing Rosa's red sandalled feet stood in a golden pool of urine. Catching Luisa's glance of reproof, Rosa's eyes filled with tears.

'Que vaya buen,' Luisa said softly, and when Rosa had almost reached the car, the flower tumbled from her hair.

Felipe tossed Rosa's suitcase in the boot and the car drove off. Watching him saunter towards her, hands in his trousers pockets, Luisa thought, he'll be living in a modern apartment block in Inca with his young wife by now. She looked him in the eye, her hands awkwardly holding the blue case in front of her, the rucksack at her feet, and she had to clear her throat before she said: 'So you're married now, Felipe?'

With a swift look down from her eyes he nodded, picked up the rucksack and led her out under a gold and green tiled archway towards the jeep.

'Julio couldn't make it,' Felipe said perfunctorily. 'He's busy getting things ready for Saint Anthony's Fest.'

On the way, she bent down to rescue Rosa's flower. How sweet it smelled, how nostalgic she suddenly felt for nameless things. She would have liked to say 'A Happy New Year, Felipe'. She had imagined saying it in Mallorcan - *'Molt D'Anys'* - as she had learned it during a seasonal lesson from the professor at a faculty drinks party before she left Barcelona. But the words stayed like small hard objects in her mouth.

As he released the hand brake, she stole a sideways glance at Felipe's stern profile. 'Do you know Rosa Sanchez?'

'Nope,' he grunted, 'but I soon will.'

He would have left it at that, but her riled curiosity made her persist: 'Who was the woman in the car?'

'My mother, Antonia Tamarit. The Colombian has come to work for my mother.' His voice filled with exaggerated patience, he added: 'Never feel sorry for *colombianos*. Quite a few make thousands of dollars when they're in Europe, wheeling and dealing for mafia bosses who work them like puppets from their hideaways in South America.'

Determined not to let him get the better of her, even if the stony sensation has shifted to her stomach, almost protectively she tells herself there's nothing crooked about Rosa Sanchez. She shifts the rose from her pocket to a buttonhole in her jacket. Rosa Sanchez, the young nurse and her brief but shocking autobiography, whose logical conclusion had been a pool of urine! One of millions of displaced people all over the world. No wonder they were pissed off. Now she was painfully aware of it; all those years, growing up in Scotland, she had been protected from the real world. Had lived in a dream world. Hadn't her father often said, 'your head's in the cloud, lass'. At university she had avoided any involvement in politics with the excuse that the world she preferred to inhabit was the natural world. The difficult lives of birds had been her preoccupation from the age of nine when she had realised that bird survival was a chancy business, largely dependent on the weather and a reliable source of food. Small birds could die overnight in sudden cold spells, even in the Mediterranean. Small birds lived such dangerous lives many were lucky to make it past the first year. People, too, were lucky to survive. Now, for the first time, the truth hit her hard. Millions of human beings lived lives as fragile as the lives of birds, though she hadn't wanted to believe it. Hadn't really thought about it until she met Rosa Sanchez.

The jeep raced up the cavernous main street, past the church square and turned right into Calle Luna.

'Don't forget Saint Anthony's Fest tomorrow,' Felipe said, half-grudging, half-mocking before he drove away.

Out of the corner of her eye, as she slipped the key into her lock, she saw the door of number eleven being closed by an unseen hand and felt a momentary stab of rejection. No welcoming committee there either.

She dumps her bags between the outer and inner doors and walks back down the precipitous main street, past the familiar honey-coloured church, its bell-tower shaped like a Turk's cap, past Bar Solitario and the curved row of stiff town houses, towards the shops. There are only four; the pharmacy, the tobacconist, the general store and the bakery called *Gloriosa*. She can hear the women chattering away in Catalan even before she enters Magdalena's store. The dictator Franco suppressed the Catalan language as well as its variant, Mallorcan, so someone had told her. Small wonder it was so widely and proudly spoken nowadays.

Three townswomen, wearing their woollen cardigans fastened by the top button like small cloaks around their shoulders, greet her with affectionate, teasing smiles and revert to Castilian: 'Why did you stay away so long, *Reina?*'

'There must've been a man in Barcelona - or was it *Escocia?*'

'At least you're back in time for Saint Anthony's Fest!'

The dimly-lit shop smells so nostalgically of earth and twine she can almost reach out and touch her child-self playing in her Scottish grandfather's old potting shed. The women shuffle their overflowing baskets around to make room for her and she stands laughing and gossiping with them among the stacked crates of tangerines, apples, greens and the first artichokes of the season. Nuts had arrived; hazelnuts, almonds and walnuts in wooden boxes, each with its silver scoop, and dates from North Africa, sticky, caramel tubes on creamy wooden stems which she stuffs into a plastic bag for Magdalena to weigh.

'A warm spell like this comes before a harsh winter, *Reina,*' asserts María Ferrer, helping Luisa to cram her purchases into her baskets.

'Warm?' Luisa protests. 'It feels really cold to me! Much colder than Barcelona.' Before too long, she thinks, we'll all be glad to tuck our arms *inside* the sleeves of cardigans and thick winter coats too.

'You should've been here last week. We had *frost!*' one if the women said and another added: 'Oh, yes, we did! And they've started pulling the town to bits, too. What's the world coming to?'

'It's quiet now only because its Saturday lunchtime,' pipes up María. 'But during the week it's hell on earth. Dust and noise all day long, *Reina*, now they've started reforming the streets with grants from the European Union.'

Reina, Reina! How she relished the name. Every woman was a queen up here in the mountain town. They treat me like one of them, whereas in truth I was here for only two weeks in December on that reconnaissance trip. How shy I was then. The new girl. Now they make me feel I belong.

Her mouth curves, remembering what her mother once told her. 'There are three kinds of gossips in any small community in Spain, Luisa. *La habladera* simply passes on news. *Las cotillas* take it in turn to hold gatherings at each other's houses, where news is passed on and decisions taken about people in the town . . . such and such *chicas* wear their miniskirts far too short; have you heard about the preparations for the wedding of the postman's daughter? . . . that kind of thing. But watch out for *la charfadera!* She's got it in for everyone!'

Magdalena suddenly says in a lowered voice: 'You'll be living next to the new woman. Keeps herself to herself. Foreign, a right mongrel. German *and* Spanish we think.'

'Better lock up your men!' Luisa jests, inducing a gale of laughter that follows her out of the shop. '*¡Hasta luego! ¡Adiós!* she calls over her shoulder as she goes through the metallic curtain, out to the narrow pavement at the same moment as a Citroën speeds down the hill. A fleeting glimpse is all she has of the driver.

'Talk of the devil. That was the new woman,' exclaims María, stepping out behind her.

Surely they know the woman's name? Luisa wondered impatiently. Why wouldn't the townsfolk use it?

With a sly little smile that says 'we'll see what she makes of life here', María presses Luisa's arm. She makes off in the direction of the bread shop leaving Luisa thinking, you're nothing but an old *charfadera*, María Ferrer! Our other neighbour will make out just fine. *A determined, unsmiling mouth in profile, gloved hands on the wheel, white woollen coat, neat blond hair.* Intrigued, she watches the car sweep round the corner until it disappears from sight, and she lingers until the noise of the engine grows fainter and fainter and silence spreads over the town.

Saturday. The church bell struck one-thirty as she walked. Everyone had disappeared off the streets during the siesta hours. At the church square she paused to look at the Betlen. Professor Bauza had alerted her to it: 'Every year it's hauled out to symbolise the manger where Jesus was born, with sculptures of the Holy Family, then in January they take the figures away and it becomes the empty cell of Saint Anthony.'

The hut was not much higher than her, a conical construction of wood and straw, and when she stooped to look inside, sure enough, the nativity sculptures of Christmas had been cleared away, leaving only a bed of straw.

'I suppose you know that Anthony was the Egyptian saint credited as the founder of Christian monasticism?' the old man had said and, to prevent a long monologue, she had nodded.

No vehicles stirred the dust of the long steep road. Struggling up the hill with her baskets, round skips piled high with broken plasterboard, shattered pantiles and the debris of gutted houses, she couldn't help wondering, are they tearing out the heart of the town or giving it new heart? The town was spending its sizeable European Community grant on the biggest building boom in anyone's memory. Silent lorries and dumper trucks filled with bags of concrete awaited Monday morning when the slabs of quarried mountain stone set on wooden platforms would become paving for the new streets of the town. Monday morning, when she herself would return to Ca'n Clot. Trudging up towards Calle Luna, María's advance weather report teased her mind. Bad weather on the mountains would stretch her as

93

never before, but why worry about the future when the here and now was so diverting?

In her absence William, an elderly expatriate from Leeds, had died in his sleep, the women had told her, and she felt surprised that Alejandro Ferrer hadn't gone too. On Twelfth Night the Three Kings had arrived at the church on the backs of *camels* rather than the usual donkeys, the women had guffawed. A child had narrowly escaped a mauling by Bernardo Ferrer's dog when it wandered out of its enclosure, Magdalena said, rousing the other women in chorus, one day that dog will kill someone, mark our words. Tomas Oleza's donkey had given birth to twins, Tomeu Matamoros had left his wife to live in the next town with Luisa Cañellas. Gossip made the world go round here, just as it did in every small community in Scotland.

Beyond the corner of Calle Luna, three large villas set in extensive landscaped ground claimed the road just before it petered out and became a mountain track leading through a steep dark pine wood. The town's *Calvario* led through the wood to the monastery she had not had the heart to visit in December, although she had walked halfway up the route, only to find it a dismal experience.

Now she stood at her own street corner, her eyes cast upwards to the building that had been erected in the fifties when Catholicism had still been a life force in the community. These days the monastery had become an enormous white elephant, out-of-scale with the modest houses of the town, and, as she had heard from Jaume at Bar Solitario, its vast interior housed only three Sisters of Mercy who took in groups of disadvantaged Palma kids during the school holidays. How the children must cringe to go there, if it's anything like my old boarding school at St Andrews, she thought, sensing a return of old anxieties. The very name of that town still spelled deprivation and grey wind-lashed sea. Rationally, she knew it was a fine place; only her idea of it, her memory, had become distorted as a result of its association in her mind with the sudden deaths of her mother and sister. It had been after that Harry Ross had 'sent her away' to boarding school.

But hey! she consoled herself, here and now, Calle Luna is splashed with sunshine. The only sign of life in the deserted street was a spry Mallorcan terrier investigating the doorstep of her rented house. She gave it a pat, then flung open the outside doors that led directly into the modest L-shaped kitchen, tiled and decorated in neutral shades. From the shorter leg of the 'L', the stone stair rose, unguarded by a balustrade, to two second floor bedrooms. During a quick check upstairs Luisa glanced out of the bedroom window and saw Tonia Ferrer bent over her work in the shed at the bottom of the neighbouring garden. Frau Lehmann must be a keen gardener, she decided, looking down on her own landscaped plot; whereas Señora Berens' back garden on the other side was a messy jumble of plants and sculpted objects. She went downstairs again, reassured that everything was immaculate and smelled of recently applied polish and floor cleaner. No telltale signs lingered of Gerda Lehmann's ownership, apart from her private locked cupboard, a few ornaments Luisa felt she could live with and some books she might be glad to read.

The house was one of several in a row, originally built out of the honey coloured local stone as homes-cum-workshops for piece workers supplying the Inca leather industry. On her previous visit Luisa had grown fond of the Ferrer family next door who frequented Bar Solitario every evening. Mute and deaf Alejandro, one of the oldest inhabitants of the town, his ancient wife Francisca, their granddaughter Tonia, and her mother María, *la charfadera*. Tonia, aged around twenty-two, worked from morning to night fabricating shoes and gloves in the shed. Many townsfolk had made small fortunes through selling their country and seaside properties off to rich foreigners, she knew, but the Ferrers were relatively poor. Tonia tap-tap-tapping nails into shoes, the older women calling out to each other, sluicing the yard, cooking up the family lunch. The smell of meat being cooked with oil and garlic infiltrated her sitting room now, and Luisa threw open another set of French doors that gave access to the garden. There she stood inhaling the wafts of scent from the lavender bushes and the white roses of the hedge, remembering how, when she had come to look over the house, she had heard old Alejandro Ferrer crying like a baby through the walls and had felt pity for him. Just as Rafael heard *me*; evidently walls in Spain were not as thick as they looked. Perhaps, being deaf and dumb, Señor Ferrer doesn't hear himself . . . old folk tend to die in winter . . . and, suddenly, she was remembering her own father's death last January, a year ago, almost to the day.

All at once, the front door bell rang out a sharp summons and through the lace curtains she could see her neighbour standing there with a neat pile of folded linen in her arms, the terrier at her feet. *Older than me, a little smaller, on the plump side but well proportioned. Attractive, high maintenance glamour, wears a lot of make-up. Notably large green eyes above bruised looking skin that suggests someone who doesn't sleep well. If she smiled her eyes would still be sad.*

'Frau Lehmann . . . Gerda . . . asked me to give you this extra linen. She hadn't time to pick it up from the laundry in Inca before she left for Munich,' the neighbour announced, her bracelets jingling as the package was passed over. 'I am Anita Berens,' she said: 'I can't stay, another time perhaps?'

When she turned to leave Luisa thought, it's so *obvious*, she wants to set a distance between us. But why?

After that, she switches on the radio in the kitchen, fooling herself that winter might never come. A harsh winter *Reina!* but surely not here, not in Mallorca? Rosa's flower lying on the counter has a wilted look. She sets it in a narrow glass of water then empties out the shopping basket. *Butter, yoghurt, cheese, into the fridge* - the rich sonorities of a Sibelius symphony from Radio Catalunya enlarge the room - *and all those lovely greens, garlic and tangerines, into a terracotta bowl.*

As if to play down a sudden rush of loneliness, she turns up the volume of the radio only to unleash flashing cadenzas and crashing chords. Dragged back through grey northern veils to the island, she rails inwardly; surely I'm allowed to feel a little homesick from time to time. But she will not weep, lighting a gas ring on the cooker. The way to look at it is this . . . I can go back to the island whenever I want, without going back to Dan.

Life with him . . . how many? yes, almost ten years . . . typing up *his* observations of the island birds, buzzard, peregrine, geese and waders, in a round about way, was a preparation for Mallorca, I see that now.

Carrots, onions, oil, garlic and coriander. Hunger aroused by the smell of soup coming to the boil, she tears off a chunk of bread. Don't dwell on Señora Berens' unfriendliness, either, she tells herself. Yet she dreads the return of the loneliness she knew in her early days in Barcelona. There are bound to be times when I'll be climbing the walls of Ca'n Clot to escape my own company. Here I am without family, without a lover, alone, very short of money and, despite a great start to the year, doubtful about the course my life is taking. Who will I be able to turn to in the bad times? Is this independence I've discovered rather late in life asking too much, is it merely foolhardy? Rafael might, or, there again, might not, fit into the future . . . Dan and my father have disappeared, more or less, down the dark tunnel of the past.

She fills a glass with tarry red Rioja and lights one of her occasional cigarettes. Spain, my mother's land, is *my* home now and I must have faith that everything else will fall into place. She struggles to convince herself, only, the music on the radio suggests fast clouds rolling in off the North Sea, heading for her lost island. She swallows the entire glass of wine then pours out another. Damn it! she thinks. Music can be so merciless, tearing open the heart's seams of longing in the most underhanded way. Like this symphony of Sibelius, its tremendous crescendos so *northern*, like the waves of the island crashing in tears.

§

'The town you're going to – my home – re-enacts, year after year, a particular ritual based on the supposition that a raven once flew onto the shoulder of Anthony. The raven symbolises the descent of the Holy Spirit, I may say. That bird brought Anthony bread so that he might survive in the desert.'

She tried to remember what the professor had told her

97

about Saint Anthony's Fest. The warm hearted patriarch who stepped onto the empty stage of my 'life after Dan' insisted I take part in the ritual of the raven's flight. This fiesta that was cruelly outlawed, like others all over Spain, by Franco. Indeed, R. R. Bauza himself had returned to this church square in his home town, in 1977, two years after the dictator died. That year, rituals observed since time immemorial could be celebrated once more, and the professor had made a point of being here among his own folk.

Saint Anthony's Fest. The church square was scented with green myrtle branches compressed under the eager feet of the crowd gathering to see the performance. A gang of adults and children dressed up as devils in red cloaks and horned masks pranced among them, their faces painted to suggest Neanderthal brows, bulging eyes and pointed teeth. Some carried sticks attached to water-filled animal bladders - sheep or goat, Luisa supposed - and as they went merrily about, bopping the crowd on shoulders and backsides, raucous waves of hilarity and pretended outrage swooped into the clear air. Never in her life had she seen anything like this.

The sun had not yet risen over the church square. Shivering a little she thrust her hands deep into her jacket pockets and looked round at the crowd. Some had brought pets for the Blessing of the Animals ceremony that was scheduled to follow the raven's flight. Lap dogs on leashes, canaries, cats and hamsters in cages, and, all of a sudden, four horseman rode into the square, caballeros in wide-brimmed hats, reigning-in their high spirited horses. Beside the Betlen there was a pen with lambs and a cage of white ducks. And she noticed, outside Bar Solitario, Felipe taking leave of his mother and a young woman, wearing a bright pink padded jacket, whom she took to be his new wife. How was Rosa settling down? Luisa wondered. Where was Felipe off to? She would have loved a coffee herself and considered going over to the bar. But the crowd seemed too dense to push through, the gang of devils too rampant on the edge of it. Then she spotted Anita Berens on the other side of the square. *Wearing a brimmed golden hat, ethnic, fashionable, yet it fails to conceal those strange green eyes that look out on the world, sad and guarded . . .* and, to her surprise, suddenly there was Rosa Sanchez, standing near Anita, scrutinising her, yet keeping her distance.

At that moment, the church bells let rip a carillon against the sharp blue sky. Standing on tiptoe to get a better view, Luisa could scarcely believe the brown robed, bearded figure of Saint Anthony approaching the Betlen was none other than Felipe Tamarit. And when she noticed his false black beard had slipped sideways she wanted to laugh out loud, only the crowd had fallen silent. This was a serious moment and no one else seemed to be amused by the crooked beard. The bells rang out the *bing! boom!* of the hour. All eyes turned upwards and Luisa focussed her binoculars on the foreshortened bell-tower, creamy against the blue sky. On the last chime of the eleventh hour, Julio appeared framed in the arch of the campanile. Like Mister Punch, she smiled to herself, watching him carefully place Cora from the Ca'n Clot aviary onto the parapet. Then, stepping beyond his hut, Felipe threw back his head, half-singing, half-shouting, *kway! kway!*

The bird cocked its head. Suspense intensified in the square. Every eye was fixed to the bird. *Kwee! kwee!* came its high-pitched response before it flew at terrific speed onto Felipe's shoulder where it steadied itself with frantically beating blue-black wings. The crowd burst into applause, and, when Felipe turned his head to the bird, although Luisa was too far away to hear, she knew he would be saying *¡qué bonita!, ¡qué bonita!* tenderly, just as he had spoken to Aquila the day they flew her.

So, Felipe has trained the raven as well as the little eagle. Despite the tension between them, she felt moved by an odd sort of pride in him. No saint certainly, yet a man who earns the trust of birds can't be all that bad. To increasing applause, the saint in his utterly false beard disappeared through the ornately carved church door, into its cavernous darkness, and at that moment, sunlight flooded the square. Perhaps, Luisa fell to thinking, the original Saint Anthony trained birds, too? Then there was a sudden tug on her sleeve, and Rosa Sanchez stood smiling at her side.

'*¡Hola, Rosa! ¿Cómo estás?*' Warmly, she kissed the girl on both cheeks.

'*Muy bien, señora.* I saw you from the other side of the square.'

'Yes, you were standing next to my neighbour at Calle Luna.'

'Can I visit you there? Take tea in the British style?' Rosa grinned.

'How's life with Señora Tamarit?'

'They treat me well,' she replied, all dimpled smiles; 'like one of the family. Now I've gotta go. We're going back to the house for Sunday lunch.'

Thrush in cabbage, no doubt, Luisa thought wryly as she watched Rosa pushing back through the crowd towards Bar Solitario. Then she found herself looking down into the bright eyes of a Mallorcan girl. They exchanged smiles, until, overcome with shyness, the child buried her face in her mother's skirt. Luisa and the woman chatted about the ceremony and the weather and Luisa found her eyes wandering to where Anita Berens had stood, but there was no sign of her.

'Look, they're coming out again,' the young mother exclaimed and they turned to see Felipe, a young servitor and the priest in his white robe trimmed with red and gold processing to the foot of the church steps, where the animals waited with their owners for the priest's blessing. Cora, in her cadge at Felipe's feet, came first. The priest waved his smoking incensor over the cadge, Cora squawked, then he handed Felipe a rolled certificate. Cora had been duly blessed. After that, fighting and barking broke out among the dogs, one of the horses reared, the lambs bleated in their pen but, one by one, each animal got its blessing, and by the time it was all over the square smelled of a peculiar mixture of myrtle, incense and dung.

Luisa felt flooded by the wonder of it all. I've taken part in an extraordinary performance. A cross between a bad B-movie and a dramatisation of a scene from the Gospels. Something fantastical made real by man's determination to remember the legends of the past. Saint Anthony and the devils, Felipe and Aquila and now this tamed raven, all seemed to her congruously linked to the Amerindian musicians, to Rafael in his winged costume and the living statues in the square in Barcelona. Suspensions of disbelief. Conjuring tricks! What an amazing world she was discovering far from her own Scottish hills. Initially, she had scoffed at the idea of the burial ceremony her flatmates had endured in the Garaff hills. Only afterwards, seeing their undisguised joy at having completed Rafael's tough training programme, she had felt great respect for his ability to convey to others his deeply felt sense of ritual. Rituals, legends, like this blessing of the animals, united a community. Now she could understand why these events were infinitely precious – and powerful – otherwise why would the cunning Franco have banished them? Sooner or later, if the world is to keep what sanity is left to it, we must all catch up with legends.

Over at Bar Solitario Felipe, dressed once more in military-style conservancy attire, sat with his trio of women. Leaning back in his seat, his cap pushed back, the raven on his shoulder, nonchalantly Felipe held court. People surrounded him, shaking his hand and a little regretfully, Luisa decided there was nowhere for her to go but back to Calle Luna. She turned to see the patient mountain that was never far from her thoughts, just visible above the pantiled roofs of the houses of the town and the pine cloaked crags. Up there, she would have the stark contrasts she had craved in Barcelona. In her mind, Massanella took on the attributes of Bauza's desert: a Godforsaken place until the early disciples brought the light of . . . what? Christianity? These days non-believers like her would call it simply love, a sort of pantheistic love, of the natural world. She walked on filled with certainty. The return to the mountains tomorrow with the wardens and this raven celebrity, *Corvus corax*, would open another extraordinary chapter in her own life. Something that would bear scant resemblance to anything she had ever known, and she could hardly wait to get on with it.

The weather was changing fast. Ominous clouds, grey against granite, held to the high reaches of the mountains. Bad weather up there, but not down here. Not yet, Luisa thinks, quickening her pace to draw level with the stocky, bandy-legged

María Ferrer ahead, and, suddenly, a white airport taxi comes rushing up the narrow street behind them, forcing them to press their bodies against the wall of a house.

'Watch your toes,' María exclaims, then chuckles. 'That taxi had to wait for an hour or more on the other side of the square while the *fest* was going on, and serves it right!'

An old crone, wearing a black dress under a floral overall of the sort my Spanish grandmother wore almost forty years ago, Luisa decided. María had removed her hair curlers this morning. Unbrushed hennaed rolls contoured her head like the fruit garlands of a gnarled old goddess. Perhaps María's bitchiness could be put down to sacrifices she'd had to make as a single parent, caring for her own ancient parents all these years?

'Did the raven of the myth *stay* on Anthony's shoulder, María?' Luisa says. 'What d'you think? Did the saint tame the raven, did he *teach* it to fly onto his shoulder like a falconer?'

María stared at Luisa as if she might have been the village idiot. 'Heaven's sakes, what a question, *Reina*!' Her face contorted in astonishment. 'None of us know, or want to know if he taught birds tricks or if he didn't, neither could we imagine a year without Saint Anthony and the raven.'

Fair enough, María . . . and to calm her down, Luisa agreed, no, of course it didn't really matter, but, all the same, she wondered if she might find a *Life of Saint Anthony* somewhere in the town library.

When they turned into Calle Luna, the taxi was pulling away from Anita Berens' door and, keen to witness the scene, both women slowed their pace. From a discreet distance they watched Anita Berens laughing, exclaiming, hugging someone – a man – who hoists up a black travelling bag, puts an arm round her shoulders then goes in with her through the door of number eleven.

'Visitor,' says María darkly. 'She doesn't get many of *those*.'

After the flurry at number eleven and the closing of its door, the street seemed even more of a deserted backwater than usual.

'By the way, I'll tell you something for nothing, *Reina*,' María piped up in the silence. 'Anthony is also the name given to the smallest pig in a litter! *Hee, hee, hee,* didn't know that, did you? For that very Anthony you saw in the square today, that Felipe, is the patron saint of swineherds along with everything else!'

With a cackle, María rushed off and disappeared into number thirteen, leaving Luisa bemused. Surely she doesn't *really* think Felipe's the patron saint of pig farmers. Talk about being dropped to earth with a thud. From the Holy Spirit to pigs, indeed.

And then the silence embraced her. Past and present seemed to fuse profoundly within her as she stood thinking, at this very moment, this is my life. A mountain called Massanella and this street called Calle Luna, where three identical arched wooden doors, just high enough so you don't have to stoop when you enter, lead to extraordinarily different worlds — to the Ferrers, to Anita Berens' and to mine. Sooner or later our stories will unfold, and not even I can begin to know the script or the outcome of my own. She bent down a little to admire the botanical pots beside Anita's door, identified bougainvillaea, though its twiggy stem was not yet in flower, miniature roses, purple and pink, and white winter pansies. And she hoped that, inside number eleven, Anita's visitor was cheering her up.

After Sunday lunch Colin Cramer and Lourdes Herreros found themselves sitting on a squat concrete block that passed for a bench, halfway up the Calvary leading to the convent on the hill behind the town.

'I've never thought to ask you this before, Colin, but where did you and Gustavo first meet?' Momentarily, he was aware of her sharp glance before she carried on drawing a pattern with a stick in the pulverised earth under their feet.

He slid a little along the seat towards her. 'Might *I* ask you the same question? Where did *you* meet Gustavo?' Colin longed to put an arm round her shoulder at that moment, if she would just lay down the stick.

'I met him at Broadcasting House in Bogotá', in the canteen, to be specific,' she said sweetly. 'A bit prosaic for Gustavo, perhaps . . . .'

'Indeed, yes,' Colin broke in with a gruff laugh. 'Gustavo

certainly has a taste for dramatic locations. He and I met for the first time, at *his* suggestion mind you, outside the late Paco Escobar's house, the Hacienda Napoles near Medellín.'

'No! That was *cheeky* - but typical, I suppose - of Gustavo!' Lourdes tossed her head with a gust of laughter. 'Talk about getting right to the heart of things! Escobar ran a perpetual fiesta at his hacienda, as you must know. In the good old days, Andreas and I often used to go to parties there with politicians, industrialists, oh, you know the scene. All sorts of freeloaders. When things got so bad in 1991, I refused to go again, but Andreas had to keep going, to keep Paco sweet.'

Colin's visits were fraught with risk and had to be planned with the utmost care. However, after twelve months with no news that Andreas Herreros had become active again, he talked of visiting Lourdes more frequently in the interests of finishing *Flight into Exile*. A real-life thriller setting the ordeal of her kidnapping, her personal story, against the backdrop of Colombia's recent drugs-running history. He himself, and Gustavo Balcázar, Lourdes' colleague at Radio Colombia, had masterminded her escape over the border in the back of a rented van. This was the drama he intended to write up during the next few days, the chapter introducing Gustavo, so he felt pleased Lourdes had brought up the subject of their mutual friend.

'Paco Escobar's Hacienda Napoles was quite extraordinary don't you think?' she was saying.

'Gustavo and I didn't get to see *inside* the compound . . . though I gather Escobar kept a zoo stocked with African giraffes and hippos. As if he had been some Renaissance prince! But what grabbed me was that small plane displayed at the entrance like some national monument. Escobar certainly had nerve. '

'Yes, I remember the plane. Wasn't it the one they used to export the first ever cocaine shipment out of Columbia?'

'The very one . . . yes,' he said, wistfully.

From the first moment he had set eyes on it, Colin had relished the plane's resemblance to the sort Antoine de Saint-Exupéry had flown on his mail flights. And it didn't escape him that both Saint-Exupéry and the first drug traffickers had shared a near-mythic aura, though for very different reasons. Many of the early traffickers had endured poverty-stricken childhoods in the slums, and later, when they made it rich through drugs, they had redirected some of their wealth into charitable works in marginal neighbourhoods. Certainly that was one of the main reasons they had enjoyed prestige in Colombian society in these naive early years. Only, ironically enough, it was that very collusion between the traffickers and the community that would foster the evil of the decades to come. He gave a little shudder, dreading to think what form that evil might take in the next generation.

Earlier, when they had set out towards the rather forbidding monastery that dominated the mountain town, Colin thought of its approach not so much as a hill but a *colline,* though he was not sure why. He felt his spirits deflated by the place to the extent that one of his headaches was coming on, yet they were not even halfway up the Calvary. Perhaps it was the grey damp afternoon, when, in the low sulky light, the bushes and small trees that hung about the route seemed dull, even a little threatening. In the absence of birdsong, it was silent as the grave. He remembered how, last time he was here, he had lain awake in the middle of the night in the tiny bedroom he now shared with Lourdes' computer. She had been maddeningly, deeply asleep next door. He could hear her breathing that was not quite a snore through his door that was slightly ajar. Couldn't he just push it wide open and go to her? Declare himself ready to give up everything and come out here to live with her? Only, once again, he had had to face the facts. He was too much of a coward. Even if he no longer loved Felice, it would be downright madness to give up Littledeane Hall and the privileged yet *dutiful* lifestyle he had inherited by way of his wife's ancestors. If only he could have persuaded Lourdes to have an affair with him . . . but it was no use. He had declared his love for her before, only to be rebuffed. I love you dearly as a friend and working colleague, *nada mas,* Colin; I couldn't handle anything more, besides, even if you're not a *happily* married man, you are a married man.

Now, clambering in front of him, up the rough path that every so often passed one of the thirteen Stations of the Cross, Lourdes seemed in good spirits, happier than he had seen her for a long time. He put this improvement down to his Christmas present, the Apple Mac that gave her access to her daughter by e-mail. Deep down he felt very pleased, despite this ghastly walk she was taking him on. Put simply, he needed to be needed, he *needed* to help her. Their relationship put an exotic spin on his predictable life in Britain. And apart from that, they both benefited from working on his book together, sharing their direct experience of the sort of criminal society Colombia had spawned, like venomous mushrooms throbbing away in a monstrous dank cave, as Gabriel García Márquez had put it in one of his books.

Walking on, lost in thought, he rehearsed the gist of the introduction to *Flight into Exile* he had drafted before he left London. He had faithfully described the state of the collective unconscious of third world societies like Colombia, where groups of disempowered, *excluded* people violently turned on the privileged as the only hope for survival left to them. And who could blame them, he often boomed to anyone who would listen. Poverty-stricken, near-illiterate, unhealthy, and remorselessly taunted by mass-media advertisements featuring the consumer goodies they could never hope to have . . . unless they got into the drugs racket or some other terrorist activity.

Terrorism had become commonplace in every part of the globe as the downside of globalisation and the Information Age. That was the key message he intended to convey to readers of his book as well as in future issues of *Ecco!*. He intended the magazine to become harder-hitting, only he would have to secure a stronger advertising base first. Couldn't afford to scare off the customers he already had in secure positions on inside front and back pages, advertising green wellies, wind generators, solar panels and the like.

Strange, he thought, following Lourdes's determined figure, his breath coming in painful short bursts as he forced himself onwards and upwards, how two people can be tracing a route at the same time and have polar opposite reactions. There she was, having a great time, when he'd much prefer walking in the valley or, better still, pruning trees at her finca. Anything rather than dragging his rather overweight, dispirited body up towards that dreary looking institution.

Every so often the track they followed met the spiralling asphalted road from town, and they had to cross it to find the start of the next bit of the path. Here was the road again, and as he stepped on to it, a black limousine with darkened windows sped swiftly by on its way down from the convent. Creepy, he thought, seeing only shadows through the subfusc glass, and he wondered, did they belong to ecclesiastical gangsters or innocent saints?

Lourdes had discovered the continuation of the path on the other side of the road. 'This way, Colin. The path's over here!' she called out. 'Why are you just standing on the verge like that? C'mon, it's not far now!'

Do we *have* to go any further, he groaned to himself? On the other hand, it was good to see her so happy. He crossed to the path where Roman numerals marked another Station to his right. Number nine. He held back from saying how ugly he found it, as hideous as every other waymarker they had passed to reach this spot. Perhaps Lourdes *liked* the look of the things. After all, though lapsed now, she had been brought up in the Catholic faith. Silently, he examined the recently constructed, monstrous piece of pink-tinted concrete inlaid with banal coloured ceramics, this one depicting Christ being given the sponge of vinegar.

Ecco homo! he mused. 'Behold, the man is become one of us, to know good and evil . . . .' A conscious echo of the words God supposedly used after he expelled Adam and Eve from the Garden of Eden. Words that had inspired the title and ethos of his magazine. Behold! *Ecco!* The reminder stirred him as he pressed on behind Lourdes, and, at the next station, he persuaded her to rest beside him on the concrete seat. Spread below in the afternoon gloom was the wide fertile valley, inscribed with near-black cypress trees, where he could see, here and there, manorial houses and farm buildings.

'There, that's better,' he told her, briskly rubbing his hands together, 'The view from here suggests we might be in Italy.'

'Italy? Why Italy? What's wrong with Mallorca?' Lourdes said sharply, and when she held his eyes with a bright glance, he felt he would like to kiss her. Love in the afternoon, back in her townhouse. Now wouldn't that be better than this?

'Nothing's *wrong* with Mallorca, my dear. It's just that so many Italian masters . . . Salvador Rosa and Claude, for example, painted landscape scenes like that valley down there, and I don't know of any Spanish artist who did, in quite the same way.'

It was after that, sitting on the grey hill, they began talking about Colombia, and Lourdes picked up her drawing stick from the path. He had gone out to Colombia to research a documentary for British television about the notorious drug baron, the late Paco Escobar, and the drug cartels' murders and kidnappings in the early 1990s. Gustavo Balcázar, the journalist and broadcaster, had been one of the first people Colin had contacted to work with him on the film. It was Gustavo who had come to him later, beside himself with worry about Lourdes' disappearance.

'Gustavo chose the hacienda at Medellín as our first meeting place,' Colin said, turning to her, wishing she'd put down the bloody stick and give him her full attention. 'Gustavo knew full well that the old aeroplane positioned at the entrance to Escobar's place . . . rather than some mammoth civic statue in a city square . . . would make a startling visual lead-in to my film. And I had to admit it, he was right. That 'plane is so symbolic of Colombia's tragic history, yet also, somehow, tragicomical; Escobar was a ridiculous yet powerful old goat. Of course, I did follow Gustavo's suggestion in the end.'

Lourdes gave one of her deep sexy laughs. 'Yeah, Gustavo is pretty insightful,' and her voice sounded so soft and sweet Colin immediately had to discount a pang of jealously.

At last, Lourdes tossed the stick into the bushes. 'Just as well you did arrive in Colombia, Colin. Otherwise I certainly wouldn't be sitting here now.' She slipped a hand through his arm. 'Oh, I'm so *glad* you're here. What would I do without you?'

Since he could not possess her, he took full advantage of getting his own way in smaller matters, and so, after a companionable pause, he said: 'Look, do we *have* to go all the way up this awful hill? Do you really want to visit that off-putting monastery or convent or whatever it is? Be a sweetie and say we can go back to the house for tea.'

She agreed straight away. 'Of course we can, Colin, if that's what you want.'

Turning to her with that bittersweet sensation of frustrated desire he knew so well, he found a stray blond hair on her collar and plucked it off. Yes, he was allowed small affectionate gestures, and that one earned him a gorgeous smile.

'That's settled then,' he said happily. 'We'll go down in a moment. Okay by you if we get working on the book for an hour or two before dinner? I want to cover that 1991 era in Medellín . . . I still find the enormity of the DEA's figures staggering, I was revising them the other day . . . *two thousand* people in the slums worked for Escobar at that time, many of them mere adolescents - like *your* minders after you were kidnapped - who earned their living hunting down and killing police with ransoms on their heads. In the first *two months* of 1991 alone there had been *twelve hundred* murders.'

She sat very still beside him, almost prayerful, so that Colin immediately regretted having prolonged their conversation. Perhaps she was remembering her journalist friends who had swelled the statistics that year? After a minute or two, a sudden skittish gust of air rustled the leaves of the gum cistus bushes near where they sat and she brightened, as if her thoughts had blown away. There'll be a storm soon, she said. A wind was getting up, the sky was growing heavier by the minute.

They rose to leave, and Colin said: 'Gustavo told me about you that first evening when we had a meal together.'

'What did he say?'

'He said you were a fabulous woman as well as an outstanding broadcaster.'

She gave him a playful shove. 'Go on! Tell, me more! What else did he say?'

'I'll tell you when we get back to Calle Luna and you've made me a nice cup of tea,' he teased, starting off down the path.

With mock petulance – 'tell me *now*, Colin, or I won't come' – she hastened to bar his way, so that they both stood grinning, impetuously daring each other like schoolchildren in the playground, darting this way and that with outstretched arms. Then, out of breath and unable to remember when he had laughed so much, yet badly needing that strong sweet tea, Colin suggested they get back before the storm.

'I have to confess Gustavo and I were a little high on tequila,' he said, leading the way down. 'Nevertheless, I had the impression that he fancied you rotten,' he added, testing her a little.

'Get off! That's ridiculous, Colin! However, we were some team in the broadcasting studio, I'll give you that.'

Arm-in-arm they went, in advance of the thickening cloud menacing the foothills. And, just as they reached the outskirts of town, taking them completely by surprise, an enormous black dog sprung against the wire fence surrounding a villa. They stared into its fanged jaws and saw the fence bulging alarmingly when it flung its weight against it, barking viciously.

'Oh, my God! What a brute,' Lourdes shrieked and, hiding her face in Colin's shoulder, burst into tears.

When they got back to the house, they had a brandy to recover.

'It wasn't there when we went up the hill,' Lourdes protested.

'No. It seemed to come out of nowhere, like a bat out of hell.'

But Lourdes didn't smile as they sat at either end of the sofa sipping their brandies, discussing the dog. Her over-reaction to the event worried him. Had the shock of the dog triggered off deeper tensions?

'Perhaps its owner was feeding it earlier?' she said with a puzzled frown. 'That's why we didn't run into it when we went up the hill?'

At last he manoeuvred the conversation round to the tea he had been promised, followed by a session on the book, and, while Lourdes went to put on the kettle, he sought refuge on the small patio above the garden where he sat listening to birdsong. He had no idea what the birds were, thrushes, finches, perhaps. And a strange tap, tap, tapping seemed to come not from the very next garden, but the one beyond it. He could hear women's voices, too, in that same garden, calling out to each other in good natured banter. Mallorcan women, he supposed. He didn't understand a word of their guttural language. Certainly not Castilian, he decided, getting up to peer over the shoulder-high bamboo fence, where he admired the small garden next to Lourdes' that reminded him of an illustration from a Renaissance manuscript.

There were cruciform paths of silver gravel, interplanted with grey green Mediterranean lavender and other herbs he couldn't identify. The fence was smothered with small white roses, and the garden ended in a secret place of trees. He felt a rush of desire to enter that place. Sitting down again, waiting patiently for tea – would it ever come? – he tuned into the voices – ¡Pa bo! ¡molt ve! these few words were all he recognised of Mallorcan; open vowels everywhere! Such a rustic language.

'Can you hear me, Lourdes?' He raised his voice. He could see her pouring out tea in the salon, on the other side of the glass doors leading to the garden.

Then suddenly he heard the squeak of hinges from the upstairs window of the house next door and he looked up just in time to see the sliver of a woman's face and her arm reaching out to close a green shutter. Intrigued by such a charming vignette, like a small oil painted by Bonnard, he decided the moment had come to think about something other than Gustavo and Colombia. Lourdes had already mentioned the new neighbour, and that must be her.

Lourdes called back, 'yes, I can hear you,' and he said 'why don't we go next door and pay your neighbour a visit?'

Lourdes' scant details had intrigued him. 'Some sort of environmentalist, maybe. Dresses in khakis, binoculars, walking boots, goes off in the conservancy jeep to the mountains. Not my type,' she had said, pulling a mock-serious face. 'Very nice but rather earnest.' Nevertheless, Lourdes needed a friend up here, someone she might come to trust enough to confide in, and he resolved to bring about a meeting.

'Are you listening, Lourdes?' he said.

'Of course I'm listening,' she replied, arriving a little irritated with a laden tea tray. Saliva rose in his mouth at the sight of a golden and glistening almond cake. 'I'm *thinking*, too,' she chided in a lowered voice. 'Only, I think I'd feel more comfortable keeping a safe distance.'

'We could just check her out. It might be good to get to know her. You spend far too much time alone. After all, you have nothing to be afraid of. You have a terrific alias. Anita Berens and her book, *A Century of Tourism in Mallorca*. Isn't it time to practise talking about it? Let's ask her in for dinner before I go back to London. Do you know, something? I've never seen Anita Berens in action as a hostess? I'll bet she's quite a severe charmer!'

When the remains of an excellent tea lay on the plates in front of them and he'd done his best to soothe her, Colin expressed his satisfaction and wiped his mouth with his napkin.

'Tell you what. I'll go and ask to borrow salt, something like that. No need to stay long,' he said, getting up and going to her. Lourdes looked tired and probably needed an afternoon nap.

'Okay,' she sighed. 'If it's what you want, go see what you make of Luisa Ross.'

Poor Lourdes, he refrained from saying, and kissed her cheek. She hated any form of pity and had shown herself to be brave in her new form of captivity in Mallorca. He relished her displays of fiery indepenence, the brave front she put on in spite of the confines of her boxed-in life in exile. Being with her, working on the book with her, challenged him in quite a different way to running *Ecco!*, and their relationship counterbalanced with considerable piquancy his rather mundane life as a family man in the Home Counties. He knew he was the one person in the world she could trust without question. And when she, challenging her emotional dependence on him, wondered why he kept coming back, he made her laugh by saying, one day

112

you'll make me very rich. When it is finally published, *Flight into Exile, your* story, will be a bestseller.

Whenever Luisa had a spare moment, she found herself documenting vignettes of the past and present in her notebook. She chose to do this at the small table at the bedroom window that overlooked the picturesque valley and the Puig de Magdalena – where there was a church named after Saint Anthony, according to a guide book she found in the house. With wry amusement, she put the finishing touches to a line-drawing of Felipe, Cora on his shoulder. Then, underneath it, she wrote: The patron saint of swineherds!

She found the ample bright bedroom, decorated in white and yellow, more appealing than the rather gloomy sitting room downstairs. Not even Frau Lehmann's considerable skill as an amateur interior designer had been able to dispel its lumpen atmosphere that the exposed, dark stone walls only emphasised. Besides, an extension pipe from the sitting room stove snaked up here and made the bedroom very cosy.

Luisa had been sitting at the table in front of the window, when suddenly an English voice startled her: 'Can you hear me, Lourdes?' A man's voice in Anita's garden. A quick look at her watch told her it was much later than she thought, in fact it was time to start packing for the week ahead. Not without curiosity, she went to close the shutters and, glancing down, for a split second her eyes met those of the man she had seen arriving in the taxi that morning. A little later, he was standing on her doorstep introducing himself as Colin Cramer and asking for salt. She suppressed a grin; an old dog with an old trick. They chatted a little as she measured out salt into an egg cup and before he left he invited her to join him and Anita for dinner the following Saturday.

Colin's visit had reopened seams of memory Lourdes struggled to keep tightly closed. Often she would link past events with herself as 'her' rather than 'I', as if they belonged to someone else. For example, she thought, staring at the damp tea leaves in the sink, 'between September 1983 and January 1991, twenty-six journalists working in various Colombian media had been murdered by the drug cartels. Lourdes Herreros had been lucky to escape that atrocious era, though she had been kidnapped at the end of the decade.' But however hard it was, the main purpose of Colin's visits was to get information out of her. She knew that, and he had made it clear that this visit was about filling in factual gaps in his manuscript.

She minded that Colin had gone next door. Why involve Luisa Ross, weren't their lives tricky enough? And she acknowledged a twinge of jealousy. Maybe Colin would fancy the *chica*. Didn't many older men prefer younger women these days? She knew she was being unreasonable, but if *she* couldn't have him she was darned sure Luisa Ross wouldn't either. Totally selfish, I may be . . . but . . . she thought, bending down to remove the rubbish bag from the bin . . . well, isn't life enough of a brute without extra complications. The bag tightly tied, she put the tea things away in the cupboard, urging herself to think more constructively. At least their project, Colin's book, was something tangible, almost concrete, something that gave a framework to her life. At least you're alive to tell the tale, she admonished herself as she tidied up the kitchen. So dig up the past, pin down the dates, remember the awful time. The *cholos!* – and sort out in your mind how you want to tell it to Colin.

She turned on the radio. Pop flamenco flowed over her, upbeat, vivacious. Colin knew a bit about Andreas' infidelities, but not about her own affair with Gustavo. How can I tell him about Gustavo when it would detract from the drama of his book?

At that moment Colin came back, softly closing behind him first the arched entrance, then the French doors. 'Luisa Ross is A-okay,' he told her, punching the air with a raised thumb then coming to put an arm round her waist. 'You'll like her. A serious type, but not, I think, a prude. Scottish people are, in general, reticent, rational, not given to showing emotion.'

She pushed him away, a little scornful, and turned off the

radio. But he didn't seem to notice her rebuff. Fishing for his glasses in a trousers pocket, he rattled on: 'The Scots I've met in my life have been warm hearted, and if they befriend you, you can trust them to the ends of the earth. Luisa's got Spanish blood in her, too. Spanish mother. As you suspected, she's a scientist, an ornithologist to be precise, carrying out field studies in the mountains to the north.'

Lourdes made no comment on Colin's verdict of Luisa Ross, but carried two glasses and a bottle of *La Ina* on a tray through to the salon where he was adding a log to the glowing embers in the fire.

'The storm that threatened seems to have passed over,' she said.

'The air feels clearer,' he agreed.

She put on a CD, turned the volume low – *her* lifeline music, Colin would hardly notice it – then she lay back, her legs drawn up on the white sofa while he took the armchair. And she thought a little regretfully, and not for the first time, they would probably have become lovers if she had fancied him in that way. There had been an awkward moment on the hill this afternoon when she wondered if he suspected the truth about Gustavo. The love of my life, who, even now, is often in my thoughts. Whereas Colin's more like a brother.

'Inch by inch, life's a cinch,' he was saying cheerily, raising one of her elegant crystal sherry glasses. 'Here's to us and the book.'

She laughed wryly: 'Yard by yard, life's very hard,'

'Well, you of all people know all about that, Lourdes!'

She pulled a face and lifted her own glass: 'As you say, here's to us and the book!'

They had come so very far. Already Colin was more than halfway through the first draft of *Flight into Exile*. Often she wondered, is he involving me in this project to keep me sane? The story was unlikely to be published as long as Andreas was active. But she squashed her concern; she *needed* Colin to keep coming to visit her whatever the pretext. Needed his companionship, needed the fun they shared even as he dug out of her painful memories she'd prefer to forget.

Two people in a small house in a remote mountain town in northern Mallorca, planning an uncertain future to the music of the Caribbean, turned down low. Writing the book as they went along. She listened out for a line in the song she knew well . . . *esperanza, esperanza* . . . and felt she might cry.

Colin clicked on his tape recorder. 'Ready to talk some more about Colombia?' he asked kindly, then added, 'yes, I like your neighbour . . . she's straightforward and serious, a little driven, perhaps. And pretty unsophisticated, when it comes to the worlds you and I have inhabited. But I think you'll like her too, and it'd be good for you to get to know her, I'm sure of that. Are you listening, Lourdes?'

'Yes,' she said flatly, wishing he'd just shut up about Luisa Ross.

5

The door of number thirteen Calle Luna burst open to reveal María in her pink candlewick dressing gown and old man Ferrer tottering down the hall behind her. 'Take Papa off my hands for a bit, *Reina*, down to the Solitario?' she implored, and Alejandro arrived at the front door, his face set like that of a child determined to break free of his minder.

Luisa nodded. She was going to the bar herself, but she couldn't stop wondering if she had forgotten something. Cameras, field glasses, notebooks, pens, books, music, batteries, first aid kit and all the food supplies? After years of preparing for field trips with Dan, surely it wasn't such a big deal to be organised?

'And, will you give my door key to Julio and Felipe?' Luisa said. 'They're coming in less than an hour to pack my stuff in the jeep.'

María slipped Luisa's key into her dressing gown pocket: 'Tell Jaume I'll come for the old boy in a couple of hours?'

They set off down the street, Luisa holding her blue case by its curved bamboo handle, Alejandro shuffling deaf and dumb at her side in his felt carpet slippers.

The old man's eyes and hands inscribed the air as they picked their way past dusty vehicles revving-up for another week's construction. He can't stand all this disruption, Luisa realised, firmly tucking the old man's arm under her own, and when they reached the bar a rowdy gang of workmen in yellow dungarees and woollen caps pushed out through the door, stiffened by their *carajillos* for a gruelling day's work ahead.

'¡Hola! ¡Bon día, Rey y Reina!' they call out boisterously, and Luisa flushed with pleasure. No one passed even a stranger in these parts without a greeting.

Alejandro totters towards the old armchair by the cheerful fire, and Jaume leaves off his reorganisation of the tables and chairs. Though it's still early the now deserted bar swirls with the mingled aroma of coffee and today's lunchtime menu.

'*¿Comó va?* Welcome back.' Eagerly, Jaume shakes Luisa's hand. 'You can have your old room back if you decide you don't like Gerda's house, *Reina*. We've missed you.'

She settles on a high stool, aimlessly flicking through *Baleares*, selected at random from a pile of daily papers on the counter. '50 kilograms of cocaine seized on yacht in Palma harbour', she reads, and: 'New survey names immigration as biggest fear of Mallorcans'. Warily, she scans the international news headlines: 'Bush means business with Iraq', 'American warship bound for Palma harbour', then turns to the local pages where a photograph of hunters attracts her attention: *The Shameful Pursuit* runs the headline. 'Every year an unacceptable level of lead enters the soil from the hunters' shot and threatens the welfare of plants, animals and birds,' she reads, surprised by an aspect of *la caça* she had never considered before. Lead poisoning.

With a keen glance at what she's reading, Jaume slides her steaming aromatic cup of coffee across the shiny maroon surface of the counter. 'Ha!' he says. *La caça*. How can we give it up, señora, when the hunt is in our blood?'

Wondering if she dare respond truthfully, she shoots him a glance. But Jaume's eyes are glued to the door where a hesitant shadow glances off the etched glass pane.

'It's the new woman . . . your neighbour,' Jaume asserts, folding his arms. 'She's never come in here before.'

Is it possible, Luisa wonders, to pick up the merest whiff of an expensive perfume through a closed door? They wait and watch. 'Maybe she'll come in, maybe she won't,' says Jaume.

Filled with ambivalence, do I want Anita Berens to come in? she wonders. I certainly don't feel like chatting, I just want to sit here peacefully for a bit. I'm a bit nervous about going back to the mountains, I suppose, yet, on the other hand I can scarcely wait to get there. Solitude is precious even if it is sometimes hard to bear . . . still, the woman is my neighbour, and I must make an effort . . . the shadow vanishes, and she returns to the newspaper with a sigh.

Only now it was hard to concentrate. Facing up to her own solitary life ahead, she wondered how Anita coped with isolation in the mountain town. Don't you find it a little *too* quiet up here? she imagined she might ask next time they met. But perhaps . . . that man? . . . was he a lover, companion, partner? What did she find to do all day when Colin Cramer wasn't around? No doubt she'd find out when she visited them next weekend.

Not that I really care, she frowned, remembering Anita's rudeness so far. Mesmerised by a strong beam of sunlight that had cast the etched pattern of the door onto the ochre-tiled floor, she found herself inventing a new description of her neighbour. *Handsome, even arresting, her haircut emphasises her long neck and her broad back, like a light-haired Nefertiti - no, even better, Ingeborg the Viking muse whose long narrow eyes are observant yet languid, whose elegant nose has a fluted tip, whose rounded cheek bones are high-set.* Most people don't notice small details when they meet someone for the first time. Yet my training, observing animals and birds in the field, also serves me well with humans. *Discernible wrinkles round her eyes and lips, like hair cracks on a fine porcelain cup.* Someone vulnerable lurks under that show of cool confidence, the generous lipsticked mouth. There was something strange, something evasive . . . was that the word? . . . about the mouth that smiled though the eyes were sad. And it was so incongruous to find a foreign woman like her living up here, so far from anywhere. Most foreigners thinking of settling in Mallorca would consider this a boring town and look for somewhere far more exotic.

Jaume returns to set out huge tarts filled with custard, raisins and nuts on the bar and tells her with a wink: 'That woman's not only got the house next to yours in Calle Luna, but a smallholding, too, in the countryside beyond the town. She goes from her house to her car, from her car to her *caseta* in the countryside, and back again, does her shopping at the Inca supermarket, and rarely shows herself in town. I dare say she must be wealthy.'

'Maybe, living next door to her, I'll get to know her?'

'Oh, I wouldn't count on that.' Jaume scoffs, 'Oh, no! She's

119

had a lot of work done out at her orchard, new olive wood gates and fences, tree pruning, the land dug up. But the workmen get their instructions over the phone. Never see her. She does everything by remote control. That's why I was surprised to see her at the door just now.'

Briskly rubbing his hands together, he prepares to develop his theme, but suddenly the door bursts open and Julio calls out: 'Morning, Jaume! . . . ready, señorita?'

She bends down to pick up her blue case and crosses the room to say good-bye to Alejandro who sits still as a stone with fathomless eyes.

Luisa would have preferred to walk up to Ca'n Clot, only there was too much to carry. The jeep was filled with her supply boxes as well as the shining raven in the cadge at her feet and two dead goats. At certain times of the winter, the very survival of mountain birds of prey might depend on regular deliveries of goat meat from the jeep she travels in with Julio and Felipe. The goats, each rusty head punctured by a single bullet, four opaque marble eyes transfixed to the moment of death stare out near where she sits, distanced as far as possible from their feral stench. It's so adamantly acrid, she doubts she'll ever get used to it.

They had driven through Casas Viejas and Pep Oleza had come out to acknowledge them with his grudging wave. 'Estate's under offer,' he called out. Then they left the town with all its commotion, and the perfumed woman with the dour face far behind. They emerged from the woods and crossed the silver plateau dominated by Massanella and the other peaks of the sierra, strewn that morning with brilliant patches of snow.

'The whole area above the tree line was under snow when you were away in Barcelona,' Julio remarked. 'It's hard to believe when it's warm like today, yet the old people said there hadn't been such cold in the mountains for fifty years.'

'Will it snow again soon, d'you think?'

'Well, something funny's happening to the weather. But

don't worry, we'll make sure you have everything you need.'

After that, everything fell strangely silent. The raven huddling on its perch with her eyes firmly closed, Julio scanning the terrain through his field glasses and Felipe negotiating a way through the boulders. He had ignored her so far, and, after they passed through the gate, he accelerated into a wooded valley so fast her supply boxes toppled onto the metal floor. The raven, previously docile after her taxing role in Saint Anthony's Fest, rose up croaking furiously, her thick bill agape.

'Felipe, for heaven's sakes, *slow down*,' Luisa cried out. 'You'll injure Cora, not to mention my equipment!'

'*Tranquila*, señora,' he smirked, his eyes glinting in the driver's mirror. 'We can always mend Cora with superglue!'

But he did slow down, and when they approached Ca'n Clot, Perro's distant wild barking made the raven bounce up and down on its perch with bristling feathers.

Kronk! kronk! Cora cried, *Kronk! kronk!* and they all laughed, even Felipe, 'I think Cora's glad to be home,' he conceded pulling up with a flourish.

Luisa got out and passed the raven's cadge to Felipe who set it on the ground and opened it. The brave bird burst out and flew up and away, over the roof of C'an Clot. After a few seconds of silence, Felipe threw back his head, opened his throat and called, *kway! kway!* Spellbound, Luisa waited beside him until the bird came shooting back and settled with a cry on the chimney stack. *Kwee! kwee!* it called at last, and darted down to Felipe's shoulder.

Felipe's continuing hostility infuriated her, but she would not let him spoil this moment, standing once more in Ca'n Clot's cobbled refectory, its vast open hearth set with logs, its central stone well with a wheel and chain ready to haul up cool spring water during summer droughts. The finca resembled a church, the fireplace its altar. It was as if nowhere else in the world existed now she had come back. Here she could be complete, here she had everything she needed, this was the haven where she could indulge her passion for the wilderness and the creatures who inhabited its secret places.

Julio helps her to carry in the boxes then goes to the kitchen. Savouring the musty odour of damp and wood smoke from old fires, she dumps a box onto one of the rough wooden tables and starts to unpack it. Cora flies into the refectory over Luisa's head, and settles on the rafters to preen herself. Then, all at once, she hears the drumbeat of Felipe's feet on the steps leading to the gallery and she sees him carrying up her rucksack.

'Thanks, but I can take that up myself,' she calls out, alarmed by what he might be up to.

When he pays her no heed but continues up the stair she senses trouble, takes her blue case and hurries after him. Why is he doing this? A glance through the split-wood balustrade reveals Julio whistling below, pulling down a kitchen pan, lighting the stove in the kitchen area, and she wonders, is he aware of this latest drama?

Four basic rooms in the gallery are kept for visiting ornithologists and conservancy workers. Just as she enters the one she slept in last December Felipe pushes out past her and says, 'I'll open up the den downstairs.'

'There's no need,' she begins, glancing in at the simply furnished room with its pine-frame bed, table and chair where her rucksack sits. Why is he doing this? Surely he's not still trying it on with me? 'As I said, there's no need . . . thanks for carrying my bag up but now, please, go away,' she calls out after him. 'Give me the key. I'll open up the den myself.'

But he's away down the stairs and she follows fast, her irritation tinged with relief at the realisation that his compelling physicality has lost its charge for her. His neat black Don Carlos beard round his anemone-like mouth seems silly rather than seductive now. The passage leads to the den, her sanctuary at the back of the finca. Felipe has no business preceding her there. In fact, strictly speaking, the den is off limits to anyone but herself. With mounting fury when she sees him unlocking the door and going in, she rushes past him to open the shutters herself.

The room floods with light and a startling view of Cuevas Negras. And, yes, here they are, the two old easy chairs, the sturdy wooden desk. The map pinned up on the wallboard beside fading photographs of vultures, ravens and falcons. The air is incensed with wood smoke and memory.

Felipe leans sullenly against the door jamb. 'Go!' she says sternly. 'What are you waiting for?' He stands with his arms folded, his eyes following her every movement.

Everything is exactly as she left it before Christmas . . . only, not quite. She glances at the list of falconry terms she pinned up on the wallboard that first enchanted week at Ca'n Clot:

mail - breast feathers of hawk

aylmeri - leather anklet

bewits - leather strips fastening bells to legs of hawk

petty singles - toes of a hawk

imping - repairing broken flight feather

creance - light line attached to partly trained hawk

Words don't lose their magic, but objects often do, she thinks. Determined to rebuff Felipe, she fishes in a pocket for the Dutch hunting hood and thrusts it towards him: 'Here, take this back,' she says crisply.

'*¡Hija de puta!*' he curses under his breath without shifting from the door.

What are you, some sort of *cholo*? she longs to retort. Stonily he stares at her, one hand placed high above his head on the door frame.

'Hell hath no fury like an airhead scorned, is that it?' she blurts out - in English, knowing he won't understand. Such a proud head he has, capless now, revealing shining hair pulled off the high, smooth brow. *Outwardly* he's a beautiful man, she thinks, inwardly a teenager. 'Don't be so infantile. Working together up here will be easier if there's a friendly atmosphere between us.'

'Is that so? Well, you'll have to sleep down here when the weather turns nasty, *cariño*. It's going to be a long cold winter.' And, with that, he turned on his heels, leaving her alone at last.

A bad winter, *Reina!* Oh, yes, she thinks, and suddenly understands. He fancies he's still in love with me. It was the way he said *cariño* . . . darling . . . mockingly, as if to remind me of how differently the word might have been delivered had I returned his advances last December.

She fumbles among dusty books on the long shelves above the desk for the key she left hidden somewhere last December. *La Serra, Mallorca Mágica, Animales y Aves de Las Sierras, Spain's Secret Wildernesses* . . . a dozen books lie scattered on the desk before the key reveals itself. She lays Rafael's case in the middle drawer of the filing cabinet, zips the key into the breast pocket of her jacket and returns to the refectory.

Pausing at the end of the passageway - foreground, Felipe reading a newspaper by the fire, the raven on his shoulder; middle-ground, Julio busily cooking; background, herself - the subfusc scene before her suggests a Velasquez oil-painting and her spirits rise. Here she was in one kind of Spanish heartland, and if Felipe was determined to hold a grudge, she must make a *compañero* of Julio. Ca'n Clot is their base as much as mine, she reminds herself, going to the kitchen. On wet afternoons, during the siesta hours, or after dropping off carcasses, mending fences, cutting wood or planting trees the men came here, often to play a game of cards or dice.

The savoury smell of potatoes, olive oil and onions cooking makes her ravenous. As if on cue Julio calls out: 'Come and have something to eat, Luisa? There's enough here to feed a family.'

Reassured, she sits at a wooden table near a vast gilded mirror that might have been rescued from the abandoned palace of some eighteenth-century aristocrat. How incongruous it seemed up here in the wilderness. And a seven-bracketed candelabra on a serving table underneath it added a further curious baroque touch to the otherwise spartan room.

When Julio comes out with three sets of cutlery, she asks where the ornaments came from.

'From the old finca at Casas Viejas, so I've heard. Long ago there was a link between the buildings. The estate manager lived here until the middle of the last century. It was a ruin when the conservancy took it over two decades ago.'

124

He returns to the kitchen and she lays the table, praying Felipe's sullenness would be short lived. She has so much to thank him for. She cannot forget the weight of the bird that day when Felipe first put it on her arm, her astonished eye-to-eye contact with Aquila's rapacious head, and she consoles herself. Soon he'll be asking me to help him fly the bird again. In a day or so he'll adjust to my return.

'If you desire to heal the wounds of the present you must bring to mind the epiphanies of the past,' Rafael had said. *Epiphany*. She had to look in the dictionary for the exact meaning of the word and discovered '*epiphany*, manifestation of a superhuman being'. Recalling the otherworldly whiff of spread wings, the fan of her pinions the moment Aquila ceremoniously left her perch to mount Felipe's arm, makes her heart skip a beat. Yes, there had been something superhuman about the little eagle. Even the raven was a harbinger of worlds beyond mortal ken.

'The grub won't be long. Have patience, señorita,' Julio calls out.

'*Tranquilo*, Julio, I'm not in a hurry.'

She slices the loaf from *Gloriosa* that lies on the table, filled with gratitude for this rich seam that was opening up in her life.

'Grub's up,' Julio shouts happily, bringing a thick black *sartén* to the table. 'This is no more than an apology for a true Spanish tortilla,' he says, filling Luisa's plate with a flourish of his spatula. 'There wasn't enough time today, but one day I'll make the real thing for you.'

When Felipe strides over to claim his plate of omelette and bread with a glass of wine, Cora flits down from the rafters and settles on his shoulder. He feeds her a morsel of bread. *Qué bonita*, he tells her, *qué bonita*, and Luisa's ears burn.

'If you like, I'll take you to my hide in the mountains to the west next week,' Julio is saying. 'It's the best place to watch vultures and ravens feasting on prey. You'll get first class photographs for your project.'

She nods. She will not allow Felipe's jealous eyes boring into her back to mar her pleasure.

125

As they eat, Julio ticks off the birds she might expect to see between now and Easter, one for every finger of his hands. Marmora's warbler, Blue Rock thrush, Eleanora's falcon, Alpine accentor . . . then, his brows meeting, he breaks off a chunk of bread and chews it thoughtfully. 'You have a few other things on your agenda, too,' he says at last. 'An ornithologist from Sardinia coming to stay here next month. A Señor Bigatti, also studying birds in areas where vultures breed, though I believe his special interest is ospreys. Small numbers of osprey overwinter in the area, as you probably know.'

'Therefore we must take him over to S'Escorca,' Felipe suddenly pipes up, and Luisa turns in time to see him swirling his bread around his plate and devouring it with relish.

'Where is this S'Escorca?' she asks.

Pretending he hasn't heard, Felipe peppers his plate with crumbs for the raven and Julio answers: 'S'Escorca's on the other side of the mountains from here. About three hours by foot. A very bleak place indeed. Once upon a time it was the haunt of smugglers and bandits . . . .'

'The Bigatti bloke'll feel at home with the bandits,' Felipe smirks, cutting the air with a swoop of his fork, sending Cora squawking in alarm back to the rafters.

'Don't listen to him, Luisa. There are no bandits now and few people either, come to that. Only mountains, woods, underground springs and hawks. Unfortunately, I'll be away when the visitor comes. But Felipe here will be your guide.'

Dismissing Julio's cue: 'D'you know what?' Felipe says. 'Spanish sparrows will mate with Italian sparrows at a push, but only in Sardinia.'

Knowing his statement to be true yet irrelevant, Julio and Luisa exchange tolerant smiles.

'What else is on the agenda, Julio?' eventually she asks.

'Let's see? The town trip up here's in February.'

She nods and drains her glass. It was another of the town's traditions. The alcalde had told her all about it at the reception when she first arrived. On a certain day in February, every able-bodied resident of the town walked up the mountainside to Ca'n Clot.

126

'Raúl Caubet, *el alcalde*, wants you to give a talk at that event, about your fieldwork.'

When she sighs, Julio lowers his wiry eyebrows with a *tutt-tutt!* of chastisement. 'Señorita Ross, you have a reputation to live up to.'

'Yes, I know. And I'll do it, of course. And I mustn't forget, I've a lecture to give to students at Palma University soon. Will you drive me to the station that day?'

For some time after the men have left she sorts out her papers in the den. The stove crackles and hisses, burning fig wood incenses the air. A small press cutting flutters out of the envelope on her lap. *Vultures' diet affected by BSE,* she reads. *Dietary changes triggered by the mad cow crisis in Europe have worked their way down to the vulture. An estimated 400 birds living near Madrid have been fed dead sheep rather than cows because of EU health regulations.* A marginal note in Dan's handwriting, made with his familiar blue-black pen, makes her smile. 'Just as well Mallorcan vultures eat goat.'

In her mind's eye, she is standing at the gate of the white cottage watching Dan sprinting towards her over brittle brown autumn leaves. Her eyes alter with emotion, remembering. 'Swans don't always mate for life,' he calls out, pausing to catch his breath, waving his arms like a desert hermit returning to the medina. 'Now I know it for a fact.' It had taken Dan over a year of habitual observation beside the swans' nesting site, in freezing winter and midge plagued summer, to reach that conclusion. And it had taken her and Dan several years of trying to have the child that might have bonded them, only to reach the painful conclusion that they hadn't mated for life either.

Later that week, Julio drove Luisa to the hypermarket at Inca to buy tinned foods and dry goods in case she became snowed-in at Ca'n Clot, an event she hoped for rather than dreaded. And, if necessary, she would take out a long pole to test the ground for snow holes as she walked. The thought amused her. For her, to be snowed in for days at a time in the wilderness would be one of life's great experiences. The wild things, their body temperatures lowered by the cold, would show themselves then, embrazened by their urgent need to find food.

They had been walking back towards the jeep, each carrying a filled cardboard box. 'Enough food here to feed an army,' Julio had grunted amiably then added with a curious look in Luisa's direction: 'By the way, you won't be seeing much of Felipe for awhile.' From the way he held her eyes with a slight crinkling of his own, she realised Julio had been well aware of Felipe's seductive tricks and wanted to be sure they belonged to the past. 'Felipe's been detailed to join a tree clearing operation from that devastated wood we took you to high in the hills,' he added. 'The work's urgent as you know; it's got to be done before summer when the woods'll be a red alert fire risk. They need every man they can get. He'll still be around to feed the birds, fly the eagle and stand in for me when I'm away.'

Luisa gave him a collusive smile: 'We'll get along just fine without him.'

They picked up Felipe, moodily kicking stones around broken paving slabs outside a newly built block of flats on the outskirts of the town. She supposed he must live there.

'He looks a bit fed up,' she said.

'Because he doesn't fancy becoming a lumberjack,' Julio growled.

To her surprise, Julio slid into the passenger seat and asked Felipe to drive: 'I'll be guiding the señorita by way of the mountain paths today,' he added. 'You can drop us off beyond the meseta, after the gate . . . you know, where the first path leads along the edge of the escarpment?'

She contained her delight, and no one spoke until they reached Casas Viejas where Pep Oleza was balancing precariously on the top rung of a long ladder, pollarding the splendid crown of one of the palm trees that fronted the main house.

'Estate's been sold,' Pep called out, waving them on.

'Pep Oleza should be in a circus,' Luisa said. 'He always seems to be up that ladder!'

'He'd be balancing on a different sort of a ladder if I

128

reported some of the things he gets up to as *amo* of this estate,' Julio responded sharply.

'Get real, man. Pep could get away with murdering his wife if he had one,' Felipe scoffed. 'He's thick as thieves with the alcalde's entourage.'

Luisa was wondering how it was that Oleza came to have such protection, and what it was he got up to when they came out of the wood, onto the meseta, and Julio suddenly announced, 'Way hay! visitors ahead.' In the middle distance, two men were picking their way across rough ground.

Julio looked puzzled: 'I didn't know there were strangers about.'

Through her binoculars Luisa saw the men turning abruptly as the jeep trundled towards them. 'Isn't it unusual to find strangers up here, walking in the direction of the reserve?' she said.

'It is, and no one passes Pep's dog without him knowing about it. I wonder why he didn't mention them. Unless . . . Oh! ho! perhaps *they're* the new owners of Casas Viejas.'

The jeep drew closer and the men stepped off the track to let it pass. *One, far older than his companion, wears walking gear in shades of brown and mossy green, with a tan leather bush hat. The other's dressed in an ill-fitting navy-blue track suit with pink flashes, of all things! and a peaked cap. They don't look like father and son.*

'Just keep going, Felipe,' Julio grunted.

Felipe kept up a steady pace and the older man raised his alpenstock in a greeting which Julio returned with a tolerant wave.

Then, for a split-second, the man peered in at Luisa through the window as the jeep proceeded past. The intensity of his gaze struck her as if by a dart and she found herself turning to look back at him as they drove on.

'Serious mountain walkers? Bird watchers? *Extranjeros* anyway,' Julio was saying. 'Pep must've given them permission to pass through the farmyard.'

'The older man's got expensive binoculars round his neck,' Luisa put in, struggling to shake off the look of the stranger. That handsome face, that autocratic, yet rather furtive, curiosity. But why had he been so curious? So absorbed had she been in the drama of that arresting head coming face-to-face with her own through the dusty window, she hadn't so much as glanced at the youth. Turning to look back again, she drew him into her binoculars, but the peak of his cap hid his face as he walked, his eyes glued to the ground. Shifting her focus, she stole another look at his companion until, gradually, the strangers disappeared behind them and they reached the padlocked gate. When Luisa got out with Julio, he opened it with uncharacteristic briskness, as if he couldn't tolerate the thought of the strangers catching up with them.

After that Julio and Luisa set off at a good pace, following the margins of the meseta until they came to a steep, sparse holm oak wood undergrown with knee-high clumps of pink heather and cistus bushes. Julio's muscular figure pressed on while she paused now and then to consult her map, part-tracing, part-memorising the way. Alone next time, she would come up through this wood to this old gate set into the drywall where Julio waited, holding his cap and mopping his brow.

'*Mira*, señorita,' he protested with a gruff laugh. 'That map of yours won't do you any good! You'll have to *learn* as much as you can of the route now, with me. Then when you trek up here alone all you have to do is trust your instincts.'

She smiled, eye level with him, appreciating his energetic responses. He seemed to be driven by unquenchable passion. A man of many dimensions, that much was certain, and she was looking forward to learning from him the hidden secrets of this wilderness.

Now he was suggesting a short detour. 'I have something to show you. Come this way, please.'

Picking their way through shoulder high boulders, he led her further up along the boundary wall until they reached the tree line where the silver and blue landscape, all stone and sky, spread expansively before them. She stood beside him, eager as a schoolgirl, and he pointed out a pine wood to the east where to her astonishment she saw a vulture's nest. Or was it? The shape and size of this balloon-like structure roughly corresponded with drawings and photographs of vulture nests in books she had studied. But she could see no evidence of the thick branches vultures use to construct their nests. This green monstrosity suggested a cancerous growth on the crown of the tree.

Keen to examine it more closely, she walked towards the edge of the cliff. But Julio grabbed her arm and pulled her back with a roughness that surprised her. 'You should be careful of edges,' he said sternly. 'Edges can be *seriously* dangerous in Mallorca. Don't do that again.'

She sucked in her cheeks, shaken. Little did Julio know her own fear of falling. *My mother falling, dying* . . .

His eyebrows met over alarmed eyes, and she knew she was in for a lecture. 'Never forget how dangerous it is to stand on any edge when you're out in the field, *vale*? Promise me that? Only last month a young father fell down a cliff face when the rock under his feet gave way, leaving his ten-year-old daughter looking down at his body far below, unable to do a thing about it. He fell a long way and never came back.'

When his voice tailed off, 'I'm sorry,' she said, and when he nodded she returned to scrutinising the bulbous, idiotic thing through her lenses. Its surface was encrusted with ivy - enough berries on the ivy to feed hundreds of thrushes and redstarts. She turned to Julio with a puzzled look: 'I give up . . . unless, is it a diseased pine tree?'

'*Mira*, it *was* a vulture's nest,' he smiled. 'Now it is what we call a 'historical site'. That is, the vultures abandoned that nest so long ago it's got overgrown with vegetation. Not so long ago, ten, fifteen years ago, it was easy enough to find vulture nests near man-made sites, sitjas, for example, and even on the edges of the mountain towns. Nowadays, with a few exceptions the birds prefer to nest on the edge of cliffs overhanging the sea.'

Intrigued by the idea of historical nesting sites, Luisa got her camera out of a waistcoat pocket. 'They abandoned old nests like this because they were disturbed by increasing numbers of visitors tramping up the mountain trails, is that right?'

'*¡Eso es!* But the good news is, now their numbers are increasing, a few birds are re-inhabiting the old sites.'

Julio waited while she took some shots, and, before they left, she found herself stealing a look at the plateau they had just crossed far below where, sure enough, there were the strangers. Two matchstick figures consulting a map laid out on the huge flat boulder between them. They'll see the red dot on the map that gives Ca'n Clot away, she thought, irritated that the mountain sanctuary might be disturbed by interlopers. But she said nothing to Julio as they went down, even when they paused to drink from their water bottles at the gate in the wall, she struggling to erase the memory of the older man's fervent gaze.

'The network of paths criss-crossing these foothills here was formed by carbon makers and hunters,' Julio was saying.

Yes, Luisa thought, charcoal made by Alejandro Ferrer in his youth and by Professor Bauza's father, also Ramón Rafal.

'At the Town Hall they have what they call a *heritage* booklet explaining how they made charcoal from these trees. Perhaps you want to know more about it than I can tell you?' Then, leaning against the gate, he added, 'you'll be glad to know this is as far as the bird hunters come. *La caça* ends here, although goats are culled from time to time on the escarpment we'll be crossing.'

The ground under their feet was littered with spent cartridges edged with brass – blue ones and red ones, some rusty with age, others newly gleaming. Enough lead shot to kill and maim thousands of birds and thoroughly dose the earth with poison according to the newspaper article she'd read at Bar Solitario.

'Think globally, act locally,' she said with a shrug and they both stooped to start clearing them.

'Hunters in Spain are often associated with the PP party, Luisa, the *Partido Popular*,' Julio said, kicking some cartridges into a neat pile. 'Franco was a famous hunter. Hunting and right wing politics often – not always! – go together in Spain. Not surprising, eh? And two senior government officials, who might have prevented the *Prestige* disaster that flooded the coast of Galicia with black, black oil a few years ago, just happened to be away hunting at the crucial moment they might have averted the tragedy.'

His voice sounded taut. Luisa knew he was reigning-in deeply felt emotion, the forceful side of his personality that lay behind his cordial exterior. Here was the steely environmentalist who had thrown himself behind the bid to save Mallorca's Black vulture, a threatened species of around twenty birds, until the last few years when its numbers had increased to eighty pairs. The success, she knew, had been thanks largely to organisations including the Balearics Ornithological Group and the Black Vulture Group but importantly, too, to Julio and others like him who had helped to organise vigilantes. These local volunteers posted themselves in the sierra during the breeding months at the beginning of every year to politely ask tourists and hikers to stick to routes well beyond nesting areas. As a researcher at Ca'n Clot, she would be required to act at all times as a vigilante, Julio had told her.

Together they collected the spent cartridges and stuffed them into their backpacks until no traces of the shameful pursuit had been left behind.

Another day, they picked their way by torchlight through a pine wood well before dawn. Out of the mysterious thicket a huge bird rose with an alarming *woosh!* of wings. Instantaneously, Luisa ducked, but not before she looked up into piercing orange eyes under jagged brows.

'Eagle owl,' Julio whispered as the bird shot away on wings a large as a buzzard's. She had heard the owls calling over the hoya at night, but now she could chalk up another first sighting. Her heart pounded from the surprise . . . the *otherworldliness* of the bird springing up so unexpectedly . . . as she followed Julio through dew-covered shrubs to his hide. 'Before we do anything else,' Julio said, 'let's get the branches off the carcass.'

The day before, they had called at various fincas in the valley searching in vain for carrion until they encountered a shepherd and his flock blocking the road. 'Here's a relic of pre-tourist boom Mallorca for you,' Julio grinned, braking to a halt.

He had spotted an old billy goat pathetically limping a good way behind the herd, a festering growth the size of a small football on a front leg. 'That's the one for us,' he said, getting out to negotiate a deal with the shepherd.

The wizened shepherd made Luisa, waiting and watching, think of an ancient, pollarded olive tree. A wild shock of curly white hair escaped the confines of a small straw hat perched above his honed, bronzed face, and he looked terribly thin under his baggy sweater and canvas trousers tied round with string. She heard snatches of Mallorcan through the open window. She could almost touch the old goat's mangy, ginger and black pelt from where she sat before, unceremoniously, the men came to hoist up the bleating animal by its legs and drop it inside over the tailgate. The stench was revolting, but when the shepherd paused at the window she hid her disgust and, with a little rush of pride, was able to greet him in Mallorcan.

'The old guy and I were recalling the time, not so long ago, when the government paid people to kill vultures,' Julio said as they drove on. 'What ignoramuses they were in those days. They didn't bother to find out that vultures are not killers, they just assumed the vultures were killing lambs. Anyone who handed in a vulture's beak at the town hall was paid a good sum of money. No wonder Black vultures were almost extinct a few years back. Mind you some people on this island still think anything with a hooked beak deserves to be shot or poisoned.'

When she looked round to see the old goat slumped behind her, its breath coming in short, shuddering moans, Julio consoled her. 'Better to put it out of its misery and feed it to rare vultures than let it go to a factory to be made into pet food.'

Two kilometres further along the rough track they stopped on a barren slope overlooking a breathtaking view. Away to the east lay Massanella, thinly powdered with snow that had fallen above the tree line in the night.

Before they got out, Julio took a handgun from the tool compartment. 'Go that way,' he said, hauling out the old goat, indicating a path through the wood with a jerk of his head. When she hesitated, 'go on, go on,' he said with mock impatience. 'What are you waiting for? I'll follow in a minute.'

Beds of pine branches and twigs crackled under her boots as she walked, sending up a strong smell of turpentine. Glumly she listened for the gunshot, and after it came, ricochetting off the crags, deafening the silence, she turned to see Julio dragging the carcass through the dense maquis shrubs. Her thoughts raced. I'm alone, miles from anywhere with a man who carries a gun. The gun had come as a surprise, and she thanked her lucky stars that Julio, rather than Felipe, was her guide today. The irascible Felipe might play a trick or two on her, but not Julio, stalwart keeper of the earth.

He came up to her with a rueful smile and led her on until they arrived at his crumpled, near-abandoned, hide on a gentle slope facing a small plateau. It was a primitive, wonky construction. A sort of hermit's lair.

'I've kept it for a long time, but haven't been up here recently,' Julio said, almost apologetic, adjusting his cap with military precision. Skilfully, he rearranged the collapsed camouflage netting covering the low canvas hide that wind and weathering had undone. The dead goat lay at his feet, a carmine rivulet trickling between its staring yellow eyes onto the stony ground.

'Help me with it, Luisa,' he said.

She grasped the hind legs, and they dragged it some distance from the hide where he took out a roll of cord and picked up a thick branch to stake it down. 'We don't want the birds pulling it all over the place,' he muttered. 'If it's fixed securely you'll get good photographs.' And, when it was done, she helped him to conceal the body under a thick pile of underbrush.

'*Perfecto*,' he declared at last. 'And now let's get out of here. I've meetings to attend at the Town Hall. But don't worry, everything's ready for your photo shoot tomorrow at dawn.'

Next day they uncovered the carcass, and, though it was still dark enough for them to need torches, the light of the new day was slowly returning. Just as they had taken off the last branches, 'hold still!' urgently Julio whispered and mayhem rent the sky. Six croaking ravens fluttered down beside the exposed carcass, and, seconds later, a pair of vultures flew in. Near-delirious to be the close witness of such an extraordinary event, Luisa cried out, and several ravens flew off with a loud *kronk! kronk!* Then, with a bewildered look, the vultures, too, leaped into the air and beat away on monstrous wings, wings so clamorous it was as if some God of the skies had been crumpling up gigantic sheets of thick brown paper.

Damn it! she thought, I've blown it. I'm no better at this game than a blinking amateur. Some scientist! Did I really think I could turn photographer as well?

But when she looked at Julio, '*No pasa nada*, they'll be back,' he said with a Charlie Chaplin-style shrug of his shoulders.

She sucked in her cheeks with relief.

Then, furtive as an Apache, Julio unhooked a knife from his belt. With one deft cut he slit open the goat's skin, dark alizarin blood gushed to the earth. Acid juices rose in Luisa's throat before she steadied herself with the thought, that was the action of a practical countryman, that's all.

'Just like opening a tin of soup,' Julio joked, cleaning off the knife on the underbrush. 'Now let's get to the cinema,' he smiled, indicating the hide.

Daylight was returning fast and they put away their torches. Now every second seemed to reveal new aspects of the purple mountains, the pale blue sky striated with rose and silver, the full complement of textured trees and sculpted rocks. She crawled on all fours into the hide, where the vegetation smelled of a peculiar mix of tin and new mown grass, and set the camera on its tripod while Julio stretched out full length on his belly beside her. He warned that they might have a long, uncomfortable wait ahead, but then, almost immediately, the *kronk!* of ravens filled the air and, seconds later, a dark shower of birds fell on the feeding ground.

'It *is* a bit like being at the cinema,' she smiled, peering through the window of the hide.

'*Blood of the Vampires*,' Julio grunted amicably, and looked at his watch. 'Almost seven thirty . . . get ready for the early morning show.'

136

She counted a dozen ravens quarrelling beside the carcass with outlandish comical noises. '*Kwark, ger ger*' was followed by '*wug, crok*' repeated several times, then a precise rendition of human burping. When her body shook with repressed laughter, Julio laid a restraining hand on her arm and she looked through the lens in time to see one of the ravens waddling over to another with a long thin piece of the goat's entrails in its beak. Its mate grabbed the other end and the two started up a tug of war.

'It's so funny,' she burst out.

'Yes, I know,' said Julio, 'but *tranquila*. You don't want to frighten them away again before we get to the big scene with the vultures.'

Another pair of ravens started a fencing match with stout black bills.

'Fighting for possession of the old goat,' Julio said.

Feeding for survival. A deeply selfish ritual, Luisa thought, remembering with a start the first time she had seen Aquila rip meat from Felipe's gauntlet. A business re-enacted, unseen by human eyes, every day on this wild sierra. Another raven pair waddled off then stood closely together as she photographed, the smaller female lowering her beak to allow the male to preen the back of her neck. 'Mating ritual,' Julio said. 'After all, it's almost spring.'

There was a lull after that when the ravens settled down to feed. Blowing warmth into her cold hands, Luisa willed the vultures to return. She took out her notebook, Julio lit a cigarette, and, in the companionable silence, some inner prompt made her ask: 'Have you discovered anything about the two strangers we passed on the meseta?'

He nodded and drew on his cigarette. She liked the smell of his black tobacco.

'Did they have permission to walk beyond Casas Viejas?'

'They didn't need to. One of them's the new proprietor of Cajas Viejas. Don Nicolas Monterey. The other's his assistant. A lad that goes by the name of Miguel, no last name given. The deal's gone through.'

'Does that mean they'll have the freedom of the Ca'n Clot territories?' A little apprehensively, she wondered, does that mean I'll have to keep looking over my shoulder wherever I go?

'Well, in theory, yes, they could *walk* to Ca'n Clot and its surrounding territory. The area we maintain. Only they would not be permitted to drive through the padlocked gate . . . unless an agreement exists in the title deeds of the Casas Viejas estate and of Ca'n Clot for privileged access. Come to think of it, I must check that out. The *possessío* of Ca'n Clot is a large tract of land, as you know, the property of the Balearic government and overseen by the conservancy. Whereas the territories of Casas Viejas, also part of the mountain, belongs to the estate. However it's vital for your work, señorita, and for ours, that the wildlife remains undisturbed and so I'll make a point of spelling out to these newcomers the regulation distance they must stay away from nesting birds.'

'I'd be grateful if you could.'

'*Tranquila*, I'll soon warn them off your patch.'

At last the sun had fully risen over the site. She felt warmth return to her body and when Julio slipped away, presumably to have a pee in the bushes, suddenly hungry, she found the sandwiches and opened the thermos flask. Carefully, she poured black coffee into two plastic mugs. The day was turning out clear, cloudless, perfect for photography – *un día precioso* as the Spanish say – a bit of luck. Bad weather was forecast for the following week when something called *una borrasca* was expected. Dense thick cloud that could settle in for days on end. Weather that made a dark hell of the mountains. You'll be glad of the Calle Luna house in such conditions, Julio had remarked.

After a few minutes she looked through the lens and held her breath. A Black vulture stood beside the carcass, massive in comparison with the ravens. What a photograph. Then, right away, a noisy raven strutted up, challenging the vulture. But the majestic newcomer held her ground, cocked her head sideways with a warning look then, with great dignity, walked away. The raven, ridiculously small beside its opponent, pursued in a series of little hops and jumps. Then it rushed forward and grasped hold of the vulture's great tail with a tweak of its beak. *Click* after satisfying *click*, Luisa captured the scene. *See everything, hear everything, document everything.*

Julio slipped back into the hide. 'Coffee time,' she beamed, pointing to his mug.

Just then, six vultures were landing near the carcass. The parametres of the hide dictated her view, straight ahead. She hadn't seen them actually fly in before they landed, and she resolved that when the time came to construct a hide nearer Ca'n Clot as part of her own research, she would choose a higher site with an open view.

Now the new vultures stood aloof, nobly waiting their turn. Two started to preen. Another courted its mate, twisting its daft head to gaze as tenderly as gimlet-like eyes permit at the female waiting beside him.

Luisa pressed the camera button. Only, at that moment the film ran out. Cursing under her breath . . . why must there be any halt to this fantastic opportunity? . . . she rummaged in her bag for a new roll. Again, Julio's hand came on her arm, watch this! With a swift look up, she saw yet another vulture sweeping onto the site with a clumsy bumping run. Its vast wings fully open, it bounded straight up to the feeding ravens with a threatening display, its head snapping this way and that, forcing the ravens to jump sideways and, seconds later, all the ravens flew off with a tremendous rustle of wings, like rain falling on dried autumn leaves.

The vultures were tearing at the carcass now. The camera was ready to capture the most recently arrived vulture as it broke away from the imbroglio with a large chunk of bright red goat meat in its yellow beak. Thinking it was safe to eat, it ravened greedily until another vulture snuck up, intent on stealing the fodder. Immediately, both birds leaped into the air, their wings cracking as they battled like giant fighting cocks until the meat-owning vulture forced off its opponent with powerful downward slashes of its claws.

Luisa turned to Julio, thinking she had never seen anything so tremendous in her life. The meat held safely between its great yellow talons, the victorious vulture stood on the alert, its wings fanned, until another of its kind came along. For a few seconds they gazed at each other with solicitous, twisting heads, before the newcomer was allowed to share the meat.

'Clearly they are a mated pair,' Julio said in a low voice, 'the ones you saw yesterday.'

Yes, this was the pair Julio had pointed out, soaring above Ca'n Clot, with small identifying 'windows' clipped out of their wings by the local ornithologists so they could be recognised in flight.

From far away, sweet as honey, came Rafael's words: *Praising is what matters.* Only now Julio was saying, 'time to go, I've an appointment at Casas Viejas.' They crawled out of the hide and she looked at her watch. They had been here for more than two hours.

'We can come back whenever you want,' Julio shouted suddenly and loudly through cupped hands, and the air filled with monstrous dark wings, beating, beating, lifting up all the the birds at once until they vanished away into spheres of their own.

6

Next morning Colin Cramer came down to a cold kitchen where he found a note from Lourdes, 'gone to the hairdresser'. He made breakfast and went to work on *Flight into Exile*. But when Lourdes hadn't returned by early afternoon he felt cooped up in the house. Pity he couldn't just drop into Bar Solitario on a whim and try out his Spanish on some poor unsuspecting local. He had to be careful for Lourdes' sake, only now – desperately – he needed a breather, and he decided to walk towards the mountains, into Luisa Ross' territory. She'd be coming down for tonight's dinner party and, having consulted a map of the area fixed to the kitchen wall, he guessed she'd take a minor road through a hamlet called Casas Viejas. With a bit of luck he'd bump into her.

Before he left, he slipped upstairs to check the books stacked in three low shelves in the corner of the guest room. Lourdes wasn't interested in birds, but the previous owner might have been, and it had been he or she who had left behind most of these books. Kneeling on the floor to make his search easier, he ran his hand over the colourful spines until he had it: *Birds of the Mediterranean*, he muttered, eagerly drawing out the book. A quick scan of the index and he soon turned to the page he wanted. Black vulture. *Aegypius monachus*, he read. Wingspan 250-295 cm. He gave a low whistle. Some size of a bird. *Rare, confined to S. Iberia, N. Greece and Turkey; readily seen on Mallorca. A huge raptor. Long, broad wings parallel-sided and square-ended; the primary feathers form distinct, splayed 'fingers'; head looks small in proportion to the body, tail relatively short. Plumage is brown, not black. Soars effortlessly at immense heights over mountains.*

In all the years he had been coming to Mallorca, he had never known about the presence of these vultures. And I must see one, he resolved, leaving a note for Lourdes on the kitchen table, 'gone for a walk'.

Luisa reached the rocky promentory high above the meseta that marked the edge of the true wilderness, a landscape virtually untouched by humans. During the past week her enthusiasm for it had been heightened by her discovery of the vulture pair, wheeling over a bowl-shaped depression filled with golden grasses. She was keen to explore the area, and her reluctance to re-enter so-called civilization made her sigh as she overlooked the distant pearly cubes of the houses of the mountain town. And she lingered, imagining Anita Berens down there, busy in the kitchen at that very moment with preparations for tonight's meal. Then, a slight movement near a high bosque to the east made her bring up her field glasses in time to draw in the back views of Don Nicolas and his Sancho Panza-like assistant who were disappearing under the cover of the trees. Would she spot them everywhere she went? she wondered uneasily, shifting her sightline to a pair of goshawks circling above the wood, the female larger than the male. White under tail feathers and yellow legs, their flight lyrical against the clear blue sky.

Then, all of a sudden a volley of gunshot ricochetted round the meseta. The entire universe seemed to shudder, and the plateau below sprang to life with men, over-excited dogs and a cross-country vehicle gone beserk. Studiously she drew each hunter into her lenses, dark against the silvery terrain. Paramilitary gear, shotguns, unshaven faces. The jeep, skidding on stones, swerving past boulders, veering away towards the wood above Casas Viejas, threw up dust in its wake. Then, when it halted, the hunters strode towards it, their guns swaying, left, right, right, left, as if they expected to see enemy action at any moment. Luisa cursed. The stationery jeep had blocked her view, and, eager to see for herself *la caça* in full swing, she hurried down the path. Her thoughts raced. Some migrant birds had arrived earlier than usual this year and in greater numbers . . . redstarts, fieldfares, redwings, chiffchaffs and goldcrests . . . all chased south by severe winter conditions in northern Europe. Small birds that preserve themselves from hawks by day only to be slaughtered in the bloody games of hunters. She arrived on the plateau in time to see beyond the jeep a solitary figure surrounded by the hunters, their arms outstretched, forbidding his passage. And, when she recognised Colin Cramer, she ran as fast as she could over the uneven ground. She wasn't concerned for herself but for Colin, who might be stubborn enough to stand his ground in what looked like an angry confrontation with these bizarre replicas of Yugoslavian militiamen she'd seen on television during the civil war.

Just within earshot, she yelled out, 'hey, Colin!' and, myopically, he craned round for the source of her voice. Seeing her approach, the hunters backed off, shouldering their shotguns, and the driver returned to his vehicle. They won't harrass him now, she thought, arriving at Colin's side, bending over, her breath coming in deep painful bursts.

'What the hell's going on?' Colin demanded, neat in his green waxed Barbour.

'They're hunting,' she said between breaths.

'*What*,' he said impatiently, 'are they hunting?'

'Thrushes mainly.'

Colin grimaced. 'You've got to be kidding.'

'It's *true*, and yes, isn't it ridiculous?' She gave a burst of ironic laughter. 'Grown men waging war on songbirds.'

She drew him, her hand on his arm, into the wood, onto the path leading to Casas Viejas, explaining as they went that most of the game that once abundantly inhabited these mountains had been shot or trapped out of existence. Nowadays, all that was left in plenty were the flocks of thrushes.

'What was the driver of the jeep saying to you?' she asked.

'He was making it clear I was trespassing.'

'You weren't. The path over the meseta is a right of way.'

'Then he said if I didn't clear out they wouldn't be responsible for my safety. Nasty bit of work he seemed. I wanted to sock him one.'

Luisa murmured sympathetically. 'I don't for a moment condone what happens up here. But you have to understand the hunt is a blood cult, a secret male preserve that's gone on since time immemorial. My take on it is that the hunters can't stand being caught in the act by outsiders because they know they look ridiculous. And they must feel something like guilt surely, going on this ritual slaughter, year after year, returning to town mudded and bloodied. It's perverse. You don't see women up here, but not because they're against the hunt. No, they're waiting in town to throw the catch in the pot, and I dare say the men get a severe telling off if they don't come up with the goods.'

Coming out into the open again, they could see other hunters making for their cars parked above Don Nicolas' house. Car doors slammed, laughter and shouts of coarse abandon rang in the darkening air. Colin and Luisa slipped past under the cover of shrubs, but when the road narrowed they had to show themselves on the verge to let a car pass, its headlights blinding, the fumes from its exhaust acrid in the pure air. Zombies, Luisa cursed under her breath, despising them. Four men in the car. One of them leers from a window in the half-light and aims his spittle at her feet. 'You can walk to town, *cariño*. It's good for foreigners to walk.'

'Not men I recognise. Not local,' she said. 'If they were, they'd be more respectful.'

Colin said nothing as they moved on, but pulled up the hood of his coat and shivered a little. Her throat felt dry with tension, her tongue like sandpaper. Another car came down, then another, and, again they waited. A battered white Fiat van came down last, and, to Luisa's dismay she recognised Felipe in the driver's seat.

He rolls down the window. '*Whoa!* Would you like a lift to town, señora?'

Her stony glance takes in the smirks of Felipe and his companions, their rifles, several braces of thrush, blood smears red against the white van floor. The feral smell of the panting dogs scunners her. She can't bring herself to look at Felipe. Now she knows it. The man, who had the trust of birds at the aviary, is also a hunter.

Tersely she said, 'thanks, we prefer to walk,' but her disdain only intensified Felipe's delight. '*Tordus tordus* for the table,' he taunted with a puerile grin. My wife wants to make *Tords en Col*

144

for Sunday lunch. You should taste it while you're in Mallorca. Why not join us tomorrow, is that a date, *cariño?*'

Their raucous departure raised a cloud of dust and her eyes stung in it. The opportune irony of Felipe's parting shout was not the least of it. Off-duty, he assumed he could be as rude to her as he liked. *Cariño!* Darling, indeed! How dare he. But worse by far, she reflected gloomily, was the realisation that a man whose paid employment was to *conserve* nature was also engaged in the slaughter of birds. Tradition be damned. In the weeks left to her, she would work out the most effective way to protest against *els caçadors.* To hell with the so-called delicacy of her position as Professor Bauza's pupil.

'Someone's standing over there,' Colin warned softly as they entered the yard at Casas Viejas. 'See, he's silhouetted under the date palm.'

It was obvious by the way Pep Oleza strode out to block their path, he had been waiting for them. One of the hunters must have tipped him off.

'You should know better, señora, than to take tourists up there during the hours of the hunt. He is trespassing,' Oleza said agressively.

Luisa struggled to stay calm. 'Señor Cramer is not a tourist,' she said, avoiding Oleza's shifty, porcine eyes. 'He's a guest of my neighbour in the town.'

'*Mira*, look here, man, you *can't* just close off roads that are marked on public maps just because it happens to suit you,' Colin said. His Spanish made Luisa wince, but his passion impressed her.

'Señor, this is a *private* road,' Oleza thundered. 'It is *not* marked on any *public* map. Only on a military survey map published in Franco's time. *¡Hombre!* You should take a closer look at your map.'

At that, Colin drew a map from his pocket and flapped it. 'You look here. This is a map put out by the town hall and it distinctly shows a route to the meseta.'

Luisa tugged Colin's arm, 'let it go,' she said. Oleza was in no mood to be trifled with. His arrogance, this exaggerated rudeness, unnerved her. Pep Oleza tolerated her but regarded her as just another unwelcome foreigner. She'd heard it said at Bar Solitario that he was a Catalan nationalist and she inferred that he saw no reason why a Catalan didn't have her job at the field base.

Now Oleza was thrusting the outstretched palm of his hand towards Colin's face. 'There's a new proprietor here who's given specific instructions. Strangers are to be kept off his land.'

'I gather the new owner's moved in already?' Luisa said.

'If he has, it's none of your business,' retorted the gamekeeper-cum-manager of Casas Viejas before he slunk away into the darkness under the palm.

Low-maintenance glamour, she tells her reflection in the mirror. A dab of make-up is in order, so glorify the oval face, the fluted nose, with a touch of foundation cream. Around puzzled mossy Scottish eyes inherited from your father, draw a touch of eyeliner. On maternal Spanish skin inclined towards sallowness, spread a fingertip full of blusher. This was all a game to her. Minimum effort was all she was prepared to make.

And why are you doing this? she asked herself. Getting involved in your neighbour's life when you've work of your own to be getting on with? And besides, wouldn't you rather be joining the merry gang at Bar Solitario than attending Anita Berens' smart dinner party. The guy, Colin, seems nice enough, but a bit public school. The sort you'd find on the A-list of guests invited in August to posh Scottish house parties. He was pretty upset by Pep Oleza. Dragging her hairbrush impatiently through tugs in the thick crimps of her dark brown hair that never seems to stay put, she went over the incident in her head. There might be a shooting accident, that's what worries Oleza, I told Colin. I tried to cheer him up, did my best. But the poor guy really felt wrong-footed and I don't suppose he's used to that.

Why did you accept this supper invitation? she frowns at her face in the mirror. But, c'mon, *remember the list*; thunderstorms, snow, isolation? Don't be so aloof. Hey, after all, it's very nice of them to invite you for a meal and no man, nor woman, is an island. No, not even you. One day you might need friends like Colin and Anita.

She went downstairs thinking Oleza's downright hostility might be a sign of the times. Too many northern Europeans coming to the island, threatening Mallorcan interests, wasn't that it? Putting their noses in where they didn't belong. Into the hidden world of *la caça*, for example, a virtually all-male club of right-wing traditionalists. On the way down she had told Colin about the concern of European ornithologists over the slaughter of migrant birds. He had seen for himself the cars coming down off the hill, had glimpsed the hunters through the dusty windows of their vans. An independent television company based in London might be interested in a proposal for a documentary about this Mediterranean blood sport, he said. Would I help with the research if he managed to push a proposal through, he asked? I told him I'd think about it. Maybe Colin Cramer is the breakthrough I need, maybe together we can help to influence Spain to get into line with the rest of Europe on animal rights?

How odd it had been meeting Colin up at Casas Viejas. Colin Cramer. He had come all that way up the hill hoping to see a vulture. Well they are quite a common sight in these parts, I said, only you have to choose the right time of day. The vultures don't just hang up there waiting for tourists. I didn't *say* that of course. The rest of the way back to town we talked mostly about environmental damage to Mallorca as a result of tourism. That, and the weather. Not surprising, really, since, suddenly, it's almost cold enough for snow below the tree line.

When we reached the church it was already dark, yet Colin seemed to want to linger. Come for a drink at Bar Solitario, Luisa? he almost pleaded. But I thought of Anita waiting for him, and for *me*, too, in a couple of hours, so I excused myself, saying I had to shower and change. However, before we parted at our respective doors in Calle Luna, he said, look, do you mind not mentioning our meeting to Anita? She's a bit overwrought these days. And at that very moment, María, *la charfadera,* peered out of her door, and seeing us standing

together under the lamplight, she let out a little chuckle and
darted back inside.

'An Indonesian stir-fry . . . that's what we're having tonight,'
Anita says crisply as she hangs up Luisa's anorak. 'Why don't
you go on through to the salon and let Colin fix you a drink?'
In the room beyond the kitchen Colin, dandyish in a bow tie,
tells her, 'good stuff this Spanish champagne, *Non Plus Ultra*,
I think you'll like it'. . . and he pops the cork through the
open doors leading into the garden. Though she's not cold, she
shivers, watching him pouring the bubbling liquid into three
glasses with the deftness of someone well practised in the art.
He hands her a glass and goes to close the doors.

'Why not sit near the fire, Luisa? Have some nuts?'

The experience of the afternoon has turned us into
conspirators, she thinks, casting him a sideways glance when they
sit side-by-side on a long white sofa, searching for something
to say. *Bulbous nose, myopic eyes, grainy skin, yet he is an attractive,*
thoroughly nice man. Curling silver hair, close cropped. You've had
a haircut since the other day when you came to look me over
on the pretext of borrowing salt, she might have said, only that
would have sounded far too familiar. *On the podgy side, needs*
exercise . . . then, *stop it!* she reprimands herself, sorting out
with her fingertips the mixed nuts in her palm. You are not
describing wildlife now. Her practice of making swift mental
notes about people had started at boarding school where she
often felt insecure. It had boosted her confidence when she felt
at a disadvantage. Like now facing this couple, and particularly
Anita with whom previous encounters had been sticky, to say
the least.

The delicious mingled aromas of garlic and ginger cooking
in virgin olive oil infiltrate the room. She watches Colin polishing
his spectacles with a corner of his burgundy cardigan and thinks,
how suddenly vulnerable he seems without them. A man with
a lot on his mind, a caring and powerful yet puzzled man. He
replaces his glasses and wonders aloud how come the people in
town are rich enough to afford the designer jeeps, the BMWs
and the Audis he has seen parked in the church square.

'It's the *women* who are rich up here. That's what I've heard anyway,' Anita breaks in, suddenly entering the salon to place a salad bowl on the dining table. She picks up her champagne, takes a sip and casts a meaningful look at Luisa: 'Gerda Lehmann - your landlady - told me, and *she* should know since she's lived in Mallorca on and off for many years. Apparently there's a tradition here of giving property to sons and daughters on marriage, and often the girls got land by the sea, infertile land, because it wasn't worth as much as the agricultural land their brothers got.'

'Then, when tourism boomed, land by the sea became the most valuable land of all?' Colin said.

'That's what I've heard. Lots of women display gold jewellery and drive expensive cars.'

With that, Anita retreated back to the kitchen as if, Luisa thought she had been a leading lady arriving on stage to deliver her lines, then hastily departing through the wings. And wasn't her salon – it was a *salon* rather than a sitting room, Luisa had to admit – something of a stage set? Its constrained opulence came as a surprising contrast to Frau Lehmann's functional, though identically constructed, room next door. Everything here looked expensive; the white leather sofa, the oriental rugs, the antique Mallorcan dresser and serving table. The central dining table was luxuriously decked out, too, with a vase of flowers, crystal wine glasses, silver cutlery, and china which, even from where she sat, looked like what her own mother would have called 'good'.

'I'm not stopping here long,' Colin says, turning to Luisa. 'Business in London doesn't permit long absences.'

His remark might be a cue to ask, what exactly do you do? Only she doesn't pick it up, but allows him to do the talking, reminding herself not to mention their encounter with the hunters, content to look round the room which seems to reflect Anita herself, who, from her manicured nails to her expensive clothes, gave the impression of a woman with substantial means and time on her hands.

'I've not been to this part of Mallorca much,' Colin continues pleasantly, 'though I've cronies with places nearer the sea over

149

Pollensa way. You get a lot of Brits out there. The valley's fertile, with lots of trees, so I suppose it must remind them of England.' Rising a little out of the sofa, he pauses to refill Luisa's glass. 'It's very different up here in the mountain towns. Rather stark and uncompromising. But I like what I've seen. Once the infernal building work stops and peace returns to the town, no doubt it'll be very restful?'

Luisa nods and smiles, her eye attracted to an object standing under a lamp on a white wood bookshelf. A stone carving of a crouched man, haloed with a feather head-dress. It looks like an antiquity from the Mayan civilization, only she isn't up on that sort of thing and doesn't feel she can ask. Dammit! she thinks, how inhibiting my inbred sense of decorum can be. All the same she hugs to herself the thought that whatever its origins might be, the object reminds her of Rafael wearing wings in the Barcelona square and it seems oddly comforting.

Anita arrives, her small dog in her arms. She settles the animal on a cushion and tells Luisa its name is Azahar. *Handsome tonight, wearing a patterned silk shirt in shades of green, a black velvet skirt, ankle-strap shoes, heels not too high, shapely legs in fishnet tights. Her near-perfect English carries hints of foreign accents. Her mouth purses, a hand flies to smooth the silky bob. Not a hair out of place.* Yet she seems edgy. Why? Luisa wonders. Are they hoping to disguise from me their affair if they're having one? Colin has the well-padded air of a married man, yet also a gleam in his eye that suggests he could be up to something.

They raise their glasses and she gives them her brightest smile. '*¡Salud!*' they say in unison. So far so good.

'That was a dramatic exit you made the other day,' Anita says.

'Who, me?' Colin asks Anita affectionately, peering over the gold rims of his spectacles.

'No, not you, silly! Luisa. She practically *fled* from Bar Solitario last week and drove away in a jeep with two men in green uniforms.'

Luisa laughed politely, but, at the same time, she realised how willing she was to dislike her hostess and resolved to try harder. After all, the champagne was already taking the edge off the effort that must be made to turn strangers into friends.

'Oh, it was nothing dramatic,' Luisa smiled. 'All part of my job, you know. The men are Julio Valente and Felipe Tamarit, the nature conservancy wardens I work alongside.'

'Are you alone up there on that mountain at night? Aren't you afraid?' Anita says.

'Yes, I'm alone a lot of the time and, no, I'm not often afraid. No one has any reason to come up there. Bird and egg thieves, perhaps, but I've never seen any. And I have daily contact with the men you saw me with. There's some risk, of course. I might sprain an ankle, or slip and fall on scree.'

Speech falters. Vividly she pictures Julio pulling her back from the edge of the escarpment the other day. She prevents herself from saying, *actually, I'm terrified of falling . . . you see, my mother fell down a flight of steps in our house, picked herself up, said she was quite alright. Only she died of internal injuries four days later.*

Colin breaks the silence, asks her to describe Ca'n Clot, and she obliges with a vivid description of its surroundings, the wood, the crag, the near views of Massanella, then, turning to Anita, 'where do you come from,' she says.

Looking thoughtful, Anita opens an enamelled cigarette case. 'Oh, I'm pretty well international by now. German in origin, but I've lived a long time in Spanish speaking countries.'

Spanish speaking countries? Luisa reflected. She didn't say Spain, therefore Latin America?

'My adult life has been lived, to a large extent, by the throw of the dice,' Anita adds enigmatically while, at the same time, she rolls a cigarette.

'You must visit Anita's wonderful orchard, Luisa,' Colin says kindly.

'Occasionally I worry about intruders coming out there, yet it's hardly remote compared to your base, I'm not sure . . . .'

Anita's voice tails off, leaving Colin to enthuse over the marvels of her finca two kilometres from town. A citrus orchard, ancient olive trees, a wild vine with sufficient *rosado* grapes to fill twenty wine bottles every autumn.

'I'd love to see it,' Luisa says.

'Well sure, why not? Sometimes I'd like to sleep over in the little cottage on my orchard but so far it hasn't been possible. I'm afraid to, I guess.'

Seeing Anita's downcast look, Luisa rallied. 'Oh, you'd be safe enough. You've got a dog after all.'

The conversation floundered while Anita lit her cigarette and Colin attended to the fire. Then Luisa found herself saying: 'Last December there was an incident that gave me a fright at first, however it turned out to be more slapstick than serious. An ageing hippie from Devon who'd come to look for holiday beaches in Mallorca found himself lost in the mountains.'

Attracted by the sound of Luisa's voice, Azahar suddenly arrived at her feet and she leaned down to make a fuss of the dog.

'Go on, Luisa, tell us more,' Colin encouraged.

'Well, God only knows how he found his way up the mountain. I would have felt more sympathetic if he hadn't been wearing an idiotic cap with sprouting horns in purple and black velvet. I was edgy at first, my flashlight beaming woefully in the darkness, the dog barking away like mad and me calling out, who's there? until he shouted out, "can you put me up for the night? I'm on the verge of hypothermia".'

'I'd have been *terrified*,' Anita grimaced.

'Well, what could I do but take pity on him and give him one of the rooms we keep for visitors? He turned out to be such a pain in the neck, I ended up locking him up overnight. When he banged on the door, "let me out, let me out", I shouted back, if I do let you out you'll go right back outside. In the morning Julio and Felipe drove him away and put him on the Palma train.'

When Anita gave a small sympathetic laugh and said: 'I think you were very brave,' Luisa thought, that's the first positive thing you've ever said to me.

'It was his silly hat that got me,' she went on. "If I wear this hat on trips," the chap pouted, "usually it makes people smile".' Then, greatly to her hosts' amusement, Luisa mimicked a Dorset accent. "'I've travelled round India. Been given food and lodgings on the strength of this hat. But in Mallorca? No one's so much as smiled at me since I got here, everyone looks away. Unfriendly bunch the Mallorcans," he dared to say.'

Colin chuckled and Anita said quietly: 'I don't find Mallorcans all that friendly either.' As if to say, don't interrupt, Colin frowned and laid a hand on Anita's arm. 'Go on, Luisa,' he urged again.

'Well, I didn't bother to explain that his stupid hat might be seen to mock a Mallorcan tradition. They wear horned hats, devil costumes in processions, particularly during the festivals after New Year, like Saint Anthony's Fest. You know, Anita, the festival you saw last weekend? It was only a hunch, I couldn't be certain. You never knows with Mallorcans. In so many ways they're just like the Scots. We don't suffer fools gladly either.'

Her story over, she felt glad to have added that small endorsement of Mallorcans whom she genuinely warmed to. Only, she hoped Anita hadn't taken her remark about not suffering fools as a slight. Leaning into the chair, what the hell! she told herself, now I've earned my dinner.

A yellow and white cloth with matching napkins, vivid blue glasses for water, crystal glasses for wine, embossed cutlery, an artful arrangement of wild flowers and candles. More than a bit over-the-top for a neighbourly meal in a country town, yet Luisa admitted to herself the event was a welcome contrast to spartan Ca'n Clot and utilitarian number twelve Calle Luna.

Colin talks breezily, yet interestingly, about the years he has spent as a foreign correspondent covering world news. Often that meant wars, he explains, South America, the Middle East. Now he has a city job as managing editor of the monthly social and culture magazine *Ecco!* he founded five years ago. He has come to Mallorca to help Anita with the book she's writing.

'It's a history of tourism in Mallorca,' Anita breaks in. 'My plan is to build up a series of books about the other Mediterranean islands, too. Ibiza and Menorca might be the second volume.'

'And I thought my work was exciting,' Luisa says, reluctantly waving away yet another helping of the delicious stir-fry Colin was offering.

Although the evening was going well, Anita discomfitted Luisa. *Her large eyes gleam, her skin looks pallid even by candlelight, her red-lipsticked mouth resembles a wound when she speaks. Perhaps she's ill?*

'After that, the Mediterranean world's my oyster – Corsica and Sardinia, Crete – and all the other islands,' Anita chirruped. 'I'm fifty-two now, so the books should keep me busy – and travelling – for the next decade at least. Perhaps even for the rest of my life.'

All this is impressive, but Anita Berens is trembling like a leaf about to fall from a branch, Luisa thinks, relinquishing her knife and fork to her empty plate. A highly strung woman rolling up the silk sleeves of her blouse, getting up to clear the table the minute the meal is over.

Colin restrains Anita with a sudden hand on her arm. 'The dinner dishes won't go away,' he says rather sharply, leading her to a seat by the fire. 'I expect Luisa'd like to hear more about your book.'

He slips a CD into the sound deck. Latin American music with a rich bass beat softly enfolds the room and Luisa asks Anita if she might include information about the impact of tourism on the mountain environment in her book.

'Well, I'd say that's a great idea, don't you think so, Lourdes?' Colin says. Taking his cue, Luisa swiftly adds, 'perhaps the coastal environment, too,' but she's thinking, how odd, he called her Lourdes.

'I'll certainly consider it,' Anita says shooting Colin a sharp glance. '*Men*, aren't they the limit sometimes? Colin, Luisa asked *me* a question, not you, and you must allow *me* to answer.'

Luisa had heard him use that name, Lourdes, the day he sat in Anita's garden, the day she met him for the first time. *Can you hear me, Lourdes?* So her real name might not be Anita. Are they having an affair? And is this house the love nest? Lourdes must be his pet name for Anita, or the other way round. Anita for Lourdes? She felt embarrassed, almost as if she had caught them *in flagrante delicto*. Though, frankly, she had no interest in

154

whether or not they were jumping in and out of bed together.

'Does your book have a title?' Luisa says to fill the silence.

'The working title's *A Century of Tourism in Mallorca*. A London publisher's interested in taking it on, but so far not sufficiently to put his money where his mouth is.'

Colin folds his arms. 'Publishers take so bloody long to make up their minds these days.'

The beat of the music claimed the room. Evidently Anita had no more to say about her book and Luisa felt sure they had noticed Colin's little slip. *Lourdes*. Tired herself, she longed for her release.

'The mountain air makes me feel sleepy,' Colin said at last, yawning and stretching his arms in the air. 'It's been quite a day,' he added with a knowing glance in Luisa's direction.

You are a very nice man, Colin Cramer, she thought. Though I need more time to get to grips with Anita.

'Living up there with vultures would bore me stiff,' Colin went on, chortling like a small boy intent on mischief, then taking Luisa's hand in his. 'No, seriously, *please*, may we come and see you in action next time I'm in Mallorca? I would give a lot to see a vulture in flight.'

Luisa's instinct was to discourage anyone without a professional interest in the mountains from visiting Ca'n Clot. The fewer people trekking up there past the padlocked gate the better for the birds. But she reckoned Colin had earned his stripes in the encounter with the hunters that afternoon.

She looked at her watch: 'I have to go. But why don't you visit Ca'n Clot during the town outing?' Then tactfully she emphasised, '*both* of you.'

§

Next morning, Luisa wakened in a dark room. After she turned on the bedside lamp and went to shower in the adjoining bathroom, its glow projected her every gesture as a distorted giant shadow on the whitewashed walls and on the ceiling. She slipped through the deserted streets under the cold grey light, hearing the rustle of the earliest birds in gardens enclosed by stout stone walls. Stealthily she jogged past the villas before their tormented dogs had time to bark. With a bit of luck she would avoid the early morning shooters, too.

Already the first cockerels were rousing the mist shrouded valley, sheep bells jingled faintly. The distant church bells were chiming the hour of seven when she paused at Casas Viejas, her breath pluming in the cold air. There was no sign of the new man or of Pep Oleza, however two unfamiliar jeeps, one red and one green, stood in the yard. The huge wrought iron gate to the finca was padlocked, the geese and ducks clucking securely in their hay-strewn compound. Nothing stirred in the innocent countryside as she walked on. Carob and olive trees under-planted with spring grass waited in the lightening dawn. Venus, damp and translucent, hung in the topaz sky, faint slivers of frost clinging to the verges, until, as if in a breath held and released from one moment to the next, the sun bursts over the hills to the west.

At an old Arab well she stops to sample the water flowing along a curved channel whose source must lie near Ca'n Clot. The shape of the stone well reminds her of the conical alpaca hats people wear in the High Andes, and her mouth curves. She scoops up a sample of the crystal water into the chalice of her hands, and, all of a sudden, a long dark shadow blocks the light. Startled, she whirls round and he lays a finger on her wet lips. 'You know as well as I do, we share this mountain now,' he whispers. Then he's gone. Nothing there, no-one. Stock-still, she ponders the uncanny moment. The proprietor of Casas Viejas. Breathing . . . breathing deeply . . . the hallucination dissolves. Christ, I've only seen him a couple of times, yet now he's jumping into my mind in this underhanded way. This is what really happened; the orbiting sun cast the shadow of the well across the *canaletta,* that's all. Mountain camomile scents the silent damp earth under her feet. Still, it's true. He and I are the only inhabitants of these high and lonely reaches on either side of the padlocked gate. We share the mountain now.

She hiked far beyond the countryside – the land tamed by centuries of labour – into the archaic wilderness where the only sign of human endeavour was the tumbling, abandoned olive terraces rising sheerly up the mountainside. Soon she would reach the meseta and she turned in the pure air to look back over the distant plain of Inca to the south, its hillocks, towns and hamlets darkly punctuated by cypress trees beneath a vast sky. Far below she saw the pantiled roofs of Casas Viejas and allowed herself to wonder if the Don was at home. Away to the east the aquarelle smudge of the Mediterranean Sea and the bays of Pollensa and Alcudia, bitten into the land, exactly as Professor Bauza's book, *La Serra de Mallorca* had described. She vowed she would go there one day, where dwarf plants like rosemary, curry, juniper and yellow horned poppy must surely grow on the dunelands.

The sun, hot on her back, cast her shadow before her, onto the silvery cutting between high rocks on the left and a sheer drop into the gorge on the right, so that momentarily she imagined she was an ant on the edge of a vast enamelled bowl. The abandoned terraces tossed down a rugged cloak to an occluded valley far below, where the chimney of a solitary farmhouse sent up a spiral of smoke. And where there is a mountain habitation, she thought, any vulture worth its salt knows it might be lucky enough to pick up something from a litter. A dead kitten, perhaps, a lamb, or a stillborn piglet.

Above her head the olive terraces sheered away so steeply she couldn't see the sky. Then, to her right, the true wilderness opened up and seemed to rejoice in the absence of the hunters. Everything here was stone. Miles of drywall terraces which Julio called *marges*. Incredible walls that must have taken many men years to construct. As she walks on, her footfall echoes the beat of her heart. The theatrical, textured meseta beckons. A brilliant composition of stone formations and gesticulating wild olives, with Massanella rising in the crystalline air, bright snow patches clinging to its barren, gritty surface.

A black and white photograph? She has to coax her mind to reconstruct the fading scene as she walks of Dan patrolling his territory, the island in the snow. Then the light fades altogether and a brilliant photomontage takes its place as if from some chemical bath in her brain. Rafael performing in Plaça Major, sitting in the kitchen of the Barcelona flat. And then, a new image imposes itself. The enigmatic proprietor of the Casas Viejas estate.

Having decided to make the Golden Bowl, around one kilometre south of Ca'n Clot, an area of special interest for her field study, she walked round the lip, listing botanical specimens and insects. She disturbed a coiled snake that had been sleeping beside a warm rock. When it reared up its yellow-brown head with a little hiss she noticed two faint dark stripes on its back. Later she looked it up in one of the reference books in the den: *Elophe scalaris*, the Ladder snake.

She had given the place a new name, *La Copa Dor*, the Golden Bowl, and had even written it on her map because its given cartographical name - just *'coma'* - seemed woefully inadequate to describe the grandeur of this extraordinary place where high golden grasses of the *Gramineae* family contrasted sensationally with the silver and greyish-green of the wider landscape.

She rejoiced in this remote and unchangeable spot where all the activities and troubles of the mountain town seemed insignificant. Nothing below the mountain – the professor's challenges, threats of bad weather, Felipe Tamarit, the hunters, the new neighbours or the worlds of Colin and Anita – could influence or worry her. Here she was free to explore the same tangled scrubland the Phoenicians and Romans discovered when they first disembarked at Mallorca. The first settlers of this timeless zone must have felt elated, too. And a few blood-drawing scratches from thorn bushes didn't bother her when she climbed down the neolithic path that ran across the depression like a hairline crack inside a bowl.

Hot with exertion and suddenly aware of perspiration seeping under her hat she took it off and ruffled her damp hair. She felt so vividly alive her blood pulsated in her veins. Her cleavage was wet, the back of her T-shirt was soaked with sweat. Stopping to gulp from her water bottle, she caught in the corner of her eye the bluish-grey coat of a mountain hare as it fled for cover in the golden grasses. Her mouth curved. Ah, so, I'm not alone after all, and vigorously she wiped forehead, cheeks and mouth with her water-soaked scarf.

When she reached the floor of the bowl and looked up into an azure sky, smooth as a wash of water-colour, she felt terribly small. The bowl resembled an abstract, post-modern painting with daubs for prickly shrubs and a stunted pine copse. And, here and there, dark strokes delineated the hideous black forms of trees maimed by lightning strikes.

If I'm lucky, they'll come, she thought, anticipating the whirr of the vultures' wings. And when she heard, faintly at first, their distant, grudging call, *AUK! Auk! . . . . AUK! Auk!*, she kneeled to anchor her body, and fixed her lenses where the sky met the rim of the bowl, rehearsing what she knew.

The Golden Bowl is steep, arduous terrain. A profound depression the vultures soar over, as if the depth of the place thrills them. But its real attraction is the wind that blows over the land and is forced upwards in thermals as soon as it encounters high ground. The warm air has a lower density than the surrounding slightly cooler air as it begins to rise. Highly skilled at finding warm air thermals, the vultures catch a ride, circling inside the thermal, gaining altitude until they are so high they can glide off and away into still air. Eventually, in the still air, they begin to lose height and are forced to discover a new source of lift.

AUK! Auk! . . . . AUK! Auk!

At last the raptors soar over the lip of the Golden Bowl, their splayed wing tips directing brain and body. *In remote places the heart soars highest, Luisa. There you have glimpses of the world of the spirit . . . .* The movement of their wings raises the air above her head. Yes, professor, I am seeing, hearing, documenting everything. This is the mature vulture pair I photographed in their mating ritual at Julio's hide, with 'windows' cut into their wings.

She analyses their flight. *The importance of the ratio of wing area to body weight . . . vultures need to glide through still air for long distances, losing relatively little altitude. This feat requires a large wing area in relation to body size.*

159

She notices how each vulture emulates the flight of its mate. Until, suddenly, they're off and away to the north-east *because the zone of rising air inside the core of a thermal is restricted, if the birds are to stay in the rising air – thus avoiding the surrounding sinking air – they have to be able to turn tightly within a small circle and manoeuvre skilfully.*

On her last field trip here she had constructed small cairns of quartzite to make the path easier to follow, but, even so, it would be impossible to move fast enough to follow the gliding birds after they left the bowl. Rooted to the ground, she trails the disappearing dark forms against the vibrating midday sky.

Mountains and hills are sources of lift . . . mountains like Massanella, or Puig Tomir . . . even Cuevas Negras is high enough to provide a source of lift. These 'standing waves' often reach altitudes far higher than the original mountain or hill obstruction that started off the wave in the air stream. In this way vultures reach considerable heights without so much as flapping their wings.

I wonder, she suddenly thought, dropping her gaze, could the nest of this pair be on the far side of Cuevas Negras? Then, looking up again, suddenly she froze. High above, a dark figure stood motionless against the opaque sky, on the ruin of the bowl. And then it disappeared. A mountain walker? The new man at Casas Viejas or his assistant Miguel? One of Pep Oleza's cronies up to no good?

At a break in the ancient wall high above the Golden Bowl, she enters a startlingly different world of smooth white rock, pine and oak woods, high above the fertile valley. Settling down at the base of a shady pine tree, she takes out her sandwiches and gives up the vulture pair for the day. Only then, the crackling of undergrowth in the sudden breeze, a little like rattling bones, brings her to her feet. Was that stranger still lurking about? Maddened to be so jumpy, that she no longer shared this landscape only with wildlife, she looks over her shoulder. The owner of Cajas Viejas or his assistant, exploring, map-reading, might suddenly come upon her. Often, she realised, she *expected* to see them, distant, yet enlarged by her field glasses. Or she would turn at the sudden snapping of twigs in the woods

160

thinking it must be them, only to discover a mountain goat staring at her out of the undergrowth.

A slight shiver made her reach for her jacket. In the course of the morning the thick bank of grey cloud had widened and deepened over the summit of Massanella and is neighbouring peaks, lowering the temperature by at least eight degrees. After consulting her map, she decided to return by an unfamiliar path, that would lead her about half a mile south of Ca'n Clot, onto the road the jeep used. The terrain was familiar now, small woods alternating with *maquis*; prickly juniper, kermes oak and pine. The path through it was so well beaten she reckoned it had been used for transporting goods to Ca'n Clot on donkeys. Faintly, as she strode she heard a sound like distant music. Yet it was too early in the afternoon for the birds to return to the woods. Only towards dusk could thrushes, finches and other migrant birds risk flocking back from the plain. The sound repeated, yet when she paused to listen there the woods fell silent.

She followed the sloping path until the trees thinned out and it turned abruptly above an incline, and, looking down into it, for a moment she faltered. An area cleared of trees, infilled with wiry brushwood supported by a huge tree trunk. This was it. The first time she had seen a trap for netting birds. Her excitement mounting, she slithered gingerly down the slope and soon stood beside the rough-and-ready construction that rose high above her head and spread far wider than her outstretched arms. She would have to climb over to the other side of the tree trunk to figure out how the trap worked. Bending one leg, she got her other foot onto the top of the trunk and, after fumbling for handholds on the thick wire supporting the brushwood, hauled herself up and over. On the other side, she found a long pole swathed in a fine black net propped against a tree. This was the trapping instrument and she had to resist an impulse to take out her knife and rip it to shreds. The hunters come here at dawn and at dusk when thrushes and migrants fly back from the plain, she reasoned. The birds are attracted to this spot because they can fly through the cleared space between the trees, right into the outspread net.

Then she found two beat-up old car seats on either side of the gap she had climbed through. The hunters sit there waiting on either side of the net ready to make a death bag of the net. Fat and contented, she imagined, anticipating their *Tords en Col*. Then she noticed a guitar leaning incongruously against one of the seats and her thoughts raced. Evidently the source of the music I heard earlier, and was the owner still lurking about? A little anxiously, her eyes searched the clearing. She shivered and, turning to leave, almost tripped over a bottle half-hidden in the earth. Hastily she yanked it out and brushed off clinging leaves and soil to reveal twiggy plants floating in a yellowish liquid. Among the trove she identified bay leaves, myrtle and juniper before she pulled off the cork and sniffed. Heady alcoholic fumes stung her nose, and, at that moment someone was saying, *buenos tardes, señorita*. She swung round and saw the owner of Casas Viejas, standing at the edge of the clearing. He, she thought, is the one who spied me at the Golden Bowl, and, uneasily the hallucination at the old well filled her mind. 'We share this mountain now.'

Yet, relief flooded through her. A couple of hunters might have been hard to tackle, but not this haunter of her unguarded moments.

'Please stay where you are,' she said crisply. 'Don't come any closer, you might be acting illegally. I am the vigilante for the Ca'n Clot *possessío* and I have to find out if this particular section of the escarpment's off limits to walkers.'

Pep Oleza's words to Colin teased her mind: *The proprietor has given strict instructions, strangers are to be kept off his land.* Was the man staring at her now, with affable bemusement, a bird hunter?

To her surprise he obeyed her instruction, and she edged back up the incline groping for the phone in her pocket. She keyed in Julio's number only to find the line was busy.

Playing for time, 'is this yours?' she said, thrusting out the bottle.

The Don had looked bemused, waiting obediently at the edge of the clearing below, but the bottle made him smile. 'No, it's not mine. However, I happen to know it's a local speciality called *Hierbas Secas*, made from pure alcohol and herbs. Pep Oleza laid down a stock of bottles in the cellars at Casas Viejas. That one must belong to the bird netters,' he said, eagerly taking a step towards her.

'No, please don't come closer,' she said, a note of authority steadying her voice. 'Perhaps you aren't aware of the rules about walking up here in the nesting season? You need to find out from Julio Valente where there are nesting birds. It's illegal to go within a certain distance of them.'

'Then I must apologise,' he said, bowing his head a little, 'I was ignorant of that. But rest assured, as the new man in town, I have no wish to cause offence.'

'That's great, but wait there, please, I'll have to check this out.'

I'm out of my depth, she thought, her heart pounding, trying Julio's number again. Waiting for him to pick up, she realised the Don was humming a tune, quite unconcerned, as if nothing had happened. Almost whispering, she told Julio where she was and whom she had encountered.

'Be nice to him,' Julio pleaded. 'He's important to the conservancy's work, and there are no sensitive nesting sites up there.'

Well, there wouldn't be would there, next to a bird trap? What an idiot I am. She rang off then tossed down the bottle in the direction of the car seats. 'Everything's okay, thanks, señor.'

With a wave of her hand, she started to climb, and, looking back over her shoulder, glimpsed him packing away the guitar in a carrying case. Stricken by her insensitivity, she swallowed hard. She hadn't spoken to anyone like that since her teaching days in Glasgow, and it wasn't as if this man was an unruly teenager learning biology. No, he was an important local landlord whose estate bordered the territories of the field base.

She walked fast, anxious to keep her headstart, but, soon, she heard him whistling behind her. Irritated and amused, both at once, she thought, when he catches up, I *will* be more civil.

He drew level and said: 'I didn't mean to disturb you earlier when you were watching the vultures. And, after that, with my strumming? I only learned to play the guitar last year, and I'm not very good yet. I like to practise in the mountains where there's no one to hear me, except the birds.' And when he added, 'I was composing a lament for the birds slaughtered at that dreadful trap,' her stride faltered. Can what he says be true, or is he teasing me? Does he mean to disarm me?

'My name is Nicolas Monterey,' he added, stopping, laying down the guitar case, his inquisitive eyes playful now. 'And yours is?'

'Luisa Ross,' she told him, accepting his outstretched hand. 'I'm a research student based at Ca'n Clot.'

It was then she noticed he had something in his other hand, and, catching her glance, he opened it to reveal the chalky white skull of a bird, flecked with leaf mould.

'It's fragile, as all beautiful things are,' he said, and, at that moment, she thought, he is poetic and emotionally generous, not merely charming. 'Can you tell me what kind of bird it belonged to?'

Eager to make amends, she ran her finger over the chalky, perfect form. 'It's the skull of a buzzard.'

'A casualty of the bird netters?'

'No, I don't think so. The nets catch smaller birds. The buzzard probably died from natural causes. Exhaustion during high winds, old age, death as the result of a damaged limb, who can tell? It might even have been poisoned.' She rattled off the alarming statistics she had read for bird deaths from poisons people were able to buy freely over the counter, in supermarkets and gasoline stations throughout Mallorca. Poisons put down to get rid of rats or mice, kittens or dogs, could all too easily find their way into the blood streams of hawks and vultures, she said.

He listened carefully, alternately scrutinising her face and the skull lying on his palm, and, when he turned it over in his palm, she was struck by the delicacy of his broad fingers that sprouted a few dark spiralling hairs. 'What are these shapes rising above the beak?' he asked, his index finger hovering over the twin domes inside the skull.

164

'They're the brain cavities. They held the brain of the bird that fixed the tilt of its wings.'

And when he said, 'it's a perfect natural sculpture, this little skull,' a rush of empathy ran through her and she wondered if his tenderness masked something deeper. Unfathomable, like anguish. Perhaps he's been through a difficult time, she thought. And watching him carefully return the skull to a cradle of leaf mould, an ache of nostalgia swept through her for the little auk on the island all those moons ago. Now he was standing back a little, looking down at the skull, almost reverential, just as she had done all those weeks ago on the North Shore.

'*Los muertos abren los ojos a los que viven,*' he said, startling her with a fierce, squinting look, baffling her, yet winning her over. Clearly, he had been affected by his own sentiment, for he gave a nervous cough before he picked up the guitar case and suggested they walk on. At a loss for words, she wondered, *the dead open the eyes of the living;* where have I heard that phrase before?

They continued along the path, he humming his earlier tune, she hoping to pluck from her mind the source of his evocative words about the living and the dead. Couldn't she just ask him? She cast him a sidelong glance, and, catching it, he responded with a quizzical smile, but she decided, after her earlier incivility, to uphold their companionable silence. When they reached a place where the path forked, he doffed his hat and she was surprised by thick dark hair rising, leonine, above a broad high brow and drawn at the back into a neat knot at the nape of his neck. And when he left her with a promise to ask Julio Valente where he could and could not walk in the wilderness, she felt swept up by his benevolent energy as if into an embrace.

§

The following Sunday, the day when people who live alone are left to make plans for themselves, despite their pleading – won't you *please* come, Luisa? . . . we'd *love* your company! . . . we're

165

taking a *delicious* picnic hamper out there! – she had turned down an invitation to Anita's finca. Only, after writing up field notes all morning, she changed her mind. She needed a walk. She ate a cheese sandwich and a bowl of soup before she set out, not minding the glowering sky that threatened rain, and she found the cross-country path on the edge of town that led to Anita's place, just as Colin had described it when they had invited her there. Perhaps they would have left the orchard by the time she arrived, but it didn't matter. It would be enough to see Anita's land and she recalled Colin's vivid description of how to get there.

A stone bridge, no more than a slab, crosses the torrente *on the edge of town, leads to a path, past a pen where four silver speckled guinea fowl with turkeys and bantam hens peck away at earth composted with their droppings . . . .* At the bridge she paused to look down into the river bed the locals called *el torrente*. Some years the *torrente* swelled with rain and melted snow, as it did now, and María Ferrer had told her it was such a rare event the entire town would turn out to see it from this bridge. Looking down into the silky golden water, she realised how much she missed Scottish rivers. In Mallorca there were only these winter *torrentes*, although underground the island seethed with lakes and springs. Moving along the path, refusing to allow Dan to leap into her mind every time she thought of Scotland, she had to negotiate a narrow path with a sheer drop down to fertile terraces on her left until she came to a track leading through open countryside.

She went at a measured pace, turning over thoughts about the odd couple. Anita had a daughter in New York, Colin had three children, two in England, one in Scotland. Just before she had left them last weekend Anita had said, 'you see, I'm a bit of a globe trotter. It matters not a jot where I live or in whose house, so long as my work is interesting.' And what about Colin's little slip? Lourdes, he had called her. Is it possible to make friends with people who may not be what they appear to be? Isn't much of what they tell you liable to be lies? I'm no prig but I don't have time to waste on dissemblers either. But Luisa had to smile when another voice countered, then what are you doing walking out to Anita's finca?

Anita Berens fascinated her, it was as simple as that. A curious combination of the showy and the severe, her broad shoulders, narrow waist and shapely rear that suggested a media star of some sort, an opera singer or a leading lady who had fallen out of the limelight. Yes, she was peculiarly *restrained*, rather like Aquila under her hood! The thought startled and intrigued her. Never before had she met anyone like Anita and couldn't imagine they'd ever become friends. Why, Anita didn't even *like* Mallorca or the Mallorcans, and she knew the women in the town didn't care for her. So why did she go on living here? Surely no one in their right mind would make such sacrifices, hide themselves away for a now and then love affair, if that's what she was having, with Colin. But even more intriguing, how could Anita write a book about the island and not be on good terms with its inhabitants?

'My adult life has been lived, to a large extent, by the throw of the dice,' was an odd comment for anyone to make. Yet Anita had said it matter-of-factly as if it didn't matter that she had no control over her own life. And how, Luisa wondered, can I respect someone who settles for that?

No cars passed her on the road as she strolled, enjoying the sweetly fertile smell of the countryside, the early wild flowers embroidering the verges. Lost in thought, she considered, on the other hand, perhaps Colin and Anita are just what they claim to be, friends and working colleagues. Perhaps Colin was sufficiently interested in Anita's book to give her his valuable time and help. And, then, wasn't it possible that Lourdes was simply her nickname, or her middle name, or even Colin's term of affection for Anita? Certainly, whether or not they're having an affair is none of my business.

Just as she was struggling to put further speculation about them from her mind, a sudden low growl made her catch her breath. Whirling round she came face to face with an enormous black dog behind a chicken wire fence. The same type as one of the guard dogs at the villas on the way up to Casas Viejas. Bared teeth, wild yellow eyes, fearsome growl. Her heart thumped heavily in her ribcage when, barking madly, the dog flung itself at the fence . . . again and again and again . . . and in those few terrifying seconds she froze, terrified the fence might give way.

It's only made of chicken wire. It's only as strong as the fence round the aviary at Ca'n Clot. First thing is don't panic, she told herself, backing off against the terrace wall, weak at the knees. Fight or flight? Too stricken to do either, moving away almost imperceptibly, she glued her eyes to the grotesquely performing dog. Then, stealthily, she took a stick off a woodpile lying beside the path. If the dog got out, came for her, she'd *hit it between the eyes!* Yes, someone had once told her that was the way to knock out a dog. Moving off slowly, very slowly, trying not to imagine what the weight of the black body might feel like pinning her to the wall . . . its teeth could rip out her throat in seconds . . . the women in Magdalena's shop said one day the brute'll kill someone. Was this that dog? There had been a headline in last week's *Diario de Mallorca* – 'Young Man Narrowly Escapes Mauling Dog in Palma'.

The beast lunged, the fence bulged and, unable to bear the torment a moment longer, she turned and ran. The barking stopped as soon as she was a few metres beyond its territory. Bending over, catching her breath, steadying her nerves, relief ran through her. Perro barks ferociously if a stranger approaches, she thought, only not with the viciousness of that dog. It must've been unspeakably badly treated as a puppy.

There was a split-wood gate at the end of the path. When she reached it, there were Colin and Anita, deep in conversation under the lintel of a charming small building the colour of honey. Azahar lay sprawled out in a patch of sun at Anita's feet.

'Hello,' Luisa called out. 'I hadn't planned to come so far.'

'Well, this is a surprise,' Colin said eagerly, and when he arrived to open the gate, she confessed immediately to her terrifying experience with the dog.

'I didn't think you'd be afraid of anything,' Anita began, then seemed to regret her barb. 'Oh, isn't it awful . . . you see, it's only just arrived. I mean, it wasn't there last week. The place next door changed hands recently and the new owner put the dog there. It scares me stiff, too.'

When her voice trailed away, Luisa went to sit beside her. To her astonishment Anita took her hand. 'It used to be so peaceful here. Now I dread coming,' she went on sadly. 'It's not just the black dog, but there's another dog chained up in there. A beautiful pointer. The chain's so tight it can only walk round in circles, round and round, howling.'

Colin paced up and down, vigorously rubbing the back of his neck with a handkerchief.

'I didn't notice there was a pointer,' Luisa said, removing her hand from Anita's with the unspoken excuse of bending down to retie a lace of her boot.

'The black dog does attract most of the attention,' Colin said. 'The pointer's obviously kept as a hunting dog. Is there anything you can do to help?' He stood still on the small patio looking down at his feet. 'You see, Luisa, it's like this. Anita needs to come out here, to paint, to garden in the tranquillity of the countryside. This is quite a crisis for her and it's hard to know how she *can* continue coming here, what with one dog barking viciously and the other howling miserably. That pointer is effectively being *tortured*. In Britain hunting dogs like that are cherished. Friends of mine breed them in Berkshire. Wonderful animals, pointers.'

Deeply sympathetic to Anita's plight after her own encounter with the dog, Luisa telephoned Julio in the early evening.

'The black dog's what they call a Mallorcan shepherd dog,' Julio said. 'Belongs to Alejandro Ferrer's nephew, Bernardo, who used to keep it at his house near the Calvary.'

'Oh, so it *is* that dog.' She told Julio she had heard the dog discussed in the bar.

'Bernardo Ferrer has inherited the finca next to Señora Berens in advance of Alejandro's death. The old man can't look after his land anymore. Bernardo's the nephew,' Julio explained, 'and he moved the dog out there last week.'

'If it wasn't upsetting Señora Berens so much, it would make sense for Bernardo Ferrer to keep the dog out there away from kids and old folk. But what about the pointer, Julio?'

He revealed that Felipe Tamarit had recently acquired the pointer to retrieve the game he hoped the Booted eagle would bring down and that Bernardo had given him permission to leave it at the orchard.

Luisa suppressed an ironic laugh. 'Can *anything* be done about the black dog, Julio?' she said.

'Unfortunately, Bernardo's away on the mainland. But the señora could go to the police station and take out a *Queja Vecinal* that would by law require to be investigated.'

A *Queja Vecinal?* . . . a neighbour's complaint, Luisa interpreted to herself and said: '*Both* dogs are being maltreated.'

'Yes, I know . . . only ill-treatment of the animals will not be the first thing on the mind of the police,' Julio explained. 'Disturbance of the peace is another matter. You see, Luisa, what northern Europeans regard as ill-treatment of animals cuts no ice in Mediterranean countries. Here many people, though by no means all, hold the view that animals exist *entirely* to do man's bidding. Bernardo's dog is guarding the property. Felipe's pointer is being kept a little deprived so's it'll be nicely tuned-up for the hunt. I've told you about that before. That's the custom with the hunters. On this island if dogs don't perform they run the risk of being shot, thrown in a pit or hung from a tree. Dogs are machines for shepherding and hunting. Few people think dogs have a soul or *feelings*. I only tell you the facts, unpleasant as they are.'

A pile of reference books lay on the table beside her bulging folder of notes. The past week of her field study to be written up before bedtime. Unwilling to be distracted by her neighbours, yet alerted by the small stab of guilt she felt about taking an easy way out, nevertheless she explained Julio's suggestion in a note which she slipped under the door of number eleven before going up to bed.

They were still awake next door – it was Colin's last evening – and, after reading aloud Luisa's note to Lourdes, he said he thought England could do with such a system as this *Queja Vecinal*. Sensible, efficient and fair, in which, as he understood it, any neighbourhood nuisance was first filtered through the local police station, then judged by a panel of other citizens. He made a mental note to get a reporter from *Ecco!* to put together a story about the way the system worked. He then tried his best to persuade Lourdes to follow Luisa's suggestion, but she would have none of it. Taking out one of these *quejas* about the dogs would just draw attention to my presence in the town, she insisted. There must be some other way to silence the brute.

'Perhaps you could persuade its owner to muzzle it,' Colin suggested. 'Besides, this Bernardo chap will soon be back in town and may well be sympathetic to your fears.'

But everything he said only served to exacerbate Lourdes' anxieties. And you could understand it, he reflected. Both dogs are effective metaphors for Lourdes' sense of having been ill-treated herself. Getting ready for bed, he reflected on the section of *Flight into Exile* he had managed to work on during this visit. At least Lourdes seemed willing enough to talk about Gustavo. At least he had been able to persuade her to take some Prozac, and, after that, he had gone upstairs himself, soothed by a jigger of whisky. For the first time since her exile, he wondered if Lourdes might be on the edge of a nervous breakdown and the implications of *that* didn't bear thinking about. His spirits buckled a little under the weight of such an imagined responsibility as he was getting himself ready for bed.

When he went to close the shutters, he glimpsed Lourdes' garden lit by a lamp over the back door. What an unruly contrast hers was to the one next door. It was a yard really, with no formal design and scattered about with strange sculpted heads, terracotta pots and the wonky bits of wood he supposed Lourdes must find artistic. All a bit of a mess really, and he couldn't help wondering if the yard was an outer manifestation of her confused state of mind. If worst came to worst, if she went to pieces, he'd have to persuade Felice to invite her home, to Littledeane. God forbid! but if it did ever come to *that* he could probably convince his retired psychotherapist friend, the Scot, Alex Baldwin, to take her on as a patient. He felt on tenterhooks at the edge of the abyss that had opened up between himself and the woman, his friend, who was the protagonist of his book. He hadn't bargained for this. Oh, he could write about the socio-politico-economic situation in Colombia as easily as a gecko darts up a wall, yet, if he failed authentically to reflect the depths of Lourdes' suffering not only in Colombia, but also *here* in her enforced Mallorcan exile, what sort of a biography would that be?

I don't want to see her flip side, he thought. Unreasonable, perhaps, but I just want her to be feisty old Lourdes Herreros sailing through my book with courage and intelligence. I'm simply not the kind of writer who can plumb psychological depths. Getting into the bed that was too small for him so that he hadn't had a decent night's sleep since he arrived in Mallorca, he felt a moment's despair about the fate of *Flight into Exile*. But at least he had someone else's book to take refuge in, and he opened it with relief: *Tinker, Tailor, Soldier, Spy*.

The following day, the vulture pair soars towards the mountain town on a thermal, searching the ground for carrion. Luisa stands on the ridge above Ca'n Clot following their flight through her field glasses.

Vultures use their excellent eyesight to spot carcasses on the ground and they also keep an eye on their neighbours in flight in case they are first to find a catch all can share in. A dead sheep perhaps, tossed by some local farmer into the corner of a field before he digs a pit to bury it or, perhaps, he might throw the carcass into the back of his van and deliver it to the conservancy.

The vultures wheel in tandem until they are lost to Luisa's sight and she returns to the finca with Perro at her heels.

Later in the day they wheel, high above Calle Luna. Azahar, lying half-asleep outside number eleven, has attracted their attention. The dog gets up and they see it's alive, a waste of their time. *Auk! auk!* they grunt. Sweeping into a rising air wave they glide away back to Cuevas Negras.

Down in the street stand two tiny figures. A tearstained Lourdes, whose task is to drive Colin to the airport. Oblivious to the fleeting presence of the vultures he longs to see, Colin tosses his suitcase into the back of the Citroën, hugs Lourdes and tells her not to worry. 'If you don't want to draw attention to yourself by taking out one of these *Queja Vecinals*, then wait until this Bernardo chap comes back and speak to him directly. Most people are reasonable, you know. When he discovers how upset you are he's bound to do something.'

His night flight leaves Palma airport via the same air route he arrived by more than a week earlier. The sky, before they rise into the ether and the island disappears from sight, is the colour of a black plum. Looking down, he can just make out the even darker humps and fissures of the Sierra de Tramuntana, and, if he studies the terrain he'll be able to make out the lights of the mountain town. Yes, surely that's it down there! Like the tiny corner of an illuminated microchip board. Yes! he can tell by the shape of floodlit church tower.

The cabin hostess touches his arm: 'A drink, sir?'

He grins widely, knots of tension dissolving in his stressed body at the very thought. '*Rather!* A gin-and-tonic, please, and make it a double'.

Taking his leave of Lourdes had thoroughly rattled him. For once he had felt powerless to help her, and had no choice but to leave her behind in a ghastly predicament that brought back to her the menacing months of her imprisonment.

He remembers what she has told him. Why had Herreros been that cruel? A few days later some comforts had arrived: two pillows, a duvet, a radio, a chair and a small table. Small comforts indeed, for although Lourdes' imprisonment would be relatively short-lived compared to Carmen Filgueira's and Diana Montoya's and all the others, *she didn't know that at the time.* That's what had been so awful. Not knowing if she'd ever get out of there. Not knowing if she'd become one of the disappeared. Not knowing how long the nightmare would last. Lourdes has never recovered from the shock of her abduction, he reflected. Never had a chance to, since she's still in a sort of a prison. He remembered a touching detail she had given him – *the shock made me sleep all though that first week; not real sleep, but fitful dozing, waking every other hour. I fell into a depression, began to forget who I was. A mirror? I begged one of my guards. Please, can I have a mirror?*

His mouth purses. Awful to wish anyone dead, yet they both thought Andreas Herreros was just the stocky, beef-eating, whisky drinking, cigar smoking type, who might easily drop dead from a heart attack one day. *Or*, Señor Herreros might be extradited to the United States, though his cunning made that unlikely. As long as the man stayed put as a declared extraditable he'd be pretty well invincible.

No one sits near him in Executive Class. The Gatwick-bound flight is not even half-filled with passengers. With a heavy sigh he takes out his laptop and sets it on the plastic table. Better spend the two-hour flight time doing a little more drafting. Back in London the next edition of *Ecco!*, Mark and Emma, his spoiled sprats as he calls them, and Felice, his ambitious wife, would command his full attention.

She drives back from the airport, swallows a couple of pills and goes straight to bed. Nevertheless, in Colin's absence, night fears penetrate her defences. Panic stricken she gropes under the bed for her slippers. *Lourdes has disappeared.* Anita Berens thinks she can leap back with a triumphant laugh just because Colin's gone away, but I won't let her. I'll kill the bitch off, yes that's what I'll do. Kill her off.

Elena, she thinks. Full-moon shimmering in a crystal sky. No angels. Downstairs in the fingering moonlight she telephones her daughter: *Hello, you have reached the home of Elena. Please leave a message.* If I reopen seams of memory will the angels reward me with their longed-for presence? For I cannot, I simply cannot, go on dragging around this shadow, this Anita Berens, whom I detest more and more with every day that passes. In the moonlit mirror the sight of Anita Berens staring back sullen and immovable makes her take up the Mayan statuette and hurl it at the mirror.

It is as if she has shattered the sky . . . *so sternklar war die Nacht* . . . the moonlight disappears. Anita Berens falls, sobbing, to her knees, and it is Lourdes who rises to examine the debris. The mirror's wooden backing board is still intact, though split

174

in places. Her feet edge round the splintered shards glinting on the floor in the moonlight. No going back now, she tells herself, running nervous hands through her hair. But isn't something written on the wood? She can't be sure. It's too dark to see properly. She finds a torch in the kitchen. Illuminated words written boldly in chalk: *Carpe diem!* Seize the day? Who the hell wrote that? she gasps, her hand flying to her throat.

7

During the night, Luisa stirred several times in her bed, half-hearing distant howls she ascribed to mating genets.

Genetta genetta: Elongated, short-legged catlike mammal. Entirely nocturnal. Favours woodland, Restricted to the Iberian Peninsula, South-west France and the Balearics.

Or, perhaps, the howl had come from a wildcat?

Felix sylvestris: Favours wooded country and rocky ground.

Another time a monotonous sonar-blip call sounded a basso continuo to her dreams. Scops owl?

Otus scops: Conspicuous ear tufts; grey brown or rufous. Favours woodlands, olive groves and the outskirts of villages.

The unfathomable silence of the wilderness. Silence so deep she sinks into it.

After daybreak, she stands in front of the map of the Serra de Tramuntana. Its place names read like double-Dutch on your first visit, remember? Indecipherable, until you discovered a glossary, faint grey print in the margin. Catalan and Spanish. With a green pen you added the English translations:

Clot	*Hoya*	*Valley*
Pont	*Puente*	*Bridge*
Rafal	*Cobertize*	*Shed, shack*

No need to refer to the words in green ink, now you've learned them by heart. *Clot, Coma, Repla, Puig* . . . Catalan words that sound right in this landscape. Every language safeguards words that are sacred to features of its own landscape. No other words will do. Take, for example, the *genius loci* of that small uncompromising cube, the deserted bothy precariously set on a spit of dunelands that will haunt you forever, no matter where you go in the world.

Recuerdas?

Remember, how sometimes you would stand at the corner where the bothy wall seemed to rise directly from the shell-strewn track? How you could smell the sea and the fields on the other side of the estuary both at once? One day, before you left Scotland for Barcelona, urgently, you had to find the right word to describe the atmosphere of the place. For a long time you searched the dictionary until you hit on 'ineffable' — unutterable, too great for words. Some things are beyond praise, beyond human understanding.

Her clothes are dry and warm on the hanging-rail near the stove. She struggles out of blue thermal pyjamas and puts on, one by one, grey sweatshirt, green sweater, moleskin trousers, repeating slowly to herself the fragment of that recently discovered poem . . .

this is where one's false and tawdry self
starts to drown

. . . how well it sounds, that word 'drown' in my mouth. But I won't let my heart *plummet,* she tells herself. Praising is what matters, and, up here there's plenty of encouragement. As her confident fingers lace up her boots she comprehends the source of her contentment. Up here I can be my unobserved self, observing the wild things. Unwilling to allow the slightest interruption of this other world, she has turned off her mobile phone. By choice, she lives without daily newspapers and listens to music rather than news reports on the radio, in accord with her mentor, Thoreau. Better by far to listen to the song of a blackbird than to fret about wars and persecution in another part of the globe when one was helpless to do anything about it. After all, human beings were not intended to act as the daily receivers of ghastly news.

Beyond the unshuttered window, the early morning sky veils the crag under an opaque mauve haze. Called outdoors by the strenuous piping of small birds, she walks to the wood of the Tree at the Edge where she picks a sheaf of heather for the painted ceramic jug on her desk. *Erica multiflora,* the Mediterranean heather, taller and more spectacular than its Scottish cousin, but with a similar honeyed scent and blossom ranging from almost white to deep purple-pink.

The sky clears to blue, the sun casts a golden circle on the terracotta tiled floor. The aroma from the coffee pot on the stove permeates the room. In the tangible silence, standing in front of the calendar above her desk, she takes up a pen to ring the date of carnival. In the middle of February, at the Barcelona carnival, she has promised Rafael, I'll be there, for better or for worse. She picks off a sprig of heather to enclose with the letter to Rafael she has not been able to resist writing. Even when, half-hearing the jeep arriving as it usually did midmorning, she writes on until Julio's footsteps sound down the dark passage leading from the refectory.

He sat down opposite her, fidgeting with the cap in hand, and staring at the floor, uncharacteristically sullen.

'What's happened, Julio?'

'It's old Alejandro,' he said lifting his head, meeting her eyes. *Wavy hair greying at the temples, mournful brown eyes.* 'He's dead and I would've told you sooner, but your mobile's switched off.'

Ignoring his veiled rebuke, she thought Alejandro was expected to die soon, is it such a tragedy?

'When did it happen?' she said, wondering at Julio's agitation.

Julio rose off his seat and started pacing the room. 'Yesterday I was patrolling the ridge along the old escarpment path. Near the old sitja, *recuerdas?*'

Yes, she remembered. Breathtakingly high up there on that ridge, the road twisting through the valley, a mere grey ribbon far below. The delicate magic of tumbled elements - holm oaks, rocks, boulders, darkness, light and fungus-encrusted emerald moss then the sitja, a circular wall overlain with moss, crowned with a neat high circle of holm oak twigs. Her first sighting of a disused charcoal burning circle, arcane, enigmatic in the sunlight beyond the shady grove. How long had the pile of meticulously positioned wood waited in vain to be reduced to charcoal? Since R. R. Bauza, the father's, last visit more than half-a-century ago? But what was Julio getting at?

When he spun round to make sure she was paying attention, she encouraged him with a nod. 'I smelled goat . . . dead goat . . . live goats smell as you expect them to, freshly dead goats smell worse, but goats that've been dead for some time smell unspeakably foul. The trail of the stench led me to the sitja. I had to take off my *pañuelo* to cover my nose and mouth.' He fished his familiar blue and red scarf out of his pocket for her to see. 'The carnage was dreadful,' he went on. 'Bodies of goats everywhere, lying in their congealed blood. A whole family including the kids. Some half-eaten by hawks and genets. I'm used to that sort of thing, but spreadeagled among them - face down, arms akimbo - lay old Alejandro.'

Luisa stood up. She covered her mouth with her hands. Vividly she could picture that sacred grove overlain with massacre. Alejandro in his old brown cardigan, the felt slippers he always wore.

'Surely he hadn't been murdered?' she said softly.

'No, well, not directly. Probably a heart attack . . . we'll never know exactly, and I'm sorry I didn't let you know sooner but, well, there was quite a stir when I got back to town . . . breaking the news to the Ferrer family, reporting the massacre of the goats to the Town Hall, arranging for the old man's body to be brought down.'

'How long had he lain there?'

'That's the best of it. He hadn't been there more than a few hours. What possessed me to go up there? Christ knows, Luisa, I've so much work to do elsewhere.'

He sat down again and she went to stand beside him, longing to lay a supportive hand on his shoulder.

'Maybe it was you, Luisa, that interested me in that path. It was one I'd ignored until that day we went along it together. Ignored it I suppose because it's on the very edge of our territory. After we walked it together, I decided to patrol it regularly as a vigilante.'

'But Alejandro. Was his death linked with the goats?'

'No, well not in an obvious way. Though at first the Town Hall got pretty excited by the possibility. But when they brought the body down there wasn't a mark on it. They say the forensic from Inca intends to write 'heart attack' on the death certificate.'

Luisa was surprised by tears in Julio's eyes. The stalwart keeper of the earth. When, lightly, she touched his shoulder he looked up at her and covered her hand with his own. 'There's a wake at the house today. The Ferrer women asked me to come and get you.'

A blue vein stood out, pulsating, on his neck. Julio's grief at this moment also has something to do with his own feelings of loss over his own family, she thought, going upstairs to throw some things into an overnight bag. That day they had driven down from his hide she had asked, are you married, Julio? I was married once, he said. I've got three children, almost grown up, but I rarely see them. My wife went off to live in Menorca with someone else two years ago. And she had been able to tell by the way he told his story, and by the way he glossed over the fact that he lived in a flat in Inca with his widowed sister, that he badly missed his wife and children.

Julio drove away fast from Ca'n Clot and gave over the wheel to Luisa when he got out to unpadlock the gate. They drove on and he said: 'I phoned you this morning, only I got the answering machine.'

She glanced at him, her mouth pursed.

'Was your 'phone turned off? You're not supposed to do that, you know,' he chastised. 'This wasn't exactly an emergency, but don't do that again, *vale*?'

'Okay, sorry. No, I won't do that again.' She shifted into first gear for the bumpy ride across the meseta and asked after a few minutes of silence: 'How did Alejandro get all the way up to the escarpment?'

'My guess is a woodcutter gave him a lift to the edge of the shooters' territory. You know, where we collected the cartridges? And, after that, he stumbled on along the track. He knew it so well, from his grandfather's knee, knew it better than anyone else in town.'

'And when he reached the sitja where the carboneros of the town used to camp out, Alejandro, with his father and his grandfather, he found the dead goats. Julio,' she said hesitantly, 'd'you think he *went* up there to die, *wanted* to die up there?'

'I know what you mean. It would be natural for anyone to want to die in the place they loved most. What's tragic is the old man wasn't able to sit there in the stone circle remembering the good times, the charcoal burning, the camaraderie of the men, the camp fire feasts and songs. No, I believe he died in shock when he saw the carnage.'

Her heart lurched a little when they drove through the yard at Casas Viejas . . . *I long to see Nicolas Monterey* . . . but the place looked deserted and the jeeps had gone. Inwardly, she chided herself for her disappointment and said: 'Who d'you think shot the goats?'

'Too soon to say, Luisa, but I have my suspicions about what sort of mentality could just leave the carcasses lying there to rot, never mind that the shooting was illegal, out of the permitted season for culling goats. The sight was enough to give *my* heart a judder, let alone an old man's.'

She drove straight to Calle Luna and, after she got out, Julio looked down at her from the open window of the jeep: 'By the way, the Ferrer family don't know about the goat slaughter, so keep it to yourself? The Town Hall's agreed to hush it up so his womenfolk can go on imagining the old man died peacefully in his ancestral paradise.'

The kitchen of number eleven Calle Luna enters directly off the street, exactly like number twelve's. There, Anita Berens is preparing casseroles and fruit pies to put in the freezer in anticipation of Colin Cramer's next visit, but it is Lourdes Herreros who looks up every time a shadow falls on the terracotta tiles in front of the double doors to the street. All morning people have come and gone past her door. All morning, Calle Luna, usually a tranquil backwater at the top of town, has been a hive of activity. It's raining a little. Everyone who passes her door wears something black, a coat, a skirt, a tie, or carries a black umbrella.

When the small sharp knife she's using to chop vegetables slips across her index finger, momentarily she stares at the oozing blood then rushes upstairs to the bathroom cabinet

181

for an elastoplast. It strikes her as fantastical that this physical wound so exactly replicates her inner pain, brought on, as usual, by her sense of exclusion. She tosses her head with a loud throaty laugh. Laughter in face of near despair. Colin gone once more . . . where two or more are gathered together . . . alone, it's a different story.

Of course, she had gone to offer the Ferrer women her condolences. However, as a foreigner they hardly knew, and cared to know even less, she had been kept on the doorstep of number thirteen while they nodded, unsmilingly accepting her condolences. Luisa Ross had come out of her door when she had been taking her leave. 'Luisa, *guapa!*' María Ferrer called out. 'How glad we are that you've come!' Then the three harpies pulled Luisa inside, and thus was I, Anita Berens, dismissed to the fringes of life as usual. Whereas in Colombia, I, Lourdes Herreros, would have been welcomed into the heart of any neighbour's crisis.

But something else was on her mind. She scribbled a fax to Gerda Lehmann . . . *I wonder if you can tell me who owned this house before me?*

Now it was a relief to pass the unreflecting oblong of wood that had been the mirror in the hall. Such a relief not to see Anita Berens' demanding, unhappy face frowning out at her. She wondered why she hadn't thought of shattering the mirror long before or, at the very least, turning it to face the wall. Now the two words written large in an elegant hand amused her - *Carpe diem!* - as if they were a message to her from some otherworldly, yet supportive source. She must discover what that was. Confined she might be to a two-bit mountain town, yet she must seize every opportunity to make the best of each day, as the chalky words dictated.

After that, moments fused with memory draw her upstairs, up the stone steps to the computer room, seized by something like passion. She must recapture her conversation with Angel Zavala.

'Why are you doing this, Angel?'
'We do it for cash, of course, what d'you think?'

'Is that all?'

If she can cling to the words in her head, tell it to Colin, she'll keep a grip on herself. Impatiently she switches on the computer, hears its promising start-up beep, opens the file.

Colin, she types, in the first house the rules were harsh. I lay on a soiled mattress on the floor, had to ask permission to sit up, stretch my legs, go to the filthy lavatory. The only window was boarded over. The room was lit day and night by a perpetual candle. Two guards sat on the floor, leaning against the wall. Their feet touched my mattress when they stretched out their legs. They smelled foul in the hot, unventilated room.

They weren't the same thugs who killed my chauffeur, Pedro. No, these were youngsters - teenagers - nasty, volatile and uneducated. Working in twos, changing shifts at six in the morning and six at night, dressed in gaudy T-shirts, trainers and cut-down denims. The uniform of *cholos!* One sat with his back against the wall, machine gun to the ready. The other sat on guard at the door. There was more space when they moved me to the second house where I made friends with one of these boys. The one that turned informer and told you and Gustavo where I was: Angel Zavala.

When the computer screen signals the arrival of an e-mail from Colin she pauses to read it: 'I'm on line with you, Lourdes. You're coming up with good stuff, keep going.' A lifeline thrown to Lourdes, not to Anita Berens!

They wore black balaclavas with eye-slits even in the house, she typed. For some reason, Angel started showing me a little kindness by trying to make me eat a mess of rice and refried beans. The other guard got jealous and butted me with his rifle: 'You're nervous, Lady. I wouldn't show it if I were you,' he said nastily. 'Nervous people get shot around here.'

Nervous? I was petrified. I had no idea how long this would go on and no idea if I would survive it. (As you know the experience left me with what that doctor I consulted later, at the sanatorium in Switzerland, called 'a depressive propensity'. That evil time still haunts me, but I'm beginning to think *Anita Berens* is the depressive, not Lourdes. If only I could throw Anita off, Lourdes might recover.)

183

Colin's reply edged onto her screen. 'One day you *will* be free of Anita Berens. So keep going, tell me more.' Colin was standing-by. Even from this distance she could depend on him.

At every opportunity . . . when his fellow guard had gone for a pee, or to bring in the dreadful food from the kitchen (there were other people in the house, a couple, man and woman, I think since I could hear, faintly, the sound of their *campesino* voices) . . . I drew Angel into conversation. Sometimes it worked, other times not.

'Why are you doing this, Angel?' I would ask and he always gave the same reply: 'We do it for cash to help the family, buy nice clothes, a motorcycle maybe . . . .'

Some sort of rapport was developing between Angel and me. He would tutt, shift his feet, look down at the floor then confess in a low voice: 'It keeps our mothers happy. And it keeps the Holy Infant and Lady of Mercy happy. They protect us and forgive us when we make vows and sacrifices to them so that our work will be successful.'

'Work? You call it *work*?' I said scathingly. 'Surely you're not *proud* of what you do?'

Angel avoided my eyes, as if to say, don't push it, lady. 'The saints bless it, anyway,' he said.

Later, [at the second house] he told me that not only the saints but a drug called Rohypnol (a tranquilliser) supported their work.

'It's fantastic how life turns into a movie when you take Rohypnol!' he boasted. 'We swallow it with beer and get high right away. Then you can do whatever you like! Fuck a *chica*! Hold up a car. What a laugh that is! You see how scared the driver looks handing over the keys and you think, man! how can anyone be scared of poor little Angel and his mates. And you think, he's a fucking idiot, and leave him standing on the road miles from anywhere!'

'That isn't work, that doesn't bring you cash, that's downright brutal,' I protested.

'Well lady, you might think so, but we gotta have some fun

in this shit life!' he replied. 'We're gonna die young, right? So we say, live for the moment. Yeah, we were born into shit, we die in shit. You're quite a nice lady, but you don't have an idea even the size of a piece of *fluff* what it is like to be born poor in Colombia.'

He was right, of course, how *could* I understand the degradation, the alienation they felt, the brutalisation that had made them loathe politicians, the government, the state, the law, the police, *all* of society?

My breakthrough with Angel came after he happened to read a newspaper article about my disappearance. (Colin, did you and Gustavo give the paper the story?) When Angel discovered I was none other than Lourdes Herreros, the radio broadcaster his mother and his sister had listened to faithfully every week in the kitchen of their pueblo hovel, he started to slip me presents. Things like a bar of soap and the plastic crucifix which I keep in my handbag to this day.

In his London flat, Colin shut down the computer and went to his filing cabinet where he stored a bottle of malt. Lourdes was on good enough form to be ironically humorous, as well as clear headed and unemotional. He felt almost weak with relief, pouring himself a measure of the spirit, admiring its soft golden colour, swirling it around in his mouth. It looked as if her crisis was over. Yet wasn't it odd, to say the least - she hadn't so much as mentioned the dogs?

§

Stealthily *la borrasca* was moving in, a vast cloud bank that stretches across the Balearics every winter, above the coast of Spain, southern Portugal and the Atlantic. You never know how long she'll linger, and how often she'll come back. She's a bitch, Julio said. Already Luisa had noticed the menacing grey mushroom cloud obscuring the summits and fingering chill into even the warmest days. Already Felipe's prediction had come to pass. Some nights it was so cold she slept on a paliasse in the den near the stove.

She had left town right after Alejandro's funeral and, apart from a brief 'hello' when they passed each other outside the Ferrer's door, had managed to dodge Anita Berens. She had walked back to Ca'n Clot, full of resolve to fulfil the schedule she had set herself for the coming week.

The next day she picnicked on the other side of the wall, beyond the Golden Bowl. She had just been zipping on her waistcoat ready to return to Ca'n Clot when she heard the distant sound of a vehicle on the road far below. The road she had driven along with Julio the day he bought the old goat for her photo session, the road that had looked like a mere grey ribbon when she looked down from the escarpment path. Now she knew it was an important linking route through the mountains between Casas Viejas and the string of towns north of Inca. Perhaps the Don is exploring his new territories? she thought with a rush of appalling desire. *It's happening, isn't it? I could easily fall in love, am falling in love, have fallen in love . . .* must talk to him again, get to know him, apologise for my rudeness that day at the bird trap. Must get Julio to invite him and his assistant to Ca'n Clot on the day of the town's visit.

Curiosity drew her towards the edge of the ridge. Few vehicles ever came into the mountains on these roads. So who was this, if it wasn't the Don? A woodcutter, a farmer, or Pep Oleza, perhaps, on his way to pick up the new guy at Inca station? Heeding Julio's warning, she went cautiously to to edge and heard the engine cutting out directly below. Hearing two car doors banging, metal on metal, she focussed on a jeep far below, identical to the reserve jeep but small as a Dinky toy in the valley. And when she moved clear of dense obscuring branches, she half-heard the vulture pair crying high overhead and didn't even look up.

Turistas in a rented jeep? . . . but no; adjusting her lenses, it was a stark surprise to come face-to-face with Felipe. Ah, so it *is* the conservancy jeep, but why isn't he up in the wood cutting lumber?

Her feet sink into the leaf mould, she has to steady herself with a hand on a tree. Then a woman fills the lenses

- a different hat, *black* today - Anita Berens and Felipe? What are they doing up here together? I should have warned Anita about my colleague. How out of place Anita looks. Silly woman wearing her white coat, a modish hat, high-heeled shoes in the mountains. Watching closely with something like relish, she sees Felipe leading Anita away from the jeep, evidently trying to persuade her of something, and feels the frisson of someone about to witness a clandestine theatrical performance put on for her benefit alone.

On the magnified stage below, Felipe takes Anita by the arm, and Luisa, scarcely able to wait to for the action, gazes voyeuristically down from the theatre box of her cliff top eyrie. But it soon becomes clear, this is no amicable tryst. Felipe faces Anita, his back turned to Luisa's bird's eye-view, hands in his pockets, shoulders heaving. High above, concealed in the silent trees, it's as if she's watching a clip from a silent movie filmed in muted colours of holm oak green, rock silver, bark brown and the black of Anita's hat.

Now Anita takes up a defiant stance, feet apart, hands on her hips, head slightly tilted back. It had been impossible to see through the field glasses anything of the face under the hat until that tilting movement revealed a grimly drawn mouth. No, this is not all fun and games, Luisa worries. Felipe takes a step towards Anita, grabs her upper arm. Then, when Anita raises her arm as if to slap his face, Luisa wants to rush to her aid. But, c'mon, you can't *rush* in this treacherous terrain, she warns herself. It'd take fifteen minutes of arduous clambering to reach the road, by which time surely they'd be gone?

With a sharp sideways flick of her arm Anita throws off Felipe's hand and steps back. He points stiffly, as if to command her to his will, but Anita turns away briskly, gives him two fingers in the air, folds her arms and marches back to the jeep with her head down.

Good for you! Luisa wants to shout, approving this side of Anita she hasn't seen before. Felipe follows her, shoulders held stiffly. Then *slam! slam!* metal on metal, comes the cymbel clap of the closing doors. After a neat three-point turn the jeep heads back towards town, leaving Luisa with the frustrating sense of curiosity aroused and unsatisfied.

The odd inexplicable scene haunted her into the next day. What had happened between Anita and Felipe to draw them to the middle of nowhere, so far from the town? An assignation, a lover's tryst that had ended badly? Surely Anita hadn't fallen for Felipe's sultry charms, yet they must have had something to hide from the watching countryside. For it was certainly true that very little could take place in the mountain town without someone picking up a scent of it, a clue, or, better still, a few embroidered details among the papery scattered blossoms of purple bougainvillaea lying in its dusty kerbs.

When Luisa was returning to Ca'n Clot after the morning patrol, the heavens opened as if some great God of the skies had decided to pour upon the world the shock of a cold shower. Rain slicked her face, soaked her hair round the edges of her hood, and she realised the temperature was almost low enough for snow. Her head down against the driving rain, she wondered uneasily how many days she might be confined to base in this bad weather. She would happily stay in the mountains for days on end if she could be out and about. Cooped up inside Ca'n Clot would be a different story. Julio had told her *la borrasca* often settled in for days at a time and, even if it moved off for a day or two, it could swiftly return, making a dark hell of the mountains.

The rain beat insistently on the surface of her oiled jacket and ran down in rivulets to soak the thick socks above her walking boots. The field base already stood in a dark hell. Just the weather for slitting your throat, she decided, her exaggerated thought making her hasten her pace. Desultory smoke wreathed the main chimney of the finca and the reserve jeep stood outside. The men are holed up for the afternoon by the fire, she thinks, running now through the deluge.

She let herself in by way of the door leading directly to the den. Her own private entrance never used by the men. Catching her breath in the darkened hall, dripping puddles onto the floor, she anticipates the hot shower she'll take in the upstairs bathroom. Only then, the muted voices of Julio and Felipe came to her down the dark passage accompanied by the *click, click,* of dominoes falling on the table. Both their ancestors originated from Andalusia as she had discovered; Julio's parents and Felipe's grandparents had come to Mallorca to work in the cement factory near Inca during the boom years of the sixties. Unlike Mallorcan country folk who prefer card games, these two frequently played dice or chess to wile away the boredom of siesta.

The door to the refectory was slightly ajar at the end of the hall, and, hearing Felipe say her name, she was drawn to it as if by a magnet. She had only to step forward a little to see clearly through the door jamb. Each man had his feet up on a bench on either side of the table, hats off, boots off, sleeves rolled up, the fire blazing, a bottle of wine, bread, cheese and olives laid out on the table between them.

Suddenly Felipe announced arrogantly in Mallorcan: 'We've got a weird one there. *La Solitaria!* What woman worth her salt would want to stay alone in this God forsaken spot?'

Dammit! he was speaking so fast, but she caught the gist of his words. She flushed with outrage then watched Julio throwing back his head with a loud laugh: 'What! Luisa weird? *¡Hombre!* you're the oddball here,' he retorted in Castilian. 'She's strange, maybe, different from us,' Julio went on: 'A scientist, prepared to work long hours alone in the wilderness to advance her career. She's a *foreigner,* man . . . you have to make allowances for that!'

She put a hand over her mouth and held her breath. Studying the scene in which Felipe puts out a hand to refill his glass from the bottle, she sensed he was up to no-good. 'Only *half*-foreign,' he said with a superior air, reverting to the Castilian which Julio had subtly insisted upon. 'Her *mother* was Spanish.' And when he added, 'she's a *bruja*,' Luisa almost gasped out loud. 'I've seen her out in the woods picking herbs, nettles, who knows what else . . . .'

Julio roared. 'Come on, man, get the real world. A lot of

189

women do that these days. It's called alternative medicine, herbs made into teas, soups. Nothing wrong with it, in fact it's a good thing.'

'*Medicina alternativa?*' Felipe guffawed. 'What about the wings she wears?' he persisted, with an air of triumph.

How had Felipe . . . *How* had he? *When* had he seen . . . . Oh, my God! She turned her head away, biting her lip, puzzled until she remembered the photograph Rafael had taken of her when he had let her try on his winged costume. It had been a lark between them the day after he returned from the Garaff hills and she kept the photograph in her notebook. Surely Felipe hadn't rummaged through it, read my most intimate thoughts? Impossible? . . . no, it was all too possible! Then she realised with a rush of relief, but, of course he doesn't understand English; at least he couldn't have understood my private jottings! And then she remembered her drawing of Felipe as Saint Anthony, patron saint of swineherds. He would have seen that. Oh, my God!

'Everyone's entitled to a peccadillo or two,' she heard Julio say.

Bless him, she thought. Still, Felipe didn't know when to stop, damn him! She dreaded to think what might be coming.

'She showed me a few of her *pecas*-what'd'you-me-call-thems when I screwed her last December.'

Clinging to her door, Luisa raged inwardly, scarcely able to prevent herself from bursting through the door and beating him with her fists. Lying fantasist! But she'd wait this out, might even hear about Felipe's assignation with Anita the day before.

Through the crack in the door she saw Felipe rising a little off the bench with a provocative tilt of his body in Julio's direction, his hand clutching the edges of the table. Perhaps it would be better not to hear the rest? Felipe's version of the erotic hours we might have had, that part of her wanted to submit to after they flew Aquila. So long since I'd felt the melding of mouths, the erotic blaze of desire, the irresistible pull of flesh to flesh. How well she remembered the next time she had seen him. He had come to the den, lighting up a *Ducados*, inhaling deeply and saying I'm engaged to be married. The way he said it . . . was the sentence meant to shock, to disappoint? It had the opposite effect. You actually laughed in his face! There he was offering to you on a plate his wedding tackle, his beautiful lithe body that was promised to someone else. Inhaling his foreign odour, you rebuffed him for the second time. When I get back in January, today will be just a memory, you said. Yesterday I wanted the same as you, to help you fly Aquila, but anything more is out of the question.

Now her darting glance between the door and its frame takes in Julio rising up, his chest expanded, his voice raised.

'*¡Hombre!* Spare me! Don't give me the details about your fucking cock!'

She took a deep silent breath, blessed Julio again, and pressed her body against the cool wall. Yes, Felipe's dashing displays with the eagle had magnetised her from the start; he was so graceful in action. Something about the hooded bird, something intensely erotic had led up to it. As erotic as the fine line of a dry stone dyke undulating over a barren hill in Scotland. Only, she soon discovered his enthusiasm for falconry had a commercial ring when, before he placed Aquila on her arm, he told her that he wanted to quit conservancy work and put his efforts into setting up a bird flight centre for the public on the other side of the island.

Outside the refectory door she stood her ground, listening. Waiting for the clue she sensed would come to yesterday's odd sighting of Felipe and Anita in the valley.

After a lengthy pause, Julio sat down and said assertively: 'As I told you the other day, I fancy the new woman in town. Señora Anita Berens. She, not Luisa, is *la solitaria*. I've spoken to her once or twice and I might ask Luisa if she would sound the woman out, to see if she would let me take her for a meal in a restaurant.' He put a cigarillo between his lips and lit it.

Luisa relaxed at the turn the conversation was taking. Anita and Julio? Well, that makes more sense than Anita and Felipe!

Felipe said scornfully: 'Ah, yes, *la solitaria*, the singer of songs of lonely desolation, Anita Berens. *¡Hombre!* that's *very* interesting . . . you fancy going out with Anita Berens the dog killer?'

Luisa stiffened, peering through the door frame to a view of Felipe pretending nonchalance as he rattled the dominoes on the table. Dog killer? Julio, as if acting out her own feelings, was staring in disbelief at Felipe dividing the spoil of the dominoes into two equal parts, a conquistadorial glint in his eyes.

'A couple of days ago I saw Señora Berens walking down the path to her finca,' he began with slow languor, stretching out his legs under the table. 'Bernardo's gone to the mainland and I'm pruning the trees in his orchard, as you know, as well as cutting the fucking fallen trees up in the high woods. The Ferrer land needs a lot of work. It's been neglected for years since old man Alejandro became too feeble to maintain it.'

He placed one of his dominoes on the table with an assertive click and looked up at Julio. Not taking his eyes of Felipe for a second, Julio clacked down one of his own dominoes: 'I hope you're not working at Bernardo's in conservancy time,' he said cuttingly.

Felipe ignored Julio's remark and studied the two dominoes on the table. 'A double-five. My turn to lead.'

'Well?' Julio growled.

'Bernardo's dog put on quite a performance I have to admit. Have you ever noticed what horrible yellow eyes it's got? Scares the living daylights out of you, that dog. And the fence it's behind isn't that strong. No wonder the woman was scared. It's only chicken wire.'

'Well? Get to the point about Señora Berens,' Julio challenged frowning, reordering his stake of dominoes into two rows of small black dykes.

'The woman, Señora Berens, was walking down the path with her dog when Bernardo's dog put on its performance. I watched, hidden behind some orchard trees, and as she drew level she took a revolver out of her jacket pocket, aimed, fired and shot the beast. I tell you, it was chilling.'

In the shocked silence after Felipe spoke, Luisa heard the hissing fire, the rain spattering against the windows, then Julio's low grunt: '¡Dios! Then what happened?'

'Then nothing, *nada mas* . . . she just put the gun back in her pocket and walked away.'

'*¡Jesus!* what d'you do then?' Julio got up and started pacing about, a wild distressed look on his face. 'Did anyone else see this?' he asked anxiously, going to stand over Felipe. 'Well?' he demanded: 'who else saw it?'

Felipe grinned stupidly, like a non-swimmer, Luisa thought, who has just realised he can't touch the sea bed with his feet. 'No one else saw it,' he said disdainfully. 'No one but me.'

Julio took Felipe by the shoulders. 'Then?' he persisted, drawing him up by his jacket to stand facing him. 'And then what happened?' His fist was clenched ready to deliver a punch.

'Then nothing much. I dug a pit on Bernardo's land and buried the brute.'

Luisa's thoughts raced . . . it might break free, maim a child . . . she'd been terrified by the dog herself, yet, for all she sympathised with Anita over the disturbance of peace at her orchard, it seemed scarcely believable that she had actually *shot* the brute through the fence. Had she flipped? You just didn't do that sort of thing in a small country town.

The men lowered their voices so that she had to strain to hear Felipe when he sat down again. Suddenly she felt chilled through, yet she had to hear this out.

'I'm the only witness. And I tell you what, I won't spill the beans, you can have the bird for all I care. Señora Berens is a scraggy hen, far too old for me, but in exchange for my silence I want a different kind of bird.'

Julio almost spat out, 'what bird?' Then it dawned on him: 'A conservancy bird? Which one? The eagle? Aquila? You've got to be joking, kiddo. D'you know how much that bird is worth?'

'A lot more than it was worth before I trained it from an eyas! *Vale*, it's your choice,' Felipe smirked. 'If I don't get the bird I'll make a police report about the killing and that woman'll be in the shit.'

How odious Felipe can be, and nothing if not cunning, Luisa thought. I suppose he'll go far one day running his own flight centre. Only now the truth was out, she would like to end this shocking vigil. Tiptoeing back to the den, she made a point of banging the door as if she had just arrived that minute, then summoning jauntiness into her footsteps, she marched down the hall into the presence of the men.

'*¡Hola!* Julio, Felipe! It's me.' Brightly, forcing a smile, she stepped into the refectory.

They turned to her like guilty schoolboys, their faces deadpan as they stood warming their backsides at the blazing fire.

'If you're thinking of flying the birds today, think again, Felipe. It's pissing down out there.'

She made a show of shaking out her waterproofs, ran her hands through her hair and went coolly to stand beside them in the fire's warm ambit, aware of their astonished eyes. '*Hace mal tiempo!*' she repeated for emphasis. 'The rain's on for the day.'

They stared at her thoughtfully; had she heard anything of their diatribe, they must be wondering? Then Julio rubbed his hands together and said, 'yes, a pity about the weather. We'll be off then. I've another appointment with Don Nicolas.' As he picked his jacket off the bench, Luisa almost blurted out, can I come with you, meet the Don, too? A flicker of confusion must have passed across her face. 'Is everything okay?' Julio said kindly and when she nodded, 'then I'll see you tomorrow morning, *vale*?' he said, running into the rain, leaving the door ajar.

Felipe lingered, insouciant, looking her up and down: 'I think you should introduce *el caballero* Valente to the bird that lives beside you in the town.'

Hiding her fury, Luisa searched for a response.

'Julio fancies the blonde bird,' Felipe added cheekily as if he was talking to a dimwit.

Luisa pointed straight to the door. 'Get out!' she said fiercely. 'Señora Berens is a *woman* not a bird!'

Dancing a side-step, mocking her with a grin, he pulled on his cap. It took every particle of her strength to reign-in her temper, to prevent herself from kicking his backside before he sauntered out and she bolted the door behind him. Hearing them driving away, great, good riddance, she thought. Anita and Julio? Who cares. I'm fed up hearing about Anita Berens.

Anita and Felipe! Anita and Julio! Anita and the dog! Anita this, Anita that. My God, you'd think up here in the mountains, so far from *anywhere*, I'd be well out of her orbit hearing not so much as a whisper about the shadows she seems bent on casting.

The relentless rain poured over the roof and spilled down the eaves, splashing the windows, entering Ca'n Clot under the refectory door in solemn puddles. That evening, she took the large shovel and dug glowing embers out of the still lively fire in the refectory. She might as well enjoy the relative comfort of the den to prepare for the Palma lecture. Nothing taxing, just an illustrated talk to students, she reassured herself.

The red hot logs in her shovel briefly illuminated the dark passageway as she passed through, and suddenly she felt lonely rather than blessedly alone. It was something to do with people wandering about, the disconcerting neighbour and his mysterious assistant, Felipe and Anita, and who or what would appear on the mountain next? Felipe's unremitting sullenness, and now his lies, were way too much. The notion that he had, if not read, then at least dared to open her private notebook, that he had held the photograph between his fingers and *looked* at it upset her far more than anything to do with Anita Berens. Felipe was a snoop. Fine, she resolved, from now on I lock *all* my personal things in the filing cabinet along with Rafael's blue case.

Fiery embers lay on the grate. She piled on mixed logs of carob, almond and olive wood, opened all the controls of the stove, then sat staring at the erupting flames. She thought about the eerily primitive bird trappers' den and her encounter with Don Nicolas. She superimposed his face upon the dancing flames and stared at his fierce amused expression, willing it to come . . . *los muertos abren los ojos de los que viven* . . . and there it was, the epigraph to a poem halfway down a page in a collected works of Scottish poets she had borrowed from the British Council library in Barcelona. A poem entitled 'Perfect'. Hugh MacDiarmid's homage to the Spanish Civil War that had somehow lodged in her brain as a tribute to her own grandfather who had been murdered in that same war. Skulls of resistance fighters. Skulls of dead birds. All perfect, 'without a crack or a flaw anywhere', as the poet observed. Would it ever be possible to explain to the neighbour who shared the dark mountain the startling coincidence of what he had said and how deeply his words had affected her?

8

The elegant bronze head of a bull labelled 'third century BC Roman Pollentia (now Mallorcan Pollensa)' drew her admiring gaze, but nowhere could she find the bull statuette excavated at the site Raúl Caubet called the Bull Mountain. She had searched the vault of the museum in Palma as efficiently as time allowed, passed through chambers dedicated to the island's history, her imagination roused by amphorae, bead necklaces and strange warrior figures less than a foot high. Eventually she gave up on the bull, but found in the display cabinets of the Islamic rooms decorated ceramic bowls, jars and heavy stone lintels deeply carved with Arabic orations.

Has Felipe Tamarit seen *these*? she wondered ironically. Surely these objects would fuel his passion for the island's Moorish past, she thought as she climbed the wide staircase in the courtyard to see the religious art. She knew she would have to confront him soon. Yet, if I face him with his deviousness, wouldn't that just feed his need to triumph over me? And, entering a new gallery, she decided her energy was too precious to waste on him.

Here were vividly painted panels that reminded her of the ones Rafael had shown her, but, apart from the fragment of a fresco, an image of men rowing a boat across the Mediterranean during the Conquest, the collection of Romanesque art here held nothing to match the art in Barcelona.

Before she went out into the sheet-like rain, still pouring down beyond the museum's grand entrance, she asked a bespectacled, nervy custodian about the missing bull.

'I think we must have loaned it to the National Museum of Madrid, señora,' he said, dancing a little in front of her as if he had been waiting a very long time to be asked such a question. 'You are English?' he added curiously.

'No, I'm from Scotland.'

That made him even more excited. Flourishing his hands in the air he said: 'I want to go to your country. I have seen a film of a castle on a lake where Spanish soldiers lived in old times.' He spoke in English, though so poorly she responded in Spanish. She happened to know he referred to Eilean Donan, that romantic loch-girt castle near Dornie. Once, on a trip to the west coast, she and Dan had been impressed by the story of the Spanish soldiers billeted in the castle during the Jacobite rising of 1719.

'A hill near the castle is named after them, *Sgurr nan Spainteach*,' she told the man, and, at his insistence, she wrote down the Gaelic name: 'You pronounce it Spain-*tach*,' she said. 'I hope you *will* come to Scotland one day,' she added, selecting her umbrella from others dripping small puddles near the entrance.

'If only I had enough money and enough time, señora!' the custodian exclaimed then put on an odd little performance, pointing to the ceiling with one hand, pulling a mournful face and giving a little kick in the air with his foot. She interpreted his gesture sympathetically; he feels trapped in a badly paid job by his bosses upstairs whom he'd like to kick.

The museum stood in a dark cavernous street, now transformed to a shallow river by ceaselessly tumbling rain. A labyrinth of a place, she thought, soon getting lost in the ancient *barrio*. If I keep to the left I should reach the old city walls, parallel to the sea, she reckoned, and, slipping through streets with evocative names like Posada del Mar and Torre de Amor, sure enough she did. The rain stopped and she followed the ancient city walls towards the cathedral, so magnificent on its elevated site overlooking the bay of Palma, she could hardly keep her eyes off it. And when small hawks came wheeling out above the spires she thought of the drying green at the Barcelona flat with a surge of nostalgia. Ah, so, you are here too, *Falco naumanni*, my companions in the city of *voladores*. When she reached El Borne, the long tree-lined street where jousting tournaments had once been held (according to the guide book she carried) she found a taxi to take her to the station.

The Palma lecture had gone well. In addition to the students, several members of the island's most important environmental group had come to hear her. As an afterword to her own lecture (titled *The Habitat of the Black Vulture* and illustrated with slides she'd found in the den) she had praised the work of the island's ornithologists in preserving the species. And, in a rehearsal of sorts for the forthcoming Alejandro Ferrer memorial talk (not far off and increasingly nagging at the back of her mind), she had put forward perceptions that had come to her unexpectedly in the train that morning.

Thoughts as well as actions are physical *things, registered as such in every cell of our bodies as well as in the bodies of birds and animals. Whenever we are cruel to each other - or to animals - that negative energy registers in every cell,* in every one of millions of cells, *including our brain cells. The result is that we become sick, both as individuals and as societies.*

There had been a hush in the hall after she said these bold words, yet the eager faces of her audience encouraged her to carry on.

Chaos is another word for this sickness. On a social level you are seeing that now in the breakdown of Mallorcan family units, in the huge influx of immigrants who flee here from evil regimes in South America and Africa, in the destruction of large parts of this beautiful island's environment and ecosystems. Now it's time for us as scientists to consider how to recreate a sane society here in Mallorca. This is not an unrealistic aim. We already have the example of the island's environmental groups who intervened to turn around ignorant government policies that, in the past, rewarded the killing of vultures and birds of prey, *and who have succeeded in reviving the near-extinct vulture population to almost two hundred birds.*

Afterwards she had taken a taxi to the museum. All in all, it had been a worthwhile day. Added to that, the plastic bag on her lap contained the developed films of the ravens and vultures at Julio's hide, and an extra set for him.

Tonight the Inca train carries office workers and shop assistants back to the country towns. Women mostly, young girls

199

and middle-aged women dressed in winter shades of brown, grey and black, some reading magazines, others dozing. Shop assistants, office workers, she supposes. A few people chat in low voices. Most seem wrapped up in themselves. One or two blow their noses; the season of colds and 'flu has arrived. The carriage window acts as a mirror reflecting the weary travellers against the dark world outside. She catches an unflattering glimpse of herself, haggard and drained of colour under the neon strip lights on the ceiling and looks away.

Far from being disappointed not to have found the bull or paintings to match the Master of Pedret's, she feels she has absorbed a rich slice of Mallorca's history in that hour or two at the museum. And, yes, she affirms, knowledge of a place's history changes the way you think about it. Startlingly so, just as familiarity with its wildlife does.

More people fill the carriage, strangers like herself, only exotic. Tall young African men with skins like black tulips. Then a group of smaller, ragged, older men speaking Arabic. Three of them sit gratefully round her in the only seats left. The others stand, holding onto the leather straps, their faces deadpan beside the radiant young Africans. Immigrants from Morocco, she thinks, too tired to meet their soulful gazes.

At last the train pulls out, and the tedious night journey begins. When she closes her eyes, almost unconsciously her thoughts return to that still-undissolved kernel in her brain. Walking across the sands, burying the little auk. And, damn it! she cannot quash insistent motifs from the *Rosamunde* overture, its regular opening beat somehow emphasising residual elements of loss dredged up, she supposed, by her present state of exhaustion. Footsteps in the snow, leading to another life in Barcelona, then, on and on, to this here and now.

She opened her eyes and unthinkingly gave one of the Arabs a fleeting smile. He didn't smile back, but solemnly nodded in recognition of her gesture. After that, she didn't know where to fix her eyes, and soon closed them again, drifting in and out of un-orchestrated thoughts. The little auk, the buzzard's skull. Tender anguish, anguished tenderness. Guitar music at the bird trap. I long to meet Nicolas again. I crave physical love. I'm too much in my head. Yes, I need new music now; otherworldly, suggesting the whirr of wings, the return of humankind's lost yet noble spirit. It's the twenty-first century after all and there's a dangerous world out there where people are maimed and killed like birds in the nets, and refugees spill out of their own countries into any others that will take them. Proud people who had homes and status once upon a time are condemned to poverty and to labour in lands whose language . . . *music*, since isn't language a form of human music? . . they must learn as part of their survival technique.

At the first station, people get off, exchanging their seats with the newly arrived. She recalls Rosa Sanchez's touching appearance at the station the last time she made this journey. Perhaps she would never see Rosa again? After all, it was unlikely she herself would ever cross the threshold of the Tamarit clan. It was then a disruptive homunculus lodged itself in her half-dreaming brain. A tiny Anita strutting round the mountains, gesticulating, jumping off rocks, falling, shouting . . . trying to attract my attention.

Her watch read six forty-five . . . Julio will be at the station to meet me . . . I'll be at Calle Luna in an hour, and tomorrow I'll walk up to Ca'n Clot. Should I call on her this evening? Momentarily she wondered, then decided, no. Absolutely no more distractions from my field work until the village trek. Oh, except for Señor Bigatti's visit.

Beyond the window, it was as if the dark countryside had ceased to exist. Her own reflected face appeared again, distorted in the window, an unlikely element in a group photograph - herself with three weary Arabs, a couple of standing Senegalese, and two rather sedate Mallorcan matrons - and she smiled inwardly. If Dan, who had never been further south than Doncaster, could see me now! How amazing it is to be here rather than in predictable old Scotland, being hurled in a machine through the night with these exotic strangers. What on earth can be on their minds, exiles like me? Have they villages back home, wives and children, neighbours and friends? What have their journeys been like across deserts and rivers and seas, days and weeks of discomfort and danger . . . even more so than Rosa . . . to get themselves here?

Her eyes shut against the bright light, the fug and the people in the carriage, she wanted to doze off, but a poignant vignette of Anita's distant figure in the mountains, upset, yet evidently taking a stand against Felipe's bullishness, haunted her. And, forcibly, it struck her; if Felipe was capable of inventing a sex scene with her, he could have invented the story about Anita shooting the dog too, to wind Julio up. After all, in both cases, Felipe was the only witness.

A few hours later, hearing something unusual, Luisa wakens with a start and decides she must have had a dream of old Alejandro sobbing through the walls . . . only Alejandro is *dead*, she chides herself and drifts back into sleep.

Giddily she goes, pacing the kitchen past midnight. A caged animal when she yells out '*hijo de puta*' and her rage rebounds off the thick walls, up the stone staircase, to the very roof of the house. And, in the shocked aftermath her thoughts run riot, her fists want to beat the whitewashed walls: *Andreas Herreros has done this to me* . . . here in this Godforsaken town, again I'm in a prison of his making *for who knows at precisely which moment he will send them to find me?*

Better get it over with, slit my wrists, swallow the pills. Or get out of this house. Find someone to help me. Luisa Ross is the only person who can. That black brute of a dog coming at me with its menacing growl, its bared fangs, out on the path. Only, now I know *who let the dog out in the first place*.

Wrapped in the cocoon of her eiderdown Luisa had considered not responding to the insistent knocking that wakened her a few minutes later. But she couldn't ignore it when it came again, and, even before she pulled on her sweater over her pyjamas and went downstairs, she knew Anita Berens would be waiting on the other side of the door. There she was, forlorn in the lamp-lit street, huddled in her white coat like the Griffon vulture in Ca'n Clot's aviary.

'I'm sorry,' Anita said, her hands wringing anxiously. 'You were asleep? Julio . . . I bumped into Julio in the church square this afternoon. He told me you'd be staying in town tonight.'

Resolving to reprimand Julio – in future, please *do not* divulge my movements to *anyone* in town, not even to Anita Berens – Luisa manages a gesture of welcome, and Anita, shrugging off her coat, fetches a white handkerchief from its pocket with a rattle of gold bracelets. A whiff of perfume. Expensive, probably French. Stifling her irritation, Luisa hangs the coat on the row of pegs beside the kitchen door. Cashmere with a yellow silk lining beside my own green waxed jacket. What different worlds we do inhabit. Wordlessly she leads the way through to the sitting room where Anita goes to lean against Frau Lehmann's worn leather armchair.

'Has Colin gone, then?'

'Yes, three days ago.'

'You must miss him.'

Anita stands massaging her upper arms with slow sad movements as if to warm herself. It does, after all, feel cold in the room.

'Why don't you sit down?' Luisa says, kneeling to coax life into the fire. Anita Berens is in a terrible state. Eyelids swollen from weeping, hair awry, and, without make-up she looks years older. Her back turned to Anita, she searches for something to say. They had been speaking English, yet they were both bilingual, and she supposed the precedent in favour of English had been set the night they had dinner with Colin.

Displacement talk in Spanish, she calculates, might help Anita Berens to unwind so she says: 'The train journey was pretty unpleasant tonight. Not like during the day when you see the mountain range and that heavenly countryside. People speak to you by day, but not at night. There were a lot of Africans and Arabs on the train. I was amazed.'

She had mentioned this to Julio who had been waiting at the station to drive her back to town. In recent years there had been a huge influx of immigrant men, he explained, to work in the construction industry and in agriculture, in fields of potatoes, artichokes, melons and beans, east of Inca. So many Mallorcans had become wealthy in recent decades, the last thing they wanted to do was work on the land like their toiling ancestors. Palma and the towns were flooded with women too, mainly South Americans, engaged as au pairs, companions to the sick and elderly and cleaners of homes, offices and restaurants.

All this she told to Anita, glancing at her over her shoulder, thinking the woman needs help . . . presumably she did kill the dog . . . .

'It seems Mallorca's full of exiles, immigrants refugees; at the station a couple of weeks ago, for instance, I met a woman from Colombia,' Luisa says, sinking into the armchair opposite Anita's. 'It was fascinating, though disturbing, to hear her story. I know nothing about Colombia.'

Anita rummages nervously in her handbag, pulls out a packet of cigarettes, then a lighter.

'I wouldn't even know where to put that country - Colombia - on a map of South America,' Luisa goes on. 'But now I intend to make it my business to know where these places are. Anyway, the woman . . . her name was Rosa Sanchez . . . told me she had lived in fear of her life in a mountain town in Colombia. She told me the country was overrun with killers and thieves. *Campesinos* were killed frequently and indiscriminately, she said, and the bodies of her friends and neighbours had been found dumped in caves near her town. How does anyone get over such a hellish experience?'

Is this some sort of a sick joke, Luisa Ross? Christ in Heaven! Am I supposed to listen to a story about someone from *Colombia*? Let me out of here! *Rewind* . . . then *Play*.

She feels she might suffocate, fights for breath. The past half-an-hour flashes onto the screen of her mind. Scenes of herself, or rather of Anita Berens, making a frantic exit from this room, backing out of this room, regaining her coat, backing out through Luisa Ross's front door, knocking on it, backing in through her own door, and shutting it, closing it firmly, then pacing up and down, back and forth, in her own kitchen, wondering whether to risk coming to Luisa at all when she might well be on the edge of a nervous breakdown. It would have been easier to swallow the pills.

'Colombia?' Anita exclaims, her voice cool and flat.

Even as she resolves to leave as soon as possible she recognises her own paranoia; this Rosa person *isn't* someone sent by the Extraditables. Still Luisa's story unnerves her. Forced to listen until the story ends with this Rosa's unshed tears, the red rose in her hair, the pool of urine, she thinks, someone else on the run . . . nothing to do with me . . . but oh, how I envy this Rosa Sanchez. At least she's free to move around Mallorca or anywhere else she chooses to go.

When Luisa asks, would you like a brandy? I wonder if she notices the tears glistening in *my* eyes. Lourdes Herreros - to whom self-pity was once an alien condition - *just can't take anymore.*

She fumbles with a trembling hand to light the cigarette between her fingers. 'Yes, thanks,' she says: 'I'd love a brandy.'

Rich bitch, Luisa thinks, then intensely dislikes herself for the thought as she goes to the kitchen to fetch the brandy bottle.

Oh, yes, Luisa Ross. I would like to be able to describe areas of Colombia in the grip of criminal gangs. *'You feel it, Señora Herreros? That's the gun that'll do the job if necessary. We're coming to a police checkpoint. If you move or say anything, we'll kill you.'*

Anita sits stiffly, puffing at her cigarette in the still-cold, graceless room where the clock mercilessly ticks off the passing seconds, her nervous exhaustion heightened by the cruel association of terrible memories with killing the dog. *The barrel of a revolver pressed into my back, my head still held in the stinking lap, I thought I might suffocate.*

If only I could risk telling Luisa Ross the truth about who I am. It would amaze her that I, Lourdes Herreros, could put Colombia on a map of South America with my eyes closed.

Then the man realised you were clutching your bag, the green mock-lizard, how well I remember.

'Hand that bag over,' he demanded.

You begged for a few seconds to get some things out. Lavender oil, tissues, Angel Zavala's plastic crucifix.

Frau Lehmann's handsome German grandfather clock chimes out the hour of midnight through the silent house.

Luisa returns: 'What did you decide about the *Queja Vecinal*, Anita?' She hands her one of the glasses: 'Have you complained to the local police about the dog yet?'

Anita's mind whirls back to her own kitchen, putting on her coat to come here. Police! Christ! Where is Luisa Ross coming from! She lifts a cushion off the armchair and clings to it, hoping not to break down. Luisa Ross is waiting for me to answer her question, watching me, under the hollow ticking of the moonfaced clock.

Luisa, in the big armchair, hugging her knees to her chest, prays this drama will soon be over.

Suddenly reverting to English, Anita says crisply: 'A *Queja* would be useless now. It's far too late for formal complaints.'

She feels more assertive in English, Luisa thinks.

'The dog's dead,' Anita said flatly. 'It tried to attack me and I had to shoot it.'

Anita clinging to the cushion, rocking a little, her hand covering her mouth. Anita preventing herself from sobbing. A neurotic woman who keeps a gun. I'm out of my depth, not very good at this sort of thing, Luisa thinks wildly. The thing is . . . keep talking to her with kindly concern. Acquiescing to the shift of language, Luisa says: 'It tried to *attack* you? You mean it wasn't in its enclosure?'

'No, it was out on the path . . . I was walking towards my finca . . . like you did that Sunday. The brute was suddenly at my heels . . . I'm *so sorry*, Luisa. To disturb you like this. Only I've been so afraid someone from the town would come to accuse me, arrest me, or I know not what.'

Anita's head went down, her shoulders heaved with deep sobs and Luisa suddenly reinhabited her own state of despair after her sister died. She uncurled in her chair, filled with the pain of remembering. *And I was too shocked for tears. And I, without mother or sister must live alone with Harry Ross and dam up my tears. Grief, said my father, was something to be borne and not discussed.* All that was a very long time ago, and now I know it, grief needs to be discussed.

'You were right to come here,' Luisa said, going to sit on the arm of Anita's chair. Felipe Tamarit's version of the story had been wide of the mark.

'It must have been terrible,' Luisa went on, laying a hand on Anita's arm. 'You don't have to worry about the town reacting to what you did. Everyone in the bar was convinced that dog would attack someone one day. The owner, Bernardo's away at the moment as you know. They'll be glad his dog's disappeared, so why should you worry? Look, why don't you tell me exactly what happened?'

Anita wiped her face with her handkerchief, and still clinging to the cushion, burst out with a little laugh: 'I haven't been able to tell a soul!'

'You can tell me now,' Luisa encouraged.

'Well, at first I walked on steadily, struggling to stay calm, not to show fear, yet feeling its breath on my legs, hearing its low growling, seeing its bared fangs. Then it started to growl viciously. My period had started. Did you know that dogs are attracted to menstruating women? They *smell* the blood. I was sure it was about to attack me.'

Hiding her astonishment, Luisa nodded.

'Well, for a few seconds I just stood there, paralysed. There seemed no way out . . . no fence low enough to jump over . . . no one to call out to.' Anita looked up at the ceiling, as if to find words there. Hesitantly she said, 'there was nothing else for it . . . I took my revolver out of my pocket, spun round, aimed between its eyes and fired.'

Luisa fumbled her way back to her own chair. How revolting it must feel to kill an animal, especially one as large as that dog. '*Your* gun? You have a *gun*?' she said. 'But why? How come? Where did you learn to shoot?' She wanted to see, to touch, this gun.

Setting aside the cushion, Anita drained her glass. 'When I was young I took part in hunting - deer mostly - at a cousin's estate in Germany.' Her voice was low, but measured now. 'My grandmother was Dutch, my mother half-Dutch and half-Spanish. Shooting birds and animals was all part of the lifestyle when I was growing up, though now I find the so-called sport quite odious.'

That's all true! Anita thought, amazed by her sudden, vivid recall of the woods beyond the landscaped park of her uncle's estate near Hamburg. This I can tell Luisa Ross with no fear whatsoever. Family and friends in tweed hacking jackets, plus-fours, Scottish brogues, the women sporting Hermés scarves. Leaves the colour of russet, red and gold scattered like potpourri on the brown earth. What laughter, what *civility* when, after the shoot, we enjoyed a cold buffet washed down with champagne in the gamekeeper's lodge. Although, later, as I grew older, how appalled I was by the slaughter of birds and animals we took for granted in those days.

'Do you know,' Anita went on, forcing a smile. 'One of my great-uncles - he had these enormous drooping whiskers fashionable at the time - demanded of his gamekeeper: "Where are all the birds that used to come to my estates?" Had they flown off somewhere else? Where were the herons, the swans, the peregrine? "You've shot them all, sir," the gamekeeper suggested and uncle was shocked. He thought that you could shoot as many birds as you fancied and *instantly* more would fly in to replace them.'

Luisa nodded with wry amusement. Victorian lairds of Scottish estates had believed exactly the same as Anita's relative. Anita smiled wanly. How good it was to be able to offer someone a *true* slice of my biography instead of all these Anita Berens lies!

'Let me get it right? You say Bernardo's dog was *on the path?*'

'Of course, someone let it out.'

Yes, and I think I know who. Luisa could picture it only too well: Felipe standing by, doing nothing, *letting* Anita go through this nightmare, *watching* all this, hidden among the trees of Bernardo's finca. Why, oh why, hadn't he rushed to her assistance, rounded up the dog and closed the gate on it? Why had he left the gate open in the first place? For a start, that path is practically never used, Luisa thought. Maddened as she was by that part of herself that sought to absolve her colleague, she couldn't believe he had *planned* this. Felipe never dreamed anyone would come down the path, that must be it, so he didn't think it was necessary to close the gate. After that, things must've happened so fast . . . and Anita's action was not only entirely justified, but necessary. No doubt about it, Anita had killed the dog in self-defence.

'Go on,' Luisa encouraged. 'What happened then?'

'Well, numbed by what I'd done, I rushed to my own finca. But it was no use running away. I had to go back and do something about the carcass, couldn't just leave it lying on the path.'

If you had, Luisa thought wryly, the vulture pair would've been at it in no time at all.

'Half-an-hour or so later I forced myself back, but the dog had disappeared and the gate was closed. Apart from spots of blood on the earth, no one would have suspected anything had happened.'

'Only *someone* must have seen it, the person who got rid of the dead dog so quickly, someone must know?'

Anita looked away, her eyes cast down, and the clock ticked on.

'What were you doing in the mountains with Felipe?' Luisa said. 'Quite by chance, I saw the two of you through my binoculars the other day when I was patrolling the ridge above the road through the pass. Felipe seemed pretty upset. So did you.'

Anita twisted the handkerchief in her hands and closed her eyes as if this new turn the story was taking was more than she could bear. Yet, after a deep sigh she said with patient determination: 'Felipe Tamarit telephoned me and asked me to drive up beyond Casas Viejas, and to keep going along the track until I met him . . . then, he said, he would drive me to a place where we could discuss the dog.'

She spoke slowly, now and then biting her lower lip: 'He was the one who removed the dead dog . . . he knew all about the shooting, he said, and, if I didn't agree to meet him, pretty soon everyone in town would know, too. It wasn't a pleasant meeting.'

'But what was he after, what were you arguing about?'

'He told me no one would believe the dog had been on the path, that he'd say he'd seen me kill it *through the fence* before I walked away. And, that as soon as I'd gone, he'd buried the brute in Bernardo's grounds. He was ready to tell this story in the town if I didn't do what he suggested.' Anita's head tilted back defiantly: 'He was attempting to blackmail me.'

'You can't be serious . . . he actually asked you for *money*?'

Anita managed a weak smile: 'Miserable bugger, isn't he? He told me he needed money to set up a bird flight centre. I told him he could just f- off.'

Luisa got up to put another log on the fire, and decided to risk confiding, '*Julio* knows you killed the dog.'

'Julio? Julio didn't say anything to me this afternoon.' Anita stiffened as if she might lose control again. 'If *Julio* knows, how can I be certain that no one *else* knows, that Felipe hasn't blabbed to the whole town?'

Luisa fell silent, playing for time to make sense of this melodrama that involved the men she worked alongside.

'When the money gambit didn't work,' Anita said, 'he told me he'd keep silent *if* I had an affair with Julio Valente. It was my choice. Work that one out, Luisa. I couldn't. I came back to town more confused than ever.'

She could work it out only too well. Felipe would stoop to anything to get Aquila. The bird he had trained from an eyas that would be the first performer in his private bird world. She gave Anita an edited version of the conversation she had overheard at Ca'n Clot, including Julio's declaration of attraction to Anita and Felipe's attempt to blackmail Julio into giving him the bird.

And that seemed to cheer her up. Anita pulled her shoulders back and pushed her hair off her face with a graceful sweep of her adorned arms and her mouth curved with a little laugh. 'No one's ever offered to exchange me for a bird before.' Smoothing out her black velvet skirt with brisk movements of her hand, she said: 'D'you think he'll get the eagle?'

'That depends how events unfold.'

Anita frowned: 'I hardly know Julio.'

'Perhaps, but that's not the point. Felipe was trading on the fact that Julio had declared his interest in *you*.'

'Felipe made me *really* livid. Between ourselves I do have a sneaking attraction to Julio, only, *never* would I start an affair with him just to shake off Felipe Tamarit! That he could even think such a thing . . . oh, it's quite ridiculous.'

The men's private lives are no concern of mine, Luisa thought, and, getting to her feet she said: 'Look, don't worry, I'll find a way to let Felipe know that I know *he*'s the guilty party. *He* left the gate open, carelessly, accidentally, the reason doesn't matter. Only, it's quite clear you shot the dog in self-defence.'

'Oh! You believe me?' Anita blurted out. 'Oh, that's such a relief.'

At that moment Luisa warmed towards her neighbour. 'Of course. Anyone would be on your side.' Then admitting her fascination for Anita's gun she said, 'do you have it with you? . . . the gun. Can I see it?'

Anita looked uncertain before she fumbled in her bag. Cautiously she drew a revolver out of a brown velvet pouch and Luisa took it, finding the thing surprisingly light and dry to the touch, not the heavy, ugly, cold thing she had expected. She turned it over, fascinated by its walnut handle, its elegant design and wondered, how can you tell if there are bullets inside?

'How do you use it?' she asked nervously, her fingers avoiding the trigger as she returned it to Anita who promised she'd show her another time. And, watching her put it away, Luisa decided not to put her neighbour on the spot by asking again, why do you keep a gun? The real reason must wait for another day, she'd had enough for one night.

Stretching her arms, she yawned. 'Look, why don't we continue this conversation in the morning?' And, still sensing the imprint of the revolver on her palm where she had held it, she led the way through the kitchen.

'Felipe won't dare to say *anything* to anyone,' she added, handing Anita her coat. 'You're quite safe there. In fact you could *challenge* his story in your own self-defence.'

Anita stiffened: 'No, I can't do that. *It's* impossible. Please Luisa. I don't want to draw attention to myself, I only want a quiet life. One day you'll understand. I know I can trust you. I *can*, can't I?'

At that moment Luisa was struck with sudden certainty: Anita . . . *Lourdes?* . . . has far more to hide than this dog business.

'Wherever I go I have to trust *someone*,' Anita was saying. 'Don't ask for details, *please*. Just believe me. At any moment my life might be in danger and I *need* that revolver!'

Luisa felt she had plunged into a place where she had no business to be. In fact, she felt exhausted, and, determined to bring the night's drama to a conclusion, she said, 'don't worry, no one'll try to take it away.' And, when Anita suddenly turned to embrace her, she felt a rush of embarrassment. Awkwardly she drew away, saying, 'everything *will* be okay. Don't worry, Felipe daren't say anything in case you make a formal contradiction of his statement. You can trust *me* not to say anything, and Julio's lips are sealed. So, really, you have nothing to worry about. As far as Bernardo and the townsfolk are concerned, the dog has simply disappeared. It happens, you know.'

It happens you know . . . with people, *too.* In Colombia, for years *people* have disappeared without trace, just like animals.

How I, Lourdes, would have loved to have been able to say that last night. To confide in Luisa Ross. To take off the damned paper bag I've been wearing over my head all those lost months.

She was sitting on a high stool in the kitchen eating a bowl of muesli when Luisa knocked on the door and looked in. 'I won't come in, Anita, got to get going to Ca'n Clot, just wanted to make sure you're alright.'

'Yes, I'm fine.' Though her heavy body trails the troubling dreams of the previous night, she feels more at peace than for a very long time. 'Thanks for listening, thanks for your friendship, last night.'

'Let's speak Spanish together from now on, *vale?*' Luisa said grinning, backing out of the door. *'¡Hasta pronto!'* she called out, then she was gone at the same moment as the telephone rang in the salon. A fax was coming through.

Anita, she read, *You asked me about the person who owned your house before you came. He was an artist, French, but I'm afraid I cannot remember his name. He painted very well, large abstract oils mostly, but he was also what he called a 'concrete poet'. He used to publish exquisitely illustrated cards printed with plays on words in different languages like* Tempus fugit, *for example, and* Esprit de l'escalier. *I hope this is helpful. Hoping to see you when I come out in the summer, Yours, Gerda Lehmann.*

Tempus fugit, Esprit de l'escalier and *Carpe diem!* Anita laughs out loud, passing the mirror that is no longer a mirror but an *objet d'art*, concrete, minimal and pertinent. Two little words in Latin. *Carpe diem!* Seize the day! A bright patch of sunlight falls on the kitchen floor and she organises a basket of provisions to take out to the finca.

Luisa follows the track towards the plateau, the chalky day moon suspended above the summit of Massanella her constant companion. Soon the moon would be full. *Luna llena.* Soon she would open Rafael's blue case in her own private ceremony. Soon it would be her thirty-ninth birthday. And later, enfolded in Ca'n Clot's generous silence, she pins her timetable up on the cork board above her desk and mischievously fixes her sketch of Felipe, patron saint of swineherds beside it. Then she removes the Dutch hood from its hook, blows off the dust and decides to put it away in the filing cabinet. A talisman that belongs to the past, only she wonders with a jolt of surprise, why does it bring Anita to mind? Anita is like an exotic bird waiting for its hood to be struck, is that it? What is she hiding from? What secrets? Why the gun, why the fear? Why do I have the sense

213

that she's trapped in her house in Calle Luna? All I know of her life so far is sketchy. A few exotic locations casually marked down as if on the back of a paper napkin. Her childhood spent in Holland and Germany, her well travelled adult life as a writer in 'Spanish-speaking countries' as she said, New York, where her grown-up daughter called Elena lives and London where her friend Colin Cramer runs his magazine.

At dawn the following day, she stands at the treeless summit of the crag they call El Escarpado de las Cuevas Negras listening to the wind soughing through the pine woods below. For a while, at least, the wind has blown *la borrasca* away. The day before she found the nest of the vulture pair, its ballooning twigs easily visible among the pine trees below. She has found the focal point of her field study, as if it had been the spot marked with an 'X' on a treasure map.

Leaning into the swirling wind, eyes half-closed, she rejoices to be so far removed from the demented world on the plain below. *I must cease to think of Don Nicolas . . . he will have a wife, of course, and several children, all waiting to arrive at their new home . . . .*

There is no sign of a vulture, but she takes up her field glasses to focus on the dark, distant buzzard she's spotted waiting in the top branches of a tall pine to catch a ride on the next convenient air current. *Buteo buteo: medium-sized raptor, widespread resident in Mallorca, favours wooded areas.* And when the expected gust comes, her lenses trace the bird's *glissando* in the direction of Casas Viejas, and hearing its mewing screech that sends shivers through the airwaves, she imagines the tremulous stir its v-shaped wings are raising over the treetops. Designs and patterns in space and time, in a universe pulsating with energy. Soundings from uncanny spheres it is her business to investigate.

When a buzzard shrieks and flies across the face of the rising sun it announces a course of action to every living creature who witnesses its aerodynamics from the camouflage of the woods. To every witness the flight is a cue, a message rich with meaning. Avian intelligence. The

214

time and direction of the flight determines each reaction the bird makes, triggers each and every individual response of all the creatures in the watching and listening bird community, as well as my own.

The development of the buzzard's screech motif comes, faint as it rings up towards airborne prey. Hushed in the cover of branches and undergrowth, alarmed warblers and finches stay silent. It's a matter of survival to wait patiently until the buzzard has found its meal further down the mountainside before breaking into song. Then out of the woods into the hushed morning three ravens ignore the buzzard, wings flapping brazenly in search of breakfast. *Cronk! cronk!* they call. Gods in the disguise of birds. *Voladores*, flyers putting on their aerobatic display, their comic mid-air tumbling and rolling.

Enthralled, she watches until hunger pangs drive her back to the finca for her own breakfast. A little later, Julio and Felipe arrive, but their activities need not concern her as, purposefully, she carries on typing notes into the computer. An island wildlife group has sought her co-operation in helping to locate abandoned vulture nests, Julio's 'historical sites'. So far she has had no luck in finding any others than the one Julio showed her, one they already know about. But now she sends the organisation an e-mail describing her discovery of the active vulture nest on the other side of Cuevas Negras.

Towards midmorning, out and about, she hears the gate of the weathering flapping in the wind. Drawn to it, she finds Felipe with Aquila attached to his gauntlet wearing the Bahraini hood, the pointer stretched elegantly at his feet.

'Will you help me fly the little eagle again?'

Meeting his eyes she shakes her head. Impossible not to think of Anita's trauma, his lies to Julio and his invasion of her notebook, and she can't contain herself: 'You are nothing but a common liar, thief and snoop. You should be ashamed of yourself.'

'Way, hey!' he says, retreating, holding the palm of his free hand out as if to defend himself. 'What's got into you?'

'If you don't know, you're beyond hope,' she says cuttingly and walks on past him.

In one of the pens she sees the Egyptian vulture tearing the red meat under her talons; the kite next door ravages a small gory bone.

'Anything you might happen to know is not your business,' he retorts, watching her retreat.

'And what about my notebook and the photograph?' She turns to face him, judging it wise to settle her own score and leave Anita out of it for the time being.

Fussing with Aquila's jesse, 'I'm over it now,' he says stiffly. But when you came back, I thought . . . .' He paused, pulling back his shoulders. 'I was *angry*. Wanted to know if you'd had a bloke in Barcelona.' He avoids her eyes. 'Okay, so I'm sorry I went into the den, looked at some things when you weren't around.'

He passes her a feather from his pocket and, stirred by the delicacy of his act of contrition, she uses it to stroke Aquila's back. He stands very still with the bird on his arm, chooses his words carefully. 'I've given it a lot of thought . . . it's hopeless trying to train Aquila up here without assistance.'

He frowns, and, despite what she has recently heard from Anita Berens, the more noble part of Felipe's nature re-engages her; the part of him that had been willing to spend hour after hour training this once wild bird, first to eat off his gloved fist, then to jump to his fist, to fly on the creance and back to the fist, to respond to the rabbit lure and, at last, to fly free. How well she remembers, Aquila reaching that stage the day Felipe asked for her help on the crag. The day her own spirit had somehow taken flight.

'I haven't the time to train her to follow on,' he says regretfully; 'to respond to a whistle as we go, from tree to tree, over the landscape, and, hopefully, to start chasing game and not just rely on food off my fist. So if you can't help, next week I'll have to take her to an austringer on the other side of the mountains. Near Valldemossa, where the Arab princes hunted with hawks before the Conquest of Mallorca.'

He crouches down, stretches out his arm and Aquila, hooded in her dark silence, obligingly steps up onto the side of her carrying case. He attaches her to the cadge and hoists it up by its strap onto his shoulder.

Her mind flirts momentarily with words that suggest his lost Arab world, *juz d'Inken, aylmeris, azahar* and the Bahraini hood, the most favoured hood of the Arabs for their *shaheens*, or peregrines. Will Aquila ever return to Ca'n Clot, or will the bird side-step neatly into Felipe's dream, his private bird centre?

'Does Julio know your plan?'

'He grumbled a lot when I told him, but he's agreed. After a lot of persuasion, he's made me sign a form that guarantees the bird will come back.'

Ah, so the astute Julio has reached a compromise with his cunning colleague.

'How's the timber felling going?' she says, changing the subject.

'I'll be glad when it's over.'

Attracted at that moment by the pointer's soulful eyes, Luisa bends down to make a fuss of it. 'Do your dog a favour, Felipe. Don't keep this beauty on a short chain all day at the finca next to Señora Berens, or tied up *anywhere* for that matter.'

Felipe steadies the cadge, his boots shuffling on the gravel. '*Mira!* I've got to be going.'

But, catching his arm, she won't leave it at that: 'Dogs feel pain and pleasure, just the same as people, Felipe. If you accept that, and it should be *obvious - ¡hombre!* just look into this one's eyes - just think about it, how would you like to be chained up alone, day and night, until your owner decided to come and give you a little grub or a little outing?'

'*¡Vamos, Tamarit! ¡Vamos!*' Julio's deep-throated call cuts short their encounter and she throws Felipe an urgent, questioning look.

'I'll think about it,' he says.

Julio hands Luisa a letter he has collected from the post office in town. A Barcelona postmark, Rafael's handwriting. Something hard inside, yes, this must be the key for the blue case.

'About the men at Casas Viejas,' Julio says, laying a hand on her arm. 'The older man's a wealthy recluse according to Pep.

217

Seems he wants to run what he calls an ecological farm. And, would you believe it, he's sacked Pep. Pep hadn't exchanged more than a few words with him before he was given his marching orders. The youth, Miguel, is to run the estate from now on. They want to employ a cleaner and a housekeeper instead of a gamekeeper. Pep's in a right lather, I can tell you. He's worked at the finca for twenty-five years and thought he had the job for life.' Julio lifted his eyebrows and gave Luisa a wry smile. 'Your guess is as good as mine, how the town will react to this news. And now, Tamarit, let's get going.'

'Where's the Don from?' Luisa longed to know.

'*Quien sabe?* Not even Pep knows that although the estate was paid for, so he tells me, in Deutschmarks.'

'Where is Monterey?'

'There are Montereys everywhere. In Spain, in South America, there's even a place by that name in California, but I don't think he comes from there. I know what you're thinking, but we can't tell where he comes from by his name,' Julio smiled, almost affectionate, like a parent to a questioning child.

The idea of an ecological farm intrigued Luisa. She wanted to know more, but Julio was anxious to be off. 'Well, I hope he doesn't start interfering up here,' she said, sucking in her cheeks against her lie. Every day now, she hoped to encounter the Don.

Interpreting her remark as a sign of alarm, Julio growled: '*¡Hombre!* If he does, just tell me. I'll see him off.'

His mock ferocity made her laugh. She stood for a few moments watching the men driving off before she perched on the stone bench outside Ca'n Clot, ripping open the envelope and bringing out a small brass key.

There was a letter.

Luisa, she read, *I have risen above the crowd that assembles every day in Plaça Major. Perhaps that suggests I have found a way to fly? Unfortunately, not. Not yet! Still, I do stand a fair way above the heads of the tourists now, on a plinth - there must be a name for such things, only I can't think of it at the moment. I constructed the thing from two circles of wood joined by a tubular strut, about three feet long. Also, I wear dark goggles now, and instead of my jousting sticks I have two silver swords, carried one on either hip.*

Two collection boxes are placed on either side of the plinth now, and I'm doubling my money for the pueblos! When a tourist drops money I hear the clink and instantaneously engage him or her with one of the swords. The cash flow from the new act is impressive.

It's also a perfect vehicle for the rage I feel about the mindlessness of the so-called developed world in relation to the disadvantaged world. Sometimes I think (rather unfairly, I admit) that these tourists represent that mindlessness. At other times I stand on the plinth thinking I've had enough of such a life and, looking out over the heads of the crowd, I dream of starting a new life somewhere else. Back in one of the pueblos, growing vegetables and roses, keeping a few animals. Does the bird life of Central America interest you?

Wings, she thinks. I am obsessed with wings. Because *all* wings, everything that flies or takes the shape of wings, symbolise the nobler aspects of the human spirit and, no matter how mad this world becomes, this will always be so.

All down the tree dappled day she picks up thick slabs of pine bark, fallen to the ground, invariably in the shape of wings. She had expected the key but not a letter. In her own letter to Rafael, lying unposted on her desk, she has described the Feast of Saint Anthony with its performing raven, symbol of the Holy Spirit or the supernatural. Universal Energy as Rafael prefers to call this power, this *poderia*. Dancing inwardly as she goes, she thinks of Saint Anthony's shoulders where the missing wings should be, and of Ezekiel in the Master of Pedret's painting, with *three* pairs of wings. She invokes the spirit of Rafael, part-avian in his winged costume, performing for tourists who little dream that the money they drop into Rafael's helmet will find its way to poverty stricken pueblos on the other side of the Atlantic Ocean.

Six feathers fan from her fist, feathers collected on her patrol for Felipe, whose earth-bound struggles dissolve every time he marvels at Aquila's upward spiralling flight. She has seen it in his face. He has requested feathers from her, a peace

219

offering, and she goes to lay them in the stone outbuilding where he manufactures Aquila's gear. On the thick wooden workbench, carefully she lays them out. Peregrine, buzzard and vulture feathers, beside his own box of feathers collected from the aviary birds during moults. Primaries, secondaries, tail, coverts and alula feathers; brown, almost-black, beige, white, spotted, striped, speckled. Here in this workshop she has learned a new dimension of bird anatomy.

'If the birds lose or break feathers, it's easy to replace them,' he had told her last December. 'First - it's obvious - choose a corresponding feather from the same bird, thrown out in a previous moult, from the same side of the body, and imp it straight back into place. If it's hanging by a thread you can secure it with superglue.'

*Super*glue? That had made her laugh.

'Sometimes, though, a complete break must be mended with a peg between the feather shaft and the replacement feather.'

Above the workbench hang exquisite drawings of wings labelled in Felipe's childish script, in bright red ink:

Primary moult sequence of a shortwing and broadwing

Primary moult sequence of a longwing

Tail moult sequence of a shortwing and broadwing

She takes out her mobile phone and taps in Julio's number.

'*¡Hola! ¡Mira!* . . . about Felipe's pointer. Is there any reason why he couldn't keep his dog up here? He could make a kennel for it next to Perro's, couldn't he? And it wouldn't have to be chained up. *Vale, gracias.* You'll mention it to him then?'

9

A silver watch lay on the ground. It looked expensive and belonged to a man, she decided, clearing off the damp leaf mould sticking to it, and she saw the hands had stopped at ten past midnight. Was that when it had fallen to the ground? Or had the battery run out? Had someone come up here yesterday? Or, did the hypothermic tourist in the jester's cap drop it all those weeks ago? But no, surely she'd have noticed the watch the very first time she went to pick heather? Could it be Felipe's watch, or Julio's? They were both up here yesterday and Felipe had actually stopped the jeep at the edge of the wood when, to her delight he had arrived with the pointer.

Luisa was gazing out of Ca'n Clot in the direction of the wood, watch in hand, when a figure suddenly emerged near the Tree on the Edge. He picks his way with the gangling, awkward gait of someone who feels the ground uncertain beneath his feet, and she trails him through her field glasses. Someone who doesn't belong here, so out of place in the wilderness, wearing these horrid so-called sports clothes, decorated with shocking-pink flashes, that seem at least a size too big for him. The unlikely assistant of the Don. Looking for the watch? She didn't like him popping up out of the blue like this and she kept her eye on him as he skirted the wood then went to phone Julio.

Around an hour ago she had taken the dogs for a walk in the woods, where clumps of new heather blossomed among silver-grey rocks speckled with bright yellow lichen. Memorial stones for carbon makers, like Alejandro, or so she had thought and, momentarily, the old man seemed to be there, reaching out his gnarled fingers to grasp the twiggy purple flowers. Of course Alejandro had not *actually* been there. But had the assistant been there? Had it been the *assistant's* presence she'd sensed at that moment? Perhaps he often watched her? The thought made her uncomfortable. It could well be the case, as she had realised more than once before. Anyone could observe me up here, for days on end if they wished, without me even knowing it.

By the time Julio answers, the youth has vanished and she takes on another tack.

'Julio? I need a hide so I can study the terrain on the other side of Las Cuevas Negras.'

'*Vale*, Luisa? *Nada mas?*'

'Yes, there is something else. Have you or Felipe lost a watch? No? I thought not. I found a man's watch lying in the wood. And I've just seen someone . . . the Don's assistant . . . lurking about near the Tree on the Edge.'

She needed to feel in control of her territory but now she was extremely rattled, standing by the desk making wild whorls on the notepad.

'You're worried, Luisa?'

'No, not worried exactly. I'm *irritated*. We can't have prowlers up here . . . the *chico* lives at Casas Viejas but that doesn't mean he isn't an egg collector or a falconer on the look out for a bird to pinch. Who knows? Many birds are nesting now, and you know how valuable trained birds are to fowlers. Maybe they'd like Aquila, Felipe's bird.'

As her voice tailed away Julio almost screeched: 'It is not *Felipe's* eagle!'

She stifled her amusement and let his outburst pass; it was not her business, after all.

'Is the guy still there, Luisa?'

'No, he seems to have gone.'

It took Julio just under an hour to drive up. He marched into the refectory, his arms swinging, then sat down beside her on one of the long benches where she was writing. He took a look at the watch lying on the table, remarked that it need a new battery, then got down to business.

'We'll start building the hide tomorrow. Oh, and by the way, I didn't pass anyone on the way up here. No sign of anyone at Casas Viejas either.'

'Did you ever discover who shot the goats that day you found old Alejandro at the sitja?' she said.

'Pep Oleza shot the goats illegally,' he said, his face grim-set.

'He didn't apply for a special permit, then?'

'No. It seems the garden at Casas Viejas had been ravaged by goats, new trees the previous owners planted destroyed, flowers and shrubs gobbled up. I suppose Oleza wanted the new owner to see him as a good *amo*, so he took the law into his own hands. He didn't expect us, or anyone else, let alone old Alejandro to come along the escarpment trail that day.'

'The Don had nothing to do with it?'

'No, in fact Pep may have been fired as a result of the cull.'

'Where's Felipe?'

'Cutting wood for Bernardo. Bernardo gets his new terraces cleared and Felipe sells the wood to the conservancy at a bargain price.'

'I see,' Luisa smiled. 'You rub my back and I'll rub yours?'

Julio took off his cap, faintly embarrassed. 'Yes, *amigismo*. You could call it that.' They both knew the arrangement with Bernardo was unofficial.

'Did Tamarit bring his dog up as you suggested?'

'He did. Yesterday. How long's he been working on Bernardo's finca, by the way?'

'Off and on for about a week, I'd say.'

Carefully she laid down her pen, avoiding Julio's eyes: 'I heard someone shot Bernardo's dog the other day. In fact, Anita Berens told me she killed the dog.' She breached Anita's confidence but needed to confide in Julio to win his support. 'Anita Berens shot the dog in self-defence,' she added.

'*Self-defence?* Julio echoed. 'What makes you say that?'

'Felipe must've left the gate open . . . accidentally, of course, *carelessly*. The dog got out onto the path that leads to Anita's orchard. Unfortunately Anita came along just at that moment. Seeing the brute there scared the living daylights out of her. She thought it would attack her and she shot it.'

'So she does keep a gun,' Julio said thoughtfully. '*He* told me the dog was shot through the fence . . . in the,' Julio turned his head away as if he risked entering a trap.

She finished his sentence. 'In the orchard? No, Julio, the dog was out on the path.'

He cast her a sharp glance and she went on toying with the watch as she spoke. 'Now you don't have to give him the eagle to buy off his silence, do you?' She threw him a knowing wink. 'Think about it. Who was guilty? Anita for shooting a dog about to viciously attack her or your colleague for letting the dog out in the first place? I'd drop Felipe a hint if I were you.'

Julio looked puzzled for a moment, then slapped his thigh. *Ho! ho! ho!* In a gale of mirth he doubled-up, shook out his handkerchief and mopped his brow.

At last, she thought, averting her amused eyes, the penny has dropped. When he calmed down he looked quizzical. He's wondering how I know about Felipe and his bid to get the Booted eagle. Luisa grinned. Time to change the subject. And to distract him from the small teasing silence that had fallen between them, vigorously she started drawing a rough map of the crag.

'*Mira*, Julio. This is the perfect site for the hide. Not one like yours, but an elevated hide with a good view of the far side of Cuevas Negras where there is a vulture nest.'

'A vulture nest?' he said, surprised.

'*Sí*, a vulture nest.' She turned the map sideways to let him see. 'There's a large tilted slab there.' She marked the place with an 'X'. 'The vultures' nest is down there.' She made another mark. 'And here's where I want you to build the hide.' She marked that site with a star and handed it over. After that, they made coffee and sat planning the impending visit of Señor Bigatti, the Sardinian ornithologist, until lunchtime.

In the afternoon she took both dogs for a run in the woods. She loved the rising smell of the fecund earth. The dogs pawed among the dank mulch like truffle hunters, with low growls of pleasure. Then, to her surprise, they suddenly raised their heads and barked. Someone must be coming along the path, unless it was a goat separated from its family. Unusual though, for the goats to roam so high, unless, sometimes, an old billy goat wandered off on a lonely forage. Like old Alejandro she thought, sucking in her cheeks with a rush of sorrow.

In the absence of sunlight, the low level of light made the wood seem eerie. She stuffed her hands into her pockets and waited until she saw with startled pleasure her neighbour striding along the path. Okay, so he's had a good press; doesn't like bird netting, plans to start an ecological farm . . . . The dogs rushed off to investigate, sniffing at his heels in their polite, well-trained way, so that he almost tripped over them.

'The dogs won't bite!' she called out.

He took off his brown leather bush hat, waved it in the air and hurried towards her. *A large, loose-limbed man, full of restless energy. Handsome, elegant, his arresting brown eyes shielded by a ridge of densely curling, greying eyebrows.* When he stood beside her he was panting for breath, beads of perspiration glinted on his brow. 'Your colleague . . . Julio Valente . . . told me he knew where I would find my watch. I lost it the other day . . . remarkable how he knew it was mine.'

'How *did* he know?' Luisa said, thinking how *right* his face seemed.

He gave a deep laugh. 'Well, as it happens, he passed through the farmyard earlier when I was out mending a fence. Hot work, had my shirtsleeves rolled up. Valente said, "you've lost a watch, señor. I can tell by the shape on your wrist that's lighter than the rest of your arm". Sure enough, there was the impression of the watch on the part of my arm that hadn't got sun-tanned. I hadn't even noticed I'd lost the thing. Time doesn't seem to be so important now that I live in Mallorca.'

'Julio's trained to be observant,' Luisa smiled. 'Don't worry. Your watch is safe at Ca'n Clot, though it might need a new battery. Why not come with me now and pick it up?'

The dogs bounded ahead and the Don loped along beside her, solidly built yet muscular and energetic. Then, just as they

225

were leaving the wood, suddenly he bent down. She turned to see what he had found, almost at the same spot where she found the watch. It flashed through her mind, if the watch is the Don's, when was he here before? And why? Now he was picking up another bird skull lying half-buried under scattered carob pods and leaf mould.

Perro raced back to them, bristling with curiosity, the pointer at his heels.

'That's where I found the watch,' she said.

He straightened up, frowning: 'I admit it, I came up the other day hoping to see you, but you weren't around. I don't usually wear a watch - the watch in question was given to me by a friend - I always seem to lose them.'

She studied his face, his vibrant brown eyes. 'Did you want to see me about anything in particular?'

'I'm keen to learn about birds,' he said, almost bashful. 'Even I can see this skull's different from the buzzard's. Can you identify it?' He laid it in her palm.

She hesitated, examining it. 'This time,' she smiled, 'you've found the skull of a raven.'

When they reached Ca'n Clot, she led him inside by way of the den, keeping the dog to heel.

'You allow the dogs inside?' he said, surprised.

'Yes, occasionally, and they can't believe their luck.'

The stove was burning and the room smelled as musty as the fungi in the woods. She asked if he would like to stay for a bit, and, after looking around approvingly, he took off his jacket. Hanging it up beside her own it pleased her to think she would have such a neighbour when she came back from Barcelona after carnival. *Carnaval* . . . the word was spelled differently in Spanish, the meaning was the same. The last night before the sacrifices of Lent . . . *carnaval; carne*-flesh; *levare*-to put away. And what a night it would be . . . *dos voladores*, she and Rafael, let loose for once, before the sacrifices of Lent. Yes, the Don would be a welcome companion during the sombre days of Lent, and by Easter she would have finished her work here.

He filled the room, as he had filled the clearing the other

day. She was glad of his company; and this time, she thought, the schoolgirl in me has been left behind. After all, he calls me señora now, not señorita, and I mustn't blow it.

'Your watch is on the desk,' she said, 'and will you have a glass of wine?'

'Thanks, I will!' He was looking all around, rubbing his hands together with brisk relish. 'I must say I admire the simplicity of your life up here. I've always longed for such sparseness in my own life.'

The timbre of his voice suggested Wagnerian heroes. Yet she knew this powerful man had another side; the sensitive soul whose fingers had traced the declivities of the bird skull at the clearing.

'So far I've cluttered every home I've ever had with bric-a-brac, antiques, Oriental vases, you name it, statues, etcetera,' he was saying.

A man somewhere between forty-eight and fifty-two, she decided, and blew the dust off a bottle. Yet his enthusiasm made him seem somehow ageless. She handed him the corkscrew saying, 'I've never been able to afford to buy any of the things you mentioned.' She took down the best two glasses from a motley collection on the bookshelves. 'And I don't suppose in my line of business I shall ever have money for luxuries. Still, this rather robust Rioja should be worth drinking.'

The cork plopped out, and she put forward two *copas* for him to fill.

'Oh, but you don't *need* luxuries. Anyone can see you're content with the simple life,' he said almost shyly. 'I can't complain either. The new finca really is splendid. You must come and see it. Here and now I invite you. What views. What peace. *And* I've indulged in rather expensive reforms of the kitchen and bathrooms.'

The armchair barely contained him when he pushed his back into it and stretched out his legs so that they almost touched her feet where she sat facing him.

'Where d'you come from?' she said, avoiding his eyes lest he read in them her desire when wasn't love the last thing she needed up here in the wilderness, where all she had in her was required for the field work?

His full lips curved determinedly: 'Oh! let's see, that's a difficult one. I've travelled so widely in my life, it's almost impossible to say where I come from,' he said. '*Now*, though, I'm looking forward to settling down here. I've just come through a painful, drawn-out divorce and buying the estate marks the beginning of the next phase of my life. I bought it off the Internet, sight unseen, and thankfully the place has turned out to be ideal for my purposes. Fortunately, I'm in a position to retire early, and Mallorca seems to be as good a place as any. Better, perhaps, than most.'

So, he was a free man after all. 'I've grown to love Mallorca,' she said, dismissing another thought. But that was okay. Rafael's tantalising hints in his letter of a possible life in South America had yet to be tested, so she allowed herself to say: 'I think I'd like to settle here myself after I've completed my doctoral thesis.'

'Oh, that's good,' he said affably 'When you and I have both settled perhaps we'll keep each other company from time to time.'

She swallowed hard and said she'd like that. On a personal level, Rafael had confused her, muddled her feelings, whereas her attraction to this man seemed to fly like an arrow from her heart. Yet the yearning he aroused discomfited her, too, since how could she tell if he felt anything other than a quasi-professional interest in her?

'They say you plan to develop your estate into an ecological farm,' she said and his face lit up.

'Yes, it's early days, it'll take years, but I'm not in a hurry. In the past I've developed similar projects in Central America. After Easter I plan to bring several cows and a bull over from Menorca. You can breed horned cattle from the animals they have there, and they are the best.'

'I haven't seen cows in Mallorca,' she put in.

'No, there are very few. But a proper organic farm needs cow dung, as the basic element for reviving soil depleted of minerals. Then vegetables, herbs and flowers can flourish. And humans who eat the vegetables will get all the vitamins and minerals they simply don't get nowadays from supermarket food.'

She urged him to tell her more, and, before he left an hour later, they had decided to go on a birding expedition after her return from Barcelona. He had no idea 'how birds work', as he said, and he listened attentively while she spoke about the big subject of bird migration, now and then questioning her about simple facts, such as where do birds sleep at night? When she offered to lend him a book about bird behaviour he seemed touchingly pleased, like a child being given a present, and he promised to learn 'a thing or two' before their trip.

It was almost dark in the room when he got up. 'Well, I must be off. I've taken up enough of your time *and* it's a long way back to Casas Viejas, though I know the road very well already!'

You can call me Luisa, she wanted to say, but the very thought in her head sounded banal and, when he stood up, almost a head taller, a powerful rush of desire made her step back a little. Her flesh tingled, as though the tips of his fingers had brushed her arm. Yet they hadn't. His fingers were zipping up his jacket, that was all. And, after that, apparently unconcerned, he switched on his torch ready to brave the dark night walk to Casas Viejas.

§

The vultures had built their nest, a giant balloon of twigs, in the top branches of a tall pine tree on the escarpment of Cuevas Negras, facing the meseta. Its dome was clearly visible fifty feet below her and, inside, hidden from her, the female vulture would be incubating her egg and would not leave the nest until her chick was hatched. There was no sign of the male who would feed her continually after that. He's out on a rekkie, Luisa supposed, patrolling his territory, getting food for his mate. Humans are the only predators he need fear since vultures fly off, leave their nests, if humans come too close.

It had been difficult to move across the sharp slabs on the rim of the crag, Perro holding to her heels, but she had persisted, wanting a vantage point over the entire area. It was so cold she wore gloves and predicted snow that clear morning, so perfect for photography. She photographed the tilted rock slab and the miniature botanical garden that surrounded it. Dwarf rosemary in vivid blue flower, yellow stonecrop and Balearic sandwort. She made a rough map of the terrain, the woods, the valleys, the scumbled grey mountain and its accomplice peaks. At this spot, where the men would construct the hide, she crouches on the slab while the obedient dog takes up a position on a smaller slab nearby, panting with joy to be freed from his kennel. Faintly, she hears above the finch-chittering trees that familiar long drawn-out wooden call: *auk! AUK! auk! AUK!*

The immense male bird is no more than a distant yet fast-moving speck in the firmament. Then it becomes a Chinese kite sailing fluently against the pure blue sky. She hears footsteps. The men bringing the materials for the hide, she thinks, setting the camera on the rock. The vulture wheels overhead. *¡Perfecto!* She must not lose the moment. The bird would descend soon. She must not scare it away. Click after satisfying click, she shoots off the roll of film as the bird obligingly hovers in the mid-distance. Then, just as she's packing up to leave, she turns and glimpses the Don's assistant stealing away down towards the meseta.

'Hey, you!' she yells angrily through cupped hands. 'You shouldn't be up here!' And, when he keeps going and doesn't even turn round, her fury mounts.

Back at the finca, the men are shouldering up tools and planks of wood.

'The youth from Casas Viejas was on the crag,' she complained, her breath coming in short bursts after her swift descent. 'Can't the Don control him? After all *he's* been made aware about sensitive nesting sites. The boy must be forbidden to come up here.'

'I'll stop at the house on the way down and remind the Don,' Julio said soothingly. 'We'll have the hide up in no time. Give us till after lunch.'

Down in the town, Anita Berens closes a file, labels it *Flight into Exile*, sends it via an e-mail to Colin, puts her computer to sleep and looks at her watch. Eleven-thirty. Her daring astonishes her. She has accepted Julio Valente's invitation to dinner this evening at a restaurant near Pollensa, and she can hardly wait for him to knock on her door at eight o'clock as he has promised. He's not a sophisticated man, but he is a civilized man with a heart of gold, she thinks, and isn't that about as good as it gets?

The newly constructed hide was everything Luisa had hoped for. She climbs the ten stout rungs into an oblong interior covered on three sides by greyish-green canvas spliced to wooden struts just under six-feet high. She walks across the platform to look through the open flap, and, sure enough, it's perfectly placed, directly above the nest. Here she could watch night and day, for hours on end, here she could film the first flight of the vulture fledgling from its nest. From the hide she could see all the way to the meseta that, today, resembled a landing strip for alien craft carrying otherworldly beings. Through her binoculars she picked out some of the peculiar rocks and boulders that had become familiar during her walks across the meseta to Ca'n Clot. Nothing stirred. It was as if she surveyed the surface of the moon itself. Chalky, impassive, infinitely expectant.

'Did you construct these treads from Bernardo's wood, Felipe?' she asks after she climbs down.

'What's it to you?' he grunts under his breath and walks away carrying unused planks of wood.

'Now *you'll* have some fences to mend with him,' Julio says with a dark look that makes her wish she'd held her tongue.

'Why not stay up here this afternoon, Felipe, and fly the eagle?' she calls, but Felipe doesn't even turn round.

Julio says: 'Ach, forget him! By the way, Luisa, the watch belongs to the Don. I stopped off to look at some broken fencing near Casas Viejas yesterday and spoke to him about it.'

'Nice bit of detective work you did there, Julio!'

'*Claro*, señora! Your Sherlock Holmes would be proud of me.'

Then he looked serious. 'Not such good news, though, for Monterey. The town is heaving with gossip about him firing Pep Oleza. Factions are gathering. Pep's supporters want him reinstated while those that never liked Pep are gloating.'

She considered this, uncertain how to reply. She intensely disliked Pep Oleza; arrogant, authoritarian, reactionary . . . labels to describe the man sprang easily to mind. Only, in the matter of this new drama involving Don Nicolas, the town and Oleza, she was out of her depth so she kept silent.

'As I mentioned the other day, the new man wants to turn Casas Viejas into an environmentally friendly estate. No chemical fertilisers are to be used, for example. A small herd of cattle will supply the dung. And he told me he's importing trees from India with oils in them, so powerful they can even heal animal wounds. *Neem* trees, I think he called them. He plans to grow the trees right here in Mallorca, on the estate . . . .'

'Yes, he told me about it, ' Luisa began.

Julio cast her a curious look: 'So you've been encountering him?'

'Yes, I'm being very nice to him,' Luisa said with a grin.

They caught up with Felipe standing with Cora on his shoulder outside the weathering. 'Old Perro's given up his kennel to my dog,' he guffawed. 'Come and see!'

Sure enough, Perro had spread his great black bulk on top of the kennel, while the pointer lay sleeping in Perro's cosy lair below. The old dog surveyed his human audience lazily through half-open, toffee-coloured eyes, then yawned contentedly.

'There you go, two's company,' Luisa said, and thought, Felipe's happy about the pointer but he must have an uncomfortable hunch I'm onto the true story regarding the fate of Bernardo's dog.

During lunch, from his fireside retreat, Felipe praised the black olives, *las pansidas*, Luisa had bought at Mercado Olivar on her trip to Palma, and the cheese from Mahon he declared superb.

'He's buttering you up for some reason,' Julio whispered.

'Bernardo's dog?' Luisa muttered.

'Leave it, Luisa.' Julio smiled faintly then said, 'We'll pick up Señor Bigatti tomorrow at the station. Then, after the trip to S'Escorca, you'll have nothing to distract you except your talk.' He sniffed his glass appreciatively. 'I've heard on the grapevine, by the way. . . .'

'Grapevine?' Luisa broke in with mock surprise.

'He means the alcalde's office,' Felipe said scathingly. 'Old Julio goes into the town hall several times a week for the sole purpose of picking up gossip.'

'Of course. Why not?' Julio practically boomed. 'Since at that office the affairs of the entire town are dealt with. There one always learns interesting information.'

'Gossip, you mean,' Felipe smirked, 'and I can give you some. Don whatever his name is, is up to something with Rosa Sanchez. Paying her for information. That's all I know, Rosa wouldn't say any more, but he's probably a spy.'

And you're a fantasist, Luisa thought, her spirits rising to the Don's defence. Yet, *could it be true?Rosa?*

Julio ignored Felipe. 'As I was trying to say, the alcalde's keen to promote your talk as the Alejandro Ferrer Memorial Lecture.'

The heel of Luisa's hand hit her forehead in mock consternation. 'Oh, my God, then I'll really have to work on it,' she groaned.

After Julio drove away, she cleared up and arranged her backpack for the afternoon patrol over to the Golden Bowl while Felipe went out to the aviary. A little later, she stood high above the hoya watching for a few minutes his stick-like figure on the plateau. Then she heard the piercing, discordant note of his Asborno whistle and followed Aquila's magisterial flight above her head until the bird turned in the air and flew like a dark missile to the distant landing strip of Felipe's outstretched hand.

That evening, the refectory glows with firelight and candlelight. In the solitary ritual she has invented for herself, she comes through from the den carrying the blue case. Alone on her birthday, but never mind. What with the fire and the candles, the setting is so theatrical this will be one to remember.

She has to sing under her breath a northern song to strengthen her nerve; *the river is wide, I cannot get o'er . . . and neither have I wings to fly.* She lays the case under the Baroque mirror; *bring me a boat to carry two . . . that we may sail, my love and I.* She inserts the brass key and the lid springs open to reveal iridescent feathers gleaming like wet silk and tinged with rainbow colours. Incredulously, she lifts them out and they tumble into a fantastic cloak. Rafael has made this for *me*, she thinks, a copy of his own wings. Her eyes blurring at his generosity, she explores the construction. Hundreds of feathers. Downy, soft white feathers around the neck and shoulders. Larger, shining dark feathers for the rest of the cloak. Carefully she spreads it on a table and, exploring the case for a message, finds something reddish-brown protruding from a side pocket. Oh, my God! she gasps, bringing out a painted bird mask such as Renaissance Venetians wore at their *Bailes Masqueras.* It's made of papier mâché and, attached to the curved golden beak, there's a slip of paper. 'Necessary equipment for life's journey and the Barcelona Carnaval,' she reads. 'Happy Birthday, Luisa.'

Dancing inwardly she puts on the cloak, admiring in the mirror the way the curving mantle feathers settle on her shoulders. Turning slightly sideways, almost coquettishly, she fixes the wings to her arms by way of leather and velcro circlets. The clinging feathers reach beyond her fingertips, and, when she swoops up her arms, they cascade down with a little hiss. She can scarcely believe such a treasure is hers. Then she slips on the eye mask, smiles at her phantasmagoric beaked shadow reflected onto the whitewashed wall, and goes out through the door where the moon casts no shadows onto the hushed landscape.

She fancied she was a huge ground-walking bird. The feathers swept and rustled when, from time to time, she spun round peering through the eye slits at elements transfigured by moonlight. Stones, rocks, trees, looming in the eerie silence.

234

High above, the sky was a pre-Gallilean dome, interlined with indigo velvet and pierced by Levantine stars. To her it was ineffable . . . beyond words . . . the map of the stars the migrant birds would follow soon. Swifts, swallows, wheatears, and all the others, across the Mediterranean from Africa on their spring journey back to the north. The aviary birds rustled, ghostly icons on their perches, their eyes half-closed when she slipped past. Perro grunted and stretched on the roof of his kennel. Felipe's dog stood up and silently fanned his tail behind the wired enclosure. The night air, chill as champagne, condensed her breath as she stole towards the crag.

Her feet hardly touched the ground, and it struck her that, by giving her these wings, Rafael was further encouraging her, just as he had her former flatmates, to stray off the beaten track of human existence. Already she had taken a wide swerve, and would she ever get back? Did it matter? Would she ever want to? His invitation made her feel so vitally alive her one thought was to climb as far as she could go, to the highest point of the crag. Now she was Bird-woman, Woman-bird, Woman disguised as *una voladora*, a flier. She was crossing a daring border, dissolving into the gullies and crevasses of El Escarpado de las Cuevas Negras, up, and further up, until the moonlit vista seemed to disengage itself from her, to roll out all around and below her like an ancient patterned carpet, opal with the dark splashes of faraway woods above the meseta. Here was a perfect stage for dreaming, and her heart bent under the pearly hushed magnificence of it all.

Standing on the rock slab beside the hide, perhaps the mountain is dreaming this stupendous adventure, she thought, stretching her winged arms above her head. But, as a matter of fact, I wouldn't mind at all waking up one day, transformed into some winged creature. Eagle owl, would do nicely. She started dancing, leaning one way then another, into the space, a hip-swaying, languorous dance. Her mouth curved. Crazy woman, anyone might be forgiven for thinking (if they could see me now) unless they realised, oh, ho! she must be rehearsing for carnival. But there *is* no one to see me, sky-gazing on this rock, seeing a star wooshing into vast eternity. Here is beauty enough to make the angels rejoice. And, over there, a revolving jewel-pin satellite. And a passenger plane trawling overhead, bound for Palma airport, flying so high you can't hear its engine but can see the winking micro-gems of its amber, yellow and green landing lights.

It was then her spirit flew. Wondrous that weightless feeling of flying and spiralling for a few heady moments, until something came hurtling towards her. A blur at first against the mountain, the inky sky flickering and lightening as it approached with terrifying speed. Half-man, half-bird, winged, with feathered legs and talons. Her urgent thought was to get back to earth and, with an involuntary shriek when she fell onto the rock, simultaneously, the apparition disappeared. For a few moments she lay disbelieving, then, dizzy with apprehension, forced herself to peer over the edge of the crag. There was nothing there. Only the dark abyss and the shadow of the pine tree and the ballooning vultures' nest.

Trembling, she felt herself all over, just a few bruises . . . *the heart soars . . . or else it plummets*. When she got up, her feet set loose a patch of scree. Fragments fell, drumming and skiffing like hailstones on a tiled roof. In the distance, Perro started barking. Someone must be in the woods or on the hoya, was her urgent thought as gingerly she returned down the crag. Perro always knows - as if his brain had been fitted with some inbuilt tracking device - exactly where I am. He knows I'm up here. He wouldn't react like that to tumbling stones, so he must be alerting me to something else. Someone prowling around Ca'n Clot, or in the wood? Someone after eggs or the birds of prey? Her throat constricted. She dreaded having to cross the plateau, and, as soon as her feet flattened on the ground, she heard the sickening scrunch of small stones shifting under someone else's feet. She had to force herself to look, and, before she could sprint away, a figure, as if it had been drawn in charcoal against the moonlit hoya, seemed to float towards her. Mesmerised, she saw it take form, heard a voice saying, 'Luisa, are you alright?'

Then Nicolas Monterey was at her side. 'You're trembling,' he said, holding her arm.

'Something weird happened up there, a trick of moonlight, but I'm okay now thanks,' she said, mustering a smile.

He kept his hand on her arm and they returned in silence to Ca'n Clot. Once inside, she went to replace some of the guttering candles and asked him to throw some logs on the fire.

'I hope you didn't mind me calling you Luisa earlier?' he said. 'And I'm Nicolas from now on, if that's okay with you.'

Soon the renewed light cast a comforting softness between them, and as they drew closer to each other her imagination replayed the apparition, part-man, part-bird on the crag. But she could not share the memory, however much she wanted to. It had been a harbinger, she thought, of the new world I have entered under Rafael's spell. Somehow associated, too, with the proximity of Nicolas' spirit in the wood below, even although I had been unaware of his presence.

As if to lighten their mood, Nicolas broke into her thoughts. 'You look marvellous in wings,' he said, 'you should always wear them.'

'I'm not sure I could handle that,' she grinned. 'They're pretty wild for everyday wear and may not be as innocent as they look.'

'Do you often go out dressed like that?' he smiled, appraising her.

The corners of her mouth puckered: 'No, in fact it's the first time. They were a present from a friend. But what are you doing up here?'

'I was walking in the woods, looking for eagle owls. I'm learning, slowly, about your birds,' he began. 'Then I heard a strange sound, not quite a scream coming from the crag. Well, it would have been foolish of me to try to get up there when I don't know the terrain, but when I reached the edge of the wood your dog started barking. I noticed dim lights in here, and when I came closer, I saw the door was open. I called your name and when there was no answer I didn't know what to do. The vibes seemed so strange, I went out to look for you and thank god you came down the crag when you did.'

'The sight must've spooked you,' she smiled, touched that he cared for her safety. And, when awkwardly she started to unfasten the cloak, 'here', he said, drawing closer, 'let me help.'

Easily, his fingers undid the fastening at the neck and she shivered a little when the cloak slid off her shoulders and rustled into a sensuous heap at her ankles. Then, stooping to pick it up, lightly his hand brushed her leg. Suffused with desire, she bent towards him, but he was straightening up saying: 'I was in the wood . . . I was in the wood, because I was trying to pluck up courage to come and visit you.'

'You need *courage* to visit me?'

'Well, you're not the sort of woman one meets everyday,' he said, meeting her eyes with utmost seriousness.

'Not many women wear wings, I guess,' she jested, going to lay the cloak on the table under the mirror. Nicolas sat down on one of the benches, and she went to him, speaking rapidly as if that might disguise the troubling range of her emotions. 'The winged cloak is a sort of symbol of my new life in Spain . . . I'm half-Spanish, you see, and in fact, to draw a line under my past, I've been thinking of changing my name to de Frutos. That was the name of my Madrid grandfather. He was assassinated during the Civil War. I never knew him, of course, but my mother told me about his death.'

Nicolas listened attentively, searching her face even when she had stopped speaking. 'How strange,' he said at last. 'You see, I, too, have reached a crossroads in my life where everything - well, as much as possible, must be changed. My grandfather, too, came from Madrid. He wasn't killed but succeeded in escaping with his family to South America. It seems we have several bonds, you and I, birds, grandfathers from Madrid, new names, and what else?'

They sat so close she could feel the solid warmth of his arm beside her own, and her lips pressed hard against the ardour she felt before she turned to him. 'There is something else,' she said, teasing a little. 'We share this mountain, Massanella, on either side of the padlocked gate.'

His face lit up. 'That's true, I've considered that more than once myself. It's rather like a fairy story. Once upon a time . . . but what will happen next?'

When, with mischievous eyes, she dared him to imagine, he put on his fierce, squinting look. 'The pity of it is we may not find out for some time. You see, I have to leave for the mainland tomorrow. I'll be gone for a couple of weeks.'

Going away? Oh, please don't, she almost blurted out . . . that day, it seemed so long ago . . . standing with the professor under the map of this area, the red dot of this finca where now she sat so wholeheartedly in the moment, compulsively drawn to this man. Yet, if he was going away she must protect herself, take another tack, and a hint of coolness returned to her voice.

'A friend, an anthropologist, brought the feathers for the cloak back from South America. I don't know which country exactly. He made the cloak himself.'

Nicolas seemed not to hear. 'And, that's not all,' he interjected, taking her hand. 'After my trip to the mainland I'll be back for a few days. Then I have no choice but to return to Central America until Easter. Promise me we'll spend time together between those two trips?'

Swamped by renewed disappointment, he has a generous spirit, she thought - I've waited this long for you in my mind, I can wait a little longer - but he's somehow mercurial, too, and I must be careful. Easily, he slipped into my life and, now, just as easily might slip away. In fact, now he saying, 'I have to go, but as soon as I get back from the mainland will you come to supper at Casas Viejas?'

There was no kiss, but the passion of his departing embrace held her spellbound. She allowed herself to be held, thinking, yes, you are the one I want, and his embrace was a balm that flowed down through all the dark tunnels of her past, breaking open their sealed-off exits and entrances, dark places that lay between her grief-filled adolescence and this moment. When, at last, they drew apart she stood watching from the door until his dusky figure grew smaller and smaller in the moonlight. He turned once to wave before he disappeared altogether at the Tree on the Edge while she lingered in the doorway of Ca'n Clot, at one with the night whose diamante firmament had drooped low its loosely threaded constellations, its planets and shooting stars.

§

Señor Bigatti was not entirely an unknown quantity. In a telephone conversation with Luisa he has conveyed his particular interest in visiting an excellent osprey site on the north side of the mountains, three hours walk from Ca'n Clot.

'Of course you can make it there and back in a day,' Julio reassured her as they drove to the station to pick up Giovanni Bigatti. 'Only you must set off early, and Felipe will be your guide since I have important meetings to attend with the Balearics Ornithological Group in Palma.'

Anita Berens drives to the halt before Inca and parks her Citroën under the shade of red pepper trees where she waits, hoping a white Opel will drive up and that out of the passenger door will step a young Colombian woman by the name of Rosa Sanchez with or without a rose in her hair. It's a remote hope, but one worth acting on. She has struggled to remember what Luisa Ross said about Rosa Sanchez that ghastly night when she almost had a breakdown. But that's all in the past.

When she rolls down the window the fronds of the dancing branches in the light breeze remind her of the sea. There's hardly anyone about. Only one swarthy bespectacled man over at the station, carrying a holdall and looking a little lost. She is prepared to wait until the next train comes in. There's no rush. Although the chances of Rosa being on the train are practically zero, what's important is she has taken action, has driven here on the first day of her new life.

It's partly the result of a great night of lovemaking that she's here, out in the world, a breeze lifting her hair. She feels restored to herself, a process that began, she supposed, when she smashed the mirror to smithereens and then dared to save herself by shooting that dog. Making a confession of sorts to Luisa had been a step along the way, too, that reached a culmination during dinner with Julio last night.

She had looked at him across the table dressed simply in a crew neck sweater and black jeans; an attractive man, not exactly handsome, a year or two younger than herself. Not once since she came to Europe had she risked eating in a public place, and Julio has chosen well. A quiet country inn near Pollensa, run by a French woman and her daughter who cook imaginative food from the freshest local ingredients. The pile of langoustine on her plate with a pot of garlic mayonnaise, and on Julio's plate a salad of bacon, pomegranate seeds and rocket, attested to their skill. The interior was tasteful, the tables covered with plain white cloths, each set with a central vase of fresh wild flowers and a lit candle. Six of a dozen tables were occupied and, of course, she recognised no one, and, to her relief, neither did Julio.

As the meal progressed their smiles grew wider. So long since she had felt like this. Attractive, sexy and unafraid. Julio is the best sort, who will take her passionately yet lovingly. *Carpe diem!* that was her motto now. Theirs would be a singing and dancing sort of love, though, of course it might not last forever. Love is what she ardently desires, sex is what she needs, throwing her head back, laughing heartily at one of his jokes.

'Shall we talk about the dog I shot?' she asked rather reluctantly as they waited for the second course. She wanted to get the subject out of the way.

'Not unless we have to,' Julio replied. 'Is there anything, really, to say? Luisa told me you shot the dog in self-defence, and, since no one in town seems anything other than pleased the dog's vanished, what more is there to say?'

When the stuffed pork arrived with its garnish of baked apple and apricots, its accompaniment of glazed carrots and tiny roast potatoes, how could they do other than forget the dog and fill their glasses to the brim with a rich dark wine.

At one point in the evening she related Luisa's encounter

with Rosa Sanchez on the train. Julio listened thoughtfully then said: 'You know, Felipe Tamarit's mother took on a young Colombian woman who works for Don Nicolas now, the owner of the mountain estate. Perhaps it's her?'

A simple enough comment, yet it turned a key in her locked-up soul. It should be possible to contact Rosa Sanchez. When she had been a broadcaster it had been young women like Rosa whom she always hoped to reach out to. Women at risk. Women who somehow kept songs in their hearts despite the most appalling abuse. Women who needed her, someone older and more experienced. No longer could she waste her life when she had so much to give.

'Could you ask Felipe the name of that woman, perhaps she's Rosa Sanchez?'

And there was the beauty of it. Julio would help her willingly with any request, however large or small, without delving into the whys and wherefores.

As they ate and laughed her *eureka!* had come as an unexpected sub-text to the evening. There could be no turning away. She, as Lourdes Herreros, would run a centre for immigrants in Palma where women could learn English, work with computers, take part in discussion groups or whatever might help them to adjust to the First World they had arrived in, as if they had dropped from the moon. Maybe she'd even get a slot on a radio station. To hell with Andreas! What a fool she'd been to hide away to the extent that she had been driven to the edge of a nervous breakdown. Now she would give Andreas and his gang two fingers and go about quite openly in Palma.

Later, driving back to Calle Luna with Julio, she continued her line of thought. Surely it would be better by far to be preoccupied, working with the immigrant women, than wondering every day in my orchard if some stranger's going to come for me, scaring hoopoes off the almond trees.

'What are you thinking?' Julio said.

'Only that I'd like you to stay over at my place tonight.'

He turned to her with a grin and accelerated down the twisting dark roads of the night, past bearded palms and conical cypresses backed by an outrageous full moon, towards Calle Luna.

'You sure drive fast,' she protested in mock-alarm.

'Señora, I can hardly *wait* to get there.'

They pulled up outside number eleven. Ever the gentleman, Julio came to help her down and she wondered, giving him her hand, if she dared to go as far as it was possible to go. Should she keep up the Anita Berens pretence a little longer or go the whole hog and reveal to the world without delay - starting right now with Julio Valente - the uninhibited, purposeful, powerful female that was Lourdes Herreros?

Now, waiting near the station, at first she didn't notice the jeep parked further down the road. But when she caught sight of activity in her driver's mirror, she paid attention. For goodness sakes, wasn't that Luisa Ross, extending her hand to the man in the specs who had been waiting over at the station? Then, to her astonishment there was Julio dressed in the civvies he had worn last night, slipping the man's case into the back of the jeep. Luisa and the man got in and drove off, and, seconds later, she and Julio were the only people left behind in the deserted street.

She couldn't resist pressing the horn. He hastened towards her and when she got out he swept her up in an embrace.

'*¡Qué sorpesa, señora!*' he exclaimed. 'I'm catching the next train to Palma. I've a meeting there. But it won't take all day. Come with me, let me show you the city?' he pleaded, searching her eyes, pressing both her hands in his.

And of course she would go to Palma with Julio Valente. Singing and dancing, all the way. There would never be a better time to start her new life.

S'Escorca, Luisa read, *is the forbidding - even sinister - heart of the Serra de Tramuntana where the scattered population living isolated in narrow valleys and ravines, suffers the harshest landscape and climate in Mallorca; low temperatures, heavy rainfall, scant sun, frequent fog and snowfalls at relatively low altitudes. It is limestone country par excellence where the process of karstification - the chemical dissolution of limestone in water - gives rise to peculiar rock formations and caves called* monges *(nuns) or* esquedars *(fissures). The subterranean landscape comprises the cave of Sa Campana (3304 metres deep) and vertical abysses like the chasms of Fermenu and Escorca, both over 100 metres deep and the pit of Es Amics (180 metres deep).*

She had made it her business to find out everything she could about S'Escorca with the help of *La Serra de Tramuntana*, touchingly inscribed on the flyleaf: *To my pupil Luisa Ross. R. R. Bauza. Barcelona.*

Señor Bigatti, or Giovanni, as she began to call her colleague, turned out to be no trouble at all and, of course, he had definite ideas about what he wanted to see. Felipe had leave from the woodcutters to come at dawn to guide them on foot over the mountains to S'Escorca and the Gorg Blau. This was Mallorca's main reservoir, well stocked with trout and bass, according to the book, its waters encouraging yellow-footed gulls, cormorants and ospreys to nest and live along the coastal cliffs as neighbours to nesting Black vultures. The evening before their trip, she fed Giovanni the dish she occasionally set aside vegetarianism for. Wild rabbit casserole cooked with rosemary and juniper berries from the wood. Nicolas was never far from her thoughts, but she relished the company and straightforward conversation of this dedicated bird man who had been one of Professor Bauza's pupils at Barcelona, in the class of 1993. And, after she wished Giovanni goodnight, she had telephoned Rafael to thank him for her magnificent birthday present.

'For you, it had to be something extraordinary,' he said. 'Something that symbolises your higher purpose in life - the welfare of birds - as well as one of life's great truths, that everything apart from our higher purpose is make believe.'

She had laughed at that and said, 'is love to be classed as make believe?'

'Of course, since we can only make sense of our intimate relationships by projecting onto them what we know of ourselves. But that doesn't mean love isn't real in the here and now. Are you in love, Luisa?'

She had found herself describing her experience on the bare mountain, the apparition of the bird-man, and Nicolas' sudden appearance. And, when Rafael said, perhaps both the bird-man and Nicolas were reminders of your need to live fully in your body as well as your spirit, she had replied, how wise you are.

Thoughts of Nicolas played on her mind during the first hour or so of their climb when Felipe led them on narrow, but well-defined, garrigue paths. Only when they crossed the high mountain pass did she leave Nicolas behind to engage fully with her companions. There, grotesque boulders sculpted as if by the hand of some devilish god led into the forbidding maquis of S'Escorca, and made Luisa appreciate the relative luxuriance of the *possessío* of Ca'n Clot. S'Escorca's desolation made her shiver so that she had to stop to put on her anorak. The very place names - S'Escorca, Fermenu, Es Amics - sounded as uncompromising to her as the landscape, unyielding as stones on her tongue. It was, she thought, the sort of place where someone could easily disappear without trace.

On a ridge high above the reservoir they halted, subdued by the mournful grandeur of the place, and after scanning the terrain through her field glasses Luisa said, 'there's a plume of smoke way over on the other side of the valley, Felipe. Can you see it? Is something on fire?'

Felipe skipped to her side, his eyes tracing the direction of her finger pointing across the wide valley. 'Yeah, it's a fire alright. It's a mountain farmer burning reed grasses to tenderise the pasture for his sheep and goats in winter.'

'It's certainly bleak here,' Giovanni said, pulling on a woollen cap, 'and damned cold. In fact the area reminds me very much of the highlands of Sardinia in winter.'

'We'll have some good sightings today,' Felipe put in cheerily. 'The reservoir's a paradise for large birds. And there's been so much rain this winter - more than we've had for six years, in fact - the reservoir's swollen to eighty per cent of its capacity. Birds like abundance, don't you agree, señores?'

She gave him a wry smile. Felipe was in his element as tour guide in Julio's absence. All good practise for his private bird centre.

Looking down, the Gorg Blau resembled a steely grey lochan in the wide valley. The sun seldom penetrated into this side of the mountains during the winter months and she felt thankful to be working over on the south facing foothills of Ca'n Clot. They had been walking for over two hours and took the opportunity of this halt to drink from their water bottles. A few cars came and went like toys on the ribbon of the far away road between Soller and Pollensa. Otherwise it was as the book had told her, an eerie, forsaken world, dominated by the reed grass *Ampelodesma mauritanicum* and hushed, but for the occasional bleating of mountain goats or the sudden screech of a hawk.

'Later in the year these ridges are carpeted with milk vetch, *astragalus*, d'you know it?' Felipe asked, turning to her with a grin. 'Its spherical shape gives it the name in Mallorca *coixenet de monja*, or the nun's pillow.'

The three of them stood motionless, field glasses raised, and Luisa's mouth curved, impressed by Felipe's botanical knowledge which he never revealed in Julio's presence, and amused by his snide reference to her own nun-like pillow. We look little different to bird-watchers photographed in this area decades ago, she thought. She had seen pre-war archival photographs, reproduced in a Balearic ornithological magazine, that bore an uncanny resemblance to Felipe, herself and Giovanni Bigatti, binoculars raised, intrepid as any old time explorers caught in the time warp of a sepia photograph. Bauza would be proud of them.

'The ancient kings of Mallorca hunted with falcons here. Imagine hunting with Aquila in this terrain.' Felipe exclaimed and gave a low whistle. 'Wow! that would be something. Leading her on with the whistle from tree to tree. She'd find plenty to eat over here.'

Luisa threw him a tolerant smile, and when he said, 'this area was part of the *Juz de Al-Yibal* in Moorish times,' she exploded with laughter.

Giovanni wanted to know why.

'Oh, it's just that Felipe's fascinated by the island's Moorish past. He's always going on about *Juz* this and *Juz* that.'

'Some Mallorcan place names indicate Arab settlements,' Felipe persisted, serious, uncertain if Luisa mocked him. 'And this area would have attracted them. The area's so impenetrable, you see. First the Moors came, then the Catholic conquerors, then the smugglers and the banditti.'

Giovanni nodded sagaciously. Being a Sardinian, as Felipe had remarked, he knew all about banditti. Only the visitor, more interested in the ospreys he had come to see, suggested briskly that they get on with their trek. They followed Felipe, Indian-file, down a narrow winding path that traced for more than a mile the route of a covered *canaletta* whose hollow chamber amplified the sound of the rushing spring water it carried down to the reservoir. Silently they walked in an unremittingly grey world until, near the Gorg Blau, they came upon the car park. Amateur ornithologists, Felipe said, come here for a good day out.

Then Luisa happened to recognise someone sitting in the driver's seat of one of the jeeps and, surprised by joy, made a detour towards it. Drawing closer she realised someone else was resting on the back seat. To her dismay she recognised Rosa Sanchez and, instinctively, turned away, but not before she had stolen a good look at Nicolas and recognised the bird book he was studying as the one she had loaned him.

He saw her and burst from the car. 'Luisa,' he exclaimed, opening his arms to her, but she murmured a protest, the palms of her hands raised to prevent his embrace. Responding to the reserve in her, his hand shifted to lightly support her elbow. 'Forgive me,' he said, a little embarrassed. 'It's only that I couldn't be more pleased to see you.'

'I'm on a field trip,' she said cooly, moving away, gesturing in the direction of her colleagues who were already through the gate leading to the reservoir. Then Rosa, too, sprung from the car. 'We're on the way to the airport, I'm driving the boss there,' she piped up, but her childlike voice held no charms for Luisa. *He pays her for information . . . .*

247

Filled with unreasonable irritation, she searched their faces, longing to believe there was no other meaning in the coincidence of discovering them together in this high and lonely place. To the airport? Is that all there was to it? She saw herself reflected in the black caverns of Nicolas' eyes - so tiny she couldn't possibly count for much - and said stiffly: 'I forgot to tell you the other night, your assistant's been illegally trespassing on El Escapardo de Cuevas Negras. If you can't control him, then we'll have to.'

'Luisa, let me . . .' Nicolas began, his face filled with consternation, but she turned away and strode towards Felipe and Giovanni who were already waist-high among the grasses at the water's edge.

10

Motherland. Eight or nine years old, I see Spain for the first time.

To me, my maternal grandmother, *abuela,* resembles a terse black bird, all bones and lampshade skin. All flapping cloth in her hilltop eerie that reminds me of Frau Lehmann's house here in Calle Luna. *Abuela* lived in a mountain town, too, with a similar view across a wide valley, its dimensions accentuated by cypress trees, geological cones and suggestive crags. They laid her on a trestle bed but she tried to fly away screeching like a banshee, her arms in the black dress pulling at the air as if she clutched at some invisible chord of life.

It's Mother's voice I hear: 'Go and play outside until supper time, Luisa.'

I played in the moonlight under the plum blossom, never taking my eyes off the lighted windows of the house until my mother came out again to tell me grandma was dead.

That was when the diffused rays of the rising sun wakened her. Turning her head on the pillow she sees bursts of red, yellow, blue and green. Floral and geometric patterns on the woven white background of the curtains. A traditional Mallorcan fabric design, but where is she? Cautiously raising her head, she takes in the bright room with its yellow painted furniture; bookshelves, desk, bedside chests and the ample wardrobe. Her fingers trace the edges of the bed linen, good quality cotton printed in a design of white and gold. I'm in the town. I have a luxurious duvet. Whereas up at Ca'n Clot it's an old navy-blue sleeping bag. I'm at Calle Luna slipping in and out of dreams and haunted by half-forgotten memories.

I can hear . . . almost hear . . . Rafael's voice. It's like this, Luisa, you must *feel* again the emotions of your childhood, you must re-encounter the people you knew, from the beginning of your life to the present if you are to understand the past and free yourself from it. Feel the *atmospheres* of scenes from childhood, relive the emotions.

Is that why I lie here, hovering in Scotland now, the Fatherland? The day my Scottish grandmother died.

'Please Daddy, *do I have to go up?*'

'Yes, yes - silly girl - up you go.'

Harry Ross' stern voice leaves no room for doubt as I climb the cold grey stairs of the Scottish grandmother's house. Keeping to the bright red Turkey runner, my hand only just reaching the balustrade of the wrought iron railings. Pausing to peer through them I want to say again, Daddy, please, must I go? But he is so unmoving below, his eyes following each step I take.

'Up you go, Luisa. Your grandmother has asked to see you.'

One year after Spanish *abuela* died, I tiptoe through the stout door leading into the Scottish grandmother's room. I stand beside the high bed, watching her tweed blanket rise and fall level with my eyes. Her face is made of papier mâché in the darkened room. Horrible, I shudder, and that wakes her up. With a puppet jerk, she sees me through opaque sheep's eyes.

'You've come, child. I want you to look over there.' Her great bony hand points to the monumental Victorian chest-of-drawers where the middle one is slightly open.

'Take out the package lying on top.'

A precisely folded embroidery wrapped in white tissue paper.

'Take it, then run off like a good girl.'

Grannie Ross' voice chokes on a whisper. Death lies beside her, I know, and I'm terrified, fingering the thin crisp paper. I don't have to unwrap it. Inside is the embroidery I worked for her last Christmas. Flowers of Scotland in bold shapes and primary colours. I flee downstairs and fling the package at my father's feet.

'I didn't want it back!' I rage. 'It was a *present*. It was to be hers forever.'

The day after Giovanni Bigatti left, Luisa had looked out from the small barred window of her room on the gallery. A thick cloud bank had descended during the night while she tossed and turned, dreaming she lay in the arms of Nicolas. *La borrasca* had moved in again, blanketing the hoya with a ghostly grey light. More weighty, greyer than Scottish fog. A dour, lifeless grey. Near Ca'n Clot, pitch black trees pierced the thick mist with their antennae-like branches. Relentless cold humidity penetrated everything, and, even after she struggled into her thermals, her entire body felt as if it had been wrapped in damp bandages.

But now she's lying in her bedroom in town, reviewing a grainy black and white silent film. Herself, a forlorn figure in a muffled landscape, groping her way on buckling legs to light the stove in the den. Then going out to feed the dogs. Nothing moving outside, no birds singing in the meteorological paralysis. Hunks of dark red rotting meat scattered in the bird pen, the birds immobile on their perches, their eyes shuttered against a day that promised no joy. The spoon clanks against the metal feeding dishes, the dogs howl and she trembles as if the din might summon havoc-wreaking forces from far above the cloud bank. Beyond the chicken wire fence the fog is so dense, she can't even see the Tree on the Edge. Carrying heavy water bowls to the waiting dogs seems an almost impossible task. Water slops over the edges, soaks the cuffs of her jersey. She does her best to reassure Perro with deep strokes along the length of his back.

Now, in the comfort of the town bedroom, she remembers. My head ached, it always does before a storm. My bones ached, too. That was unusual and my one thought was, must get off the mountain. Yet I hadn't the strength to pack, let alone walk to town. That was the awful bit. Knowing I couldn't leave even if I wanted to. Sleep was all I craved, creeping back into bed and when I wakened hours later, eerie flashes of soundless light suffused the white walls of my cell, over and over again.

Recuerdas? Yes, how vividly I remember. My terror of

lightning storms. One . . . two . . . three. . . then - *crash!* over the mountains. Earth's unconscionable energy streaking upwards to meet the charge of the solar system . . . flash! *crash!* flash! . . . thunder claps and bursts of lightning as if some God of the skies was announcing an end to everything. Releasing chnothic forces to spew out boulders, hurl trees sky high, set avalanches of stones hurtling down Cuevas Negras, scorch trees, crack open others, releasing memories of weather, age and time as they fell to the ground or burned to cinders. A sign of Armageddon, Dad would have said, believing the Old Testament prophecy that one day, out of the blue, the world would end with bolts of lightning and terrible fire. Well, I don't buy that, sinking deeper into Frau Lehmann's luxurious duvet.

Sometime later, sinister light cylinders penetrate the cloud mass and the storm is over. I try to slip from the chrysalis of my sleeping bag as moths do after a storm, to haul myself up to the chair beside the stove, opening all its vents to make the fire roar, hiss and rage red heat, to stop the shivering.

Then the phone rings: 'That was one *helluva* storm, Luisa. It hit the town hard. Several roofs've been whipped off, trees've blown over . . . is everything all right up there?' Julio says.

'I don't feel too good.'

'You sound terrible. You can't stay up there when you're ill. I'm coming to fetch you, Luisa, and don't argue with me please!'

What a relief, that someone, *anyone* cared enough to release me from the dark hell of the mountains.

Now, looking round Frau Lehmann's bright bedroom with its delicate posy of flowers on a yellow shelf of the bookcase, she faces her disappointment - so much work to do up there - only there's nothing to be gained by denial. I couldn't have taken it, all night up there alone, storm after storm. Sometimes it's better for humans not to witness the havoc of the Gods . . . . better get out of the way and leave them to it. And better for me to admit it, I'm a scientist not a heroine.

On the painted yellow bedside chest, an open packet of tissues, a large tumbler of water, a packet of paracetamol tablets, three tangerines. A still-life painting entitled 'Illness'. The clink-clank of movement in the kitchen downstairs. Someone is looking after me . . . I really am ill . . . the 'flu? *la gripe?* . . . I must've caught it on the Inca train with all its snivelling passengers. And have the dreaming Africans and Arabs in their bobbly hats caught it, too? And have they, too, been rescued by a caring hand, and wrapped in a cocoon, like me? No, not much chance of that.

Lapsing back against the ample pillow, her fevered brain holds to fragments of the dream she has just wakened from. Chaotic figures in a spacious, bitterly bright landscape. Identical figures, rushing about in a pattern with no discernible meaning; tall, thin, hairless, with perfect, colourless features and oval heads. Like unprogrammed robots. Like people in cities. The very opposite of Arabs and Africans in the sensuous compounds of the homelands they abandoned to become hopeful migrants in Europe.

Her anxious eyes take in the half-empty yellow bookshelves where a pale green stem-glass holds a spray of honeysuckle and a branch of creamy wild clematis. Its beauty holds her spellbound. Who has put it there? Who has opened the curtains, tiptoeing in when I was asleep? Whoever was downstairs has left. The house has fallen silent. Restlessly, she turns her head from side to side on the pillows. To begin with I thought of Julio as someone who does his duty to the letter - *iy basta!* nothing more. But lately I've come to think of him as extraordinary. Could Julio have left the tissues, the oranges, the water, the pills? And the flowers?

Nothing matters more than my recovery. I must outwit this predator, this virus that pins my body, inert and sweating to the mattress. My dissociated brain, a floating ball of white light on the ceiling, registering, as if for the very first time, the scene beyond this bedroom window. The flinty wall at the bottom of the garden, the pantiled roofs of village houses beyond, a helmeted Gaudí chimney oozing smoke, the Caspar Frederic crag, its scraggy pine trees tearing at the pewter sky.

The mayor said, this is the crag where people worshipped the bull.

Not so long ago, they dug up a figurine, but it's not in Palma museum.

Weightless, disencumbered by my body, my spirit clothed in wings, I fly over the dome of the church that was once a Moorish mosque. Centuries dissolve under the wand of my flight; Christianity, Hellenism, Zoroastrianism, Gods and Heroes, Moses, Abraham, until I alight on the moonlit Hill of the Bull, hearing the regular beat of loud impertinent drumming. I have to fold my wings over my ears. Then, sudden, God-awful bellowing makes me peer over the edge of the crag where a great bull stomps on a silver ledge, invisibly black. The drumming gets louder, pounds my bird brain, drives me crazy.

STOP! *¡BASTA!* I shriek. Kill the beast!

Four priests in white robes surround the bull. One plunges a knife between the shoulder blades. A flock of screeching ravens flees the pine copse. The thunderous weight of the murdered bull falls . . . *R-O-A-R* . . . . A stony avalanche hurtles into the valley.

In Rafael's wings I fly over the body of the bull. I spy on the priests through my bird mask. If only they'd get lost, back to their oratories, I'd attack its flesh, the good bits first, then the sinews. But they hold me off, raising their hands above their upturned bearded faces, shaking their fists. No women allowed in here! I recognise their faces: Ezekiel, Moses, Abraham . . . my gimlet eyes watch them creeping about in candlelight, shrouding the bull carcass in a red cloth before they haul it away to an east-facing burial pit at dawn, and the people of the mountain town waken from their oblivious sleep.

Early sun rays steal through the patterned curtains. Sweat-soaked sheets, feverish head encircled with metal braces.

'Luisa, I'm here.'

Lady Ingeborg at my bedside.

'Why doesn't that damned drumming stop?' *¡basta!* . . . if it did I might get off the ceiling.'

'What drumming, Luisa?'

'Don't you hear it?'

'Oh, *that*? It's only Tonia Ferrer, hammering nails into the shoes. She's working in the hut at the bottom of their garden.'

Anita's hand holding mine earths me to the surface of the white and gold eiderdown. I was a raptor devouring the flesh of the moon-bull, I tell her. Ha! ha! that should scare her off! But no, her hand flies to my forehead. Then I hear running water in the bathroom, feel a cool cloth on my brow, and Anita says: 'Doctor Colom is here'.

'She has influenza, not just a viral infection,' the doctor says. 'Probably of the type brought into Mallorca recently by tourists. She'll be better by *Carnaval*.'

My eyes scrutinise Doctor Colom's hairy hand writing out a prescription, leaning his pad on the bookshelf under the flowers where Anita stands. Then their voices shuffle out of the room leaving me thinking, nothing matters more than my recovery. Spanish 'flu killed more people in Britain after the First World War than the war itself. Viral cruelty. I have *la gripe* in Spain, but it's not Spanish 'flu. It's a strain of Oriental 'flu! Laugh? But I can't even cry, lying helpless, beyond sleeping or dreaming, my mind obsessively drawing maps on the bitter ceiling.

'Can't you sleep, Luisa?'

His voice, the one who said: *I'm coming to bring you to town.*

Why is Julio here? Pinioned under the taught white sheet, too feeble to protest, my eyes following his inexplicable dark form invading my room until he reaches the bedside table and by the light coming in from the window I study his face that has become dear to me.

'*Antibiótico y codeina.*' He reads the labels aloud and lays down two slim packets. 'Better than paracetamol for reducing such a fever as yours, Luisa. That's what the doctor said.'

Motherland - Spain. Fatherland - Scotland. My land - Mallorca. Vetch and cranesbill grow here as well as there.

Here the robin redbreast is *el petitrojo*.

There *el tordus* is the thrush.

Exotic difference enthrals me to Mallorca

date palms, wisteria, bougainvillaea

azahar of citrus trees

azure, tourmaline, and turquoise seas.

Perhaps I'll live here till the day I die; yes, that's it, I'll get a little finca like Anita's with an almond, fig and citrus orchard. Yes, that's what I'll do. The only trouble is, this 'flu might kill me prematurely.

Anita Berens and Julio come into the room. They pull me up onto raised pillows, one of them on either side. Julio slips away and I feel another cool cloth on my forehead.

'Who let you in, Anita?'

'Julio came to ask me if I would nurse you, the night he brought you down from the mountains. After the storm, three days ago.'

'You brought the supplies . . . the pills, the water, the flowers?'

Anita stops plumping up my pillows, looks at me and nods: 'Yes, Julio and I.'

I don't like this intrusion, I'll make her go by saying, thanks Anita, you're very kind, but I'll manage by myself from now on. It's just a case of lying low and getting on my feet again. I'll be fine by tomorrow.

'Huh! With a temperature of 103 degrees I hardly think so.'

Put these two pills on your tongue, she insists, holding my head as I gulp down the water. She tucks a hot water bottle under my feet. Sleep, Luisa. That's the best medicine. And don't worry about a thing. I'll be back later.

Softly, she closes the door.

Why is Julio here? I don't have to ask, listening to them cavorting downstairs.

'Stop, Julio! *¡Basta!*' Anita shrieks in the kitchen.

That woman has been nothing but trouble since I arrived in town, and now she's messing about with Julio, and I want them both out of the house.

The whitewashed wall behind the open bookshelf is embroidered with the yellow pollen heads of mimosa and the fronded, almond green tracery of its leaves. Someone has added another floral tribute to the honeysuckle and clematis, also in a slim stem-glass. A thoroughly inventive use of the German woman's hollow glass candlesticks from the dining table downstairs.

Was it Anita or Julio? Which of them came stealthily into the room bringing me floral tributes as I hovered on the ceiling thinking of death?

Someone switches on the bedside lamp. Lovely lady, that Ingeborg. Or is she Nefertiti, full of duplicity and cunning with her walnut handled gun?

'I've come to take your temperature,' she says.

What a smile she has, leaning over me until I feel her mercurial rod between my teeth.

Anita is me, I am Evie, ill after the death of our mother. Poor kid, ten years old with meningitis, the hospital corridors long and cruel under neon lighting until I find her ward. 'You are *not going to die, Evie,*' I tell her, leaning over her bed, clutching her hand that's wet with my tears. 'I won't let you.'

Anita says: 'Your temperature is down a little, Luisa. It's a hundred degrees. Now you won't have to stare at the ceiling. You'll be able to sleep.'

Ceiling maps. *Cartas de navegación.* Largs, St Andrews, Glasgow, Barcelona, Mallorca. Clean cut holiday maps: Edinburgh, Maeshowe. Maps in an obsolete gazetteer that once belonged to Dan and I, lately of a bothy on an island cut off by the tide.

A bird might fly swiftly from any one of these places and back, to another place and back, and another, faster and faster, defying time, memorising these maps, superimposing layer upon layer of memory until the result resembles no other map in the entire universe. It is My Map - Luisa Ross's - alone. A map of my life, as unique as my fingerprint. The question is, when dreamers die, what happens to their maps?

I'm not going to die but I do need a map with instructions for escape. Isolated on this bed, search-lighting the white ceiling, I have no end and no beginning. I'm no more than an element in a still-life painting of a yellow table with a bowl of tangerines. That is all I am and all is always now, this suspension of time. Did that thought occur to people dying with Spanish influenza, or to my ancestral bog people waiting to be cast into peaty waterlogged graves the colour of dried blood? In their so called unenlightened Dark Age did they meet their fate without questioning their belief that this was how life must be?

Three days? Four days? Medicine, water, hot water bottles, piss pot. Yes, I need a map to escape. A map the size of reality overwhelms me. Yet, a well-felt landscape needs no map. Old carboneros like Alejandro Ferrer needed no maps. With memory of a landscape you can make a map; I can get there with my eyes closed:

Casas Viejas - the meseta - the oak wood
the precipitous path on the edge -
the Golden Bowl - Ca'n Clot - the hide
Hiding place

Beyond the curtained window, another day dies. Skye. Dan and I. Julio and Anita. Felipe and his birds. Rafael and my wings. *Cartas de navegación. Casa Viejas*, Nicolas. Swept away by profound longing for his embrace, Luisa burst into tears.

Late at night Lourdes sends contributions to *Flight into Exile* via 'computer share'. She keeps an eye on Luisa during the day, and sleeps over in the spare bedroom of Gerda Lehmann's house, where she has installed the computer. Now that someone is in the next room, anyone - even someone as ill as Luisa - she sleeps soundly, all through the night.

Waking at dawn . . . the curtains have been left open . . . the valley is a river of silver mist. The Puig de Magdalena in the centre of *La Pla* is a purple-black hummock under a dark violet sky. The cockerels are already crowing, dogs bark distantly from several directions. Hearing the guns go off she turns her head uneasily on the pillows. *Fly away little birds!* Then the church bell rings out the hour twice as it always does. Why it that, I once asked Julio? So that if you don't hear it the first time you might hear it the next, he replied. Now it chimes the hour of seven and a sliver of red steals up the western flank of the Puig. The vermilion gesture of a painterly God. The red stain swells like a red balloon pulling away, rising gloriously free of its proscribed axis,

Later, Luisa sits up against the pillows exhausted as if by a long journey watching Anita tidying the room.

'The flowers are lovely, Anita.'

They have wilted a little, the honeysuckle on its twiggy stem, the mimosa and the miniature bough of wild clematis, look dry and peppery.

'Did you bring them?'

'I brought the first posy. Julio picked the mimosa for you.'

'Julio? You two?'

'Yes. ' Anita averts her amused eyes.

Luisa notices. Anita looks so vivacious you'd scarcely recognise her, her hair pulled back as if to cradle a red rose. 'But you are so unlike, he's so . . . .'

Anita's cuts off her remark with an enigmatic smile. 'Yes, perhaps, but he makes me feel alive.'

They smile at each other in the silence before Anita says sweetly: 'We'll talk soon, Luisa, when you're stronger. But would you like a little breakfast now?'

'How long have I been here? Four days?'

'No, this is day five and the good news is your temperature is normal. Later you might like a warm bath.'

'Have I been talking in my sleep?'

Anita considered this. 'Yes . . . quite a bit. It was nonsensical, I didn't really pay much attention.'

'I had one of those flying dreams.' Luisa said. How can one dismiss the nurse who has kept vigil? The moment has long passed, several days ago, when I hadn't the strength.

Dawn over the bothy on my island, followed by a radiant sun. Dawn at Maeshowe, the sun illuminating the runes that say 'Ingeborg is the loveliest of women'. Without Anita to nurse me they would have taken me to the hospital in Inca. As it is, I'm feeling almost well and next week, ready or not, I'll be back in the mountains. My first report to the professor already late.

Today marks the dawning of a new era. I am Luisa Ross, 39 years old as of a few days ago, a biologist working towards a doctorate in ornithology. I arrived in Mallorca a short time ago to complete my observations of the habitat of *Aegypius monachus*, the indigenous Black vulture. I've lost precious time through no fault of my own . . . hey, wait a minute . . . you didn't have to go back to town or to have supper with Anita and her friend Colin, did you? Or stay up half the night listening to her drama? Or indulge in romantic fantasies about the Don? The Palma lecture was unavoidable, certainly, and this 'flu was beyond your control . . . and now here's Anita bringing in the breakfast tray. Tea, toast, a boiled egg. I'm ravenous.

Accept her without question. Humility, like forgiveness, is endless. You've a lot to be grateful for. Hasn't she seen you through from dark to light?

'You've had several phone calls,' she says. 'From someone calling himself Monterey. He says he'd like to speak to you when you're well enough.'

In the bath, how sweet the warm lavender bubbles frothing its smooth surface. Mountain lavender. How frail my body, how glad my heart. I'm getting well, really I am!

Julio and Anita, ah! ha! . . . *I* can scarcely remember what sex feels like, I'm dead between the legs, yet love's restorative grace radiates from Anita bringing me tangerines, picked, she tells me, from a tree in her own orchard, and I'm filled with hope.

Anita hands me my mobile phone: 'It's him again.'

I rise up, throw off the bedclothes and tell him, yes, yes, I'm better. Yes, I'm remembering our supper date. I was so rude at the reservoir the other day. I don't know what came over me. I must have been in that sensitive state before illness hits, but didn't know it. You're falling in love with me? What can I say? Yes, see you not this Sunday but the next.'

For an entire day thick snow falls fast, blanketing the German woman's garden, the roof pantiles and the distant Hill of the Bull, as it does once or twice a year in the mountain towns of Mallorca. Anita has lit the stove downstairs whose pipe shoots up through the bedroom delivering heat, melting away the last remnants of illness. She turns her head to watch the surprising snow falling, soft as eider feathers against the window pane.

María Ferrer brought nourishing dishes every day. *Sopes Mallorquines* (soup with cabbage, other vegetables and soggy brown bread), *Arroç Brut* (rice with bits of rabbit or chicken and vegetables) and *Caldo con Fideos* (chicken broth with noodles). To begin with Luisa stayed upstairs, hearing Anita and María cracking jokes downstairs in the kitchen. Then, when she was stronger, she ate lunch with Anita on the small terrace above Frau Lehmann's narrow garden in bright and sunny weather after the freak days of snow. Sounds from next door spilled over the rose hedge as the Ferrer women bustled and chuckled in the yard and Tonia tap-tapped in the woodshed. Everything was returning to normal.

One day during lunch, Anita nudged Luisa and said in a low voice, 'Tonia was the result of a one-night stand many years ago after the Inca fair. The man vanished off the island when he heard the child was due.'

'And now Tonia is banished to the woodshed?' Luisa suppressed a grin. After all, it was far from funny that María's chances of marrying someone else in those days would have been ruined. And Tonia had grown up without a father. Still, she thought, she'd been fortunate to have had passionate old Alejandro as a father substitute.

'But how do you know about María?'

'She told me yesterday. It's common knowledge in the village so Luisa had better know. That's what she said.'

Anita returned in the evenings after her regular rendezvous with Julio. One evening she blurted out: 'Julio and I are going to Ibiza for a few days after you're better. To celebrate Carlos' birth. As of today I am a grandmother! Elena had a boy at a New York clinic last night.'

At the same time as she was offering her congratulations, Luisa felt an ache of loss. She hadn't even achieved motherhood.

'Being a grandmother is the most wonderful feeling,' Anita went on. 'I can't express it. It's different from giving birth yourself. Oh, I can't wait to see him! One day he'll inherit my

Mallorcan properties. All the planting, pruning, construction I'm doing out there is for him. I knew he would be born one day.'

Will I ever know Anita's 'inexpressible' feeling? she wondered, then took comfort in a memory of her own, the feeling of being enfolded in Nicolas' arms after she came down from the crag . . . despite his long absence, their encounters lingered, dreamlike, in her mind, and she found herself confiding in Anita her interest in the new owner of the estate on the mountainside.

'Mysterious Monterey of the telephone calls?' said Anita.

Yes, she nodded, but, lest the magical quality of her speculation become lost in further disclosure, she refused to be drawn further.

For the first time in almost two weeks, she had been able to prepare her own supper and, afterwards lay resting on the sofa next to the fire. She tried to thrust from her thoughts the work she could have done if she hadn't become ill, and sent off a fax to Professor Bauza.

'The hospitals of Spain are filled with the victims of influenza,' came his reply. '*No te preocupes*. Of course you may extend the deadline for your field study. Furthermore, you must not return to base until you have fully recovered. My old school friend Doctor Colom will keep an eye on your progress.'

A goshawk wheeled above wild land at the far end of Anita's orchard when they came in through the gate. They went past the ochre stone building to stand under the almond blossom. During her illness, the spectacular mist of white and pink blossom had erupted all over the valley, and now she felt she could have lingered forever under that canopy of delicate, billowing floral tents, raised high above the red earth on snaking black tree trunks. The orange trees were fruiting, too, among gnarled old olive trees and well-mulched beds of herbs and vegetables, their leaves radiating back the early afternoon light.

Luisa's eyes narrowed, tracing the goshawk ringing up against the mountains, its flight linking the tender acres of foreground blossom with the grainy backdrop of the uncompromising, snow-girt Massanella. And, when the bird shrieked at the top of its spiral, she knew it again. It is for moments like this that I live; the winged dreams of childhood. Eagerly, her eyes sought Casas Viejas, a distant cube below the white mountain and she swelled with longing to re-engage with Nicolas, their footprints criss-crossing the spoor of animals and birds, composing together a song without words.

She went through the rickety door with Anita, where the island's agricultural past staked its claim in the form of ancient wooden farm implements hanging against the parchment coloured walls. Fronds of drying red peppers, tomatoes and herbs hung from a platform above their heads. Since there was no electricity, Anita lit candles in their dusty green bottles and, after that, set light to the paper twists and sticks lying in the stove.

'We'll come in here again if you feel cold. You must be careful not to get chilled.'

'You sound just like my mother,' Luisa grinned.

The sweet musky scent of burning fig wood incensed the room.

'Will you visit me up in the mountains, Anita? Stay overnight as a thank you for all you've done for me?'

Anita considered this: 'Mountains aren't exactly my cup of tea. They *scare* me. But I might come up on the day of your talk to the townsfolk and stay on after that.'

Another day they reached Anita's finca, arm-in-arm at midmorning, Anita carrying her drawing materials in an old wooden box. Julio was to pick them up later so that Luisa, on her first full day out, only had to walk one way.

'Van Gogh and Utrillo would have rejoiced in this landscape,' Anita said, striding through the gate, while Luisa wandered on further, past hedgerows ribboned with bearded clematis and pale blue periwinkle, picking stalks of wild asparagus and fennel. When she returned to the orchard Anita was drawing, her eyes squinting between the paper and her oblique view of the orchard to determine its shape and form.

'In a few weeks, when the blossom has given way to almond green leaves, the colour of the earth will look quite different,' she said thoughtfully. 'No longer offset by layer upon layer of shades of pink and white blossom, the earth will appear much darker against the green trees.'

Luisa sees Anita with different eyes, marvelling that Anita the artist, Anita in love, Anita the nurse, Anita the grandmother, could be one and the same person as Anita the hysteric who had arrived around midnight not so long ago to tell her she had shot the dog.

Bernardo had returned and seemed to accept the verdict of the town. Someone had let his dog out. The dog had gone missing, it was as simple as that. *How* it might have gone missing provoked endless speculation in the bar, and the rustic Bernardo, generous and open-hearted in every way except in his treatment of dogs - *phff!* God made dogs to serve man, to guard *his* property, to hunt for *him*, *iy basta!* - reported the disappearance to the alcalde's office and, unwilling to point a finger at his *amigo* Tamarit, left it at that. Here was another of those open-ended events that absorbed the small community's imagination for days on end before they grew bored and picked up the thread of something new. Anita, and Luisa, too, had almost forgotten the incident. One day Anita had remarked on the blissful peace that had returned to the orchard, but that was all. And, although Luisa wondered if Anita had told Colin Cramer she had shot the dog, she thought it better not to ask.

They sat together in companionable silence, until Luisa said: 'Anita, isn't time you told me about your life?' Anita's hand hovered over her drawing: 'What d'you want to know?'

'Well, why are you here in the mountain town alone? The *real* reason, I mean? You promised you'd tell me one day . . . you said you might, don't you remember? That night you were so upset, after you shot the dog?'

Anita got up and brusquely began packing away her materials. Alarmed by such a dramatic alteration in the atmosphere between them, 'have I said something wrong?' Luisa added anxiously.

'No, but let's go inside . . . to the stove . . . we'll have coffee. It's getting chilly.'

It was as if a mirror reflecting Anita's face had cracked. From light to dark, from one moment to the next. 'We need more than candlelight, but where are the matches?' Anita muttered.

Since she hadn't a clue where to find matches, Luisa lowered herself into a rickety old chair, filled with dismay. I'm not to enquire further, she thought, tracing with her eyes the lines and fissures of the old stone floor. I must wait to be told only what she wants to divulge in her own good time.

'I'm sorry I asked why you live here. Drop it if you want.'

Anita grimaced: 'No, I *want* to tell you.' Then, with a triumphant cry, she seized the matchbox from its hiding place. The paraffin lamp burst into life and Anita laid the kettle on the stove saying 'I live here because I'm on the run.'

'You're *what*?'

'It's true. I'm in hiding . . . on the run, in hiding.' Anita stumbled over the absurd contradiction of her words but she didn't smile.

'In hiding? So that's how you come to have a revolver.'

Anita folded her arms over her stomach as if to contain herself: 'Yes, it's for protection.' She gave a disdainful laugh. 'You see, my husband had me seized and locked up in Colombia until Colin and a friend got me out almost three years ago. And, unless my so-called *husband* dies, it looks like I'll be on the run for the rest of my life. That's what makes me act demented sometimes, like the night I came to you for help. And it would be the same wherever I lived. Mallorca, this town, is better than most I've tried.'

Overcome with a sense of ignorant dismay, 'oh, my God,' Luisa murmured. 'It must've been awful for you that night, me rabbiting on about Rosa and Colombia, while you . . . .'

'Oh, I don't hold that against you,' Anita broke in. 'It *was* a rather bizarre coincidence. I'd no idea how many exiles from South America, refugees, immigrants, asylum seekers . . . call them what you like, have fled to Mallorca and the rest of Spain. I imagined I was the only one.'

Struggling to adjust to Anita's revelation, Luisa watched her making coffee in an old red enamelled pot. And when she handed her a coffee mug and sat down stiffly in the chair beside her own, she said: 'Do you feel like telling me more?'

'Yes, I do. But where to begin? . . . When we first met, Andreas, my estranged husband, was Adonis for me. Handsome, charming, with the wild heart of a boy. Only soon after our marriage it became clear to me just how emotionally vulnerable he really was. He was part-Jewish, with Sephardic ancestors from Toledo, a Spanish father and a German mother. Both parents died in concentration camps when he was very young. The Nazis had been jealous of the family's wealth - they had a shipping empire based in Hamburg - and before his parents were murdered . . . after *Kristallnacht* . . . they lost everything. I was only nineteen when we met in Paris in 1971. Andreas was a refugee, as poor as a church mouse, but full of energy and determination, when he wasn't in the grip of one of his weighty depressions that could last for days. In the end you felt you were dealing with two separate and essentially different personalities.'

'What were you doing in Paris?'

'Studying art. My background was fairly privileged. My family got out of Europe in the late 1930s and spent the war years in America where I was born in 1952. My father was a diplomat. After Andreas and I married we moved to Central America where Andreas told me we would live the lives of the super-rich. All that rubbish was important to me as a young bride. Designer dresses, fancy parties, mingling with superstars, the international emigrant set. Now I know better. Give me the simple life! Anyway, Andreas told me that in Colombia, the shapes, colours and textures of the landscape would inspire my painting. And I *was* inspired, and I was happy on the ranch he bought. Elena was born there and in a few years he had become a wealthy industrialist. We had the large estate near Bogotá and divided our time between it and London and Paris where we also owned properties. Quite the little globetrotters we were.'

'And then?'

'Andreas became increasingly determined to turn himself into a millionaire; he was *driven* to recoup his family fortunes, and in the early days of the drugs cartels Colombia was the place to make easy money. He travelled a lot and I was left alone a great deal, living the life of a socialite, riding, partying, taking drugs. In time I came to see it as a useless, wasted life, and I was sick of the flirtatious fortune hunters that hung about our house in Andreas' absence. In later years I suspected him of having affairs during his trips to the Far East. I had one or two myself. On the face of it he owned a shipping line with offices world-wide, from Hong Kong to Buenos Aires. As a matter of fact, until relatively recently I believed our money came from shipping deals. It did, but the drugs racket augmented it. The two activities tied in well, you see. He was sending cocaine and other drugs all over the world with cargoes of more innocent goods, even over here to Mallorca. This island's awash with drugs, did you know? It's as corrupted as anywhere on earth. It's ironic, really, that my properties here in Mallorca were bought with the allowances Andreas gave me. I deposited large sums over the years in a Swiss bank account, unaware of how black the money was.

'It's a long story, but since Julio'll be here any minute to collect us, I'll cut it short. Before the awful day I was abducted, I had decided to clean up my act, to create a new life before it was too late. I started working in radio. Developing programmes for Colombian women about health and education. Yet all the time I was plotting to get away. Colombia can be a nasty place. I couldn't just walk out, I had a teenage daughter to consider, my departure had to be carefully planned. Only Andreas struck first and had me seized.'

'Andreas couldn't just let you go? You knew too much about his drugs dealing?'

'Well, yes, that, and because he was very dependent on me. I alone knew about his depressions. The result of losing his parents when he was a baby, I suppose. Seemingly powerful men are often weak emotionally, and the wife has to prop them up. Yes, I knew too much. But I had fallen in love, too, with one of my colleagues, and someone must have tipped Andreas off. The watching countryside in Colombia is merciless, I can tell you! Andreas knew I might leave Colombia with my lover and, I suppose, his pride just couldn't take it. That's what I think. He wanted to punish me but the method he chose was outrageous.'

'It certainly seems so,' Luisa said and added hesitantly: 'But if, as you say, you're on the run, how have you stayed out of their clutches? Surely it's quite easy to track someone down just by asking in local bars, for example?'

'Well, they almost found me a year or so back when I was living near Zaragoza. Colin happened to pick up information that one of Andreas' men was in Spain and tipped me off in the nick of time.' Anita laughed dryly then said, 'haven't you realised I'm *disguised*.'

Startled by confused emotions, Luisa stared at Anita in disbelief.

'This hair, the contact lenses, the clothes my real self wouldn't be seen dead in . . . and, of course, my name is not Anita Berens, and not even you, *amiga mía*, can know my real name. Perhaps soon, but not yet'

Cradling the warm coffee mug between her hands, Luisa felt she might cry. It must be that I'm still weak from the 'flu. I'm overreacting . . . but all that *empathy* I've been feeling for Anita, who wasn't Anita after all? For these past weeks I have been deceived. It wasn't *Anita* who came to tell me about the dog that night, but someone else. It was someone else who shot the dog, someone else who met Felipe in the mountains, someone else who nursed me, and someone else is sitting beside me now.

Anita almost whispered: 'I had to trust you absolutely before I could tell you all this.'

The contentment, deep happiness even, I've felt these past days in Anita's company, was that real or illusory?

Anita said softly: 'I'm sorry. Please believe me, these past few days with you I have felt closer to my true self than I've done for a very long time. Somehow, since I shot that dog, I've stopped being afraid of Andreas. I've realised I have to shed the disguise, get on and live life to the full regardless of the consequences.'

'Well, then,' Luisa said, almost petulant, 'surely you can tell me your real name? Colin Cramer called you Lourdes. I overheard him that day, it was Saint Anthony's Fest, when he sat in your garden. And it slipped out again that evening we had supper together. Is you real name Lourdes?'

'Yes, I'm Lourdes Herreros,' she said awkwardly, and to Luisa's consternation, burst into tears.

This is, and is not, the same person I comforted that night at Calle Luna. It's different now. We are *friends*, and she is *Lourdes* . . . the name sounded so strange, how would it be possible to *say* it? . . . who, for the first time in months, has been able to tell the truth to another human being apart from Colin: I am Lourdes Herreros. But right now I need to be practical.

'Is there any booze here?' Luisa said mustering what she could of forgiveness.

'We're always at the bottle you and I,' Lourdes burst out, smiling through her tears.

There was plum brandy. When they went out to watch the sun setting over the orchard, glasses in hand, Luisa tried to picture the real woman. Black hair or brown hair, definitely not blonde. Brown eyes or dark blue eyes, definitely not green eyes hooded by coloured contact lenses.

'What about your book?' she asked. 'The history of tourism in Mallorca?'

'I'm afraid that's just a front, like my name. I'm no writer,' Anita said wistfully. 'After I got to Europe Colin made an appointment for me in Paris with a disguise expert. Someone who had skillfully altered the looks of pop stars as well as international criminals including old Nazis.'

'Did you have plastic surgery, anything like that?'

'No, nothing as drastic. It's all cosmetic, although he gave me language and posture coaching, tips on concealment and stealth. We came up with the Anita Berens name, and, of course, a new passport. Look, this must be difficult for you, Luisa. But if it's any comfort, I feel one helluva lot better now that the cat's out of the bag. I've had more than enough of such a life, it's been a strain wearing this disguise, and now I'm ready to drop it.'

'When will you do it?' *People do change,* she reminded herself . . . but her question trailed away when they heard Julio driving up and Lourdes rushed to the gate to meet him.

After he had left them at Calle Luna, Lourdes said: 'It might help you to come to terms with what I've told you if you read a draft of the book Colin's writing about my escape from Colombia. It's all on my computer upstairs.' And when Luisa looked doubtful, she insisted: 'Colin won't mind at all. In fact he *urged* me to tell you the truth after the three of us had dinner together. Right from the start he knew we could trust you.'

In the days before she returned to Ca'n Clot, Luisa devoted time to *Flight Into Exile.* On the bookshelves in the computer room she found a World Atlas showing Colombia south of Belize, its coastline bordering the southern Atlantic Ocean. When she pulled herself away from the computer and went downstairs to find Lourdes, sometimes they would discuss at length a scene from the book, at other times Lourdes would shrug and say, 'well, you know, it's not a pretty world!' or, 'there you go, that's life!' and it would be obvious to Luisa that she wasn't in the mood to talk. Continually, she thanked Luisa for her support. 'Now I don't feel alone in the world,' she would say with her strange sad smile.

There were moments in the book Luisa couldn't get out of her mind: ' . . . *it happened with lightning speed* . . . the unimaginable became reality *de entre la nada.'* A discordant note, she thought, one mighty blast on the Asborno whistle and the hawk seizes the prey. Lourdes Herreros. She struggled to get used to the name. Someone who inhabited a world similar to Rosa's. Despite the vast differences in their social and financial status, each woman had taken flight from a terror-stalked country.

Determined to understand the political momentum that underpinned Colin's story she re-read parts of the book. Drugs empires had taken off almost innocently with a few small aeroplanes, but gradually Colombia had become, to quote from the book, a criminal society 'spawning evil like venomous mushrooms throbbing away in a dank cave'. His conclusion had the force of something obvious she had never realised before.

'Terrorism has become commonplace in every part of the globe as the downside of globalisation and the information age.'

Parts of *Flight Into Exile* read like a novel. The character Angel Zavala particularly fascinated her . . . he'd be just like one of those *cholos* that seized Rosa's home in the countryside. On the other hand, couldn't he also have been one of the youths Rafael had told her about, driven from his poverty stricken pueblo to find money in the cities, to survive by whatever means.

'We're gonna die young, right? So we say, live for the moment . . . you're quite a nice lady, but you don't have an idea even the size of a piece of *fluff* what it is like to be born poor in Colombia.'

She winced at that. Angel Zavala might as well have been talking to her. Unable to shift particular vignettes from her mind, they returned at odd moments. Sentences and moments haunted her unbidden before she fell asleep. Even when she was working upstairs on her own research notes, she would relive episodes from Lourdes' story. An uncanny world, so hazardous, so fragile that hooded men with guns might burst in at any moment and smash a life to pieces. Fragmented lives, broken pale blue fragments like the shattered eggs of thrushes, or nestlings whose parents have been seized by hawk or hunter.

§

Pockets of snow clung stubbornly to the highest reaches of the mountain but all around Ca'n Clot the stony ground lay clear. Recent days had been cold and bright and *la borrasca* had moved off. Thankful for the radiant day, Luisa walked briskly to the Golden Bowl for the first time since her illness, aware of her lingering weakness and the rasping cough she hoped the exercise might shift.

Eventually, Doctor Colom had signed her off, his bony face lengthening with a warning. 'In theory you have recovered. However you must take it easy for another week or two. These influenza viruses linger in our bodies for some time after we

271

feel well . . . rest is the key to sending them packing, my dear Señora Ross. You must promise to rest.'

The day before, when Felipe arrived to feed the aviary birds, she had gone out to tell him she would be working indoors.

'But, hey!' he protested: 'I've brought you an ostrich egg.'

And there it was, blossoming out of his palm, his fingers cradling its chalky smoothness. Felipe Tamarit's way of saying he has buried the past with Bernardo's dog, and she had gone with him to watch the Egyptian vulture performing its astonishing feat. Studiously the brave creature stood not much taller than the egg, then aimed the flinty stone, also provided by Felipe. What an extraordinary world I have come to inhabit, she thought, seeing yolk and albumen spill out over the grey gravel. After that, back in the den, she read a research paper on the hatching of vulture chicks in captivity. There were photographs of a featherless hatchling emerging - extremely ugly, she had to admit, yet touching as any new-born - through the broken membrane of its shell.

How swiftly her life was altering. Sometimes she felt events were running away with her so that the long stretches of time she craved for the fieldwork that had engaged her more than anything else in her life to date, seemed increasingly to lie beyond her reach. Yes, there were far too many distractions; the world of Lourdes Herreros that was and was not what it seemed, illness . . . and love. But illness is unavoidable, and isn't falling in love unavoidable too? Now I feel driven, for once in my life, to leap into the life of another in a small victory over self-effacement. Nicolas had sent a voicemail message to remind her of their meeting on Sunday. 'We will be alone, and that's good since I have something very important to tell you . . . I can hardly wait to see you'. Thoughts of him played like musical sequences in her mind. Fragments that could not be banished by willpower. Fragments that insinuated themselves, over and over again. He had magnetised her so that, not only in her dreams but in waking moments, too, her spirit flew out to re-encounter his. Passionate dreams wakened her, almost sick with longing, dreams that engulfed her entire being even as she slept. Dreams that unleashed such erotic desire, their remembrance shocked her and elated her, both at once. Yet, occasionally, a small voice of warning would dance into her thoughts like a little red devil brandishing a pitchfork; isn't this all make-believe? You scarcely know the man.

In England it was a public holiday. Colin Cramer was ensconced in his study, working on *Flight into Exile*. He could hear the joyful cries of Felice and the children rising from the snow girt lawn where they had the sledge. Peering out of the window earlier, he had seen the huge snowman they had made with its carrot nose. Ahoy! he had called and they had all looked up, waving and laughing, but not begging him to come down. They respected without question his right to work undisturbed in his study.

He read over the first paragraph of chapter three and decided it would do as a next-to-final draft: 'Lourdes Herreros, a radio journalist, had never openly attacked the drugs trade in her popular broadcasts aimed at promoting self-awareness in Colombian women. How could she when she knew each minute, each second of every programme was being monitored? How could she when her own husband, Andreas Herreros, profited on the edges of the game? Above all, how could she when she had a teenage daughter to protect? No, the issues aired on her programme were strictly confined to health, well-being and self-improvement. In some broadcasts she touched on abuse, both physical and mental. Many of her listeners suffered from that in towns and villages run by criminal gangs of the drugs cartels.'

More must be included about the lives of these women, he decided, typing a memo. *Ask Gustavo to send taped versions of some of Lourdes' broadcasts.* Then he found himself typing an additional paragraph. 'Despite her impeccable approach on air, for sometime before her kidnapping Lourdes Herreros *had* become a potential target of the cartels, not because they feared she might attack them in her top-rating broadcasts but because her husband had realised she had cuckolded him and that every day she was becoming more desperate to leave him and he could not allow that to happen. Lourdes Herreros had wounded his pride by embarking on an affair with one of her radio colleagues and must take the consequences.'

Gustavo and Lourdes! In consternation, he re-read what he had just written. Yes, he thought, I know it to be true. In fact I have always known it to be true. It wasn't like him to trust intuition over hard facts, but there it was, the words had, well, just *arrived*. And, after all, hadn't he read them in Lourdes' face every time Gustavo's name had come up on his last trip to Mallorca?

Next morning, the London office was a hive of activity where next month's *Ecco!* was being put to bed. Colin had approved James Denton's article 'Spanish Smugglers of White Mischief'' and was waiting to see him. He tossed the typescript onto the mounting pile of proofs then, approved with his blue pencil his own editorial, flicked through the set pages covering national environmental issues, and scrutinised the international pages carrying the piece he had asked the news editor to research on the Scot, Callum Kerr, who had been held in Colombia for over six hundred days. The news had come through that morning: a prominent guerrilla group had just released him. Almost two years of a young life wasted, waiting in a vacuum of Colombian terror.

'Your piece is fine,' he said when James came in. 'Only, the photograph's deadly dull. We need something more dramatic. See if you can come up with a pic of the *Vega II* at sea, crew on board, customs men coming alongside, that sort of thing. Try *El Pais*. They're sure to have something they can lend us from their photo library. See if you can get a pic of Callum Kerr, too. Oh, and James, I want to move the Kerr piece up beside yours and add a companion piece I'll write myself.'

'But, Colin . . . *sir*. The magazine's already stuffed to the gunnels. There simply *isn't* room. There isn't enough time either.'

'We'll *make* room. We'll *make* time. Drop a half-page advertisement if necessary.'

James' mouth fell open and Colin guessed he was thinking, it's not like the boss to entertain even a slight drop in advertising revenue. He surprised himself then by saying, 'stepping out of line now and again, taking a little risk adds zest to life, don't you agree? Oh, and by the way, how's your research coming along.'

James responded by handing Colin a memo: 'I thought this might interest you'.

'What is it?'

'A list of Colombian Extraditables.'

Colin felt a blood-pumping rush of anxiety. He put on his spectacles to scan the list. The As, the Bs, the Cs - there were a hell of a lot of names - until he arrived at the H's. And, there it was: Andreas Herreros.

'How'd you get this information?'

'Through the Drugs Enforcement Agency using my NUJ documents. They gave me a Net link to the guys.'

'Did you succeed in contacting any of them?'

'Alvaro, Estrellas and Herreros, sir.'

'Take Herreros, for example? How did that go?' Colin said, jabbing his pencil at the one name that mattered.

'Oh, Herreros wouldn't agree to a telephone interview. He sent me an e-mail asking for my credentials and I faxed him copies of my NUJ creds and a couple of extracts from *Ecco!* When he asked to speak to the managing editor, I told him you were away in Mallorca.'

Colin held to his seat, inwardly wrecked by a bizarre mixture of fear and anger. 'Cramer's in Mallorca! You told him *that*?'

'Yes, well . . . you *were* in Mallorca, sir, everyone knew that here in the office. It wasn't a secret was it?'

'I've been over to Mallorca several times in recent weeks,' Colin said stiffly. Fear peppered his mind. Lourdes. Was she in danger because of this? Surely Herreros would've put two and two together, would've linked the name Cramer with his documentary which had been screened internationally in 2001.

He needed time to think. 'James, get this clear and straight in your mind right now. I expressly forbid you to reopen *any* of your contacts in Colombia. Finish writing the *Vega II* story and after that you're to stick to British stories under the supervision of Guy Pascoe. Guy will vet all your external contacts from now on. Draw a line under the Vega story right away. And bring me *all* your files on Colombia, hard and floppy. *Now!*'

'After that initial contact I couldn't get through to Herreros,' James said, unaccountably lamed. 'His telephone link went dead. He didn't respond to e-mails. The other two, Alvaro and Estrellas, were more promising though, and . . . .'

'Kill these stories too. That'll be all for now.'

He had badly underestimated the intelligence of his old friend Jimmie Denton's son. His own lack of judgement had led to this.

Guy Pascoe came in and laid a set of galley proofs on Colin's desk with a look that said 'can we discuss'? Colin realised he had been murdering his pencil. Broken pieces lay on his desk. With an embarrassed laugh he swept aside the debris and told his exasperated editor, not now, later. I need to cool off.

He walked up the Bayswater Road in the mizzling rain under his umbrella, his mood as foul as the weather. He entered the park and trailed round a circuit of paths. Near the pond a posse of scrawny, grey pigeons attacking an abandoned chip bag blocked his path. He wanted to rout them with his foot, but the thought of their horrid grey fluttering round his head sent him on a detour to the other side of the pond. Then he gave up on the great outdoors and took himself off to the comfort of his cafe, a copy of *The Indepenent* under his arm. A few minutes later he was staring at a headline on the International News pages: 'US on alert as Colombia frees cocaine barons'. Swiftly, he read the short article: *A decision by a Colombian judge to order the early release from prison of two of the world's most notorious drug traffickers has appalled American officials and raised fears of fresh confrontations with the cocaine smuggling empires. The news comes after the early release of several Extraditables from prison this month, some of whom are believed to have left the country.*

Back at the office he kept his cool - *after the early release of several Extraditables this month* - fielded a hundred and one questions while agonising inwardly over the best way to break the news to Lourdes.

For much of the night he had lain awake in his flat overlooking Tower Bridge . . . *some of whom are believed to have left the country* . . . Gustavo's phone had rung on an on until the line went dead and he remembered it was Gustavo's habit to quit Bogotá and walk in the mountains whenever he could. He had sent an e-mail then, 'Urgent. Can we discover A. H's. whereabouts?'

The next morning his computer screen displayed fifteen messages from different parts of the world but none from Colombia. Saturday in London . . . Friday night in Colombia . . . Saturday morning in Mallorca. Over there, they were one hour behind London. He looked at his watch. It would be nine-thirty in Mallorca and, consistent as ever, Lourdes would be getting ready to leave Calle Luna for her finca. He stretched out his arm and dialled her number for the umpteenth time.

C'mon, c'mon, he urged. She'll be out there pruning almond trees, he guessed. *I hope*, he said under his breath, or, perhaps she's with Luisa Ross? The tone rang out. Putting down the handset he cursed under his breath remembering: isn't Luisa's talk this coming Monday . . . only I've booked my flight for *Tuesday*? Damn shame, still it can't be helped. And he added two more things to his growing list of self-reproaches: he should have persuaded Lourdes to get a mobile phone and he should have noted down Luisa Ross's number for just such an eventuality as this. Now he would have to carry the worry - was Lourdes safe? - until he finally tracked her down.

Just as he hung up Guy Pascoe reappeared: 'We need to finalise the galleys now.' The digital clock above the door signalled two hours to go before noon.

'I'm doing it now,' Colin muttered, drawing the pages towards him that had lain unread on his desk overnight. But his computer was flashing a message. A reply from Gustavo in his Inbox.

'Hi, there, Colin - I've just discovered Herreros gave himself up to state protection pending an investigation of his affairs around the same date as he had Lourdes abducted. What d'you make of that?'

I have no idea, he muttered under his breath then sent a reply. 'Urgent. Has A. H. left the country?'

If he hadn't heard from Lourdes within twenty-four hours he would have no choice but to warn her via another e-mail about Andreas' possible defection, and to reassure her of his arrival on Tuesday. If Herreros had left Colombia, she might have to face the prospect of moving on again. To the English countryside, perhaps, with him and Felice? There would be time, next week, to work that one out. After he'd seen the first copies of March's *Ecco!* rolling off the press - with the *Vega II* plying the high seas on a centrefold spread - he'd be on the first plane to Mallorca.

11

Music keeps time to my heartbeat, asserts its motifs from some crevice deep within my brain. When I'm in the field, walking can be a pure unthinking state, a moving meditation. Music and walking magnetise memory. Each note, each footstep, as sure and full of grace as the slow movement of a particular Schubert piano sonata. Occasionally, thoughts of the past - of my dead parents and sister, of Scotland and of Dan - merge with the music. But nowadays, overwhelmingly, the motifs crystallise thoughts of the future and of Nicolas' return. Notes so familiar, my listening heart takes flight. I'm no musician, but I do have photographic recall of my mother's score resting on the open piano of the childhood house. And sometimes, when I'm alone in the landscape, I hear echoes of the opening moments of the Schubert sonata she played so passionately, as clearly as if a piano had been set up for her in the wood I'm passing through.

Massanella lies suspended in its blinding cloak of snow under a Cézanne-blue sky. Halfway up the crag, on the way to the hide, a figure stealing, dark as a fox, down a snowbound slope half-a-kilometre to the west fills her with a sickening sense of déja vu. She bites her lip. Hasn't Nicolas warned his assistant off this area? When Julio got back they'd have no choice but to confront Miguel. Right now, though, she would not let irritation spoil the spiralling wonder of the day. Only, after she climbed the ladder and she stood inside the hide, her resolve evaporated in a cloud of dark fury when, in a corner, she saw empty coke cans and snack food wrappers. One thought seized her; *has he scared off the vultures?* How long has that *cholo* been coming here? All the time I've been ill? Leaving the rubbish as evidence of his trespass, she went to the edge of the platform to look down on the nest.

Footprints encircled the pine tree, and a stark irrational thought frightened her; *if the vultures abandon the nest, Nicolas and I might never make it.* She scrambled down the ladder to examine the red earth mixed with snow above Miguel's descending place like a blind person rehearsing braille. Footprints at the edge of the crag where the idiot had climbed down. For what seemed a long time, she sat on the rock slab praying for a sign of life from sky or tree, but none came, and, her recent illness forgotten, she rose up determined to drive directly to Casas Viejas.

There was no snow down there. It was as if she had travelled from winter to balmy springtime in the blink of an eye. Unintimidated by the high ornate gate, she drew back its bolt and marched up to the grand entrance door. It stood open. She could see through glass interior doors into a richly furnished hall and, propelled by her anger, she didn't hesitate to pass through into a spacious salon, calling loudly.

'Hello, anyone at home?'

It was Rosa Sanchez who appeared, all smiles, carrying a mop and pail.

'Where's Miguel,' Luisa demanded.

'*Que pasa, señora?*'

In no mood for bonhomie, 'can you get him right now?' she said and Rosa went off with a bewildered look.

A little calmer now her mission was underway, Luisa absorbed Nicolas' surroundings. The room was roughly half the size of the refectory at Ca'n Clot, but there any resemblance ended. The refectory was spartan. This room smelling of flowers, firewood and beeswax polish was luxurious. How had he made his money? she wondered, standing at one of four high windows that gave a wide view over the purpling plain, the distant Puig de Magdalena and the terraced gardens where Miguel was digging a trench through an ornamental orange orchard. Haven't I always distrusted rich men? she thought, the heady scent of lilies, spikenard and roses from the Oriental vase on the table drawing her back into the room.

Ample draped sofas made focal points, each flanked with carved olive wood side tables piled with magazines and books.

The shelved wall opposite the fireplace held his library, fronted by a metal grille from floor to ceiling. Oriental rugs and runners relieved the geometry of the black and white tiled floor. A polished walnut secretaire stood handsome beside the door she had just come through, and she observed that its patina and craftsmanship matched not only the round pedestal table in the centre of the room where flowers and photographs were displayed, but also the carved sideboard under the refectory mirror at Ca'n Clot.

On Sunday we'll be here together, a fire blazing under the white marble mantelpiece. I'll discover more about him then, she reassured herself, wandering about the room, picking up a book here and there off the side tables. A Vargas LLosa novel, books about wind farms and ecological husbandry. And then the volume titled *Poems of the Spanish Civil War*, identical to the one she had borrowed in Barcelona. She riffled through the index of first lines, and there it was: *I found a pigeon's skull on the machair*. The perfect little skull, she thinks, her mouth curving. Nicolas evidently valued Hugh MacDiarmid's poem so much he'd learned something from it by heart. Her eyes blur. Fragile, as all beautiful things are, he had said. Like love, she thinks, like music.

Through the windows she can see Rosa gesticulating to Miguel and, inspired by love rather than confrontation, resolves to deal magnanimously with the boy. Can you leave us, please? she says when Rosa leads him into the room and, pacing a half-circle round the flower decked central table she considers how to begin.

'Miguel, did Don Nicolas not tell you it's against the law to wander near nesting birds on the mountains?' She forces out a sharp look at him where he loiters near the door. This is the first time she has seen him close to, and his deprived aspect strikes her so forcibly Angel Zavala springs to her mind: *why are you doing this, Angel? . . . it keeps our mothers happy. And it keeps the Holy Infant and Lady of Mercy happy.*

Her hand falters on the edge of the table, 'Don Nicolas will have to hear about . . . .' She starts to speak but her eyes are fixed to a silver framed photograph displayed on the table.

A woman with familiar, sad eyes.

Miguel forgotten, she takes it into her hands. Time stops, she swallows hard. Only this woman's eyes are not hooded. After all, this hair is wavy, it's dark brown, only, yes it must be her. The image slips and shatters at her feet. For a second or two she stares down at the mess of broken glass, the enigmatic face smiling on the black floor tile. Nearly overwhelmed by sickening disappointment, she backs away from the treacherous shards and blurts out, 'it's Anita . . . it's Lourdes Herreros.'

Out of the depths of the grimly defended fortress of her being she wants to say to Miguel, tell your boss there will be no meeting on Sunday, but the words won't come. Pushing past the baffled-looking youth she reaches the safe haven of the jeep and doesn't stop driving until she's through the padlocked gate where she hunkers down on the snow-peppered verge, flowing with tears.

She had been wandering near the summit of Massanella wearing snow goggles before disaster struck. But there had been someone up there with me, hadn't there? Someone willing to save me, she thought. He? She? There had been no indication, the feeling of the presence had been so shadowy its sex hardly mattered. Here and there, prominent stone slabs penetrated the blinding whiteness. Gigantic stepping stones that somehow reassured her as she went, testing the ground for snowholes with a stick over six feet high.

Luisa struggled to bring back the nightmare. *For some reason I bent down to examine one of the slabs and at that moment the snow underneath my feet gave way and I was sucked - terrifyingly fast - into the underworld of the snow.* The shadowy companion above would try to rescue me, I knew, but in vain. Spinning down, down, down through the icy vortex, frozen flakes flew upwards at my passing. I willed myself to submit, not to struggle against this fate. The icy cold would numb the life out of me soon enough. Let go, submit . . . life, death; it no longer mattered.

Desperate both to remember and to forget, when she sits up in bed she realises her sleeping bag has slipped to the floor in the night. I'm chilled to the bone and frozen emotionally, too, she muttered, slithering back into the bag where she slept until dawn.

It was a local fiesta. Felipe was off-duty. Anita - no longer Anita, but Lourdes - was in Ibiza with Julio. She struggled to throw off the aftermath of the near-death dream and the incident that had prompted it. Anita, Lourdes deceived me once. That was understandable. Yet how can I forgive this bitter deception that directly involves me. Who but a husband or a lover would place a photograph of Lourdes on the central table of his house? And what are they up to, he and she? I dread to discover.

There was a companion in the nightmare who tried to save me from that snowhole. I'm sure of that. But who is there to save me from the pain I'm drowning in at this moment? Hadn't the 'flu been bad enough without this? Hasn't it been lies, all lies? Anita's lies, Lourdes' lies, Nicolas' lies. Isn't my love for Nicolas, acute, prescient, nevertheless only a mere projection of some unfathomable desire, since I have no idea who he really is? A con man tricking me with a phoney interest in birds, honeyed phrases, a fragment of Scottish poetry, when all the time Lourdes had been on his mind?

And then, faintly, she heard Rafael's voice: *Lift the phone, call me!*

She began by recounting the dream and protested that, ever since she had first worn the cloak on the crag, her life had seemed to fall to pieces and come to a symbolic end in a snowhole.

Snow, cold, represents absence of love and warmth. An emotional desert. Sometimes we have to fall a long way into sensory deprivation before we can transform ourselves, Rafael said.

Was it you, Rafael, who had been my shadowy companion in the snowbound landscape?

If that's what you think, Luisa, then perhaps I was.

Before that, there had been my illness.

Illness invades our bodies at times of stress, so do terrifying dreams.

Rafael heard how Miguel threatening the vultures' nest had led to the discovery of Lourdes' photograph in Nicolas' house. She deceived me once before and now I find he has tricked me too, Luisa lamented. I'm afraid he's some sort of conman.

Rafael laughed, but kindly: *A conman, Luisa? And what is a conman? Don't we all have an undesirable, a conperson if you like, living within us? We come up with all kinds of tricks to keep this unpalatable part of us hidden, but everyone has a shadow side, you know.*

Unassuaged, she related Lourdes' story of exile and disguise. They may be using me for their own ends. But why? What am I dealing with here, a hornet's nest?

I doubt it; from what you told me a week or so back, Nicolas sounds like a great guy. He might be worth taking a risk for . . . Luisa, are you still there? *Why not indulge in a bit of make believe with him? After all, your highest purpose in life is not Nicolas, but yourself. Your work with the birds, the angelic realms. You can never lose that. Whatever happens no one can take that from you. I suggest you put on your wings, metaphorically speaking. Give him a chance, discover the truth, you've got nothing to lose.*

Somehow it wasn't surprising when, that afternoon, she glimpsed Nicolas trudging towards the finca through the falling snow. Standing at the window of the den, she held her breath. Rafael was right in a sense, of course he was. Her field study was, after all, the reason she was here on this mountain. His words had steadied her during their conversation, and now, watching Nicolas draw nearer, her heart filled with tenderness. Despite everything, I don't want to lose him. Filled with the sense that joy and heartbreak hung in the balance on finely tuned scales, she opened the door.

'I came to you right away. I've just got back,' he said gruffly. 'It seems I have some explaining to do. Rosa told me you saw the photograph.'

She made no reply but looked on while he knocked impacted snow off the soles of his boots and shook out his hat and jacket. Then, after she had closed the door, he turned to her with the fierce, right-on look she had come to recognise as the way he disguised emotion.

'The source of all the trouble?' he said, drawing the photograph out of his jacket pocket before he hung it up. Then brusquely he laid the photograph on the desk, face down, glassless now in its silver frame. 'Your next door neighbour, Lourdes Herreros,' he said. 'I can guess what you must be thinking and I'm so sorry you've been through this.'

He came towards her but she moved away to the window saying, 'it was a shock, seeing that photograph in your room.'

'Luisa,' he implored, 'you were on the brink of knowing everything. I planned to tell you about this on Sunday.'

'Fine, so tell me now,' she said, daring him with bright eyes, adding with a dry laugh, 'and it had better be good.'

She turns to see the snow falling thick and white against the darkening night beyond the window, and the reflection of him in it, behind her, watching her. Even in these distressing circumstances, she recognises something beyond mere sensation - unfathomable, unknowable, yet concrete and reassuring - created simply by their being together.

'What you need to know is that I have never set eyes on Señora Herreros,' he says. She can see him reflected in the window, fingertips massaging his forehead as if to discover how to reach her.

He has never met Lourdes, she thinks, softening with relief, turning to lean against the windowsill. Perhaps I haven't fallen in love with an intimate of Lourdes, after all.

For the first time since he entered the room she allowed herself to meet his eyes and he said: 'I left Miguel and Rosa with the task of emptying the crates of my belongings that arrived here a few weeks ago. I told them to distribute things around the house and to put my photographs out on the table in the salon. And I instructed them to study the one of Señora Herreros. You see, we're looking for her on behalf of her husband. Rosa saw the photograph a few days ago and when I got back from Madrid a couple of hours ago, she told me she thought the woman was living in town and that she was your friend and neighbour. The next thing you need to know is that Andreas did not have his wife abducted.'

285

Luisa gave an alarmed cry. 'If her husband didn't put her through that hell, who did?' Why are they looking for Lourdes? she worried.

'For years I was on nodding acquaintance with Andreas Herreros,' Nicolas was saying, 'but, as I shall explain, some time ago, circumstances threw us together. Then, recently Andreas contacted me. He'd heard I was planning a move to Europe and he asked me to keep a lookout for his wife and, of course, I agreed to help.'

A silence fell between them and Luisa went to her seat by the stove. Her mind raced as she struggled to re-order the world. Was Lourdes in danger? Was Nicolas a double-dealer, too, a crook like Andreas Herreros? 'They say you *pay* Rosa Sanchez for information,' she said at last.

He cast her a sharp look. 'Yes, of course, since without help how could I have hoped to find Señora Herreros? Don't knock it, Luisa. Some youngsters who escape from South America to Europe just wouldn't survive here if they couldn't make extra cash by various means.'

'Were you looking for Lourdes that day when we passed you on the meseta, when you looked into the jeep?'

'I suppose so, though not consciously. Having just bought the estate I wanted to discover everything I could about the terrain. No one knew for certain if Lourdes was here. Andreas' contacts in different parts of Spain have been searching for her too. As a matter of fact, I investigated a tip off when I was in Madrid last week only it turned out to be a complete red herring. Then Andreas sent an e-mail saying he had picked up clues from a London journalist that suggested Lourdes might be in Mallorca. As a matter of fact, I didn't even know for sure if Rosa's woman was Lourdes until you identified her in the photograph the day you came to see Miguel.'

Luisa swelled with indignation. 'I identified her? But I thought Rosa . . . you're saying it was *I* who confirmed the photo was of Lourdes?'

'Yes, that's right, you did. But don't worry. Rosa was already onto Lourdes.'

She looks away, and, as if respecting her need to steady herself, he waits.

'It wasn't meant to happen this way,' he said at last. 'I was waiting for the right moment to tell you everything about myself and this situation. I was afraid of losing you. I knew it wouldn't be easy, but, desperately, I wanted you to assess the facts for yourself, to start our relationship on the basis of trust. Of course, I had no idea you already knew about Andreas and Lourdes Herreros.'

Listening to him, her mind spins. The bird trap, his visits to Ca'n Clot. Their epiphanies. And above everything else, she clings to that 'something' - fixed, immovable between them, ineffable, enlarging them both. This has come as a shock to him as well as me, she thinks, reading the distress in his eyes.

He gropes for a way to continue and she helps him. 'You came to buy the estate rather than to find Lourdes?'

'Of course. Lourdes is a secondary issue, though I do hope to meet her soon.'

'How d'you know Andreas Herreros?'

'Well, it's like this. My background bears many similarities to Andreas'. We're both Europeans with Latin American connections and each of us spent most of our adult lives there. I have a son and a daughter, both in their early twenties, one living in Madrid, the other in Miami. I'd known Andreas by sight for many years. We first met at a party thrown by the dealer Paco Escobar. Everyone knew Andreas augmented his income by drugs dealing, petty in comparison with the big guys like Escobar, but . . . .' His voice tailed away and he met Luisa's eyes. 'I, for one, never condoned it. I give you my promise, I have never dealt in drugs.'

'Did Herreros mention the hell he put Lourdes through?' she says a little scathingly.

'Yes, he told me everything. However, as always, truth is often far more complex than it seems at face value. And the truth I want you to hear is that, by an awful twist of fate, Lourdes was seized, not by Andreas, but by others, the very day Andreas was taken in for investigation. His plan had been to hold her

287

only for a day, to give her a fright for cuckolding him. Perhaps you know, she was having an affair and he feared she might leave Colombia for Europe with her lover, Gustavo Balcázar?'

He paused, and when Luisa made no sign of responding, went on: 'The details of Andreas' plan regarding Lourdes were spilled out by a double-dealer to one of Andreas' rivals, a long-time sworn enemy. Terrified that under investigation Andreas would spill the beans about his cartel, the guy hijacked Lourdes' kidnapping. He paid off Andreas' pranksters and sent seriously dangerous men from his own cartel to do the dirty work. They followed some basic master plan for kidnappings. They murdered the chauffeur and hid Lourdes in an awful dump.'

From time to time as she listens she bites her lower lip. *Can all this be true?* Andreas Herreros didn't kidnap Lourdes? Colin's book is built on falsity?

'As I mentioned earlier, Andreas and I were taken in for questioning at the same time, by Government agents operating under the direction of the FBI. Pending their investigation of my affairs I wasn't permitted contact with the outside world. Neither was Andreas. A few days later an informer brought Andreas a message from the rival gang. Lourdes might be freed in exchange for a substantial ransom. Blackmail, hush money, you could call it. Only Andreas' bank account, like mine, had been frozen and he couldn't come up with the cash. Andreas then promised to pay a large bribe if Lourdes' captors moved her to a comfortable house where all her needs would be met, and he arranged for a crony in the outside world to pay that smaller sum. It was the best he could do in such dire circumstances.'

'Why were *you* under investigation?' she says, searching his features for a thug, a bully, a gangster. But her heart finds the one face that matters to her, the generous mouth, the right human face. Neither wholly good nor bad, but striving to balance the two, groping now for words to convince her not to desert him.

'Like Andreas, but for different reasons, I had been ambitious to make my fortune as a younger man. The route

I took was to wheel and deal in property ventures. Buying up South American mansions whose former owners had become millionaires in the entourages of one or other of the old dictators, and who had fallen out of favour. Buying buildings for a song, in other words, from desperate owners, turning them into hideous luxury tourist hotels by fairly savage construction methods, I confess, and selling out when the time was right. Not too much wrong in that, you might think, but I indulged in an element of money laundering, too, that took me into the super-rich bracket. When I became a Colombian resident a decade or so ago, the government must have suspected drugs dealing augmented my wealth. It didn't, Luisa, I've never, ever done drugs,' he repeated adamantly.

At a loss – since how could she possibly judge such goings-on in the nether world he had just described – her mouth puckered. 'I believe you,' she said softly, and the tension between them evaporated.

'Well then, that's pretty much it,' he said, risking a smile. 'As you see, I'm no saint. But, now you've heard the gist of my story, can we have a drink?' His appeal was so endearing she returned his smile and got up to re-enact the ritual of wine bottle, corkscrew and glasses: *he's been a petty crook . . . a few months ago I'd not have stayed in the same room with him . . . but these days the world seems not to be so black and white as it once was . . . .*

'All our lives you and I have inhabited very different worlds,' Nicolas said kindly, as if he read her thoughts. 'Yours has been blameless in comparison to mine, innocent almost. However, these days my motto is, those who love the world do not destroy it. I'm trying hard to make amends, I want to live in your world, so help me please.'

'I *hate* innocence, except, of course, in children,' Luisa said vehemently, discomfited yet again by her lack of awareness of the world that Nicolas' story had only emphasised. 'Naivety in adults leads to all kinds of trouble. And I'm certainly not blameless either.'

Surprised by her own protest, she felt the tangle of her emotions unravel. He knows I trust him. *People do change.* In her mind she's walking out across the snow covered dunes on the island. Then she's dancing tangos in Rafael's kitchen. And she sees herself heading for the crag, wearing the wings, stepping way beyond any lines she had previously drawn for her life.

'Confined up there in the mountains, Andreas broke down in fear and guilt over what had happened. He fell into a severe depression,' Nicolas said, accepting the glass Luisa was offering him. 'You see, he was, and still is, a manic depressive. The boy in him dreamed up the prank of the abduction the man in him would later have reason to abhor. Beside himself with remorse over Lourdes and the chauffeur, he attempted to hang himself. Fortunately a fellow detainee discovered him in the latrines in the nick of time. That guy was a musician, but also a small time pedlar under investigation. The compound doctor put Andreas on medication and the musician and I kept an eye on him. During his convalescence Andreas read books on Hispano-American history while the musician and I sat under the banyan trees.'

Nicolas gave a gruff laugh, remembering. 'I've never met such a patient guy as that guitarist. Slowly but surely he taught me to play his own guitar, and even to compose my own songs, day after day, between meals of refried beans and rice. Music healed my life. Music and the peace of the mountain landscape. I had time to take a good look at myself up there and felt appalled by most of what I saw. I had made loads of money alright, with a bit of pushing from a greedy wife - the one I've just divorced - but I hadn't seen what was under my nose, or preferred not to see, the criminal society one of this planet's most beautiful places - Colombia - had become.'

'Your assistant?' she says. 'Who is he?'

'A boy from the slums of Bogotá, Miguel García, an orphan, intelligent, well meaning, yet he had become a lackey of the drugs cartels simply to survive. A sort of urban Colombian wild boy of Aveyron. I came across him before I left Bogotá. His eagerness impressed me. I wanted to give him a new start in life and now I'm training him to run the estate. So far, his progress has been encouraging. And, as I said, I plan to stop bird hunting, since, it's clear to me that people who feel the need to hunt animals in this day and age are sick. That they suffer from aggression and paranoia.'

Her surprised glance prompts him. 'Does that sound extreme, Luisa?'

'No, not at all. It's just that I didn't know your feelings were so strong. It's a pity the dead birds don't open the eyes of the hunters.'

'Ah! There you have it,' he smiles and, after a small silence, pleads, 'look at me? Don't let what's happened come between us. My intentions towards Señora Herreros are honourable.'

Yes, despite all this, yes, I believe you. And you are the one I want. Her thought was almost a prayer.

'In the meantime will you help me secure a meeting with Lourdes? Will you do that? Arrange for us to meet at a neutral place like Ca'n Clot?'

She accepted the hand he offered, but, still, she had to adjust to the world he was inviting her to enter. 'I need time to take all this in. Let's talk again tomorrow at your place? However, bear in mind that Lourdes has been living a lie for almost two years, blaming Andreas for kidnapping her. In the short term, she may not be capable of adjusting to a new view of her history.'

'All we can do is try,' he said. 'Far more important to me is how you feel about us now.'

'Let's start afresh tomorrow?'

He got up to go, assuring her that he understood how she must feel, that he looked forward to her visit to Casas Viejas. But, when he opened the door the blizzard had heaped snow three feet high against his exit and he ducked back from the cold blast exclaiming, 'can we really be snowed in?'

Luisa looked out at the black and white night and laughed aloud in sudden, wholehearted acceptance of their predicament. 'Put it this way, I wouldn't let one of my colleagues go out in a snowstorm like that. Snow doesn't lie long up here, though. It comes and goes like *la borrasca*, like the thunderstorms over the mountains. You might get away in the morning.'

'Casas Viejas is below the snowline,' he said, catching her amused eyes.

'Yes, but there's no hope of making it from here to there tonight. You can have one of the cells we keep for visiting ornithologists and I've a rabbit stew in the pot.'

'It seems I have no choice, señora,' he smiled. 'Only, no more talk about Lourdes and Andreas, please, I beg you. Let's talk about us, and birds and mountains.'

In the chilly refectory he helps her gather the elements of their meal. Little does he know, she thinks, how often, half-dreaming I have lain in his arms. If he invites me there again, my longing will squash my usual protests. She beguiles him with a look, and each carries a laden tray back to the stove-heated den. In my limited experience of men, she muses, their caresses have somehow felt disappointing. Lingered on my surfaces, breasts, belly, lips and skin, as if they had been afraid to unleash my deep-red, visceral desires. Laying the casserole on the stove, she feels nearly overwhelmed by the prospect of a far deeper satisfaction with this man. If only he knew what I was thinking. But perhaps he did know, since now he was saying: 'Luisa, we might perish with cold in the gallery rooms. Why don't we drag down a couple of mattresses and lie side-by-side near the fire?' And she shivered when his touch, urging her into action, teased the last vestige of resistance from the soft declivity at the base of her spine.

The following evening, they stayed entwined for a few moments on the high terrace beyond Nicolas' observatory, watching the earnest bird flapping huge wings, russet against the inky night, in its flight towards the town.

'I'm sure that's an eagle owl,' he says and jokingly she awards him full marks.

Earlier, she had driven to Calle Luna to prepare for their supper date. The one dress she possessed - yellow silk, calf-length, body-hugging - had been hastily ironed to be worn with the turquoise earrings and bracelet her Spanish grandmother had bequeathed to her. In Frau Lehmann's full-length mirror she scarcely recognised herself. Nor, it seemed, did Nicolas, who drew back a little with a low whistle when she arrived at

Casas Viejas. In his farmhouse-style kitchen, they had eaten a simple supper of bean stew and salad prepared by Rosa earlier in the day. And, although Luisa waited a little apprehensively to discuss how Lourdes might be approached, she rejoiced that her own nightmare seemed to belong to the past.

They had been sharing an exotic dessert of papaya, mango and kiwi fruits when he surprised her by saying that the night sky, so glorious at that particular hour, would not wait for them a minute longer. And he had urged her up the narrow spiral staircase set into the tower of Casas Viejas that led to his observatory. It was a high ceilinged cube of a room where an impressive telescope stood dead centre, directed towards the wide open window. A powerful instrument, so that, one by one, she could read the major constellations as never before. He stood close, prompting her, sharing his passion for astronomy, while she described to him the night map of the migrating birds. The stars give human beings perspective too, he said. They remind us that our own planet, like our lives, turns in a void without any master. Together they observed the brilliant constellation of the Pleiades. The seven daughters of Atlas, Nicolas said, placed as stars in the sky to save them from the pursuit of Orion.

It's no wonder, Luisa said, men have always wanted to put on wings, to emulate birds, hoping to leave the earth behind in favour of brilliant guides like Cassiopeia, the Great and Little Bear, Orion's Belt, all the other constellations and the circling planets, too . . . no wonder they gave beasts wings as well, the mythical winged beasts of the ancients . . . . When her voice tailed off he said softly, 'and, you, Luisa, were you flying up there in your wings, that night on the crag?'

'I'll tell you about that another time,' she grinned. Then, when she shivered, he took her hand and led her back down the turnpike stair to the salon where the flickering flames of the fire he had lit earlier shadow-danced on the mellow walls.

She went to stand beside it and said: 'The bird shooting on your estate must upset you?'

'Oh, yes, and I will put a stop to it. I used to hunt myself. Loved the thrill of the chase. I hunted animals a number of

293

times in Africa, in Europe and South America. But those days are over. It sickens me to see grown men shooting animals and birds. Tolstoy wrote a story about a hunting man, an aristocrat who, as he grows older, becomes more miserable in his opposition to any form of cruelty and puts away his guns. I'm not an aristocrat, Luisa, but in every other way I could be the man in that story. All these guns going off around my home at dawn and dusk. Ach! I've put up with it so far, but now it's become intolerable.'

Then, seeing his guitar waiting on a ladder-backed chair, she begged him to play for her. Readily he agrees, picking up the instrument, sitting on the stiff chair - a chair with no arms to get in the way, he smiles - then his face fills with careful concern. When he plucks the strings, his long body curves into the instrument, as if to coax from it more than it has ever given before. And listening, she recognises *Recuerdos de la Alhambra,* the composition her mother played in a piano version many moons ago. In Scotland. Memories of the Alhambra. *Recuerdas?*

Oh, yes. And how well I remember the day this man and I first met. There he had been saying, *buenos tardes, señorita.* Going to stand beside his chair, he is so familiar yet so strange, she thinks affectionately. He faltered once or twice, his fingers groping for their correct position, but those brief human errors only underlined the enchantment. And when the music ended and the room fell terribly silent, they both stayed still, as if they held their breaths, before she begged him to play the lament she had heard distantly, that day at the bird trap. This time there was no stumbling over notes, and, hearing the quivering vibrations, fragile, tenuous as the call of migrant warblers, Luisa walked again towards the destiny that had been waiting to ensnare her, improbable as any dream.

She wants this seance never to end. But he has already stopped playing, and, rising out of his chair, catches her in a playful embrace. 'I'm going to fetch us a night-cap from the kitchen. Will hot chocolate do? Then we'll talk about Lourdes.'

And with that he slips away, leaving her alone once more in the scented room that seems mysteriously to have expanded in his absence. Drawn again to the photographs on the central table she sees with relief, Lourdes' photograph has gone. She takes up another. *Mysterious Monterey*, she smiles. Nicolas captured as a beautiful boy of around ten years old, posed centre-stage. He stares seriously out of a group of other youngsters, all wearing sailor-style white summer clothes, sitting on a flight of steps leading to a rather severe looking manor house. His birthday, perhaps? Evidently he had had a privileged upbringing. Then she selects a portrait of a couple wearing the clothes of the 'forties. His parents, perhaps? The young woman looks touchingly content, holding a spray of flowers. The man, tall and proud in evening dress, resembles Nicolas, though he's balding and wears a goatee beard.

Then she's looking at a face that is and is not Nicolas'. The setting is tropical. He stands under a palm tree in an exotic garden, a cigar clenched in his crooked smile. 'Is that *you*?' she blurts out, seeing Nicolas re-enter the room.

Swiftly recapturing it out of her hand, he claps it face down on the table. 'That *was* me,' he says with a hint of disdain: 'the photograph was taken some time ago. It's a photograph of the man I told you about. Myself when younger, addicted to whisky, cigars and making money. A self-centred playboy,' he added disparagingly. 'Perhaps it's better out of sight. Though I'll keep it to remind me there's no going back. Up in that compound where I was held with Andreas I devised a list of good intentions. I kept a diary, made notes about how I might radically alter my life after the investigation. An important aspect of the transformation would be to live in Europe, and to live a life of voluntary simplicity.'

'Voluntary simplicity!' Luisa couldn't help exclaiming. 'Take a look round this room. Your house is filled with *complexity*.'

'Will you help me to clear it out when I get back from Colombia?'

Looking down, uncertain, her mouth puckers, resisting a smile.

'It's alright, I don't expect you to answer that now,' he says. 'Come back to the fire. Let's discuss Lourdes.'

Hesitant at first, Luisa became increasingly convinced as they talked that the part Nicolas asked her to play was justified. If there was a chance that her involvement in such a meeting might free Lourdes fully and finally from the falsehoods she had harboured and embellished these past two years it was a chance worth taking. They discussed how a meeting might be brought off. There was not much time, since, in a few days, Luisa would leave for Barcelona and Nicolas for Colombia. At last they agreed that, since Lourdes planned to attend tomorrow's Alejandro Ferrer memorial talk, Nicolas would not. In any case, he said, he had urgent business to attend to in Palma in the morning. After the talk Luisa expected Lourdes to stay overnight as the two women had planned out at Lourdes' orchard. It would be important, Luisa insisted, for her to spend some time alone with Lourdes when, gently, she hoped to break the news of Nicolas' desire to meet her. And he would arrive at Ca'n Clot after the townsfolk had all gone away, just as if he was dropping by on a neighbourly visit.

'You'll have to be incredibly subtle. Lourdes is, let's say, a bit overwrought at the moment. After what she's been through, she's unlikely to welcome anyone associated with Andreas.'

Nicolas got up, suddenly brisk, and went to the secretaire. He drew a paper out of a drawer and brought it to her.

'This document proves the dates Andreas was held under investigation, and that's what Andreas looks like.' It was a photocopy of an official paper with a photograph of Andreas Herreros, over-stamped like a visa in a passport. Luisa studied the rather bovine face framed by thick curling hair, the shrewd eyes, the unsmiling mouth part-hidden by a neat moustache.

'Is he quite a small man?' she said, surprised.

'Small and vigorous, yes,' Nicolas said, and urged her to read the document. The officialese meant little to her until Nicolas interpreted the dates that mattered. The date Andreas was detained for investigation, the date he was released and the information that his release from the investigation had been followed by a prison sentence.

'Do you think this'll convince Señora Herreros that I bring the truth?'

Luisa shrugged: 'Who knows, she's just as likely to shoot the messenger.' And when Nicolas raised surprised eyebrows she added, 'after all, her story is the one she wants to believe, has invented all those months. I've never thought to ask, but how did Andreas get wind of Lourdes' whereabouts?'

'Soon after we were first held at the compound, Andreas got a tip-off that Lourdes had been rescued by two journalists, her lover and a British documentary film maker.'

Colin Cramer, Luisa smiled inwardly. I know Colin Cramer, she almost said, before a moment of uncertainty made her hold back.

'Herreros was so relieved to hear she had escaped the clutches of his rivals he wept on and off for days,' Nicolas was saying. 'He craves Lourdes' understanding of how it all went dreadfully wrong. Andreas told me when he pleaded with me to help him find her, "If I am to live the rest of my life with a modicum of peace of mind and self-respect, Lourdes must know exactly what happened. I don't expect her to forgive me, only to know the truth and that I'd give anything to undo what happened."'

'What's his position now?'

'Well these days he's a free man. No longer an Extraditable. D'you know what that term means?'

When she nodded he said: 'I must say, I'm impressed by your knowledge of the Central American underworld. How d'you know so much?'

Again she hesitated, her secret smile unwilling to betray the existence of *Flight into Exile*. 'One day I'll tell you, not now.'

'So be it. At any rate, I'm in the clear with the authorities too, though I've still got a mountain of paperwork to finalise in Colombia. I should be there now. In fact I shouldn't have left the country for another month, only when this estate came up for sale I couldn't risk losing it.'

Here was another truth to swallow, hard as stone. He would be leaving in a day or two.

'The animals, the sheep, the ducks and geese have already been shifted to a temporary home at a neighbouring farm, since Miguel has no knowledge of animal husbandry.'

'He'll stay on here while you're in Colombia?'

'Yes, keeping a low profile, I hope. Miguel has strict instructions to keep away from the town, where, as you may know, Pep Oleza and some others are up in arms about me sacking him.'

She nodded, pensive, then returned to the subject of Lourdes: 'If she reacts hysterically, she might raise the alert that you're out of the country?'

'Yes, that's a possibility.'

'You're willing to risk this for Andreas?'

'Yes, of course. It's a small risk to take for a friend. However, as I said, I'm already at risk by being out of Colombia before my clearance papers are in order.'

She worried. Since, if returning to Colombia posed the slightest risk, didn't that mean he might not make it back to Mallorca?

He read her expression and drew her to him. 'Don't worry. I have friends in high places, I'm pretty well invincible. I give you my promise. Nothing shall prevent me coming back by Easter. Our home is this mountain, Massanella. I knew that the first time we met, when you nearly had me arrested for trespassing. And I hope you'll agree, we'll bring up our children here at Casas Viejas.'

'Children?' she echoed, shocked and amused both at once. 'Aren't you being a bit hasty?'

'No,' he insisted with studied seriousness. 'One can never be too hasty when love leaps into the heart. Our children will be born to the wilderness. We'll show them the birds, the flowers, the stars, the planets.'

Her mouth curved, hearing the sounds of the night beyond the windows. Eagle owls marking their territories, the palm trees rustling in the skittish wind. Any lingering doubts melted in a sensation of warmth, sweet as honey, flowing through her body. *All will be well.* Insignificant we might be down here, two microcosmic elements, not even as large as grains of sand in the infinitely complex bedrock of this world, yet how significant we are to each other.

12

'We'll make a *Mallorquina* of you yet,' was the verdict of one of the jesting women, and the others agreed in unison. But their warm-hearted banter only intensified Luisa's apprehension as they bustled around her, setting vats of water to boil on the cooker, chopping vegetables and meat, filling dishes with shining black and green olives and cutting bread. They refused to let her help with the prodigious task of laying the tables for over a hundred guests. 'No, *Reina*,' they insisted. '*You* are the guest of honour today.' The refectory was a hive of activity but she could find no place in it.

The weather was fine. The snow had disappeared and the day had dawned with Felipe arriving from town in a jeep laden with fresh food supplies, complaining loudly that there had been no word from Julio. He repeated 'where the hell's he got to' so urgently and so many times Luisa was almost tempted to give the Ibiza game away. Felipe tried, again and again, to contact Julio on his mobile phone and she had to turn away her head more than once in case he read the crooked expression on her face.

Julio's absence had to be reported to the town hall, and the alcalde organised two extra men with jeeps to help with the preparations for the day and to transport back to town the frail and elderly who couldn't make the journey on foot. Felipe also requested an additional conservancy man to act as custodian of the aviary while he was engaged in other duties. The aviary was to be opened up to the visitors today. Before lunch Felipe would put Aquila through her paces and demonstrate the Egyptian vulture shattering ostrich eggs in what he called 'an entertainment for the crowd'. Luisa had smiled at that, giving him full marks for never missing an opportunity to market research his private birds of prey centre. Today Aquila would soar for the last time above Ca'n Clot before her transference to Valldemossa for further training by Felipe's austringer friend. And after that, Felipe had announced with gleaming, determined eyes, he would be breaking free from conservancy work, with or without Aquila. Already he had put down a deposit on a piece of land in the mountains west of Ca'n Clot that would make an ideal flight centre.

She stayed hobnobbing with the cooks until her anxiety began to take the form of a pain in the back of her neck. Was the content of her talk too provocative? And where, oh where, had Lourdes and Julio got to? Why hadn't they turned up as promised? The suspense had become so unbearable she had trailed her anxieties to the Golden Bowl where she sat on a billowing rock, a little dazed.

Last night after the weekend's disclosures, she had sat far into the night feeding logs into the stove in the den, pondering the near impossibility, or so it seemed to her, of human beings sustaining happiness or even consistency and balance in the course of daily living. Everything is always in flux, the shadows must fall even on the most supreme moments, shadows like old memorials linking past and present. Was this the message of the mountain that patiently endured under the blazing heat of summer and the raging storms of winter?

Seeing the first walkers appear on the lip of the Golden Bowl, she took up her binoculars. At least the action was underway, and in a few hours her trial would be over. The touching procession would have set out from the town hall more than two hours earlier, tracing the ancient route along the edge of the escarpment under the leadership of the alcalde who had learned it from his grandfather, another old carbonero. The first to come were the slowest, who were always placed first in line, older folk and the overweight, pressing on with the help of olive wood staffs. Watching the silent walkers, she wondered how many of them, passing through the terraces, the woods and the valleys, must have acknowledged the prayers of their ancestors that had been answered here, once upon a time, in the form of abundant timber, olives, wild animals and birds.

How, otherwise, could the people of the mountain town have survived?

Her lenses enlarged the first pilgrims: María Ferrer stoutly plodding along among them, her face a study in doggedness. Francisca was far too old to take part, and Tonia would be bringing up the rear with the younger folk. Then she focussed on Raúl Caubet, pink and panting, the damp stump of a cigar clenched between his teeth. Leading the people like Moses with the Children of Israel, stepping off the path to prop himself against his stick and encourage them on with a wave of his hand. He's another man with his eye always on the main chance, like Felipe, she reckoned. Overweight the alcalde might be, but power gave him boundless energy. Come to think of it haven't mayors, alcaldes, politicians and so-called media stars taken over from priests in our godless world? This one has the town in the palm of his hand, counting them now, one by one, as they walk past him. Each person represents a vote he'll get at the next local election if this day goes off well. And she worried a little. Although the Caubet regime represented a left-wing party, it was known to be very pale green. So pale you could hardly see it and it would disappear altogether on a cloudy day, she thought ironically. The alcalde, a Mallorcan traditionalist, had set aside hunt-free areas for recreation around the town at the same time as he backed the hunt, the expansion of island motorways and *zonas urbanizadas*. Blind to the impossibility of harmonising such conflicting aims, his credo was to keep as many people happy as possible, particularly his pals in the building trade. The result? The least good for the smallest number.

One by one they trickled down the narrow track, pausing on their footsore way to shake the alcalde's hand. Reduced by the expansive dimensions of the Golden Bowl, they picked out the route Luisa had marked with small piles of stones, thus avoiding the worst of the prickly shrubs and other pitfalls. This was a day out for the town, not a flight, nevertheless scenes of exodus filled her mind, not only of Moses but of her Scots ancestors reluctantly leaving their crofting homelands, and of displaced peoples all over the world fleeing their persecutors. But these

Mallorcans are not vulnerable in the least, she thought, getting to her feet, and, although her headache had dissipated, she realised how very tense she was. Again, she looked for Lourdes in the ever lengthening procession below, fretting about her friend's inevitable reaction to Nicolas' news and to her as his accomplice. Another voice countered, you have to do it. She has to know the truth. Through the binoculars she saw the stragglers included Rosa, clambering behind Felipe's mother, and Jaume and Paquita from Bar Solitario, only there was still no sign of Lourdes. And turning in the direction of Ca'n Clot, she felt a tug of disappointment on Nicolas' behalf, since how could his plan materialise in Lourdes' absence?

Felipe stood at the entrance to Ca'n Clot, chatting with Mónica and the photographer who arranged a group shot the minute Luisa arrived. Felipe growled 'still no word from Julio' and Luisa shrugged and slipped away to the haven of the den until lunch was announced when she chose to sit beside Rosa. Hissing little ladder snake. *Elophe scalaris*, the informer, not an innocuous Ingrés reproduction after all, she thought. Yet hasn't Rosa's secret activity led me to face my own vapid sentimentality about the world? Just then Felipe arrived at her side and whispered in her ear, 'you must've given Julio the 'flu. He's in Inca with his sister.'

Suddenly a flurry of gasps invaded the room. Laughter and clapping broke out, and all eyes fixed on the alcalde emerging from the dark passageway, flushed and wreathed in beaming smiles as if he had been Bacchus himself. His arms cradled bottles of brandy and whisky. Mónica followed carrying more bottles and Luisa, admiring Caubet's sense of theatre, found herself rising to her feet, applauding with everyone else. Of course, the photographer stepped forward to capture the moment for the local newspaper. People were stamping their feet, there were shouts of 'over here', 'you get my vote, alcalde!' and 'don't mind if I do', as glasses were thrust forward to receive a dram of golden liquor. Half-an-hour later, the merry crowd left the tables and Felipe and his team set to, reorganising the refectory and setting up the slide screen for Luisa.

All through her presentation she could hear the eager whispering of one neighbour to another when they spotted images they recognised. There was even the occasional snore, but she didn't mind. And, after she had shown the last image of the Black vulture pair soaring against a clear blue sky (when she referred to the birds as 'jewels of Mallorca', she got a round of applause) she gave Felipe the signal to open the shutters. Faces reappeared in the diffuse light, one or two old folk shook themselves out of sleep, chattering recommenced until the alcalde rose from his seat and commanded silence. Bang, bang, bang, went his stick on the floor.

Don't panic, Luisa told herself, moving to the lectern. You're going to upset some of them . . . but don't fudge it . . . Alejandro hated cruelty and this address is in memory of him. *Begin with exactly that sentence.* Swallow a glass of water, pitch your voice low and firm.

'Friends,' she began: 'Alejandro Ferrer hated any form of cruelty to animals and, as you know, my talk today is in his memory.'

There was a flutter of applause. Then, suddenly the refectory door creaked open and everyone craned round to watch the entrance of Professor Bauza. Luisa waited apprehensively while the alcalde rushed to bring her mentor to a seat in the front row. But his familiar wise eyes, when they met her own, were filled with such kindly complicity, she relaxed and began again.

'Señores, *compañeros*, the country folk of Mallorca live in exciting times. As you know, yours was a feudal society, even for some years after Franco's dictatorship. In those days the countryside and the mountains had to be exploited for survival. Anything and everything was needed for the cooking pot. The majority of Mallorcans were very poor and had to grow their own food. In that sense you were hunter gatherers well into the twentieth century, then, in no time at all, with the advent of tourism, the island became one of the wealthiest provinces in Spain.

'In the 'sixties, still in Franco's time, Mallorca began to be exploited as a prime Mediterranean tourist venue. Some of you sold off your lands to foreigners for increasingly large sums of money, other people diversified and put to good use in the booming building trade skills learned in the countryside. You built new houses and walls of local stone, made shutters, windows, doors and gates with your carpentry skills. You aspired to have a car; in fact now, it is said, every Mallorcan family aspires to have *three* cars. And there are more cars per capita in Palma than any other city in Europe.'

Amusement ran through the audience, and she stole a look at the alcalde and the professor, neither of whom were smiling. Raúl Caubet's staff was firmly planted between his outspread legs, a challenge sparkling in his eyes. The professor sat with great dignity, holding his walking stick at right angles before him.

'I hope that statistic about car ownership is an exaggeration,' she added to a ripple of renewed laughter. Waiting for the disturbance to subside, I could go on for hours about your mindless carmaggedon, she thought. But, fond as I am of you, today I'm going to do my best to rub your faces in the muck of *la caça*.

'Nowadays you are so well supplied with markets, supermarkets and hypermarkets, with bus and train services, with beaches, marinas, restaurants, golf courses and entertainment complexes, you are the envy of Europe. You have reformed many of your wonderful old palaces and farmsteads, you have planted and replanted gardens, set up tree nurseries, you grow some of the finest fruits and vegetables in Europe. In fact, as I reminded you earlier, the province is one of the wealthiest in Spain. However, *señores*, there has been a price to pay - a huge price - for this amazing development; the loss or destruction of large tracts of the environment, of your territories, of the land entrusted to you by your ancestors, which is undeniably one of the most beautiful places in the world.

'*Compañeros*, the study of birds and the welfare of birds is my life. Some of you know that I and my colleagues in the island's nature conservancy organisations are set against *la caça*, the hunt, which once upon a time killed anything that walked on four legs - animals now extinct in Mallorca - as well as the birds of the mountains.

'Thrushes were more abundant and olives were more precious once when, for example, oil was needed to light lamps and to make soap. Thrushes *used to* threaten one of the mainstays of your diet . . . the supply of olives which they love to eat. But, *amigos*, they are no longer a threat because you have olives in plenty. Thrushes themselves provided essential food once. But you don't need to eat them now that you enjoy pork, chicken, beef and all the food that spills out of the supermarkets. Yet the hunt goes on.'

Her moment of daring approached. She felt her legs might buckle under her. Pockets of restlessness - shuffling feet, coughing, whispering - spread through the audience. Professor Bauza and Raúl Caubet sat unmoving in the front row and her mind leaped to discover a supportive crutch elsewhere. Rafael Vargas obliged, whispering in her ear: *We must do everything in our power to bring changes for the better to this mutilated world.*

'Each dawn and dusk during spring and autumn, the racket of gunshot invades the mountain foothills in the thrush hunt which slaughters migrant birds, too, some of them rare,' she said. 'Birds are caught in netting traps in the woods near towns and villages. But the government seems reluctant to give conservation organisations, and those of you who consider the practice uncivilised, the same degree of power as your counterparts in northern Europe to put a stop to these practices. The hunt is a traditional male preserve throughout the Mediterranean world. But these days sensible people regard it as outmoded and uncivilized. The conclusion is inescapable. It is extremely difficult to give up old traditions. However I urge you, as my friend Alejandro would surely have done had he been with us today: *Think globally, act locally.* Think of Mallorca's reputation in the rest of Europe and put your guns and nets away.'

Señor Caubet rose off his seat as if he had been ignited. The professor's shaky old hand flew upwards to pull him back, but the alcalde was already striding towards the lectern. He's about

305

to cut me off, Luisa thought, bemused and dismayed, both at once. He thinks I've gone too far. Seeing him applauding, slowly, with raised, outstretched hands and hesitantly at first, some of the audience starting to mimic him, helpless to save the rest of her talk, Luisa could only retrieve her notes and stand aside coolly while the alcalde took possession of the lectern.

'It is an honour to have our esteemed Professor Bauza with us today,' he began.

The panache of Mark Anthony, Luisa thought wryly. *Friends, Romans, country folk, lend me your ears!* Then, when he turned towards her with a small bow his eyes seemed to bear the message: *We come to bury Señora Ross, not to praise her!*

'His student, whom we have come to know as Luisa, will soon be Doctor Ross,' he went on. 'She has talked very well today about the habitat of our vultures, one of Mallorca's many jewels as she has correctly said.' Señor Caubet flourished an arm in Luisa's direction and she resolved: *I refuse to be buried by this wee bully of a man.*

With a theatrical pause, he smiled collusively at the audience: 'Some of us might wonder though, if - *perhaps* - Señora Ross has exaggerated Mallorca's . . . how shall we say it? . . . Mallorca's environmental problems. We don't have problems, *señores*! Only challenges. After all, we have many organisations working at national and at local level to protect and preserve our beautiful island. *Respecte la Terra* and *Non Embrutem la Terra* are our slogans. Isn't it true, don't you see these words written on notices everywhere? There is nothing, dear lady, that cannot be put right if we continue to respect our territories as we do.'

With that, he prompted another round of applause, briskly this time. Most of the audience followed his lead until, his upturned hands beating up and down, he brought them to their feet. Luisa put on a smile. He's put me in my place with that 'dear lady' remark, she thought fiercely, watching him stride off the platform. I've been censured, but far from defeated by a pompous, self-interested politician. I stuck my neck out too far, but at least I got over my punch line: *Think of Mallorca's reputation in the rest of Europe and put your guns away.* The applause tailed off and she, pretending serenity when inwardly she was blazing, thought, fine, there's nothing that can't be put right. But how long will it take? Contention replaced the fading applause. *The unruly sparks from the bonfire I've lit.* Giddily, she wondered, where do I go from here? She had no idea, and after the fieldwork was over would it matter?

Then, someone else was calling for silence, tapping on the floor with his walking stick. Everyone sat down again and the professor slowly approached Luisa.

'I don't intend to comment on the views Señora Ross has expressed today,' he announced, standing at her side, 'but, I may say, one day soon she will be an outstanding ornithologist. I simply want to remind you that it is important, vital even, given the world we find ourselves living in, to respect views that differ from our own. As Luisa said, we live in times of great transition even at local level. Let me give you one example. Only this morning I learned from the authorities in Palma that the hunting estate of Casas Viejas is to become an ecological farm. Most of us don't even know what that is. Yet the lands of our ancestors were entirely ecological once upon a time. Our forebears knew that the struggle to conserve the environment is essentially a *moral* matter and it's evident that we have forgotten their conviction. What is mankind up to? I ask you. What is Mallorca up to when our noxious gas emissions from aeroplanes and cars are four times the limit set down by the Kyoto Agreement? Well, it seems that the owner of Casas Viejas is respecting his territories, and he has also banned hunting on his estate. No doubt his act will be controversial, but it is his right and it must be respected.

'The main purpose of my homecoming, as some of you know, is to visit my sister Paula, who is poorly,' the professor went on. 'However, I am delighted to be here to pass on the good news in person that a German university has presented the Ca'n Clot project with a clutch of vulture chicks which Luisa here will be responsible for raising with her colleagues in the weeks before Easter. And with that wonderful news dear friends, I bring today's event to a close.'

Professor Bauza kissed Luisa on both cheeks and, recompensed after the stresses of the day, she felt she might burst into tears of gratitude. 'Julio has raised chicks before. He'll give you all the help you need,' the old man whispered in her ear.

'This is a feather in the cap of us all,' the alcalde shouted out loudly over the heads of the audience before he stepped down to take possession of the professor. Arm-in-arm, they walked out of the hall. Well, Luisa thought, at least I've stirred the debate, and suddenly she felt exhausted. A small band began to gather round her, including members of the island's ornithological groups and students she recognised from her Palma University lecture. They shook her hand, they kissed her cheeks, they offered congratulations. Even some townsfolk came up to her saying, well done, we agree with you. Some embraced her while others walked away. Jaume came up with Paquita at his side. 'We understand your views, only, what can I do, the hunt is in my blood? It was a good talk, though.'

The jeeps were waiting to drive those who couldn't make it back to town on foot. Already they were forming a procession outside Ca'n Clot. Caught up in the swell of the departing, Luisa longed for everyone to leave. Then, suddenly, a hand fell on her shoulder.

'You were brave to say all that, even if I am a *caçador.*'

She turned to see Felipe with Cora preening on his shoulder.

'Has it ever occurred to you, Felipe, that *'caça'* and *'caca'* are spelled the same way? Only a little grammatical symbol alters the meaning. The first means 'the hunt', the second means 'shit'.'

When he pulled his shoulders back, soldier fashion, and fixed her with a shocked cross-eyed look, Cora cawed and fled upwards to the chimney stack.

'How long are you going to deal in shit, eh, Felipe?' she added sharply.

He crumbled a little, like an admonished schoolboy shuffling his feet, at a loss for words and she smiled. 'Look, don't worry, it's difficult to override tradition, to refuse to eat *Tords en Col* at Sunday lunch. But I know you'll want to do it one day.'

'You're a weird one, Luisa,' he said, stiffly, before they both broke into grins, and, playfully, he took out his Asborno whistle and blasted the air with a discordant note.

'Go on, get out!' she teased, pushing him in the direction of his jeep where pale elderly faces were looking out, longing to be driven home.

A profound silence reclaimed Ca'n Clot after the day's invasion. It enfolded her like a protective cloak when she went to release the dogs, and, looking up, she noticed drifts of mist teasing the summit of Massanella. The dogs kept close, growling with pleasure, rooting in the damp mulch under the trees when they skirted the wood. Then, all at once, they fled down the path barking uproariously. Nicolas is coming, she thought, unless someone else has lingered in the woods instead of returning with the others to town. She was about to run to meet him when the familiar ditty of her phone brought the dogs rushing back to her.

'Luisa?' Lourdes said: 'You've heard about Julio's 'flu? Sorry we didn't make it . . . how'd your talk go?'

'I'll tell you later. I'm *whacked*! But did you enjoy Ibiza?'

Momentarily the dogs sat studying her face with concerned, velvety eyes before they sped off again.

'Ibiza was heaven, *cariño* . . . look, I've got something rather urgent to tell you. Can you pop by and see me tomorrow before you go to Barcelona?'

'Yes, of course, it'll be around midmorning.'

'That's fine by me. Oh, and, by the way, Colin's arriving tomorrow too. Says to tell you he's sorry he missed your talk.'

Nicolas was coming round the bend of the path, the dogs at his heels and she sprinted towards him. 'Your dogs know me now, I'm accepted,' he said happily. 'Is Lourdes at Ca'n Clot? Can we get that out of the way then spend some time alone?'

'No, I'm afraid she's not coming.'

She expected him to look crestfallen, but, instead he smiled.

'Great,' he said, 'we'll do it tomorrow and spend time together now.'

Do it tomorrow? Did he really think it would be that simple? Again she had to squash her own opinion when they turned towards Ca'n Clot. It was extremely unlikely Lourdes would be won over to Andreas' version of the truth. But when his arm slid flirtatiously round her waist, she put Lourdes out of her mind.

'Have you come to collect your watch?' she teased.

'Perhaps I'll remember to take it this time,' he burst out good-humouredly. 'It isn't my watch, by the way, but Andreas'. He urged me to take it, to give it to Lourdes if I should find her. No, damn the watch! Now that Lourdes is out of the picture, tell me, please, how your talk went . . . .'

The sound of their animated voices faded in the darkening wood and when they reached the finca Nicolas fetched out of his jacket a bottle wrapped in a green waterproof bag.

'Something special?' she smiled, reading out the label, '*Non Plus Ultra*', and the cork flew towards the ceiling. 'To celebrate our love and our achievements today,' he said, his face aglow with affection as he poured out the bubbling liquid, and she thought, I have done with talking now. Reaching up to run her index finger over the curve of his wet lips, she watched his eyes softly narrow, heard his sigh before their mouths met. And, after that, when nothing seemed to exist in the world but they themselves, this is our private *Carnaval* before Lent, she thought, when our weeks of separation will be our sacrifice.

Later, when they were eating beside the stove in the den, he tried again to discover how she knew so much about Central American drugs dealing. But she refused to say more than 'I read a book about it recently.' His shrewd glance told her he suspected there was more to it than that, but he didn't press her, and they continued their meal in companionable silence until Luisa suddenly said, damn it! Perro looked up out of his feigned sleep, and Luisa stroked his dark coat, hearing the sound of a wind getting up, blowing down the stovepipe into the fire, the crackle of disturbed logs in the grate.

'What's up?' Nicolas said, and she told him she had meant to check the vulture's nest before leaving for Barcelona. There wouldn't be time to climb the crag tomorrow, and now it was dark outside.

'You're leaving, I'm leaving . . . but surely the vultures won't leave too? I can see why you're worried, but, believe me Miguel won't set foot up there again.'

Yes, she worried about the vultures abandoning their nest, creating another historical site. And she worried about her impending separation from Nicolas. Both felt inextricably bound together in her mind. 'I expect I'll find them there when I get back from Barcelona,' she said, as if wishing it to be so might bring it about.

'That's the spirit. And if you're up to it, there's something else we should talk about, *cariño*.'

'What's that?'

'Well, how do we approach Lourdes now?'

'Much more effectively than we'd have been able to if she'd come up here today,' Luisa said, yawning and stretching her arms in the air with a sleepy smile. 'You see, tomorrow a close friend of Lourdes is due to arrive. He's called Colin Cramer, a nice man, a British journalist. It's good news. She's much more likely to listen to you with Colin around.'

After Nicolas left, when she was packing her rucksack for Barcelona, Luisa had the odd sensation that something in the room was begging for her attention. Puzzled, she ran her hand over the books on the shelves, then searched the three drawers of the filing cabinet. Of course the wings would travel with her tomorrow, and she laid the blue case beside her rucksack. But the urgent something wasn't that. Only when she started sorting out the mess of papers on top of her desk and looked down into the face of the watch gathering dust on the desk, did she pinpoint the 'something'. How curious, she thought picking up Andreas Herreros' watch.

At that moment, the phone rang and Felipe complained into her ear: 'Julio might have phoned-in sooner to tell us about his wretched 'flu.'

311

No, she thought, the early stages of influenza make you too weak even to raise your head. And Lourdes could hardly have risked making her association with Julio common knowledge by phoning Felipe herself. Toying with the watch suspened between her fingers, 'I'll feed the aviary birds before I leave,' she said. 'Pick me up at the bar in time to get the two o'clock train to Palma?'

The watch swung under the desk lamp and, all at once, she noticed an engraving on the rim. Intertwined initials, *LH* and *AH*, above the date *2 Marzo 1974, Paris*. Presumably the date of their marriage. And the words: *'an ever fix'd mark'*. Lourdes choice, presumably. Shakespeare indeed. Nothing if not romantic, yet how hollow the words seemed now. Readily Luisa's mind supplied the lines she had learned by rote at boarding school: *Let me not to the marriage of true minds admit impediments/ Love is not love that alters when it alteration finds/ Oh, no. It is an ever fix'd mark that looks on tempests and is never shaken . . . .* Ever fix'd marks laid down forever in the brain of a schoolgirl in a blazer, she smiled, and zipped the watch into a pocket of her jacket.

After that she sorted out papers and notebooks into the filing cabinet. Her research notes would wait there until her return when, with all she had in her, when Nicolas would be drawing his life in Colombia to a close, she would prevent any further disturbances to her field work. And, in the final stages of her assignment, around Easter, the vulture chicks would learn to fly and Nicolas would return. *All will be well.*

During the night, distant owls screeched in the wood. *Bubo bubo*, the eagle owl. *Europe's largest owl. Widespread, but scarce resident in cliffs and gorges.* There are sufficient woods to sustain you here, my beauty, she thought sleepily. Whatever happened in this irrational human world, the owl pair and their descendants would continue to patrol the margins of this territory for ever and ever, amen. Then a cry came directly overhead and, realising what day it was, with one hasty motion she threw aside her sleeping bag. Soon, very soon, the enigmas inherent in *Flight into Exile* would move towards their resolution and Nicolas would depart.

Fragments of memory come to her in the kitchen, swallowing

coffee, gulping down cereal and toast. Anita . . . Lourdes, *the almond blossom, the goshawk ringing up, shrieking at the top of its spiral.* Then, hearing Nicolas' jeep arriving across the hoya, she rushes to let him in by way of the den.

As if to draw strength for their separation they hold each other close, until the urgency of the morning's business makes them practical. 'Shall we go?' Luisa says at last.

Nicolas parked in Calle Luna and agreed to stay in the jeep while Luisa made overtures to Lourdes. Outside number eleven, Azahar sat with drooping ears and a sad expression beside packing cases and household rubbish. Then suddenly Felipe came bursting out, carrying cardboard boxes and Luisa stepped back startled.

'What's going on?' she said. 'What are you doing here, where's the señora?'

Felipe put down the boxes and wiped his brow. 'She's gone. Phoned me late last night, said she'd make it worth my while if I rented a van, cleared out her house and took the dog to Julio's sister in Inca.' Grinning widely he pulled an envelope from a pocket stuffed with euro notes.

'Where's she gone?'

'No idea, but she left this message for you.' He took it out of the envelope, handed it to Luisa and staggered with the boxes to the van.

Luisa, she read, Colin sent an e-mail last night saying Andreas might be on his way to Europe and I decided not to stick around. I'm putting my furniture etc. into storage since I may be gone for some time. Andreas or no Andreas it's high time I got on with my life. Keep it to yourself, but I'm going to New York to see my grandson. Sorry I couldn't wait to say goodbye. Will contact you when I return to open a centre for immigrant women in Palma. Thank you for everything, With love and in haste, Lourdes.

Luisa stood staring up the street, lost in thought until Nicolas arrived at her side. 'We've missed her,' she said, making a ball of the note in her fist. 'She's left town.'

For a few moments they stood awkwardly together at the entrance to Lourdes house. Nicolas deserves a proper explanation, she thought, yet I simply can't tell him about Colin's e-mail or where Lourdes has gone to. She looked at him, beseeching him a little to understand. 'Is it okay with you if we put off discussing this until you get back at Easter?'

'Of course,' he said affectionately, looking down into her eyes. He took her hand. 'Poor Andreas. Will he ever catch up with his wife? Will he ever know her forgiveness?'

Felipe, coming and going from the house to the van, cast them a curious look.

'Will she ever know the truth? I feel a little bit cheated, don't you?' he added as they walked arm-in-arm back to the jeep.

'Yes, and no, since we did all we could and now it's out of our hands. Besides the past belongs to the past and I suspect their grandson will bring Lourdes and Andreas together sooner rather than later.'

Before Nicolas left for the airport they repeated their vows to each other. They would be together at Easter, together they would climb the mountain of Massanella. Yet, watching the jeep drive away, a chilling sense of loss swept through her. What if he never came back? A vulture abandoning its nest? *But it's not going to be like that*, she reassured herself turning into her own house.

'I'm off to the storage place in Palma,' Felipe shouted after her. 'I'll be back later to pick you up for the train.'

She went to sit in the garden feeling bereft. She imagined how it might have been. Nicolas patiently recounting the whole story, the whole truth. And Lourdes listening defensively then saying: 'You're asking me to accept that the past two years of my life have been lived on a lie. How can I do that? Not only one lie, but two. Andreas didn't kidnap me after all, you say. Lie number one. I lived all those months as Anita Berens. Lie number two. Two years of my life wasted.' And Luisa imagined she might have consoled her. Not wasted, Lourdes. You have learned how to be alone, you have learned how to be brave, you made Julio feel like a man again, you have created one of the most beautiful orchards in the Massanella valley . . . but none of that mattered now. Sitting in the garden among the lavender and roses she felt the warmth of relief run through her. Regardless of wherein lay the truth, Lourdes had freed herself.

On the way to the bar she meets Miguel.

'I'm sure Don Nicolas explained to you, you must keep away from the town.'

'I'm allowed to come to *la Gloriosa* for bread,' Miguel countered then added with a curious, sideways smile, 'are you the Don's new bird?'

Smiling, she met his eyes. 'Yes, I do believe I am.' How could she object to the term 'bird' when it came from the lips of a reformed *cholo*?

'He told me nesting birds don't like human beings. I'll not go beyond the padlocked gate again, señora.'

'*Vale*,' she said kindly, and turned into the bar. Wearily she dropped her rucksack, grabbed a newspaper and ordered a coffee before she noticed Colin Cramer sitting at one of the tables with a faraway look in his eyes. When she went up to him she saw his eyes were bright with unshed tears but, Luisa supposed, Colin's the sort of man who never cries. He registered her presence with a start and rose to greet her.

'She's gone,' he said, drawing away. 'Quite an emotional morning,' he mumbled, regaining his seat. 'Quite a turn of events.' He explained that he had arrived at the house only to find it being cleared out. Lourdes had gone leaving only a note.

'She left one for me too,' Luisa said.

'She didn't have to go, you know,' he went on. 'Actually, between ourselves, I may have bungled things by sending her an e-mail last night. She overreacted to it, I'm afraid.'

'Don't blame yourself,' Luisa consoled. 'It really was time for Lourdes to put the past behind her and move on.' She had no intention of telling Colin about Nicolas' desire to bring the truth to Lourdes, or what that truth was. This was neither the time, nor the place.

'After we became friends Lourdes wanted me to read *Flight into Exile*,' she said. 'She insisted you wouldn't mind.'

'I don't. I'm glad you did,' Colin began, and, at that moment Paquita came to their table with a dish of *Tords en Col* and a terracotta jug filled with the wine of the house.

'The documentary about bird hunting in Mallorca, Colin?' Luisa couldn't resist saying. 'You could film the opening scene right here in Bar Solitario. With Paquita cooking up a recipe for freshly trapped thrush carcasses wrapped in cabbage.'

Colin pressed his lips together and eagerly began cutting up the little parcels: 'I understand your squeamishness, Luisa. But don't you agree it smells rather good?'

He poured them each a glass of wine, and as they sat discussing the documentary, the tensions of the morning dissipated, at least a little. When, at one moment, inadvertently Luisa let out a small sigh, Colin glanced at her curiously.

'Anything up?' he asked, and momentarily she had to look away, shaking her head, biting the edge of her mouth. She had been thinking of Nicolas. Unable to meet Colin's eyes, she took a sip of wine and said: 'The new owner of Casas Viejas has put an end to shooting on his estate, by the way.'

She knew she was being wicked, but she simply couldn't resist the delicious irony that Colin might become involved in making a film in which Nicolas Monterey, *amigo* of Andreas Herreros, figured as the good guy. The very thought made her almost splutter into her wineglass.

She wiped her wine-wet mouth with the back of her hand. 'It's wonderful news, this shooting ban, since, as you've seen for yourself, Mediterranean wildlife habitats are extremely vulnerable to change, often at the whim of an ignorant landowner or developer. And here, a few miles up the road, we have an example of a landowner who has had the courage to take a stand against the hunt. Understandably, he's not too popular with some of the town *políticos*.'

'Oh, indeed? Well, I'll certainly investigate the feasibility of a documentary as soon as I get back to London. I'll be in touch. Where can I get hold of you by the way?'

She reached over the table to write her mobile phone number on his notepad.

'You *had* one of these all along?' he exclaimed, dabbing at the corners of his mouth with his napkin. 'I might have saved myself *hours* of worry about Lourdes. She left me the key to her house, so I'll close it up. She didn't mention the dog so I'll take it to the kennels near Inca.'

When Luisa said: 'I expect you'll find Azahar's gone when you go back there after lunch,' Colin's fork stayed for a split second in the air: 'But who could possibly be taking the dog at such short notice?'

'Julio Valente's sister in Inca is to have Azahar. Much better for the dog to go to friends than to kennels. You might as well know, Colin. Lourdes and Julio became a bit more than just good friends.' Taking out her pen she added Julio's phone number to her own. 'Julio Valente will be invaluable when it comes to making the film.'

With a grunt of thanks, he tucked it in his jacket, then lingered pensively in a moment of his own. Adjusting, Luisa supposed, to the wee bombshell she had just dropped about Julio.

At that moment Felipe burst into the bar. 'Speak of the devil,' Luisa exclaimed and when Colin looked baffled, 'my colleague Felipe Tamarit,' she grinned. 'He's come to drive me to the station.'

'*Vamos*, Luisa?' Felipe called impatiently.

When Colin helped her to put on her rucksack, he said: 'He's the man who cleared Lourdes' house. Isn't he also one of the hunters we saw on the mountain that day?'

'Yes, but I'm working on him. Pretty soon he'll be *un volador* rather than *un caçador*!'

She gave Colin a hug, and when she drew away he said: 'She's very loyal you know . . . Lourdes. She'll contact us again one day. Tomorrow, perhaps next week, or next month . . . .'

His voice tailed off and Luisa said: 'I'm so sorry about your book, Colin. All the work you've put into it.'

'Yes, well . . . oh, I'll think of a different approach, something. A different ending.'

317

He looked so forlorn, sitting down again, polishing his spectacles, she picked up the blue case and found herself saying 'Why don't you come to Barcelona? It's *Carnaval*, Colin. Don't you think you deserve a bit of fun?'

He looked puzzled for a moment then smiled broadly: 'Barcelona, might I? Could I really?' he said, getting up, pulling his shoulders back.

'All you have to do is get yourself to Palma airport for the five o'clock flight. I'll introduce you to a friend of mine in Barcelona. See you there?' And, her blue case firmly in her hand, she disappeared through the door.

§

A sudden stir in the dark wood alerts the gliding bird. It brakes in its thermal, hovers high on outstretched wings and caws with indecision. Its yellow eyes trace the oblong roof of the conservancy jeep emerging beyond the trees that edge the forsaken meseta, and it cries again. The vulture had been heading for the sea cliffs, but now it might swerve into a different source of lift and trail the jeep with its reeking cargo of feral goat.

The jeep starts to trace a path across the plateau of strewn rocks, and the driver heaves round in his seat to catch the eye of the woman sitting behind him.

'Did you hear that?' Julio Valente says. 'He's up there. *Aegypius monachus* waiting for you.' Then, pensive, slightly hunched, he peers up through the dusty windscreen to locate the wheeling vulture. 'Pity I missed your talk last week,' he adds after a small silence. 'It was contentious, I hear. The town's split in two over it, but I wouldn't have expected anything less of you.'

She smiles and lays a comradely hand on Julio's shoulder: 'I'll give you the details later.'

After that he concentrates on the uneven track ahead. Two goat carcasses and three people travelling in the jeep: himself, the señorita, and his colleague Felipe Tamarit, with his head in a magazine. To Felipe, the avian drama is tediously routine, but

318

the woman has been waiting for it. She leans against the side of the jeep, raises her binoculars and trawls the air until she finds the black speck that punctuates the pewter sky. A speck that resembles a bee, she thinks, until the great hovering body fills the circle of her powerful lenses. Daft piebald head, terse yellow beak and mad incisive eyes. Usually, she can't get over the wonder of it, the unlikely grace of Mallorca's Black vulture. Only right now something else is on her mind and she shifts her focus to the tangle of trees below the summit of the crag.

The vulture's usual response when he spies the jeep is to squall and glide after it, only now he hesitates, a vigilante protecting the nest where his female sits on El Escarpado de las Cuevas Negras. That's what the woman conjectures, watching the bird, what she fervently hopes. The Crag of the Black Caves. Keeping the bird in focus, steadying her hands, she watches until the merest deflection of its huge splayed wings carries it into a *glissando* . . . then *¡mira!*, a new air current swoops it away towards the sea cliffs.

Damn it! she thinks. Not to the town, not to Cuevas Negras, but to the sea cliffs. Now I don't know what it's up to. When it comes to abnormal sensitivity about bird-life, about twigs and spittle, feathers and eggs, I'm a company of one, she reflected wryly. Even the gallant Julio might be forgiven for wondering if I go too far.

Her eyes narrow, searching the crag. *Cuevas negras*. Black gaping cave mouths, rough barked pine trees, fallen trunks of dead trees clinging to the tufaceous rocks. The vulture's not following the jeep in the direction of the nest, she worries. If the pair *have* left the nest, it'll be too late in the season for them to hatch another chick.

She scans the cliff. Binocular enlargement. Magnified details, so close she might put out a hand to touch a contorted tree with dead feathered branches, a phantasmagoric boulder. Details that trigger images of carnival streets, where she and Rafael, resplendent in wings, and Colin wearing an improvised Sheikh costume, had lived it up with other revellers performing *danses macabres* in skull and bird masks. And yesterday, when she and

319

Colin had joined Rafael for lunch on the Barcelona waterfront, 'Luisa was so aloof before,' she overhead Rafael confiding in Colin. 'Now she's really involved in life. It's wonderful to see.' And she had thought, yes, from the moment I put on Rafael's wings I came truly to life. Not like one of Doctor Faustus' mechanical dolls, but from the depth of my soul. I came face to face with myself for the first time.

Delightful as it is to bring Barcelona to mind, now she must discover the truth about the vultures' nest. Her lenses reveal its partly concealed crown ballooning above the tangle of the crag, but nothing else unusual, and she brings them down. Today it was impossible to relish their journey through the true wilderness when the nest might have been abandoned in her absence. It had been bad enough driving through the forsaken yard at Casas Viejas, knowing Nicolas would be gone for five long weeks. Edging her feet round the limp bodies of the goats, tomorrow, she resolves, tomorrow I'll take a good look at the nest from the hide. She will not give up hope, even though, high and away to the north, the bird has become almost invisible to her naked eye. A discordant note running off a manuscript stave into vast cold silence.

The jeep trundles on until, quite unexpectedly, Julio turns off the ignition. She can't believe it. He's getting out, slamming his door. The noise shakes the ponderous wilderness out of its silver slumber. Edgy, she makes for the tailgate. Why is he doing this, raising his binoculars? Searching the tree line before I've had a chance to find out what's going on myself? She jumps down and only narrowly prevents herself from skidding on small loose stones.

Catching the unearthly reverberations, the bird wings back, inviolable in its heaven. Luisa sees it circling, hears it proclaiming, *Auk! Auk!* It's mocking us, she thinks, a tantalising Chinese kite, black against the pewter sky.

¡Julio! she calls out. 'D'you think the vulture's some sort of *tourist* attraction? Do me a favour, let's get going? As it is, we'll be lucky to get to the finca before dark.'

He lowers his binoculars: 'The bird's intent on the sea cliffs.'

'Yes, that's what worries me . . . .'

'*¡Hombre!* don't worry, it's only flying out there to forage for its mate.'

Concealing the relief in her eyes - yet, how could Julio be so certain? - she looks down, kicking at stones embedded underfoot. 'Let's just get the gear up to Ca'n Clot, *vale?*'

He obliges her with a good-natured shrug. Only she feels a little dizzy clambering back to her seat near the stinking goats, saying: 'How d'you know? About the sea cliffs, I mean?'

'The male was flying above the crag yesterday.'

The jeep trundles on, and her spirits rise with the sudden consolation of sun streaking through the innocent trees that mark the jeep's noisy passage through the wood. *Gloria, gloria* . . . . She takes a swig from her water bottle and spits out over the tailgate. Then, 'Julio?' she says, hesitantly, leaning forward to attract his attention. 'I'll have to work hard now . . . to make up for lost time in Barcelona.'

Their eyes meet through the driver's mirror.

'*Tranquila*, señorita! I hope you had a good time. *¡Hombre!* Luisa, I think you must be in love?'

An exchange of smiles, conspiratorial this time. Good, my abruptness a few moments ago hasn't put him out in the least. In fact he means to reassure me.

'*Primavera* . . . it's almost spring,' Julio adds cheerily. 'Fine days lie ahead on the mountain. And the vulture chicks will be arriving from Germany any day now.'

For the first time she notices Julio's eyes reflected in the mirror are rimmed red. He's not yet over his recent bout of 'flu, but he's suffering, too, and why should she be surprised? After all, isn't Julio the man who fell for Lourdes? Hadn't she, Luisa, minimised his part in the drama, underestimated the passion of this self-possessed man? Nevertheless, here he is putting on a good show, telling me in his grizzly voice, 'our own vultures have started to lay their eggs, the peregrines are mating, some migrants will soon be leaving for the north. For Scotland, perhaps?'

Okay, fine Julio, keep the conversation light. Give or take

one or two lovers, the show must go on. When, leaning back in her seat, she wonders how much he knew about last week's drama, as if he can read her thoughts he flashes her a swift look of complicity then steers the jeep through the last holm oak wood before the field base. But, when Ca'n Clot comes into view, the sight of a strange figure in the landscape fools her for one split second into believing Nicolas has never left.

'Who's that walking towards the door?' she can't help saying, her voice rising even as she realises her imagination has tricked her.

It was Felipe who answered, tossing aside his magazine. 'I'm afraid he's not who you'd like him to be. It's only that Sardinian bird man. *Recuerdas*? Señor Bigatti, who raved about the ospreys over at the reservoir and vowed he'd come back?'

Live in the present, she admonished herself. It's all you can be certain of up here in the wilderness. Rafael is right. From the great height of these mountains, the world and all its conceits belong to the realms of make-believe. Sometimes it's as if I'm a solitary bird, hawk or vulture, reading a map of the past from this tremendous height. And on that map men and women, and I myself, begin to move about, homunculi, coming and going, in and out of the streets and houses of the mountain town, etching on the landscape their various hopes and dreams.

Julio brakes to a halt and Perro barks out an uproarious welcome. Wordlessly handing Felipe cameras, rucksack and food supplies she resolves, whatever the future holds, dealing with this here and now is all that matters. So jump down from the jeep, wave cheerily in the direction of Giovanni Bigatti, an engaging colleague, reassuringly ordinary, smoking his pipe in the sunset.

Acknowledgements

The mountain town in *Rafael's Wings* does not exist in reality. Neither does the nature conservancy organisation Luisa Ross works alongside. However, in the course of writing the novel I spent many months living in several of the towns north and north-east of Inca and exploring the mountains. There I discovered an extraordinary landscape, abundant in flora and fauna, and came to realise the extent to which the dedication of various island organisations has contributed to the protection of the area. Although I had no direct contact with the Balearic Ornithological Group and minimal contact with the Black Vulture Group, what I read and heard about their work was one of the strongest inspirations - and motivations - behind my novel. My gratitude to them, and to every other environmental group and green-thinking Mallorcan, is boundless.

Ardent thanks to family, friends and colleagues who showed unflagging interest in the progress of *Rafael's Wings*. May they find within its pages something to echo their generosity. Ariane Burgess introduced me to the world of shamanism and to many other alternative ways of perceiving the world; conversations with Stephen Burgess enhanced my ability to 'think green'; Jim Crumley helped deepen my appreciation of the mysterious world of birds; Geoff MacEwan was my stalwart, quixotic companion for most of the journey. Fionna Simmonds' enthusiastic response to a mid-term draft of the manuscript (when the going was tough) succoured me more than words can say. My thanks to Nicki Dunwell for her warm hospitality, to Yolande de la Valle, Maria Eugenia Zapata Ocampo, Aihnoa Goñi, Caroline Irwin and Jane Gibbons for 'being there' and to Sverre Koxvold who, true to form, took the cover shot at precisely the right moment.

My publisher deserves my heartfelt gratitude for taking *Rafael's Wings* on its first flight and for his long-suffering acceptance of the fact that, for many authors, producing a novel is akin to the process of giving birth.

Printed in the United Kingdom
by Lightning Source UK Ltd.
129523UK00001BC/97-120/A